FATE'S TETHER

FATE'S TETHER

BOOK ONE IN THE

FRAYED THREADS SERIES

JADE NIOMA

Content Warning:

Fate's Tether is an adult fantasy novel with darker themes and is not suitable for those under the age of 18. This is *not* a dark romance novel. Please be advised of the following:

This book contains domestic violence/abusive relationships, swearing, drug use, blood and gore, violence and death, explicit consensual sex, swearing, mentions of sexual assault (no graphic on-page depictions), slavery, abduction, sexism and misogyny, mentions of suicidal thoughts, and mental health topics such as panic attacks, PTSD, and depression.

The main character is in an abusive relationship with her husband—however, this is not where her story ends. *Fate's Tether* is about her reclamation of her power, her life, and her hopes.

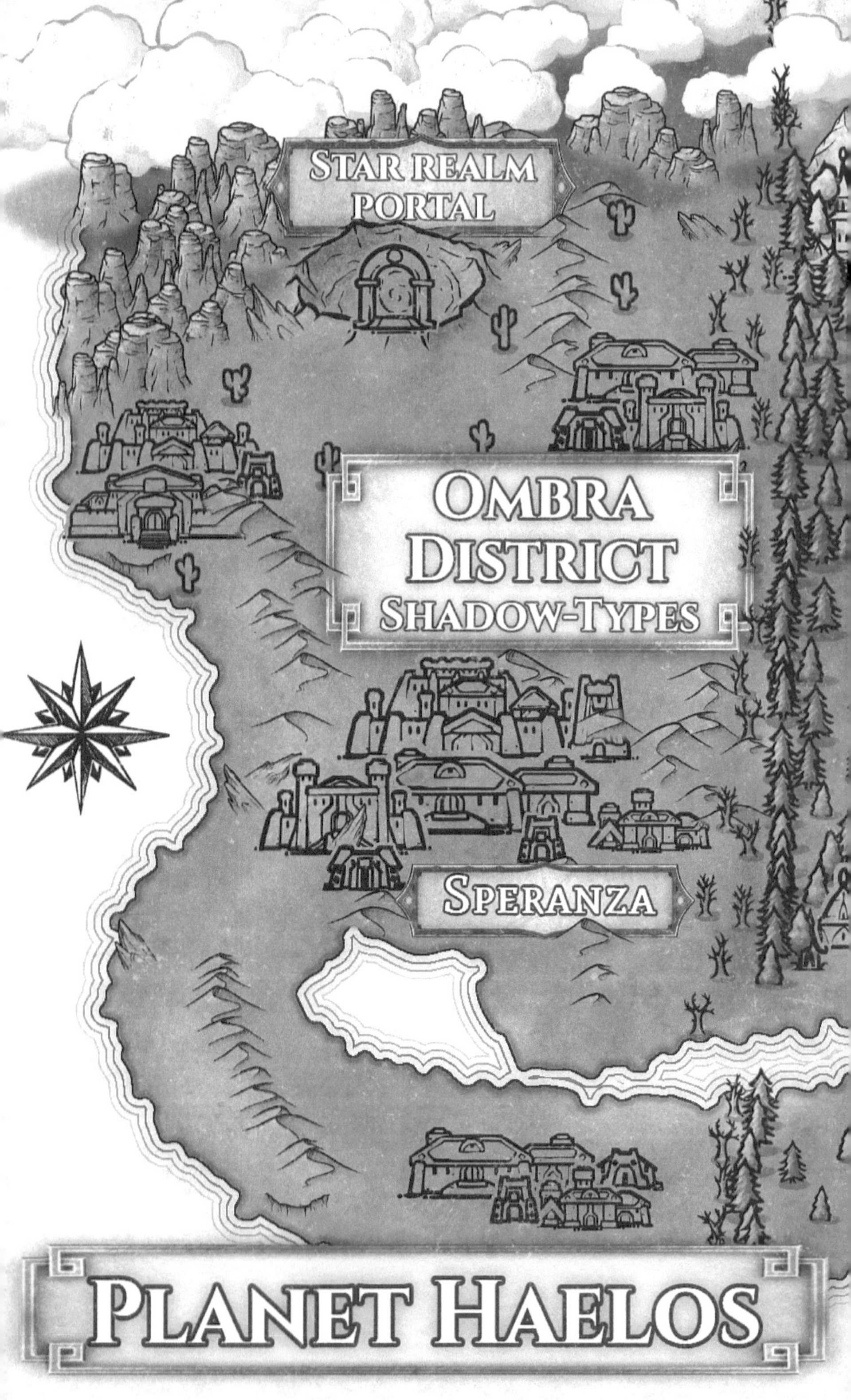

STAR REALM PORTAL
OMBRA DISTRICT
SHADOW-TYPES
SPERANZA
PLANET HAELOS

PALACE
PRISMA DISTRICT
HUMANS
ETERNITA DISTRICT
FAERIES
PALACE
PRISONS

Astral Athenaeum
Iridicenza
Innamorati

Main Palace
Innamorati
Perpetuo
The Aeria Archipelago

Name Pronunciation Guide

Aeria Archipelago
Rani- Rah-knee
Ambrosi- Ahm-BRo-zee
Cosima- Koh-ZI-mah
Aurelio- Ow-RE-leo
Caelian- SAY-lee-un
Ehses- EHs-ess
Ginevra - Geen-ev-rah
Tomasso- Toh-MAH-Soh
Lucrezia- Luw-KREH-TSYaa
Ermete- Er-met-eh
Ulrico- Ul-ree-koh
Eugenio- Yew-gen-ee-oh
Volfango- Vohl-fahn-goh
Remo- Reh-moh
Peltrasia- Pehl-trah-see-ah
Yadira- Yah-Deer-ah
Costanza- Koh-stahn-zah

Ombra District
Vincenzo- Vin-CHEN-zoh
Calix- Kay-lix
Monte- Mohn-tee
Alma- Ahl-mah
Grimaldo- Gree-mahl-doh
Odilia- Oh-dill-uh

Eternita District
Silana- Sih-lah-nah
Solara- Soh-lar-ah
Tasia- TAY-zee-ah
Aspasia- ahs-PAY-zee-ah
Ioannis- Yoh-ahn-is
Adelmo- Ah-dehl-moh

Locations
Aeria- Air-ee-ah
Sotto il Cielo- soh-toh eel chehl-oh
Ombra- Ohm-bra
Eternita- Eh-TEHR-ni-tah
Prisma- Prees-mah
Innamorati- in-am-or-ah-tea
Iridescenza - ir-e-de-chen-za
Perpetuo - Per-peh-too-oh
Nuvola Palace- New-voh-lah
Portale del regno stellare - Pohr-tah-leh del rey-gno stellar-ay

(Glossary of terms located in the back of the book)

*For the women who lose their way
and come back stronger than before.*

Author's Note

Fate's Tether contains domestic violence, which may be unsuitable for some readers. As a survivor, I wrote this novel to tackle difficult, but very real, abusive relationships. While this novel is a work of fiction, set in a fantasy world, every day in our world, those who are meant to love and protect subject their victims to horrible treatment. Intimate partner violence is isolating, traumatic, and extremely dangerous.

As a survivor of an abusive relationship, this story was created to bring awareness to not only domestic violence, but to the lasting effects it can have on a person. Cosima's story does not end with her escape. Instead, *Fate's Tether* follows her through all the difficult emotions after being free, as well as her reclamation of her inner power. This novel aims to depict a healthy relationship in contrast to an abusive one, and highlight proper treatment from a partner.

If you are a victim of domestic violence, help is available. You are not alone. There is no world in which you deserve to be treated with disrespect, or mental, physical, or emotional abuse. You deserve to be treated with softness and care. You deserve to find a loving relationship where your safety is prioritized. You deserve your peace. You are strong, you are capable, and your story is not over. In the US the National Domestic Violence Hotline is 800-799-7233.

$1 from every sale of this novel will be donated to "Control Alt Delete LLC", an organization that helps survivors flee abusive relationships. It is located in the Phoenix, AZ area. As per their website, they provide "emergency cab rides, hotel accommodations, home security, lock change assistance, meals, storage, and assistance with moving expenses". My hope is to expand these donations to more organizations with time. Thank you for helping me donate to a cause that means so much to me.

1

The Inevitable

"When the unraveling of their lives kissed them with sweetness, they called me *fortune, luck, justice.*
When the unraveling struck them with change, they called me *destiny,* believing their divine purpose was threaded amongst the constellations.
When the unraveling revealed frayed edges and mayhem, they called me *chaos, disorder, evil.*
Some call me *Mother*, or *God*, which I certainly am not either.
What is a God to the very breath of the universe?"

Chapter 1

Born in the sky, with wings unfurled, Rani Guardians were born to protect the world. Everlasting tides, with power true and bright, Ambrosi were born to guide all life.

The chant echoed in Cosima Aphelion's mind clearer than ever as she ascended to her throne. As an immortal, duty slid through her veins alongside blood, every beat a dedication. There would be no escaping the Fate laid out before her, and with sour resignation, she played her part.

The sun lit a small path in front of her along the dais, causing the brilliant maroon carpeting to showcase finely stitched detailing. She ran her eyes along the flowered borders, the swirls, the leaves, and delicate petals. Sima admitted her husband, Aurelio, absolutely had an eye for all things beautiful. Today, elaborate decor consumed the entire throne room to a near-nauseating level of perfection. Flowers littered every inch, foliage dancing under streams of sunlight from the floor-to-ceiling windows. A deliciously warm stream of light snaked across her lap. Sima allowed its heat to fill her palms, hair as black as tourmaline pooling beside her.

The throne beneath her was rigid and cold, crafted from carnelian, a fiery stone with rich red and brown hues. Hers was a perfect match to the one beside her. Within it, her kingdom's captor sat stiffly. Whether he, too, was uncomfortable from the stone thrones, or because today he would be required to play king, Cosima was unsure. He could keep them in line with force, but it was easier to placate his victims, dulling the confines of their cages with beautiful craftsmanship.

Much of the aesthetics of the Aeria Archipelago had changed rapidly after his coup. Sima eyed the red agate flooring sprawling beneath ribbons of gold fabric to mark pathways. The ripples of color were remarkably similar to the waves of blood that had coated the floors of her home. The Aeria Archipelago, from where it sat miles above the surface of planet Haelos, no longer resembled the halls she had run in as a child.

It was the Giving—a "holiday" in which every immortal citizen in the Aeria Archipelago took turns kneeling before the crown and surrendering a sliver of their magic in testament to their loyalty. Beneath the mask of 'honorable' King Aurelio Aphelion, he struggled to disguise the snake that slithered beneath his flesh.

Unwilling to peer at the lion beside her, Sima picked at the edges of her silk violet dress. Its hemline reached far beyond her toes and pooled beneath her, concealing the purple shoes strapped at the ankles. As the Rani Guardians put themselves into position around her, Sima noticed her reflection in one of the men's armor. Her dark hooded eyes were slender, hidden beneath swoops of velvety hues her servant, and friend, Ivo had placed prior to today's celebration. Even beneath the masterful make-up, Sima looked as pitiful as she felt.

As if he noticed it as well, Aurelio coughed beside her. Crowded with gold adornments, his red suit bore depictions of mock constellations threaded in the quality fabric. Intimidating gray feathered wings towered above him, a rarity for immortals. His ivory hair lay with every strand precisely tucked in line, unmoving as he turned to her. Golden eyes slithered over her, and Sima clenched her jaw. Before he could speak, a Guardian approached.

"My King," Caelian said. The Rani Guardian stood before them dressed to the nines, his feathers a rich burgundy complimented by the deep navy of his suit. Caelian's eyes shifted to Sima, a smile dancing across his lips, before he met the King's gaze. Sima shivered and averted her eyes.

"Speak," Aurelio said, as two Hexia girls, witches enslaved to the kingdom, began bringing in the lofty ceremony bowl. Their muscles strained, earning a contemptuous glance from the King.

"Apologies for disrupting," Caelian said, rising from his bow. He tucked the brown hair swishing around his temples behind his ear. "The Founders are here, and all Guardians are in position, sir."

Frail arms shook as they attempted to lift the bowl onto the pedestal, puffs of air escaping the girls' cheeks. The selenite bowl had been in use for forty years, almost as long as Aurelio had laid claim on their world, and if it were to break—Sima swallowed hard. It was irresponsible to use her magic, but it flickered at the tips of her fingers, anyway. At the precise moment Sima spotted the bowl tilting to an angle it would not come back from, time halted. Sima found the threads swiftly, the spools appearing in her mind.

When time resumed, Sima was back to picking at the hem of her dress. The girls hoisted the bowl into place at the same moment a large vase near the back wall fell from its display, shattering loudly.

"Caelian," Aurelio sighed, "if you cannot keep your bird brothers from breaking things, I won't hesitate to clip their wings."

Caelian offered a nervous laugh. "You two," he said, gesturing to the girls wiping sweat from their brows. "Get to cleaning."

After properly attending to the mess, Caelian began the ceremony by allowing in the citizens.

Sima would have preferred to break nothing, but her power to manipulate fate often came with drawbacks. By selecting another item to break, she saved the girls from her husband's wrath. Immortal Ambrosi filed in, forming lines that slithered through the room, and Sima could not ignore the preferential treatment they received.

Ambrosi men and women sauntered in, exposed necks full of fine crystals. Jade, emerald, ruby, and sapphire sparkled beneath the sheens of light dribbling from the windows. Sima touched the amethyst dangling from her ears with a frown.

The Founders of Aeria, Tomasso and Ginevra, made their way

to the front of the throne room, and Sima shifted in her seat. They inspired nearly as much fear as the King himself. The crowd bowed, foreheads inches from touching their kneecaps in respect.

In his usual black-on-black suit, Tomasso looked primed with youth, despite the duet being the only Ambrosi to predate the building of the Archipelago. His hair was like gypsum, the only indicator of his age, which complimented his umber skin well.

"Rise," Tomasso said, his silk voice careening far throughout the throne room. Whispers of respect and gratitude fluttered throughout the crowd. Even the smallest slight could have them killed should the Founders wish it. Tomasso cleansed the bowl with a silk cloth from the breast pocket of his suit.

Ginevra was a remarkable sight, as always. She was beautiful, as all immortals were. Smooth russet skin spilled out from beneath her citrine gown, bouncy brown curls toppled across her shoulders. A ring sat on her right hand, matching the sunstone used to construct the pillars beside the dais. She was one of the few women with a position of power in Aeria. Aurelio's disdain for the opposite sex led to most positions being stripped from Ambrosi and Guardian women.

It left Sima powerless as well. Beyond official appearances where Aurelio desired to show off his chained dog, she no longer held the esteemed position of a princess. Although officially a queen now, she considered herself as much a prisoner as the Hexia girls.

"This year, like all others before it," Tomasso began, "gives us the opportunity to contribute personally to the prosperity of our kingdom. This is the chance to assist our brothers and sisters in living an abundant life. When the Spirit Goddess gifted Aeria to the Ambrosi for safekeeping, she entrusted us with the lives of everyone in Sotto il Cielo—those beneath the sky. We keep them safe and lead them toward their souls' missions here on planet Haelos. Aeria's islands may exist as cities within the clouds, but we are certain that their grace extends to other realms."

With a smile that showcased her white perfect teeth, Ginevra stated, "We feel honored to be the first each year to prove our devotion." Ginevra's magic poured from her palm, swirling within the container before forming into a solid, glowing sphere. The Founders held up the balls of pure energy harnessed for their Archipelago. "Without contributions from the citizens, Aeria would have no way to power itself. Empty reserves for our islands means the world beneath us would suffer undoubtedly."

"As most of you know, there is a privilege that comes with living in Aeria. Those who are under our care in the Sotto il Cielo, namely the humans, have their myths and legends about the Ambrosi, naming us as Gods and Goddesses." At that, a laugh reverberated through the crowd, "But we immortals know our proper place here. We are not creators. To creatures large and small, delightful or fearsome, to a life as long as a breath or as everlasting as our realm, we are their guardians, their sworn protectors. It is not a job we take lightly. Remember this, even on days when your sacrifice for Aeria is not so obvious."

Applause came in lengthy waves. Tomasso and Ginevra held hands and waved as King Aurelio strode toward them.

"Thank you for the lovely speeches, Tomasso and Ginevra. Please, everyone, rise and let us begin the next portion." He turned and shooed the two most respected elders away. "Please, yes, all right." They hadn't seemed to mind, though, as Sima was sure they, too, became bored with the same regurgitated nonsense they said every year.

When you've already lived for an eternity, Sima thought, *nothing is more maddening than the repetitive passing of the years.*

"Let us just dive right in! Caelian! Commence the Giving, please! I have only a few short words, I promise." Aurelio clapped his hands together tightly as Caelian began leading the nobility to the front of the dais.

Sima's family deigned a solitary glance her way from where they stood in line, faces blank and unemotional. The former King of Aeria, her father, lived a pleasant life here. In usual circumstances, an enemy may not be so keen on allowing threats to live. However, her father was no threat.

Cosima's mother and father meandered to the ceremony bowl

made of carved and polished selenite. The bowl represented the cleansing of forfeited power, ensuring none of the energy of the person it came from would remain. Behind them trailed Sima's older sister, Matilde, who wore a long blush pink gown with gold butterflies adorning the skirts. Her hair, as midnight black as Sima's, was tied back into a tasteful knot, two loose strands framing her face. She looked sad, but Sima couldn't discern why. Cosima was never very close with her parents, but Matilde was always kind to her, even if they had grown distant.

"As you all may know," Aurelio said, placing a hand over his heart, "I am committed to my role, leading the Aeria Archipelago into a time of wonder and advancement. The three islands of Aeria: Iridicenza, Perpetuo, and Innamorati—where we stand today— exist only so we may care for the people of Haelos." A flicker of disdain scampered across his golden gaze. "It is time for me to read the commandments from the Goddess, lest we forget our vital roles."

"Commandment One: each creature and person created by the Goddess is to be respected and cared for by Ambrosi, and fiercely protected by Rani Guardians. Two: no Ambrosi or Rani Guardian may bring harm upon those they swear to protect, unless it is for the greater good of planet Haelos." A sickly smile crossed his lips. "Three: the ruling family will maintain and operate the Archipelago."

Sima's stomach turned. The third commandment was precisely the one he exploited when he came to Aeria. Only the ruling family could hold power over the Archipelago, and by marrying Sima, he guaranteed himself the ability to control them all.

"Four: all citizens of the Archipelago must contribute once per year at the Giving in order to provide the Archipelago with the energy to operate. Finally, five: any Ambrosi, Rani Guardian, or citizen of the planet that interferes with these commandments shall be subject to cosmic retribution from the Eternal Kingdom in the Ethereal Realm, and if deemed a threat, they will eliminate the planet."

Sima stiffened. Aurelio turned to her, golden eyes ablaze with impatience. His finger curled with his silent command. She rose, careful not to trip on the flowing fabrics of her dress as she made her way beside him. His rough hand slipped into hers, clasping tightly around her flesh as he raised them in the air. She scanned the opulently dressed crowd, pretending to be unaware of the incredulous looks Ambrosi gave her. Some flashed sympathetic smiles, others wore expressions of disdain, either for her husband or for Sima herself.

She and Aurelio took their free hands and hovered them above the bowl. Cosima's eyelashes felt heavy as she gave way to a tendril of her power. The forfeiture of power was hardly noticeable. A faint tremble coming from her fingers was the solitary response from her body to the exchange.

"To Aeria: *per la prosperità, per la fortuna, per la protezione,*" Caelian's voice boomed through the Throne Room. Cries repeating the phrase found their way back, as if they were but an echo.

For the prosperity, for the fortune, for the protection, Sima thought, *for the King, and no one else.*

Her ball of energy slowed to a stop beside Aurelio's as Sima lamented every reminder of their connectedness. To her relief, Aurelio dropped the hand he held, providing one last "For Aeria!"

With that, the King turned on his heel and immediately found his way back to the throne, where he needed only to smile and wave every so often. Sima followed numbly behind him, returning with a quiet sigh.

Huddles of nobility gathered in a circle and each ceremoniously lifted their right arms to the sky, the side of giving, and placed their left hands on their hearts, the side of receiving. "For Aeria!" they cried, as bursts of light tore from each of their right hands before congealing into spheres.

"For Aeria!" those remaining in the crowd cried.

As the waves of thousands came and went, Aurelio became increasingly unbearable next to her. He simmered, though Sima wondered if his desire to smoke his drug-filled cigars motivated him, or if his capacity for well-mannered behavior was running thin. Alas, only two hours remained, and the sun had set. There was a beautiful breeze wafting the scent of the nearby lavender patches planted along the Nuvola Palace.

One by one, the Hexia girls opened the enormous windows, letting in even more of the pleasant scent. The girl Sima saved from invoking her husband's wrath by breaking the ceremony bowl strained her muscles again as she twisted the mechanism. The sight tugged on her heart.

She tracked Caelian and the other Guardians through their protective sweeps. They moved in expertly timed formations, displaying their extensive training and practice. Though the Rani Guardians' wings were unique in their color, feathering, and span, they all sent the same fearful message—they would protect at all costs. As Caelian and the other Rani Guardians escorted another drove of immortal citizens into the throne room, Aurelio cleared his throat.

"Since I desperately need some entertainment, how about I give you some more news from the other realms?"

"Certainly, my King," she said through her teeth as she forced a smile.

He returned one, though his seemed less forced. "I thought you would be interested. You've always been that kind of girl, Sima, never satisfied with what you have. You're almost as bad as that scum from the Below," he said, picking a piece of lint off his coat. "Though this world is not enough for me, either. I don't think any world could hold my attention forever."

"I have located two of my brothers. I have been observing them, though they have not tempted me enough to dare a visit. From the original Sacred Twelve, there are only six of us that remain. With any luck, it shall be just me within time."

Aurelio was one of twelve powerful brothers. Rumors circulated about the Sacred Twelve, but no one in Aeria knew more than what Aurelio provided, and he was far from dependable.

The Spirit Goddess created us, gave us roles to fill, and left us all the same.

Aurelio turned to Caelian as he approached. "What is it?"

The Guardian whispered into the King's ear, the information

surprising enough that Aurelio was soon flushed with anger.

"Then deal with it," he said, shooing the Guardian with a wave. He narrowed his eyes, and a hint of a sneer scampered across his face.

"As I was saying." He inspected his fingertips as he spoke. "About my brother, Carmine, from Uperath. I am luring him in, though I cannot guarantee he will be foolish enough to come close enough for me to eviscerate him." He shifted, causing his feathers to brush against her skin. Cosima shrunk away.

"I see you're wearing that dress I had tailored for you." He waved his hand and spoke through a smile painted on for the sake of the last rounds of the Giving. They had once done it one at a time, but as the population grew, Aeria had no choice but to bring them in batches.

"Yes, I like this one," she said, shifting in her seat.

"I knew you would. The women dress like whores where they designed it. I bet you wish you could be them. I know how much you like it when all the attention is on you," he said. His smile did not falter. "Just like the last time I brought a couple friends for playtime. Didn't you love it?"

"Aurelio," Sima whispered, unable to hide her wince.

"They can't hear me, *Cosima*." Her name was a warning across his tongue. "Not one show of affection for me in front of our people. Do you wish to sow the seeds of doubt into our kingdom? What will everyone think when I demand loyalty of them and beside me on the throne lies a harlot?"

"Please, can we do this later?" She shook her head, letting full strands of her dark hair float before her face. She bit her lip to fight the tears of humiliation. Leaving would only prove him right; people would talk. Not that it mattered what they thought of her. Some felt sorry for her, but most felt she was complicit in Aurelio's crimes. That she had allowed him into their kingdom, and her people paid in mountains of corpses. Her fists curled at her sides, though she forced a breath.

"I'll call the servants and ask them to scour this planet until they find the clothes for the lowest sluts, then perhaps you'll be happy."

"Aurel—" The sounds of gasps through the crowd interrupted Sima. A man held what looked like a scroll, or a rolled painting, while shoving his way to the front of the throne room.

"King Aurelio, tell them the truth! You say you are a man of dignity. Prove it to us now," an Ambrosi man shouted. Whispers rustled through the crowd, transforming it into a living conscious whole, no longer made up of individuals. "I call you a liar and a disgrace to the throne," he said, spitting at their feet from where they sat upon the dais.

No one dared step to Aurelio.

Those who did died.

Perhaps others were not aware of this, but as the one doing Aurelio's bidding, Sima knew this was a death sentence in the making.

Rani Guardians made their way to the man, but Aurelio did exactly as Sima expected and waved them off. The King would sit and allow the man to say his piece, if for nothing more than a laugh.

Denial and saccharine smiles, the rolling heads of nay-sayers. All in a day's work for the King.

Aurelio was standing now, ushering the man up the few steps to the top of the dais. He put his hand across the shivering man's shoulder and gestured to the crowd. "We shall hear this man. I want each of you to know you are safe here and you can bring your indiscretions to me. We may know each other through tense beginnings, but we have known peace for nearly fifty years. Let us not ruin that." He turned to the man. "Perhaps we have a misunderstanding."

The man's pale skin turned pink at his cheeks. He tried to slip beneath Aurelio's grasp, like prey caught in the talons of a predator.

"Speak, boy," Aurelio said, tightening his grip.

"I know what you are trying to hide, King Aurelio. I know why we are being asked to give more this year and why you have allowed a flood of citizenships to be granted two months ago." The scroll in his hand crumpled as he spoke.

"To boost the economy and greatness of Aeria, of course!" Aurelio beamed.

Cheers erupted from the crowd.

Sima didn't know where the man was going with this, but it would not be hard to dig up dirt on Aurelio. He was proficient at deception, painfully skilled at persuasion. Manipulators got cocky, failing to cover their tracks. Sima couldn't stop herself from leaning forward to hear him better.

"No!" the man cried, finally escaping from beneath Aurelio's hold. "No, that is not it at all." Shock tore through Sima at the realization there were tears in the man's eyes. "There are horrid monsters down there. Sotto il Cielo may look beautiful and untouched and like the haven that you say it is when you are standing here in the sky. But I went there, I went Below. I saw it with my own eyes. There are dreadful creatures overtaking the planet and Aurelio is doing nothing to stop them. Our Guardians should be here to protect the people of Haelos. Instead, they fight the repulsive beasts coming from the veil themselves."

Ambrosi from the crowd wheezed, their astonishment as palpable as Sima's.

It was true.

There were beasts coming through the veil, attacking people Below.

"He hides this from you. What else is he keeping in the dark?"

A powerful push of Caelian's wings and he was atop the dissenter. The scroll he held skidded across the red agate flooring until it sat at Sima's feet. She tore her eyes from it as the man began hollering.

"You cannot silence the truth forever! You have lied to them all Aurelio, and you will pay with your life!" He whipped his head wildly side to side, evading Caelian's attempts to silence him. "There are beasts down there. They are out of control. The Districts have sealed themselves off from one another. What would the Spirit Goddess think of this? You spit in the face of Ehses!"

Aurelio merely laughed, and though dazed, the crowd soon mirrored his response, cackling in the face of the flustered man being restrained. It would take more than a crazed man for the citizens to turn their backs on their king. If there were truly beasts crowding the surface of the planet, maiming citizens, surely the Spirit Goddess wouldn't hesitate to murder every Ambrosi and Rani involved. The planet itself lay at risk of being demolished if their deity wished it so.

Forces emerging from the shadows escorted citizens before they could hear anymore. Caelian hoisted the man to his feet as another snapped restraints around his limbs.

"What happens in the dark always comes to the light, *King!*" the man shouted as Guardians dragged him toward the prisons.

Chapter 2

A flushed wave of dread had her fingertips numbing, yet the shell she had become refused to obey, refused to show her fear. Her body cooled into unnatural stillness, daring not even a blink as she awaited him.

Her husband.

Cosima Aphelion swallowed hard as the outer door to her bedroom chambers unlocked. The clutter of footsteps from the Guardians outside meant he was truly there. Beyond sheer ribbons of the finest silks and dedicated selections of artworks lay a torture chamber—one her husband, Aurelio, crafted with his presence.

There were few nights like this, but he was in a foul mood, his brown leather shoes clicking harshly on the rose quartz flooring as he approached. Her eyes flicked to the door, as if the Rani Guardians outside would come to her rescue. They would not. In fact, a handful of them took Aurelio up on the chance to join in torturing her. They took advantage of the opportunity to release pent up aggression or act out twisted desires. Though, their opportunity to do so came because Aurelio allowed it.

His impressive wings shook as he stretched them outward, fixing the cuffs of his overpriced navy suit. Though Ambrosi wings were rare, above his powerful muscles lay delicate gray feathers. Cosima resisted the urge to shrink further into the sea of blankets atop her bed.

To her dismay, her heartbeat was so fierce that as still as she tried to be, the subtle rocking from its pounding gave her away. His golden gaze registered it in an instant. The invasiveness of his glare worsened the issue. Her chest rose unnaturally from her shuddered breaths. He was relishing in the way he scared her, in the way only *he* could scare her, a sickly smile across his lips.

The King was many things, but he was not kind.

King Aurelio Aphelion of the Aeria Archipelago, the conqueror of Cosima's once honorable kingdom, lit a cigar, billows of smoke floating against his ivory hair. He scowled at her, clenching his powerful jaw.

"Cosima," he said, inhaling once again. "You won't even look at me, *Yin*."

Sima swallowed her objection to his use of his nickname for her. Aurelio found it amusing to name her *Yin*. Aurelio had traveled to many planets within many realms before deciding on planet Haelos, and ultimately, the Aeria Archipelago. One in particular Aurelio called *Gaia*. There, *Yin* and *Yang* represented, from what Sima understood, duality. The King made mentions of her hair, how it was deep like the cosmos, making her *Yin*, and his hair was nearly white, making him *Yang*. He reminded her of the other associations for *Yin*—known for representing the weak, the passive, the negative.

"You really don't like me anymore? After all I've done for you, Cosima?"

Her body had still not moved beyond the subtle sway of her panic. His eyes were on her again, though she refused to confirm by meeting his gaze. There was no escape. The demands he had would not be easy. As he neared, Sima turned her head, eyes fixated on the velvet green comforter beneath her.

Aurelio sat beside her, gingerly stroking her hair. She refrained from ducking beneath his touch, a lesson she had long since learned. Fighting back would change nothing. He would be as nice as he willed or as mean as he desired to be. Aurelio's wings enveloped her, pushing her body closer to his.

"You can only be so cold to me," he whispered against her neck. "I try to spoil you, give you the finest life imaginable, all in exchange for one little thing." He ran a finger up the length of her thigh, stalling near the curve of her hip and stomach. "Still, you refuse, still you make my job harder than it needs to be."

"I'm sorry," she muttered.

"I'm sure you thought that would help," he said, leaning back until their eyes met. She did not recoil as he pressed further, stopping only a hair from her nose. "Unfortunately, I can smell right through your pathetic lies."

He stood abruptly then, a small wave of surprise causing her to break her paralyzed mask.

"Get up," he said, "we have more work to do."

She stood up, her violet nightgown swishing around her ankles as she found her way to the sofa chair, his preferred place. Having this play out in her rooms was the easiest option for him. That way, he could leave her behind without concerns for returning her, or cleaning up after himself.

The bruises encircling both her wrists had barely faded from their last session. Her chin dipped, her lip trembling as he brought the heavy chains before her.

"You know how this goes, don't you, dear? Come on now, let's play nice."

The metal was cold against her skin as he clamped on the oversized iron cuffs. A matching pair found their way around her ankles. She sat back in the chair and dropped her jaw. Two capsules tumbled across her tongue. She swallowed them quickly before opening her mouth and allowing him to inspect. He forced her to swallow them, whether voluntarily or otherwise.

Cosima always had.

Powdered *Mortoid* caps filled the pills, a type of mushroom most Ambrosi lovingly called Death's Mirror. It had only taken one dose through her half-Ambrosi veins to make her realize why. Those who took *Mortoid* often found themselves amongst a flurry of Fates, all streams of potential ways they might die. Killing the immortals was nearly impossible, and for some, they assumed it would be the only way for them to experience death.

This proximity to the Fates allowed Cosima to tap into the threads, accessing her magic to pull the strings whichever way Aurelio commanded. He handed her a blindfold, which she placed over her eyes, and tried to find a position in the chair that minimized the pain from the chains.

"I'll be right here if you need me, *Yin*," he said, as chair legs from the desk squeaked. She always liked it better when she couldn't see him. It let her focus better, anyway. His wings ruffled.

A small gasp escaped her as he was suddenly at her side, moving with speed only the King of the Ambrosi could possess. He grabbed a fistful of her hair and twisted her neck back. Between her panting and the searing pain, she only caught bits of what he was saying.

"…better not forget it, you understand?"

She nodded. She knew what she was here for. He released her and resumed his position at the desk, the chair legs screeching across the floor again.

The darkness and quiet swirled around her. Unrest grew thickly in her gut, the nausea a sure sign the drugs had entered her system. Her ability to glimpse into potential futures had the King performing all kinds of experiments on her. At first, it was to assess if she really could change Fate. Confirmation of her abilities only solidified her imprisonment.

Sima flexed her fingers gently as the tingling sensations that had started at the tips of her digits now crept their way up her knuckles.

Death's Mirror, Sima thought bitterly, *what was the Goddess thinking when she made this drug?*

To an immortal Ambrosi, there were few things more interesting than death. The Ambrosi remained in control over their world, the Founders hundreds of thousands of years old. Throughout their reign, they had borne witness to the many creations of the Goddesses.

Aeria was not perfect, but within the three sky-bound islands composing the Archipelago, every citizen—whether Ambrosi or Rani Guardian—would protect and care for those Below.

Until Aurelio arrived, that is.

Only five or ten more minutes, she thought, resisting the urge to adjust the chains once again. Soon she would lose all sensation in her physical body. Then she was to fulfill Aurelio's wishes.

The mushrooms made her body pulse and twitch. The heavy chaining was a necessary facet to keep her from escaping or attacking her husband. Despite being far within another realm, her body became possessed with energy, the fear driving her senses mad, urging her to flee.

She thought not of the room where her tormentor sat.

No, for now, she focused on the path ahead.

Still, images of her home stitched themselves alongside images of fearsome beasts and chilling faces in her mind. Melded of stone and soil, the islands once bore vegetation along every building. All that came to her today were depictions of Aurelio's Aeria. A sterile, crystalline cloud above the planet Haelos.

The Ambrosi here referred to it as Sotto il Cielo—*beneath the sky.* Their world, planet Haelos, was vast—full of diverse magic, herbs, and awe-inspiring landscapes. Not that Sima had seen much of it. Many Ambrosi never left Aeria, but she could imagine nothing she wanted more. There were animals and insects with lifespans so short, knowledge of it had nearly broken her. Their life cycles mimicked the rising and falling of the sun. She studied them intently. She smiled as dragonflies zipped around her, unfazed by the demons she saw beside them.

Fighting through the cloudy storm became increasingly difficult as the hallucinations amped up. Hot steam and smoke toiled through her veins, threatening to turn her blood into mist. The pressure beneath her skin pulled her flesh taut against her deteriorated muscles, tugging on the last confounds of elasticity. She was close.

More bugs from books she had read floated behind her eyelids. Her mind used the psychedelic nature of the drugs to bring the drawings to life. The tingling had long since turned to burning, and she knew she had only a few moments of peace left before it took her. Cosima waded through the thick recesses of her mind. It was the only place she could go to escape. Instead of harsh memories, she found serene emptiness. No ruminating spirals, no twisted paranoia. Only quiet.

Her spirit floated in the vast emptiness.

There.

A door. In front of her lay a single wooden door.

Sima wrapped her hand around the silver handle, the rosewood door revealing a swirling orchid pink portal within as she pulled it open. A pause overtook her, the way it did each time she conceded to do her husband's bidding. Somewhere within, her soul begged her to revolt, to disobey.

Thousands of her previous attempts had returned nothing meaningful, yet she was not so broken she did not dream. She was not so traumatized that she was numb to her crimes. Each time she obeyed and thwarted attacks on her husband, she merely sowed a deeper seed of hate for herself.

A coward, a fool, an unfortunate soul intertwined with cosmic powers of unforgivable proportions, she thought as her hand hovered an inch before the portal. She sighed, knowing there would be no turning back. If Aurelio's problems remained unsolved when she returned, reprimand and torture were all that would await.

Herbal scents of foxglove, elderberry, clover tickled her nose as she stepped through. She embraced the smell of the Alfrii lands. The Alfrii, beautiful creatures with pointed ears, once had a close alliance with the kingdom. It had disintegrated the night the streets of the Archipelago dribbled blood from the sky.

The Alfrii lands were home to all faerie kinds in the Eternita District of the Below. Sima peered around the room she found herself in. Her objective lay in uncovering those involved in a rebel movement against Aeria.

Though her husband crafted lies, attempting to shield her from the truth, she was not blind to the fact that the existence of rebels meant Aeria was not upholding its duties. Still, she witnessed the memory her intuition guided her towards, pulling taut the invisible ties. The ending destination of these threads was unknown to Sima, as was the result. Only resurfacing would allow the changes to come to fruition, or to snap if the bonds were too weak to secure themselves to the person's path.

An Alfrii man with long, frizzled brown hair tucked a lock of it behind his pointed ear before continuing his task. In front of him, in the cozy, yet spacious room lit by enchantments, the man stitched a phrase into the back of a jacket.

Oh, death, bring me pardon from the judgment of the living.

Sima peered over his shoulder at it. The jacket was comprised of tightly knitted black fabric, its interior made of some sort of wool. The thread he used was a rusty color, the needle expertly crafting the letters as his hands moved.

Her hand trembled as she held it before him, allowing her magic to crawl over his Fate, picking out what it deemed useful, leaving the rest unscathed. Limits to her magic meant there could be no truly forced actions. Every thread was required to be connected to another existing path. She could weave redirections, guiding people along a particular path, though what they did with it was their own.

Two viable options slithered to the surface, yet one rose above the other, drawing her in with a captivating call. Unable to ignore it, Sima seized the filaments of Fate she saw before her, gently stitching her own ties into the man's future. With sure hands, she changed the unchangeable. A horrid power, one of weight she was too weak to seize properly.

As a child, her powers had been a clumsy thing. In rare moments, it had come with easy waves, shudders of internal songs with notes she had heard perhaps in lifetimes before. Even now, she hummed along, allowing the mysterious beats to guide her weaving.

"No longer decided, no longer true," she whispered to herself. "The tides of destiny wash you through and through."

Guilt streaked the insides of her soul, forever changing who she knew herself to be. Victim to a captor with twisted desires, and victim to the cruel irony that Cosima could not alter her own future. Rendered helpless, Cosima had learned there would be no undoing once she made these changes, and still she wove, still the ribbons attached themselves to the Fae man. The unlucky target. The man now frightfully exposed as a rebel.

It was plainly visible, the jacket the motto of the movement, the Devout Rising. Belief motivated their plots against King Aurelio, belief that their actions brought closer days of respite from an evil conqueror. Yet, with each stitch, she pried that opportunity from their desperate hands.

The Fae man was partial to rages, bordering on psychopathy when faced with the lives of those he loved at stake. A quality Cosima could admire, though would now exploit. She tipped his fervor for vengeance to absurd bounds, aligning him with constant reminders of loved ones he watched perish. He would not find peace, instead he would find determination, building until it burst from every pore.

Until he ultimately got himself captured by the kingdom and sentenced to death.

She closed the door behind her and let the waves of anguish wash her home.

Chapter 3

Reunited with her physical body, Cosima's eyes settled on the pool of blood she found herself in. She gasped for air, rolling onto her back as she attempted to muffle her screams with crimson iron-soaked hands. The *Mortoid* led her body to panic, her instincts lashing at anything within range. Chained down, with no ability to choose self-preservation, gouge wounds in her muscle and flesh were common.

Restraints existed for Aurelio's safety, not Cosima's. The King would allow her to be hurt within inches of her life. She was half-Ambrosi, and therefore, gifted with the immortal ability to heal herself. However, when her magic stores depleted, like they were now, she could not fix herself. Aurelio would eventually send a healer—she hoped. She swallowed hard. Her reserves were hours from being useful.

How long until he sends someone for me? Could he have forgotten?

Maybe he enjoyed this part of it, Sima reasoned as her body writhed. Her hands trembled as she attempted to assess the large wounds on her thighs. Outside, commotion rang through the halls. Despite her chambers being well guarded, her body trembled from blood loss and regret. Unable to ignore the blood—and flesh—beneath her fingernails, a sob rocked her chest.

The chains created the worst wounds around her wrists and

ankles. Sima wondered if she had tried to pry them off herself, at all costs. She was lightheaded. She would either vomit or pass out before she made any progress toward healing.

Sweat dripped down onto her thighs, splattering like rain as it mixed with her tears. The commotion beyond her chambers echoed, likely coming from the main stairwell down the hallway. She questioned calling for her Guardians, another sob catching in her throat. It would only worsen her misery. Either she would go unanswered, or they would take advantage of her weakened state as they had before.

Her magic sputtered at the end of her fingertips as she tried to heal enough to take the edge off. Enough for her to think straight. A voice sounded. Was someone speaking to her?

Footsteps cluttered somewhere around her. She knew her eyes were open, but all she could see beyond the piercing pain was a bright, blinding light.

"Cosima," someone shouted, "Cosima."

Her head rolled back, the person in her chambers grasping wildly at her legs.

Were they trying to make it worse? Kill her? Or were they helping?

Lightning scorched through her muscles.

And then, nothing.

Down pillows asphyxiated her, the myriad of luxurious blankets stacked high atop her aching body. For all appearances' sake, the King of Aeria took kindly to spoiling her. The extravagance did little to numb what he did to her in the dark.

It was not Aurelio waiting in her chambers, for which she was grateful.

"Ivo," Sima said, trying not to flinch when she saw the fury that plagued the usually calm girl. Anger cast her full brows inward, a scowl attached to her full lips. Eyes as blue as the sky floated against her pale skin, and hair as dark as the new moon nights swirled down to her waist. Her arms lay crossed in front of her chest, a light khaki uniform with Aeria's crest along the shoulders and back loosely rested over her thin frame.

"What happened to you this time? This is the worst I've seen you. What is he making you do that requires *chains*, Cosima?" Ivo's face was pale as she stared hard at Sima.

Sima knew there was no getting around that stare. Ivo was *Hexia*, and like Sima, enslaved to Aurelio, as all witches were in Aeria. The girl served the Ambrosi here. It was a better assignment than most received. But Ivo was strong, and she knew how to thrive, even in a place like this.

"*Mortoid*," Sima said, shaking her head, and reflexively reaching down to touch where her wounds had been. "He is making me take it in order to access my powers fully. Did you—how did I get healed? Did he call for a healer?"

"He sent for another, but my gut would not leave me be. I told my sister to take on others in need of healing. He may have restricted my power, but I have my ways around his rules. The med-witch was not skilled enough for this sort of injury. It is because of me you are alive."

"He wouldn't let me die, Ivo."

"Oh," Ivo said, throwing her hands up, "I suppose that makes it all right. By the Spirit, Cosima, why do you need those drugs to use your power?"

Sima's head fell as she studied her hands. No blood remained beneath her nails. Ivo had cleansed Cosima's skin.

"Do you remember what I told you? That I was planning to make my move soon? I told you how I have had enough, and how I wish to flee."

Ivo nodded slowly.

"I am scared. The longer I wait, the longer I fall victim to his wicked ways, the harder it feels to drag myself from beneath the misery. I question my powers, I question if I am right for this. I question why the Spirit Goddess cursed me."

"She has not cursed you," Ivo whispered. "She chose you to lead this kingdom for a reason. Upon your birth, the Goddess blessed you. Everyone in Aeria knows the story."

"It is precisely her binding declaration that keeps me prisoner. Without me, Aurelio has no way of accessing the magic of the Archipelago. When he came through the veil, and chose our world to conquer, his marriage to me gave him the key to our home."

"Do not fight the life laid in your hands. Perhaps she has chosen you precisely because you are the only one who can stop him. I believe in you, the way I always have. We are friends, not merely because you show me mercy when I serve you. You have shown me you have the heart and determination required to save us from him. I am terribly sorry this has happened to you," Ivo's voice cracked, "but when you decide it is time to move against the King, know it will be me by your side."

Sima sighed. Her friend's faith in her abilities touched her, yet still she was unnerved.

"I feel as though I am damned by the Cosmos for choosing to alter the Fates they have laid for us all. A wretched power it is, the ability to change outcomes how I see fit. My home is far from what I imagined it would be."

"What did you want the Aeria Archipelago to look like before him?" Ivo asked, returning to the cleaning she had been attending to prior to Sima waking up. As Ivo mopped, Sima considered her question.

Her belief in a greater reason for existing was the only tether between her and the darkness that lay beyond. Cosima felt as though the Spirit Goddess Ehses blessed her as the next queen, a sign the Goddess saw enormous potential in her. She thought it meant she harnessed a destiny of astronomical proportions. It was a fickle belief, though the flame never truly extinguished.

"I craved further connection between us and the people. Aurelio has brought change, luxury to the Ambrosi. Yet, he shows us no proof that those Below are thriving. I have read many books about Sotto il Cielo, and like most Ambrosi, I have never stepped foot on Haelos. Still, I dream of running through fields of clover in the Eternita District or catching snakes in the desert of the Ombra District with the *Viipir*."

Ivo laughed. "As you know, I was born in the Ombra District. Those vampires you speak of love their dangerous assortments of animals."

"I wanted to be a queen that embraces her people exactly as they are. I believed that together we could grow into something more than we could ever be apart. I would never stand for cruel extensions of control, or the enslavement of my planet's people."

Ivo stopped her mopping, gazing at Sima with a sad sort of pride. "You are an incredible queen. You will be the leader you have dreamed of, and one day, my sisters and I will be free at last."

The pin on Ivo's hood gained Sima's attention. A viper coiled tightly around a blade. At the tip, a venomous, viridescent drop. It was the only reminder of their coven. The King poured so much effort into destroying their history and still they fought to remember.

"How will I know when it is the right time to make my move? What if he captures me like he has before?"

"Let us plan something together," Ivo said, walking up to Sima's side. Ivo reached into her pocket, withdrawing a small, folded piece of paper. "Here," she said, handing it to her. "You need to see what I've found."

Cosima unfolded the paper and began reading. "Where did you find this?" she asked. "How did you get your hands on such a thing?" Her hands trembled as she read, her friend silent as she resumed her task of mopping away the remnants of Sima's blood from the rose quartz floor.

Sima could hardly believe her eyes. It was a letter from the King's desk. It outlined the next stages of change for the Archipelago. She felt dizzy. *How could there still be more of my home he wants to destroy?*

"There are servants' tunnels, though I am the only one who has been brave enough to explore them all. There are primary routes each of my sisters uses to carry out their assignments. However, with a bit of luck, I came upon an open door to somewhere I had never been before."

Metal rustled in Ivo's pocket. She reached in and revealed a dozen bronze keys. Sima shook her head. Her friend had been risking her life to explore the servants' tunnels and had used them to steal something from Aurelio's desk.

"Ivo. What were you thinking? Exploring is one thing, but thievery will get you killed."

Ivo smiled, her blue eyes brighter than Sima had ever seen them.

"It was a rush. I found my way into the city, and truthfully, I could make it as far as the other island, Iridicenza, if I tried. I had to see it for myself what he planned to do with it."

Sima gasped, eyes rapidly scanning through the text, hoping she would not find the name of her last sacred place in Aeria on the list of structures to be altered. Air left her in a half-sob as she read the words *Astral Atheneum demolition orders.*

"Aurelio can't do this!" Sima shouted between heaves of tears. "He has taken *everything* from me. He can't take Aeria's largest library too. The artifacts, the literary works, historical texts. The Atheneum protects it all from outside forces, as it has done for centuries."

"This is how you know it is the time to act. If he follows through with those plans, he will erase thousands of years of history in an instant. The demolition occurs after the Day of Return."

"Why is he in such a rush?"

"I am unsure, though I could search for more information," Ivo flashed a sheepish grin, "if you wanted."

Sima shook her head, wiping the tears from her eyes.

"No," Cosima said, "I want you to stay inside the Palace, Ivo. It is extremely dangerous for you out there. There is no way I can save you if Aurelio catches wind of what you are doing."

Ivo nodded, though Sima doubted she would listen. Her free-spirited friend did not take well to being told what to do. It was only a matter of time before she was plotting to overthrow King Aurelio all on her own.

"I want you to show me," Sima said suddenly. "One day, I would like to explore the tunnels with you. Then, if you run into trouble, perhaps it will not fall solely on your head. He won't kill me, and neither will the others."

Ivo's eyes widened. "You would truly do that for me? I am a stubborn servant, certainly not worth as much as the queen herself."

"I would not want to be queen if it meant leaving you to fend for yourself. You are worth everything, and at the minimum, you are worth everything to me. Our friendship has saved me. Through all the abuse from Aurelio, through all the times he used my body and my power, it has been you that helped me to the light again."

Ivo smiled. "You have saved me, as well. I must go, or my duties for the day will be unfinished. I am not interested in punishment for tasks undone," she said with a nervous laugh. "You will know when the time is right to take back your kingdom, Queen Cosima Aphelion."

"Thank you," Sima said, "I promise to seize it should I come across it."

"One last thing," Ivo said, reaching beneath Cosima's bed, and retrieving two novels. "Two more for you. I will exchange them soon for more new ones. You've worked yourself through a quarter of the Nuvola Palace's library already," she added with a smile.

Ivo bowed respectfully before exiting her chambers.

For the past two years, Aurelio had confined Sima to her rooms, leaving her unable to leave without his explicit approval. Her chambers lay just one floor beneath Aurelio's and one floor above the Rani Guardians quarters who were stationed within the Palace. Sima found her way to the balcony, unlatching the cherry wood doors. It would be quite some time before she could roam the halls again, her ability to do so hinging on her husband's unstable whims.

From where she stood, the sky was open and endless before her. Only three crystalline statues and fields of grass took up space in her vision. The Nuvola Palace's placement so high in the sky made it impossible to see mountains, trees, or animals. She did, however, occasionally get a few visitors.

A white bird flapped its wings, casting it further above the Palace. In awe as it circled, swooped, and glided in the open expanse of sky before her, she let out a sigh.

What would it be like to be that free? she wondered.

Sima couldn't help but think about her relationship with Aurelio. In the beginning, he arrived, impressing everyone in Aeria with his ability to travel through the veil. He brimmed with pride as he told everyone the history of Ambrosi with wings.

The Sacred Twelve are the only Ambrosi born with wings in nine centuries, he had told them. Sima shook her head at the memory, knowing they had all been fools to welcome him, to admire him. He spent months courting Cosima, all while she handed over everything he needed to take over the Archipelago. He seized Aeria because it had been Cosima who led him through the halls. It was her hand he held when he met her father, the former King of Aeria.

A tear slid down her cheek, though she refused to wipe it away, to acknowledge its existence. The guilt plagued her daily. Never could she escape the reality that she was the one who had given her kingdom this Fate. Though she could never have guessed Aurelio would slaughter hundreds of Guardians, armed with nothing but two twin swords. He was ruthless, brutal beyond comprehension. His cruelty only spread, attaching itself to every inch of Aeria.

He told no lies. The Sacred Twelve must be unimaginably powerful, if he were any indication. Yet, Sima refused to believe he was invincible. There was a way to stop him. She had just not found it yet. The others believed revolt to be futile—yet it was Cosima's own powers which made it so. Perhaps her path toward freedom began closer to the rebels than she thought.

The bird flew closer, landing gently on a statue Aurelio had constructed of himself. Composed of tiger's tye, it was one of Aurelio's favorite stones. The vivid golds and browns swirled beneath the feet of Sima's new friend.

"I am envious of you," she said aloud, "of how free you are. The way you can taste the open air, the way you may move as you desire. Tell me, how does the quiet sound when you are not afraid of what awaits you within it? I yearn for your life, one where I, too, can allow every whim to come to fruition."

As if the bird could hear her, it turned to her, spreading its ivory feathers wide and sang. The chirps from it were carefree and beautiful. Sima closed her eyes, enjoying the tune.

Then, suddenly, it stopped. When she opened her eyes, she was horrified to see it had dropped beside the crystal statue.

Sima covered her mouth with her hand as she gasped.

It had died.

Chapter 4

Through endless smoky quartz hallways plastered with imposing portraits of Aurelio, Sima made her way to the dining hall. The King's commitment to his narcissism was revolting. Sima could not raise her eyes from the crystal shimmering beneath her feet as she walked. She knew these halls well, and as a girl, she spent many empty summer days gazing out the tall windows, daydreaming about Haelos—daydreaming about anything other than the open sky before her.

It had been a week since the Giving, and the renewed energy of the Archipelago was already at work as more changes popped up across the Palace. It pained her to imagine the day Aurelio's desires fully consumed her home.

Sima hesitated as she passed an open window, the breeze magnetizing with scents of rain soon to come. She leaned against the black windowsill, peering outside. The Rani Guardian escorting her watched her tensely, afraid she would dart out of the opening, feet flying for freedom. She scoffed quietly; Sima had learned well enough from prior attempts that her legs could not outrun the winged powerhouses that were the Rani Guardians.

Cosima would not escape Aurelio's detestable vanity outside either. In the grassy courtyard lay stone seating crafted of brilliant Lapis Lazuli, its vivid blues splattered with flecks of gold, sparkling in the moonlight. Surrounding the three stone benches were fluffy blue hydrangeas and another tiger's eye statue of Aurelio. This one was a full-body warrior stance, every lock of hair painstakingly hand-carved.

How has more changed each time I leave my rooms? she wondered.

Sima huffed, pulling herself away from the window with clenched fists, when she noticed a bird. It was remarkably similar to the one Sima had seen before, and she smiled at seeing a familiar friend.

"Hello," she whispered, ignoring the impatient Guardian by her side.

The bird reacted precisely how it had before, planting itself atop the head of the statue and singing. This time, Sima backed away from the window slowly. Horror coated her insides as the bird turned, revealing a mass of fungus bursting from its little ribcage.

Sima quickly made her way to the dining hall, her escort oblivious to the mysterious, infected bird. She swallowed her fear, wondering if perhaps she had not been healed to the extent she originally thought.

As she rounded the corner, smoky quartz floors gave way to sodalite, another blue-hued stone with webs of gold, yellow, and white that spiraled mesmerizing paths beneath the large clear quartz tables. Lengthy slabs of the clear stone glimmered with trails of rainbows as they caught the light.

The ornate table bore considerable lengths of silk fabric, adorned with a patchwork of candles. Gold leaves scattered, fallen from unseen branches, drifting with an unperceivable wind. The food would have been enough to feed a thousand, yet only two hundred would dine with them tonight. It was a small dinner aimed at appeasing his flock rather than an official event. The waste of food would concern King Aurelio little.

Sima took a seat as a Rani Guardian pushed in her chair. He walked off without another word as she glanced at the food before her. An array of red meats, steaming beneath butter and garlic. Heaps of colorful green, purple, and red vegetables cluttered the remaining serving trays.

Immortal food gleamed with perfection, yet it always rubbed Sima the wrong way. It was undoubtedly delicious. Ambrosi spent a millennium perfecting it, though it was simultaneously artificial. Chefs added magic during the preparation, replacing true tastes with crafted ones.

A servant girl with long brown hair appeared, gathering food onto a plate to serve Sima.

"Thank you," Sima said with a smile.

The girl returned one, bowing her head slightly as she filled Sima's glass to the brim with wine. She shot Sima an amused glance before continuing on to serve others. Sima continued to smile to herself as she took a small sip, savoring the taste. Alcohol was a mercy, drunkenness the perfect avenue to numbness.

She picked at the enchanted food on her plate, wondering when her husband would arrive. The meal felt fake, fattened with magical energy. She took a bite of the red meat, shoving it into her mouth with a grimace. Its artificial aftertaste lingered long after she swallowed.

Ambrosi could never run out of magic—deplete it, sure—but even in events such as the Giving, nothing lasted forever. The regeneration period depended on the individual. Sima's own intervals leaned toward the high end of the spectrum. Immortal Ambrosi with lower reserves were of similar strength to the Alfrii on Haelos. The Spirit Goddess, Ehses, created hundreds of magic types for their planet—except for humans, who were powerless.

Aurelio had not only rigorously changed the appearance of Aeria, he had turned his control over Aeria into something more religious in practice. Ambrosi were now obedient, pliable to fit his needs. If for no other reason than he had promised them luxury, re-quiescence from the harsh demands of a species constructed to serve others.

As she chewed, she spotted him and his entourage arriving.

The King's flawlessly tailored black-on-black suit adorned him well. His massive gray wings sat menacingly across his back. Aurelio was one of the few Ambrosi on this planet not created within Haelos, and his magic was unparalleled to even the powerful Guardians. Rumors fluttered of the Sacred Twelve being half-Gods and not mere Ambrosi. Sima wondered if that union granted them wings nearly twice those of the Rani.

Aurelio took his usual spot at the head of the table, Sima to his left. To his right, Remo, the Emblem Chief, and second-in-command, Volfango. Both Emblems were impossibly lazy. Control of the Rani Guardians rested more in the city Captains, Lucrezia, Ermete, and Ulrico. The city Captains could not dine, though Sima spotted their wings toiling through the dining room in protective sweeps.

Caelian's seat, to her surprise, sat empty beside the Emblems. His usual stance of drooling at their toes was upheld tonight by another hopeful Guardian, Eugenio. He winked at her and rolled a toothpick with his tongue as he slipped into the chair. Sima angled her head toward her plate, focusing on forcing small, polite bites.

Several Guardians had become deeply ingrained in the torture Aurelio crafted for her. The last words Eugenio said to her echoed through her mind.

"Fight for your fucking life, bitch."

He had said it with his hands on her throat, lying between her legs.

A hand involuntarily floated to her neck, encouraging a sick grin from the Guardian.

Aurelio and the Emblems paid no mind to their exchange, focusing instead on spewing hate for all who lived in Sotto il Cielo. Servants quickly brought each of them a plate loaded with heaps of the best slices of meat. Aurelio sighed after sucking back a full glass of wine.

"Listen, and I like those Hexia, I do. They're helpful," Volfango said, smacking away as he ate. "But the Viipir are the worst to come from Ombra. How many rebels were Viipir? Almost all of them! How could we deny the proof? There is something sinister about them."

"If realms full of savage creatures exist, how do we know *they* are not parasites? Could it be true that they slipped onto the precious planet, and that the Spirit did not create them?" asked Remo, swirling his wine.

"No," King Aurelio said, "The Spirit Goddess has made many questionable species. Haelos is teeming with all kinds of shifters, worse than the Viipir. One day, our great planet, Haelos, will be free of the vermin."

Sima rolled her eyes as she ate. Her husband deigned not even the faintest acknowledgment in her direction.

"What about the Alfrii?" Eugenio asked. "Those guys are no better."

At that, the King laughed. "Oh, but they are certainly more useful. Like the Hexia, they can cast some powerful enchantments with the right tweaks. Hexia, though, are much more pliable. As it stands, the Alfrii are becoming a bigger headache than any of the creatures Below."

"What magic types do they have on the other planets?" asked Remo.

"Creatures from other planets are not as fickle as those from Haelos. Their powers are stronger than any we've seen here. The humans are laughable. What reason is there to defend them? What the Goddess Ehses planned to do with them is beside me. Toying with their little minds is the only use they bring me," said the King as he stared at Cosima's forest green dress, another of his choice. Sima shifted slightly beneath his gaze. He smiled, redirecting his attention to the Emblem Chief.

"Humans," Remo said. "I can rip their limbs clean off. Other Guardians protect prestigious commanders, not sacks of flesh. Such worthless beings are beneath us. Though, I will admit, my King, the luxury I know in Aeria is not one my kind have experienced before. They raise us to be bloodthirsty killers, but we, too, enjoy the finer aspects of this world." He lifted his wineglass, the others laughing as he took a large gulp.

Why Ehses had created humans and left them defenseless was anyone's guess. None praised the Goddesses for their forthcoming nature.

Power rippled off Aurelio as he stuffed his face, cheeks pink from too much wine. The intensity of it only increased as he drank, unable to maintain a sober grip on his magic.

"Tomorrow, I am making a trip to the Below."

Sima looked up from the vegetable she had been pushing around her plate. *He's going to the Below?* Sima thought with panic. Ambrosi rarely touched the surface of the planet. Most immortals would never contact the world beneath their sky cities.

"I must assess the gate," Aurelio said. The others dropped their chins, all suddenly very interested in their plates. "I don't believe a word of the dissenter, but I promised our wonderful Ambrosi that I would inspect it myself. Who knows, perhaps I'll make some upgrades."

"What changes can you make?" Eugenio asked eagerly.

The King laughed. "Thanks to my lovely wife here," he said, "I have access to all immortal magic granted to the royalty of the Archipelago. What I say goes. I can keep anyone out if I wanted."

"I knew there were no beasts attacking citizens," Remo said with a greasy smile.

Aurelio beamed. "Of course not!" He turned to her, sliding a finger beneath her chin. "You shall be on your best behavior, little dove."

His pet names tortured her, but *dove*. Her fingers clawed the armrests, nails digging into the velvet upholstery. He called her *dove* only when he wanted to remind her of their forgone love. Aurelio smiled, clearly satisfied. He spun his ring a few times around his finger, soaking up her anger.

Long ago, she had truly fallen for him in every sense of the word. They shared a frenzied, desperate kind of love. Her hand reached for her glass, finishing its contents before the servant came and filled it to the brim once again.

"Remo and I will contact the Guardians stationed near Portale del Regno Stellare," Volfango said, picking his teeth. "We will ensure your work is conducted uninterrupted. A group of Guardians are being reassigned to Sotto il Cielo, anyway. They can function as extra security detail."

Portale del Regno Stellare. The Star Realm Portal.

It was their only connection to other realms. The rebellion and the decrepit creatures put the King at risk. If it were true that his neglect had bred egregious consequences, a cosmic demon could slaughter him in retaliation.

"No females," he said after taking a long drink of wine. "Why they let the wombs become Guardians, I do not know. Your species' only chance at reproduction, callous enough to believe themselves above breeding and rearing brats." His tongue flicked over his teeth as he spun his glass. "You women always have to feel like the hero. Can't sit back and let men take care of things."

"Yadira is on the detail, sir. Would you like me to exclude her?" Remo asked tightly.

Aurelio's golden eyes simmered as they met Sima's gaze.

"That worthless girl is hardly a Guardian."

"She is more than capable of being a Guardian," Sima said, mouth twitching. So, he had suspected their friendship, then. That meant Yadira's life was at risk. He handled her friendships with lethal punishment—so much so that Ivo and Yadira were the only friends she had known in years.

"I forgot," he droned, "females also don't know when it is in their best interest to shut up. Fantastic job, *Yin.*" He turned his attention back to his followers. "Leave her behind. If you wish to reassign her to the inferno, I won't stop you, but she isn't coming anywhere near me."

Her fist balled beneath the table, the other hand stabbing her fork fiercely into a hunk of red meat. She chewed loudly, as far from ladylike as she could manage. Aurelio's face was calm as he reached beneath the table, snatching her knee in his hand, her flesh throbbing in response. She chewed slower, mouth closed this time. He continued chatting, releasing her knee.

"Carmine, my brother, has been telling me the latest updates from his realm. Of interesting inventions they are working on over there. They call life force the 'life seed', isn't that mad? The life force is the primary connection the Spirit Goddess has to the people of Haelos. It contains their magic, and without it, they perish."

"Do the humans have life force?" Eugenio asked.

"They have trace amounts. Enough for Ehses to keep track of them, but hardly adequate for producing magic."

The men laughed. As the meal continued, the number of attendees dwindled. Soon, it was only Aurelio and his drunken goons sitting around Sima. She picked at the dessert the servant brought. The King slurred onward. Rivers of red wine stained the silk cloths.

"Carmine thinks his world is the most interesting, bragging to me about the riches Uperath holds. He got lucky! We all had to find our own way through, no telling what we would find. He picks Uperath, and surprise, it's incredible. The Queen of Uperath is as tasty as they get, of course. Yet, he is still unsatisfied. He believes he will be meeting a merchant with plenty of money, but it is me who is luring him. Wait until he witnesses what my own two hands can claw from this wretched planet. I have big plans for Haelos, and his rotting corpse nourishes all of them."

"What does Carmine know of you and the others?" Remo asked, running a sweaty hand through his hair, cheeks flush.

Aurelio smiled, the silverware clinking against his wineglass as it tumbled onto the table.

"That is the best part. He knows nothing. I have been able to keep it all hidden from prying eyes."

"Even from the Goddess?" Sima asked.

His expression soured.

"I hide nothing from the Goddess, *Yin*. Shut up and eat."

As the conversation continued, mostly long-winded rambling about perceived political tension, Aurelio did not require her to speak again. It was getting late, and he had still not excused her from the table, even after the servants cleared all the dishes away. Everything except the wine. Her head hurt.

She looked up from her haze to find Aurelio staring at her.

He sat in his favorite black suit, with its rose-gold accents and tie. The buttons and cuff links resembled suns and stars. It reminded Sima how much he loved to pretend he was as powerful as Ehses, capable of putting stars in the sky.

But he was merely Ambrosi.

Something many would kill to be, but never would.

Something that never satisfied him, and never could.

The wine made her dizzy. Her eyes fluttered shut only briefly, but her husband's hand drifted lazily, caressing her forearm like an idle action from a lover. Dulled beneath the heavy blanket of alcohol coursing through her veins was the urge to swipe his hand away.

"Gentlemen," Aurelio said, "we are taking our leave. The missus has gorged herself, and I would never miss an opportunity to spend the evening with a pliant wife."

Chapter 5

The air smelled of iron and salt.

She knew immediately where they were.

Aurelio's personal chambers, and her personal hell hole. Whatever plan he had concocted now was especially vicious. An impossibly skimpy nightgown hung on her body. The wine from last night ensured she didn't remember getting out of her previous dress and into this. Nor did she remember anything that happened in between. It was the preferable route.

She didn't need to move to know there were heavy chains on not just her wrists, but her ankles. She was inside a walk-in closet he had transformed into his own torture pit, and she was anchored to the wall. A private little room for Aurelio to do whatever he pleased. Guardians would dismiss her screams as a husband taking what was his, and nothing more.

The scent of his cigar filled the room. Thick Void Vine plumes of smoke filled his bedroom chamber. Some of the fog made its way into the closet, and Sima stifled a cough. He had a drug habit, and it was a secret from no one. His little cigars were a ritual of sorts, always lighting up just before unleashing himself on Sima.

His footsteps sounded as he made his way toward her. Chains rumbled with soft clinks as she sat up, the dense cloud of smoke obscuring her husband from view. Dark slacks and brown leather shoes meandered to a stop just before her.

"Hi, little dove," he cooed. "I was wondering when you'd finally wake up. Open," he commanded.

Compliance was the favored option, and once her jaw fell open, capsules plopped onto her tongue.

This time, something was wrong.

He flinched as the pills full of *Mortoid* flew from her lips and hit him square in the face. Searing pain struck her cheek, sending her toppling across the chains. Aurelio seethed as he gathered the pills. All three of them.

"I said, open your fucking mouth," he growled.

"I won't do it," she said, squeezing her eyes shut.

"Oh, yes, you fucking will." His golden eyes stewed. He reached down, trailing his thumb across her lip. How many times had he done that before?

"Aurelio, we don't know what that kind of dose will do to me. It took us months to work up from one capsule to two. Please." Her lips trembled.

His fingers brushed her skin lightly as he took another long puff of his cigar. He squatted down, locking her gaze, before exhaling in her face. She peddled backward, flush with the wall. Void Vine was mild as far as drugs went. It increased the users' senses, and with enough of it, users also reported euphoria. On the downside, it could make someone incredibly anxious.

He twisted the cigar between his fingers. "Alfrii. Fucking puny little Faeries with heavy egos. They are always preaching about the planet—they bitch and moan that it is imperative we rehabilitate nature, restore the former glory of Haelos." He took another puff, savoring the draw. "Paws of devil spawn stomped all over my shipments. It wasn't enough to satisfy them. No, slaughtering my messengers, attacking loading docks, spewing fabricated nonsense about my destruction of the planet. It was just the beginning. They're playing big games for pointy-eared nothings. They forget Haelos is mine to command! I'll do what I see fit, and if it means exterminating them…"

"No," Sima whispered.

Ashy vermilion glimmered as he inhaled. "You can keep that from happening. You can save all those worthless, insignificant lives. All you have to do is take one more capsule. That's all. One more little cap, a job well done, and I'll even let you out of your rooms once a day again. If you're a good girl, I might even let you back into the library."

Sima shivered at the mention of her favorite place. Ivo had been sneaking her books, but Cosima longed to be roaming through the shelves on her own.

"Why do I have to do this?" Sima asked, voice soft, head down in resignation. She had no choice. Quiet resolve that lay within Aurelio's eyes, the type of ease made possible only by utter faith that he would get his way.

"Planet Haelos has an exorbitant number of valuable resources, and I suspect Eternita is harboring a great deal of them. Alfrii are clever, and as it stands, I cannot make it inside of Eternita because of an enchantment similar to the one that exists around Aeria to protect us." His lips met the cigar for another puff.

"Guardians I send in never come back. Either they are dead, or they are soon to be. If they are traitors, I will release their souls from this dimension myself. Sealing me from their district solidified Eternita's destiny. I will slaughter every pest Haelos has borne, and perhaps then this planet shall progress to the future it deserves. Ones without lowly magic types."

"Why do you hate them so much?" Sima asked. Studying what she could about Haelos from books failed to compare to real-life experience, yet Sima was sure he was wrong about them.

A toothy grin met her in response. Sima screamed as he plunged the burning tip of his smoke directly into the flesh of her forearm. Muscle sizzled, the scent of burned skin joining the Void Vine in the air. He stood, flicking the bud away from them. Sima hissed as she clamped a hand over her wound.

Aurelio produced a gem from his pocket, smiling as he rolled it between his fingertips. "Do you know what this is?"

Muted red hues swam along the outer borders of a crystal. The stone was small and polished. Smooth curves replaced jagged, natural corners to form a sphere. It was a rich, dark green with flecks that matched its aura.

"No," Sima shuddered as the pain dulled, her healing powers knitting her wound back together. Crystals of all kinds adorned Aeria, an addition Aurelio was proud of. However, this was not one she was familiar with.

"This is heliotrope, also known as Bloodstone. History of this small mineral claims it possesses powers of invisibility, rain summoning, health divination. This stone has special abilities imbued within. If used properly, it can grant humans magic."

Sima gasped. "That's not true, right? They just believe the crystals have power," she said, covering her eyes with her hands.

"It is true. All the crystals have power. Why do you think I chose your pitiful planet in the first place? I can traverse through realms, I am the strongest of all my brothers. Do not think I wasted my time when I came here. The power within these crystals is the exact power the Spirit Goddess used when she crafted the people of the Below."

"As such," the King said, lip curled in disgust, "they each have unique abilities, just as the stones do. The crystals I have erected around the Archipelago have beneficial properties. The people of this planet are inferior compared to those Ambrosi and Rani Guardians normally oversee. It is a mockery of what Ehses has crafted here and commanded the Archipelago to manage. I believe I am doing the Ambrosi here a service."

"This is their only opportunity to wield magic, my King," she said, not meeting his gaze. "Why do you wish to take that from them?"

"If the Spirit wanted the humans to have magic, she would have given it to them. Besides, you truly believe these stones are capable of power, yet have not inquired about their detriment. Every being on Haelos has a life force. Our meat sacks make up the vessel, souls and life force jammed within. Humans, lacking power, have an astonishingly low reserve. If the crystal contains more energy than the vessel can withstand..." He sighed. "It ruptures, causing an egregiously long-winded demise. Occasionally, when dealing with particularly energetic gems, these lethal outcomes become probable for all of Spirit's creations. Not even Ambrosi are strong enough to bear it."

"It can kill Ambrosi?" Sima's mind swirled. There was no known way to kill Ambrosi—at least, not one Sima was aware of. "If it is that dangerous, then all the people in Sotto il Cielo are at risk as well as the people of Aeria. We must save them, King."

He laughed, throwing his head back. "I have given you the opportunity to do so. I suspect they are collecting more of these crystals to come here and bring our Archipelago to its knees. They bombarded the Messengers sent to retrieve a shipment of crystals confiscated by the Rani Guardians stationed Below. Crates stuffed with thousands of crystal shards each, all hijacked by the Devout Rising." His lip tugged into a sneer. "Pity all the bodies Eternita will be responsible for."

Icy apprehension nipped at her neck. Her mind drifted to the Fae man Aurelio had forced her to expose.

"Why are they coming after you, Aurelio?" She flinched at the glare she received in return. "If there are beasts and their people are dying, why would they not come for you? We are sworn—"

"I know precisely what we are here to do!" he shouted. "There are no beasts. Those idiots just want every problem solved by the kingdom, and we are not here to pander to them. They are angry, but they are not in danger from anything beyond the crystals."

Persuasion was a strong suit of his, but she knew the truth. She studied him as any might study a captor—with spiteful diligence. She knew he would gain nothing from saving the humans. It was fear Aurelio felt. The crystals put his life at risk, too.

"What do you want me to do?" Sima said, sighing. She could not risk the lives of those in Aeria if magic that could kill immortals existed in those crystals.

He extended his hand towards her, before unfolding his fingers and revealing the three capsules.

"Solara is the name of the target. She is an Alfrii woman from the Eternita District. I am cleaning the world of rulers like her, and all the insolent followers she has gained. Waste no time down there. Destroy that pathetic excuse for a woman. I don't care how you do it."

Sima frowned. "You're letting *me* choose how to change it?"

"You have no other choice. Unfortunately, coming across information has been painstaking to say the least. She is a small, useless blip of life, and I want you to exterminate her as such."

Trembling fingers wrapped their way around the three capsules. She jostled them in her palm, the shells colliding with gentle clatters. Three capsules would have a more profound effect on her. The transition from one to two had proved that. Three would keep her under longer, a fact which had bile streaking her throat.

One. Two. Three.

The capsules gelled together as they mixed with her saliva, Sima grimacing as she swallowed them whole. Hallucinations came in a faster wave than she was used to, though the depictions were her usual nightmare fuel. The faces of monsters and demons, all across the spectrum from strange to maddening, distorted behind her eyelids.

The drugs took her, her mind and consciousness slipping through the fabric of the surrounding reality, Sima releasing all grips on her body. She floated there in a weightless dream.

Until she felt something grab her shoulder.

Strange.

In here, there were no connections to her body. There would be no way for Sima to determine if something was happening to her on the outside. Whatever touched her had somehow slipped through. Uneasy heaviness replaced buoyancy as her body hurdled faster through the vat of darkness around her. This is how she imagined falling out of the sky might feel. Well, maybe without all the horrid faces fluttering by.

She slammed onto a grassy field, her body contorting unnaturally as it ricocheted off the ground.

A field?

Why was there a field here? She hadn't chosen a door yet. *Did I take too many?*

Something in the air smelled stale, ancient. Sima sat

encapsulated in dread. She was in a field, illuminated by a small speckle of stars in the sky. Whatever portal she had come through was now closed, and all she could hear was the sounds of her breathing.

Well, the sounds of Sima *and* someone else breathing.

Cosima thrusted backward, a small shriek escaping her lips. Razor-sharp claws shredded the fabric of her blouse. Thick beads of blood pooled across her wounds, though no pain registered on her nerves. Sima clamped her eyes shut as she felt the hot breath of something leaning over her and sniffing her.

"Oh, what a joy *this* is," the creature said, perfectly mimicking the accent of those in Aeria. "I know where you're from, tiny one. You're from Haelos."

With that, a thin, serpent-like tongue flicked across her chin.

"Oh, but from Haelos, only in residence. You certainly smell just like the immortals," the creature said, its tongue flicking across her again, as if it were trying to discern her entire heritage from a lick. "Yet something more delicious runs through your veins, and I bet you don't even know it. I know who you are now."

"I've seen you here," the creature said, as its grip on Sima tightened. As the shock began wearing off, Sima floundered beneath his grip, desperate for freedom. "You scamper around doing someone else's dirty work, yet your energy is pure, not a shadow in sight. Pray tell, my dearest prize, why do you come to the Valley of the Dead?"

"This must be a mistake, I-I—this can't be real," Sima stuttered, regretting every word that left her mouth. Her erratic disposition only intrigued the beast more. Sima glanced around his body. Entities surrounded them. She shrieked, peddling backward at the sight of the shadowed figures with glowing white eyes that stood all around them.

"How you got here is a mystery to me, little gift, but I am much more interested in *what* you are doing in my home?"

She looked around frantically, though the shadowed figures came no closer.

"Someone sent me on a small quest," Sima said, hoping to talk her way out of his jaws. "I think I came to your home by mistake. I-I can leave."

"You won't be leaving, not yet. Most of the people here are souls waiting to be re-birthed. You have come to the in-between. *Tra paradiso e inferno.*" That Sima recognized. *Between heaven and hell.* "You come here to glimpse the truth, to alter a bit of destiny. No harm done, you think. You are changing a very delicate process." It smiled then. The creature actually smiled at her. Its teeth dripped in saliva during the display, each razor-sharp ivory projection bigger than her palms. She couldn't fight him off if she wanted to.

"I didn't know, I didn't mean to—"

The creature's body shook as it laughed, revealing fine feathered wings, twice the size of Sima, dipped in red at the tips. Though she only saw the glimmers of red through the limited light from the stars, her entire body stilled. She knew what he was.

"You're… you're a Drago."

"One of the last, I'll have you know." As the creature rose, he finally released Sima. Her hands reflexively flew to her wounds to assess them. "Relax, injuries to you here will not remain when you return to Haelos. You are here in spirit, not in flesh." He began walking, his powerful legs showing muscle even through his thick scaled skin. His wings were not just massive, they were beautiful. The veins along the underside showed intricate webbings, sprawling like city streets. As if he could sense her stare, he closed them, holding them tighter to his long body, tail swaying as he continued. "Come, there is something you must see."

Sima rose quickly to her feet and followed the Drago. Between the closing of her eyelids, things changed rapidly around them. At first, the field faded into nothingness. Then nothingness was replaced with flurries of light, which were replaced with flashes of mountain tops, rivers, and even buildings, just like those in Haelos, but not quite right.

"What's happening?"

"You tell me, realm-walker."

Before she could respond, the words and the very breath from her lungs vanished.

A scene unfolded, the birth of a small Alfrii baby, a room buzzing with fear and excitement. The scent of blood and triumph in the air.

"The children," the Drago said, "they are rare. They are much like the Ambrosi in their limited fertility, choosing lifespan over reproduction. The baby, she is the one you seek, yes?"

Sima knew immediately that it was. The mother of the child wept over her new bundle of joy, repeating her name in celebratory whispers. The mother lovingly wiped the blood and tissue from her baby's fuzzy golden hairs.

Solara, the future Queen of Eternita.

Solara, Sima thought, *the Queen robbed of the throne of Eternita.*

Sima reached a hand for her, willing herself to get this part of the trip over with. Something stopped her.

"Why did you bring me here if the changes I make are so disastrous?"

"Do you know what the Drago are for?"

"Protection."

"Yes, of all the souls in my jurisdiction. Do you know what you are to me?"

Sima stayed silent. She knew the answer. *A threat.*

"An opportunity," he said when she did not reply.

"For what?" Sima asked.

"For silence."

The Drago did not explain further, but they stood there for some time. The extra caps extended the time she could spend here, but they wouldn't last forever. Time was ticking, and every moment brought her closer to the surface.

The scene unfolded over and over, magic spilling from her fingertips to bring her to what caught her interest. Sima's powers simmered, straining to bypass the barrier enough to assess Solara's heart. There was a strange pit in her stomach as her magic skittered across the future queen's body. Her heart thumped loudly beneath her blouse, an invisible wind sweeping in smells of a variety of herbs as the scene began again.

It was a large room and appeared to be within a private

infirmary. Limited supplies were around, beyond a rainbow selection of tonics, the language on the labels indecipherable for Sima. The bottles appeared deftly out of place. The Alfrii healed primarily at the hands of descendants blessed with healing magic.

The woman, Solara's mother, pulled her tired body from the bed, determined to hold her child. She stroked the fuzzy nest of now clean hair atop Solara's head as tears spilled from her eyes. She tucked a lock of hair, perfectly matching the color of her daughter's, behind her elongated ear.

"Solara," the mother said, pride swelling in her throat as she spoke, "you are finally here, my baby. Do you know how we have wished for you? How many nights I have spent dreaming—yearning—for a moment just like this?"

She wiped the tears from her eyes then.

"I hope you can forgive me," she whispered across her forehead, beneath a gentle kiss. "I have run out of time. It will be up to you now." Strange chants came in hushed breaths. The mother's slender hand wavered just an inch above the babe's chest, her magic spilling out in gentle waves. The infant's chest illuminated, receiving the offering. "If not you, Solara, then the next."

Sima's breath caught. It was *life force*.

The mother was giving over a portion of her life force. The infant's eyebrows gently flicked upward, the only sign the sleeping girl had noticed anything. The mother gave and gave until the flood slowed to a trickle.

She had nearly drained herself dry.

The Drago spun in a circle like a canine, before settling down beside her.

"How can she do that?" Sima asked.

"How can you do this?" the Drago responded simply, not even bothering to look in her direction.

"How is she transferring her life force? It should be impossible. The Goddess gives the people of this planet magic. She is the only one who can transfer it."

"Whoever told you that was lying."

"And what makes you so sure?" Sima asked. Though Aurelio kept her away from the records about their world in the Astral Atheneum, her parents had been preparing her for the throne. They, too, believed only the Spirit Goddess could transfer life force.

He lifted his massive, scaled head then, letting a huff of smoke escape his nostrils, gesturing toward the scene playing on repeat before them.

"Probably that," he said, his snout jerking toward the infirmary. A huge emerald eye met hers. For the first time, she was aware of exactly how colossal the Drago was. "Their kind appears to have unlocked some way to transfer life force."

"What need would they have for that? Aurelio instructed me to keep her from the throne. Does it have to do with this transferring of life force?"

He snorted, glaring at her.

"I told you I wanted silence. You are creating messes you cannot fathom, mayhem that ripples beyond your world. *She* appointed them for a reason. Those threads are *delicate*. Have you heard the tale of Kismet?"

Sima shook her head, despite the pounding in her mind that erupted upon the mention of her name.

"Kismet is the name given to the deity with powers of predestination, the appointing of the stars. Fortuity for all, not just the people of your realm. Cosmic is the only way to describe her powers. How many who rest here spent their days questioning their creation? Your Eternal Kingdom believes themselves to be the ceiling, for even they cannot cope with the reality of Kismet, of Existence, of Oblivion. Three sisters who rule beyond what even your Empress, your Goddess, your Priestess could imagine."

The Drago huffed. "Where do you think Ehses, the Spirit Goddess, got her powers of creation? Where does the cycle begin and from where do the Gods absorb their power? How long do you have to follow the thread to find the end? How far can you zoom out before being satisfied with the endless enigma? We are not to understand why Kismet decides what she does. Whatever destruction you enact, who can tell the balance needed to restore Fate's rule?"

She paled. There were more repercussions for her actions than Sima accounted for, though she suspected her powers had been angering the Gods.

He stood, shaking his thick neck, outstretched wings obscuring Sima's view of Solara and her mother. Sima followed him as he made his way out of the memory, evaporating into the shadows. A door came without call, open for her to exit as well. She took one last peek at Solara.

Sima would not interrupt destiny today. Aurelio would be angry.

"She will always seek to bring balance, for our universe, however expansive, cannot exist without it. You are not the only person capable of accessing what lay beyond the veil, though your world remains isolated, untouchable. Something is preventing the planet Haelos from being accessed, yet it seems you can travel outside of it."

She followed his voice, echoes scampering across her eardrums as she trekked through the darkness. The crunch of grass beneath her feet told her she was in the field again. Sima racked her brain for information on the veil, yet she came up short. Few understood how the veil operated, herself included.

He ignored her, dredging toward a door that had been erected from the thin air.

"Your door," the Drago said, careening his long neck to peer at the side of it. "Should you choose to no longer be blind, Cosima, *realm-walker.*"

Cosima had never seen her own future, yet within that portal lay an opportunity. The chance to see what no other oracle could tell her, to see what Ehses, the Spirit Goddess, kept hidden from her.

As her body slipped through the portal, bright smells and colors accosted her. Children frolicked not through city streets, but through open clover fields spanning miles, gigantic trees offering shade with their canopies. Behind them sat an impressive Palace carved from a mesmerizing selection of gigantic quartz crystals.

Large prismatic towers of quartz marked the four corners. The hues seemed to entangle themselves effortlessly, creating a mirage of rose, carnelian, citrine. The crystals bore intricate designs, sigils of some sort. Beside Sima sat a foreign version of herself. The woman was identical to Sima, but she had never seen this place before. The scent of lavender hit her then, nearly knocking her from her paralyzed position. Behind her, the door latched, leaving her to bear witness to the truth.

"Cosima!" shouted a small girl, rising from the horizon like the sun. "You're back! You're finally home. We've been waiting for you."

Her confusion only grew as she watched her mirror image greet the girl with a smile.

"Come, I am happy to be home," Cosima of another world said.

When the darkness came to pull her back up then as she reached the limits of her stay, Sima let it take her, feeling adrift in an ocean of agony.

Chapter 6

Consciousness found her before air did.

Her hands scrambled to her throat, desperate to peel back her skin if it meant letting air in.

The chains. One link of the iron chains had sprung open along the weld, causing it to spear straight through her side, making it ever the more obvious that the problem was *not* her throat, it was her lung.

Her most likely punctured lung.

Air rattled from her body as she tried to breathe. There would be no licking her wounds like a broken animal. There would be no prying his wretched grasp from her beautiful home, saving her people from his toxic influence.

Perhaps death could be sweet.

She wouldn't get to find out.

Aurelio, ever her savior, was suddenly upon her, his muscular hands hoisting her from her position on the floor to his arms, the heavy iron falling free except for the link trapped between two of her ribs, grinding the bone.

He couldn't let his conduit to actual power perish, could he?

Cosima attempted a small laugh, pain wafting her senses as humor clouded her mind. She hoped it would be quick; she hadn't even hoped for painless. The seconds without air were all the agony and sensory overload that her body could manage. She wouldn't feel much more than this.

Sima danced along the line of consciousness, finding her eyes impossibly difficult to open. She had a vague understanding of being set down before an unfamiliar pain interrupted her demise.

A healer's needle full of tonic found its way into her veins. Ambrosi circumvented the magic stores needed to heal wounds—and jumped straight to a metamorphosis of bone, skin, and flesh. It required only a skilled witch healer. A whirling of organic tissue frenzied in reaction to the tonic reaching her heart, setting her healing off in a fleshy pink tornado.

Her head grew dizzy at the sight, either from the trauma, the restorative, or both.

The first few breaths were like gulping for air in a pit of mud. As her body stitched back together, her magic accumulated, the tonic working in tandem with it to restore her. With unrestricted breaths came panic.

She was hyperventilating.

Fingers intertwined themselves with hers. Her breath caught, not from relief, but from fear. She swallowed her panic. There would be no place for it here.

"What happened down there?" Aurelio said, with a familiar darkness to his glare. His fingernails, though expertly filed, dug small indents into the surface of her skin.

You're finally home. We've been waiting for you.

"I failed," Sima said softly.

"What do you mean, you *failed?* We do this for the Above and Below. Do you not appreciate the way you can be a part of that wonder? I hope you know I saved your life out of spite. You will never escape me and failing me will only lead to more drastic punishments."

Sima knew he didn't mean it. He always saved her life, even if he left her to suffer for some time first. He needed her, needed his control over her and the marriage that granted him even more power.

"Why do you give me those drugs, Aurelio?" Sima tried to

maintain eye contact with him but found her eyes flicking away after only a few tense seconds. He seemed amused at that.

"What do you mean? You have seen Aeria has thrived in ways it never has before, because of me and those little caps."

"What does it cost?" Sima whispered as she picked around her nails, leaving little trails of crimson among the fields of broken skin.

"What does it *cost?* Typical of you to be so negative, always dwelling on the dreariest bits of the vision. It costs *lives*, don't you get that?"

Of course that is the cost. It is the only thing expendable to him, Sima thought bitterly.

"Can you go into the veil?" Sima asked. "Is that why you use me?"

"You know I can't, *Yin*," his tone was harsh, and his stronghold on her hand left pockets of pain where she felt her flesh smash against her bones. "Only the ruling royalty can maintain the Portale del Regno Stellare, but I can't go through it, or my brothers will know where I am. That is why it has to be you. You should be so lucky to have found use in Aeria. I could have wiped your entire family line when I took it from your father's pathetic hands. Your line is so weak, so powerless. Those drugs you hate so much are the only things that give you any worth around here. Be proud you can provide for Aeria."

His words were hurtful, and perhaps if she weren't so numb, she would have felt the daggers deeper. Instead, they felt like pins. Her mind barely acknowledged it. She focused on the rage that bubbled in her.

"I am tired of doing your bidding. I want to be done," she said through her teeth, fear gripping her still-weakened body. Fear and anger.

He leaned in, inches from her face, and whispered, "No."

A tear slid down Sima's face as he stood. "Whether today or the next, you will break. Remember that. I can *break* you. You will have no choice. I go to Ombra today. When your Guardian arrives, you will go to your rooms, and you will not even have hallway privileges while I'm gone."

Although Aurelio had long released her hand, the dents from his grip remained. She was in one of Aeria's infirmaries outside the Palace, newly built and complete with an apothecary catering to all forms of life. Sour gratitude bit at her that he took her to proper help this time. She was closer to the edge than she had ever been before.

Yet she encountered no fear. There was a certain dullness to it. Like a threat that lost its bite with time. Life here with Aurelio was already worse than any death could be.

The scent of his Whisper Leaf cigarillo wafted from where he stood in the hallway, having a hushed conversation with a healer, her aprons covered in Sima's blood. He had gone with a concoction capable of soothing himself. The Whisper Leaf's gentle earthy aroma washed over the room.

Sima wished Ivo was here.

She didn't need to hear the conversation to know the poor healer was probably being threatened within an inch of her life to say nothing about what she had seen here. The girl was young, walking as if she was still getting used to her legs.

It reminded Sima of herself. By many standards, Sima was still considered young, at just a hair over one hundred years old. Her coronation took place only days after Aurelio's coup. She was finally of age to take the throne, as was destined for her. The Spirit Goddess had told a trusted Oracle that Cosima was to become the queen.

A ritual among the immortals had them each before an Oracle prior to reaching adulthood. The Oracle Sima saw cemented into minds of all within Aeria that Cosima would lead the Archipelago. This left no question. Their Goddess had denied Sima's sister, Matilde, the role.

The healer held Sima's attention. Her eyebrows were bushy, the color matching her brunette locks, save for the matted tips coated with bloody evidence of Sima's ordeal. Moon-like eyes, gray and round, stayed composed as Aurelio spoke to her, yet Sima noted the subtle flicker of fear in them.

Another figure waited in the shadows. At first, Sima dismissed it as just another Rani Guardian.

She was right that the figure was indeed a Rani Guardian, a fact which was hard to dismiss with the presence of an overtly terrifying set of feathered wings the race all carried, sprouting from their shoulders as if meant only to be in the sky.

Yet it wasn't just any other Rani; it was Yadira, Sima's only other friend. Beneath tight brown curls lay warm eyes, only a shade darker than her hair. Full lips complimented her strong facial features. She looked as picturesque as the fabled warriors Sima read about.

Yadira certainly wasn't as gentle as Ivo, but she was sturdy and non-judgmental as she helped Sima into a fresh set of clothes her Captain had asked her to bring. She did not allow her eyes to linger on Sima's still-healing scars.

Evidence of today's wounds would be gone by sunset, but the events weighed heavily on her heart.

As she looped her arm through Yadira's, thankful for the extra mobility the assistance allowed, Sima shuddered at the maddening eruption brewing within her psyche. She just had to make it back to her rooms. She could rest, cry, scream. Sima could do whatever it took to piece herself back together, if only to keep Aurelio from having the satisfaction of thinking he had won.

The only sound between them on their way back from the infirmary was the muffled song her gold and silver armor sang, like wind chimes, as the metals connected to one another. The biggest city in Innamorati, the main island in Aeria, was Via del Profeta—Way of the Prophet. Thirty thousand lived here, yet the streets remained flooded with silence.

Looking in the distance, Cosima realized why. The street where they walked was due for more construction soon—the entire area was marked with bright red and orange signs and barricades. Even more of her home sacrificed to the image in the King's mind, and yet the changes were more sinister than she thought. Viewing the building constructed of pure malachite set alarm bells off in her head.

"Yadira," Sima said, "have you ever heard of these crystals

having magic powers?"

The Guardian eyed her suspiciously. "No," she said, turning her head forward again, marching toward the Palace.

The massive Nuvola Palace loomed in the distance, as it did not matter where people stood in Aeria. Aurelio insisted on the magic it took to make it completely seamless, a perfect illusion. He wanted everyone to know he was there, and he wanted them to never forget.

The unspoken rule in Aeria.

"The King told me something. I don't know if it is wise to share with you, but there is no one else I can think to tell."

"You can trust me," Yadira said, eyes still fixated ahead of them.

"He told me of crystals that are imbued with strange, ancient power. He claims they have magic in the same way that the people created by Ehses do," Sima said, eyes scanning the malachite before them. "What power do you think these have for him to be constructing buildings out of it?"

Yadira shook her head. "I don't believe it," Yadira said. "He must be lying. If there was magic in these stones, wouldn't we have seen it already?"

Sima pondered it as they made their way to an open street without a work in progress, one more populated. Three Ambrosi girls ran in front of her, the presence of immortal children more plentiful than ever before. Each had their hair pulled into braided ponytails, wearing peach and yellow-colored dresses. Aurelio had thrust the Aeria Archipelago into three tremendously beautiful islands and had given the immortals peaceful lives. Cosima could not shake the nagging feeling that it was at the expense of those Below.

"Come," Yadira said, "let us grab you something. You need to build your strength up."

The Guardian's wide pearl wings settled compactly across her back as she slipped through the crowd. Waves of immortals drenched in color and fine jewelry flooded the square. Along the edges, Cosima spied the Temple for offerings to Ehses, the school she attended as a child, and a spray of food vendors.

At least this piece of her home had not changed. The lively gatherings depended not on the riches lining their throats and wrists, but on their connected, social nature. Scents of bread, pastries, and sugar floated toward them.

Yadira shoved a box filled with an assortment of pastries into Cosima's arms, the icing composed of vivid shades of emerald and sapphire, the colors of the Archipelago. The shop owner continually flashed Cosima apologetic smiles. It confused Sima at first until she spoke to her.

"You are a good leader, Queen Aphelion," the vendor said. Her blond, straight hair flicked backward across her shoulder as she spoke, her bracelets jingling as her hands moved.

She stared at the Ambrosi woman, unsure of what motivated her to say such a thing. She thought of the crystals, the rumored beasts, the story of Kismet. A melancholy smile found its way to Sima's face.

"That's not the opinion most hold, but thank you," Sima responded as Yadira extended payment to the vendor.

"That's not true," she replied, putting a hand up to motion her refusal of Yadira's money. "It is on the house, the least we could do for the throne." She met Sima's eyes. "Ambrosi enjoy the easy times, yes, but I think most are too afraid to say anything negative."

Sima looked away, thanking the woman again, before Yadira grabbed her hand and led them to an open bench near a sizable water fountain.

As the two of them munched through their sweet pastries, children played and danced nearby. The chatter of the crowd grew calmer as the sun set. Sima sighed. Soon they would have no choice but to return to the Palace. He had restricted her to her rooms, which meant this could be the last time she saw the city for quite some time.

"Why were you in the infirmary?" Yadira asked.

The silence ruptured, startling Cosima. Yadira's fist balled tightly. How long had she been stewing without Sima noticing? A dark expression engulfed her features. She wasn't necessarily a friendly woman, but Sima had only known a deep level of platonic love and devotion from her.

"It was nothing," Sima said, shaking her head.

"Do not lie to me," Yadira said, sweeping sugar from her lap. Her mouth pressed into a firm line, her jaw ground tightly enough to make her statuesque. Yadira was the strongest person Sima knew, and one of the deadliest. Yet, the way the wind rustled her hair, the way sorrow bit at her normally stoic features, Sima's stomach turned.

The one secret Yadira didn't know—that no one but Ivo and her tormentor himself knew—was about the trips, the drugs, the meddling of lives. Sima was unsure how her morally loyal friend would respond. Yadira took immense pride in being a Guardian, and for a moment, Cosima considered if that was the same reason she should tell the Rani the truth.

"My friend," Cosima said, staring down at her palms. "Aurelio has not changed. He is the same man he was when he took the Archipelago, when he ripped the Crown from my father's scalp. He may lull everyone into suspending their suspicions over him by giving them freedom and uncomplicated lives," Sima swallowed, "But he is forcing me to use my powers. My family kept my powers a secret because they believed they were evil, and now…"

Sima glanced up to find Yadira staring at her intently. Her chin dipped in a silent signal to Cosima to keep speaking.

"He forces me to change the Fate of others and uses horrible drugs to help me access that power."

Surprise smoldered in the Guardian's eyes.

"The hearth of the Guardians bore me, an ember of a greater mission. I have shed my immature skin, I have tamed my sharpest weapons. I can admit that the web of lies he spun caught me, too. He forbid the Guardians from mentioning his coup, and it worked." She paced incessantly in front of Sima. "With time, my brothers and sisters have become jaded about what it meant to be honorable, just as the Ambrosi embraced their new ruler. Extravagance dispatched their benevolence in hasty surges, leaving the future of Haelos uncertain. He is a power-drunk psychopath, putting his hands on someone already beaten into submission. I was one of the lucky ones to make it out unscathed, and still I suffered through every noxious manipulation he fed this once impermeable city." Shame cast her a physical weight to carry.

"Do you know, my friend?" Yadira took a shivering step toward her. "Do you know the monsters the man from the Giving spoke of are real? I went to the prisons myself. I remember the way the world seemed dimmer, so muddled compared to the life I was used to, after I heard him in his cell, whispering his accounts to another. They spoke of you, Cosima."

"Me?"

"He said he was waiting for the moment King Aurelio would force you into destroying him through changing his life-path. I refused to believe it at first, yet now I know it to be true. How have you kept this a secret for so long?"

"I have no choice. Either he tortures me," Sima blinked away a tear, unable to tell her friend the unspeakable acts committed by her Rani brothers, "or threatens the people I care about. He has threatened my family, the innocent children of Aeria, everything I care about. How can I object when I cannot change my own Fate, nor his?"

"This is not what Aeria is, what it is supposed to be. I have trusted connections to those on the other islands. A Guardian friend of mine was interested in the Below. A position in the Shadow District is shameful, a death sentence. Still, my friend risked his life to head to Ombra, to see if the reports of beasts were true. We spoke and…" She trailed off.

"He saw them."

"Yes, friend, he saw hundreds of them. Horrid beasts that don't even exist in the kinds of tales they sell in those bookstores."

Sima's eyes widened.

If this were true, there would be more consequences for Aurelio than just what he would face in Aeria. He would be subject to cosmic retribution, as mentioned in the Spirit Goddesses' commandments. Whatever that entailed, Sima was not in a hurry to find out.

"Where are they coming from?"

"Potentially the veil, but the people of the Ombra District have taken it upon themselves to fight back. They are the only defense between us and demons from other realms drifting through. Souls returning home have only one exit, but it also means it creates an opening. The Day of Return could wipe out thousands of people if too many enter our world."

"How could Aurelio let this happen?" Sima's lip trembled. It was true, the people fought beasts Rani Guardians were bred to eliminate. Their entire purpose revolved around protecting the people of the planet, and yet, they wasted their resources protecting immortals.

Waves of moderate winds swept past them, the chill nature's warning that soon nightfall would come. Aeria had known peace for hundreds of years, the locals lazy with the luxury of safety. Aurelio was striking them at their weakest, yet again.

Sensing her hesitation, Yadira cupped Sima's face in her hands and looked at her with tenderness.

"He is the one who forced you to do those things. One day, when we are far from him, and this kingdom has recovered from the hell that will find us, you will tell me it all. You will allow me to share those burdens with you, so we may dissolve their holds on you. I can see the light in there yet, Cosima."

With that, her friend released her, the warmth of her embrace lingering, even as the wind chill nipped at her skin.

It wasn't often someone touched her with such care, and suddenly Sima was much more aware of the deep hole within her.

The chance to change everything lay in Ombra—the Shadow District. Haelos was a place she had only seen from the edges of the sky. The unknown could give way to a world of experiences for her, and yet she was terrified. As a child, she had wanted to become queen, even if she despised her abilities. That was still true.

"Even if he locks me in my rooms," Sima said, staring up at the Palace in the distance, "he won't be able to stop me. He has betrayed our purpose, and I will not stand for it any longer."

Chapter 7

The King did not send for her once she returned to her rooms. Whether he knew she had come back late or failed to notice, Sima was unsure. Yadira dropped her off at her door. The Guardians who normally flanked the entrance sneered at Cosima as she made her way inside. They latched the door behind her, securing the lock into place.

A hand trailed the phantom scar, smooth skin in place of the jagged wound. All evidence that anything had happened to her was gone. The only injury that remained was soul-side. Sima stewed the entire night, finding muddled dreams between heart-pounding rage. Though confined to her rooms many times before, with all she had just learned, Cosima felt compelled to twist the tides in her own favor for once.

Yadira had confirmed the hordes of monstrous beasts Below, and now the King of Aeria was heading amongst his lambs, as if he were a livestock canine. He truly enjoyed playing the part of the noble, brave king. His obsession with image had truly distorted his grasp of reality.

I must assess the gate, he had said. Going to the Ombra District for the sake of proving his innocence to the Ambrosi was a bold move. He absolutely despised the people there, yet he would have to walk amongst them. Sima could only wonder what the District held, could only guess how the people had suffered beneath Aurelio.

Her arms flopped dramatically to her sides and into the overly stuffed comforter, a puff of air escaping from between the clasps of the duvet cover. As her body slowly sank further and further into the nest of pillows she endured nightly, Sima thought of what she had seen before coming back up.

Kismet would seek to balance all the mayhem Cosima was causing. Though Sima could not recall when exactly, she knew she had been told Kismet's story; it came to her mind with a familiarity that caused Sima to pause. Those on the Archipelago knew of other Goddesses that existed in the Ethereal Realm, but they only worshiped Ehses on Planet Haelos.

Kismet must align what I have unbalanced, Sima thought. Fear prickled in the back of her throat at the thought of what Cosmic Retribution could entail. Her parents had spared her nothing when expressing their criticisms of her power. Yet Matilde believed Cosima was good, and so was her power, as Ivo did. Sima could not decide if Aurelio or Kismet deserved her fear more.

Her mind flicked across the memory of the crystal Aurelio showed her. She could barely comprehend what it meant. Yadira had been dismissive, believing his claims to be false, yet too much would lay in the balance should he be telling the truth. Cosima sat up and walked over to her desk, digging into a drawer until she recovered the letter Ivo had stolen from the King's desk.

The Astral Atheneum was his next target. The library on the other island, Iridicenza, held every highly coveted piece of work, ceremonious artifact, and vital historical text their planet offered. Historian Ambrosi spent the entirety of their immortal lives tracking and recording the people of the Below.

Cosima crunched the letter in her fist. She needed to get inside the Astral Atheneum. If more information existed on crystals and Kismet, she would find it there. Her eyes fell on the entrance to her rooms. The Guardians were to keep her confined to her bedroom chambers. If she desired to leave while Aurelio was away from the island, she would have to be creative.

Sima made her way to the small kitchenette within her rooms, rifling through the cabinets to locate a proper snack. On nights when Aurelio's business was not for her eyes, he confined her in her rooms for the night with a meal. She stored shelf-stable snacks within a cabinet above the sink.

As she munched on the berry and seed mix, Cosima thought through her options. The servants' passageways Ivo mentioned would be difficult to locate. Ivo possessed keys, though Sima doubted she would be patient enough to wait until Ivo came to clean her bedroom chambers and refresh her linens.

The berries she ate had been grown in Aeria, tasting like fresh mountain breezes, releasing a subtle tartness when they slid down her throat. Enchantments in the food kept them fresh for longer than nature would have it, but not everything kept the same taste with time. She sighed, setting the food aside as her eyes settled on her balcony door.

Climbing over the railing to her balcony had been the straightforward part.

However, she had failed to consider precisely how high up her balcony was. There were four stories beneath her, and she tried to ignore the sweat that accumulated along her brow as she wiggled a toe toward the railing of the one beneath. When she couldn't reach, she did the only thing she could think of.

Slowly swaying her legs back and forth, her body gained momentum, until she had enough energy to let go on the swing inward, her feet landing just within the boundary of the balcony. Her elbows had both mercilessly collided with the railing, but she had made it. Yadira's quarters were directly beneath Sima's. It was how they had communicated in the past, the Guardian flying up to Sima's balcony for late night chats, and occasionally, gossip.

Before she could position herself properly, planning to use the flower box as a step, a shadowed figure appeared behind the billowing curtains. Sima cursed herself for not considering the people occupying the rooms during the day. She hadn't exactly gone into any of this with much of a plan and ducked behind some overly fluffed outdoor furniture that rested on the balcony. It was the same as all the others, each room a carbon copy.

It lent some use, the familiarity, as the neighboring stranger now exited their chambers, embracing the fresh air. Sima panicked, concerned the Guardians would find her immediately.

As luck would have it, a much better outcome saved Sima.

The door behind the sofa chair creaked, Sima slowly turning her neck and peering into the eyes of Yadira.

Her friend's muscular arms tossed her into the chambers, the door latching behind them.

A haze across the warrior's face told Sima she was not happy to see her.

"When I suggested you do something," Yadira said, her Rani armor only half buckled—she was getting ready for the changing of the Guardians. "I didn't mean nearly killing yourself scaling the sides of palaces."

Sima merely shrugged, though her pounding heart reminded her why she had come.

"What do you suggest I do then? He won't let me leave and I won't be a cooped-up farm animal. I won't be his pawn for another moment, Yadira. I am done."

Yadira's eyebrow raised at that.

"Comparing your situation to the culinary creatures of Haelos is fitting. Though he handles you more roughly, I presume. I must admit, I enjoy the show of bravado. Today, you had the audacity to try. Tomorrow, you will harness the audacity to win. Come, I will make do with the circumstances Fate gave us."

Yadira threw her old training armor onto Sima, tucking her dark hair beneath the hood and shielding her face within the shadows its fabric created. It wouldn't keep others from realizing it was their queen if they looked closely enough, but she had been lucky once. Perhaps they would make it to their destination without being found out.

The armor was ill-fitting, causing the bits of metal plating around her shins to clank, a beacon marking her every move. Yet it did not slow them, as they made it to the Palace library without even a second glance from the Guardians.

"Why here?" Cosima asked.

"I would have preferred to take you to the Astral Atheneum, but I know better than to test our limits. The Palace library is limited, but..." She met Sima's gaze.

"You heard about the King's plans for it," Sima said, following Yadira through the aisles of the Palace library. It, too, transformed into a grandiose display of green and peach aventurine. Ash wood tables and chairs provided ample seating.

Bookcases constructed of purple-green fluorite held considerable literary collections, though they marched right past Cosima's preferred Fiction section and headed straight to the educational and historical texts.

"Few can enter inside now," Yadira said, pages fanning as she flipped through a text. "Goddess Ehses constructed it to refuse entry to all not born of the planet and put the warding in place. It is formidable enough to forbid even Tomasso and Ginevra since they were not born on Haelos. Its restrictions have doubled; the only permissible entity now is the King."

"Not even Guardians go inside? Has anyone ever broken in?"

Yadira shook her head, her brown curls swaying. It was strange to see someone so powerful look relaxed for once. She had seen Yadira rip out a man's throat with her bare hands, and now here she was, looking studious. It was a treat for Sima, even if she didn't bring it up out loud.

"No, but there has been one case of someone making it inside the library who is not from Aeria. We never informed the King, because, well," she paused, "he just disappeared. The Guardians can defend the library from the outside. At the minimum, we thought we could keep him from leaving with anything important. An elite Ambrosi made it inside, but the cloaked man was gone. I nearly thought we imagined the whole thing, especially when the report finally came in that nothing appeared tampered with."

Sima's head swiveled as they waded through the library. The scent of the paper had her floating through the aisles as she trailed behind her friend. She would give anything to have the power to travel like the cloaked stranger from Yadira's tale.

"Maybe he just wanted to see if he could do it," Sima said with a shy smile.

The weight of their situation hung in the air between them. The Guardian turned to look at Sima, Yadira's eyes glittering with evidence of her heartbreak.

"It has been some time since you have been here, hasn't it?" Yadira asked.

Sima's chin dipped, yet a ghost of a smile hit her lips. "Yes, quite some time."

"I wish I could do more for you," Yadira said, voice just above a whisper. "I have been thinking about what you told me, how he forces you to take *Mortoid* to access your powers," she sighed, brushing a curl from her face. "All this time, I was blind. Certainly, I understood he was not kind, friend, but it is incomprehensible what he is doing behind closed doors."

Sima blew out a puff of air. "He began using the drugs because I refused to use my powers. With the drugs, I have no choice. *Mortoid* shows its users their potential deaths, and I believe, somehow, I am tapping into the threads of Fate."

Yadira studied her face. "What happens when you alter someone's path?"

Sima shrugged, though the weight of her friend's question was not lost on her. "I remember struggling with my power a lot as a child. It took me years to realize there were varying levels of fallout from my decisions. Once I realized, I explained it all to my parents, who immediately chastised me."

"Yes, you've told me how your family disapproved of your powers. They believed using your powers would cause problems. Is that what you mean by fallout?"

"Well, the smaller the change, the less likely it'll have major repercussions," she said as she followed Yadira up a set of stairs. "Occasionally, people dress differently, or the surrounding decorations become altered. Sometimes, though, ripple effects happen, and different people appear in the world around me."

The higher they went, the more cramped the sections became. Sima walked mindful of her arms, already having knocked a teetering stack of books from the shelves.

"Interesting," Yadira said, glancing over her shoulder. "It's right up here. I believe I have just the book for you."

"What are we looking for?"

Yadira ignored her, setting up yet another flight of stairs. She wished they could've simply floated to the top, but the way Sima and Yadira pressed together told her there wouldn't have been enough space. The powerful Rani woman hardly fit as is.

At last, they reached a strangely-lit series of shelves. An invisible source illuminated the spines.

"They light themselves," Yadira said, reading the question on her face easily. "These are the only enchanted books one can find within this Palace, but they tell enough that I should think this trip worth it. The King destroyed most enchanted works. He did a thorough job eliminating ancient wisdom from Haelos, yet some survive."

Yadira plucked a book from the shelf, setting it in Sima's hand with a thud. Two more found their way to the stack before they were marching again, Yadira carrying her own set of hefty books.

The enchantments in the book Sima had in her hands cast three-dimensional photographs into the air above the pages. Her book thrilled her at first, but now she saw the utility. It had allowed the pictures to be offered with unparalleled quality, adding to the tales within.

"The page says here," Yadira said, pointing to a line of text on the page before her, "The Eternal Kingdom grants twelve High

Priestesses the ability to create worlds and fill them with people. The Kingdom assigns a High Priestess to each new world. 'It is within their skill set to craft life and grant power, and to construct an Archipelago for immortals and Guardians', it says. Apparently, Ehses is a High Priestess."

Sima glanced over at the page and saw an Archipelago that looked similar to their own. "Do all of them look alike, too?"

"Perhaps only the ones created by Ehses," Yadira said with a laugh. "Here, this is what I wished to show you."

Sima paled as she read the words Yadira was pointing to— *Kismet, the Celestial Empress of Fate.* Sima pulled the book from Yadira's hands and into her lap as she quickly scanned paragraphs worth of information.

"Kismet was the Goddess gifted with the power to apportion Fate to the creations of the High Priestesses. Even those living in the Eternal Realm are endowed with predetermined lives," Sima read. Her heart beat faster in her chest as she fluttered through the pages, hungry for more information. The Drago had mentioned Kismet.

Sima searched for any information on the wrath of Kismet, though it felt selfish to do so. Worry racked her brain of what the High Priestess would think of her changes to the Fate of others.

Yadira flipped open another book off the stack, thumbing through it as Sima grew frustrated. Nothing else was of use in the book. She tossed it to the side with a huff before Yadira caught her attention once again.

"Humans," Yadira said, "I forgot about the humans. Their kind live in the Prisma District, Below. Here," she pointed at the land marked on the left side of the map on the page. "Ombra is for the shadow-types. Viipir are fanged bat-shifters. Hexia, the witches. Echos—animal shifters." Her hand drifted to the middle District. "This is Eternita. All inhabitants must be of Faerie heritage." Sima knew the Alfrii lived there. She had seen glimpses of the Eternita District through her meddling with rebels for the King. Yadira pointed to the right side of the map at the final District. "The humans."

Sima read the page and gasped. "Is it true? Did the humans actually craft weapons to fight the other magic types?"

"Yes," she said, flipping to another page. The three-dimensional picture from the book depicted strange metal weapons capable of launching projectiles. "The humans grew tired of being at the mercy of the stronger magic types. Your father originally crafted Prisma to be a safe place for the humans to retreat to." Yadira looked around, before speaking in a lower voice, "The Guardian I mentioned before who ventured Below states the humans are now confined to it, unable to leave their District."

Sima continued reading. The humans had relinquished the weapons they crafted to the kingdom upon the creation of the three Districts. She could recall her father discussing the crafting of the Districts, but she had not known it was because the humans became lethal of their own accord.

"How do they protect themselves against the beasts coming through the veil if they surrendered their only means of protection?"

Yadira sighed. "We must do something. They do not stand a chance."

Sima knew that to be true. The education received growing up in Aeria about the magic types harped on the fact that humans were weaker, with no magic like the others.

"I meant what I said. I am done taking Aurelio's word for it. There must be some way to find out more about what is happening down there," Sima said.

"I am being reassigned to Ombra, Cosima."

"Yadira, by the Spirit, no." Sima said. "You can't go. We have to fix this from here."

"There is no fixing it here, friend. I cannot deny an order. I am a Guardian, bound to follow directions. Whether the King suspects I will be in the belly of a beast, or at least far from you, I do not know."

Cosima was stunned. "What if something happens to you?"

"This is what I live for, Cosima. Planet Haelos is one of millions of planets where they station Guardians to defend the veil and the inhabitants. I see nothing more honorable than facing the beasts and bringing them down with my own blades. If the King will not protect them, then I will pave the way."

This attitude was precisely why the two of them had become friends all those years ago. Doubt gnawed at Cosima's insides, forcing upon her a brutal flurry of emotion and insecurity. Sensing her plight, Yadira rested a hand on Sima's shoulder.

"I wish I was brave the way you are," Sima said softly.

"You are brave."

"Not the way you are," Sima said, resting her head in her hands as Yadira began packing up their books. "When he first took Aeria, I fought back as much as I could, but I never trained for combat. I cannot compete with his strength. They raised me to be seated on the throne, not chained to it. I believed myself capable of more, capable of something greater. Over time, he erased all I knew myself to be. I thought myself to be intelligent, caring, competent. He crafted lesson after lesson on why I was anything but. It is selfish of me, but I have let myself stop fighting back, and I have freely become his to command, all to lessen my pain even a fraction."

"Your faith in a future free of your tormentor is worth hanging on to. You can't blame yourself for how you survived him this far. I don't believe many who have endured what you have would have the strength to keep fighting."

"I believed I would never be free of him. I hid myself away, biding my time until someone came to release me from beneath him. Yet now clarity cups my eyes. I know I have the power to free myself, even if I have not yet figured out how."

Chapter 8

Yadira was persistent there was one more place they would need to visit. The Nuvola Palace gallery was hand-curated. Pieces vital to the history of planet Haelos laid within, meaning they were priceless. The gallery consumed four stories of space, a mixture of sculptures, paintings, and other mediums by which various artists had expressed themselves through the years.

Art sourced from Sotto il Cielo had its own floor, but Ambrosi had created a portion of the pieces, as well. Maintaining Haelos had become more efficient, and though she hated to admit it, a great deal of that innovation was Aurelio's doing. This meant those in Aeria often could fulfill their duties in just a couple of hours every day. The only people constantly working were the Rani Guardians and a few select Ambrosi who operated as Messengers for the kingdom.

It had benefited them all, causing a boom in the economy of Aeria as entertainment and leisure became the forefront of the transformation under Aurelio's vision. He had ripped the crown from her father's hands, but in five short decades, he had completely reformed their society. One from overwhelming responsibility to one of rest and relaxation.

"How can the Ambrosi here enjoy such untouched, gentle lives, when the people Below fight to become warriors to defend their loved ones?" Sima asked.

Yadira walked silently next to her, and though she showed no signs of it on her face, there was an energy so tense around them, it surprised Sima her vibration alone didn't send the others visiting the gallery today to flee. Instead, Ambrosi roamed, some hand-in-hand, pointing to various works. In the less populated chambers stuffed with art, two Hexia girls performed their daily cleaning. Sima frequently wondered why others permitted the servitude of the Hexia, and now, having seen them all wearing a pin with a similar design to Ivo's, she cringed.

Could they all be of one coven?

As she followed loyally behind her friend, one Hexia girl looked up and met Sima's eyes. A small pendant on the collar of the woman's uniform displayed a viper swirled around an arrow, the sharp point of the blade dripping with a single green drop. The girl let a small smile loose, as if she knew something Sima didn't. Sima locked eyes with another Hexia girl, who repeated the knowing smile.

Their eyes stayed focused on Cosima. So much so, one with round black glasses bumped into an Ambrosi couple wandering by.

"Watch it," the man hissed. "These damn witches are as bad as the King says."

"Yes," the man's date replied, twirling a lock of her red hair. "They find themselves in the way often, don't they, dear?"

Sima's lip curled, magic twitching along her fingertips. She was capable of minor changes without the *Mortoid* caps, and though the desire was great, Sima did not interfere. Yadira had slowed to watch the interaction as well.

"It's not fair," Sima said. "They treat them so poorly. These girls are talented, magnificent witches. Imprisoned alongside their sisters without magic was not enough punishment, it seems."

Before Yadira could respond, the woman shoved by the Hexia girls, causing the one with glasses to slam against the floor. Her frames, broken and limp, laid across the bridge of her nose. Sima hardly registered the strings were in her hand when time resumed.

Yadira and Cosima walked, the two Hexia girls intensely staring at the pair. This time, the girl with glasses held a mop, a steaming hot bucket of soapy water at her ankles. The girls moved to follow Cosima when the Ambrosi couple crossed their path, the man's foot landing directly in the steaming water.

He hollered, the two Hexia girls taking off down the hall as his date looked around helplessly. When Sima turned back toward Yadira, her friend wore an indiscernible expression.

"He should watch where he's going," Sima said tightly. "Come, what is it you wanted to show me?"

Yadira nodded, remembering they had come for a reason. After what felt like walking for miles, the endless rows of art became nothing more than blurs of colors. Yadira lifted her arm, her palm facing a patch of blank wall.

Paint along the walls peeled backwards in finely spiraled ribbons, leaving the wood bare. Sima knew the Rani Guardians had secret access to every location, but she had never seen it performed in person. Within an instant, an archway appeared, revealing yet another chamber to the gallery.

Towers of stacked art threatened to tip in plentiful rows along the back wall. In front of them lay statues concealed with large white tarps. Crates stuffed with packaging material sat to her left, and a large stamp on the front stated:

PRISMA DISTRICT: RECOVERED WORKS

Along the outside were other various labels. It was littered with evidence of the Messengers who ensured the crates made it to Aeria.

"Are these painted by humans?" Sima asked.

"Yes, these recovered works are recent. Aurelio has a habit of stealing large batches of work from Sotto il Cielo, disposing of what he doesn't like. Someone tipped me off that this shipment would be of interest."

Aurelio had a habit of stealing anything from anyone, as long as it piqued his interest or, perhaps, merely made him appear more interesting. Fear prickled along her fingertips as strange energy wafted from the crate.

"He has time to go hunting for artwork but not properly assign Guardians to save lives?" Sima asked. Anger warmed her palms and face.

"There are approximately one hundred missing Guardians in Eternita, as the District has sealed the King out. That leaves a mere two hundred Guardians spread between Prisma and Ombra."

"*Two hundred?*" Sima slapped a hand over her mouth. There were thousands of Rani Guardians living in the Archipelago, and the King could not spare even five hundred. "What defense could two hundred Guardians offer?"

"None. King Aurelio has paired all Guardians to Messengers—Ambrosi that seek to locate valuable items and return them to the kingdom."

"How do you know all of this?"

"That Rani friend of mine swears there is a rebellion brewing in the Ombra district. The shadow-types may have teamed up with a group of brave Guardians. I wish to join them."

"Yadira," Sima said, "No, how can you say that? Becoming a traitor—"

"I am doing the right thing, Cosima, and I do not care if I am killed for it."

Sima sighed. "When do you transfer to the Ombra District?"

"In two days."

"Two days!" Sima yelled.

"Hush," Yadira said, motioning for Sima to calm down with her hands. "I arranged for this. I asked Remo, the Emblem Chief, to transfer me. The King agreed, and now I have my chance to join the rebellion and realize my divine purpose."

"What if something happens to you?"

"I am a Guardian, Cosima. The Eternal Kingdom built me for things such as this. Why do you think so many fear us?"

"You don't scare me that much, friend," Sima laughed, though it was half empty. She eyed the Rani's impressive wings. Even while held in a compact position, they were impossible to miss. Yet, she never really feared her. Other Guardians, sure, especially with the brutal way they trained them to protect. But never Yadira.

"That is a nice sentiment, but I am an elite killer before I am your friend."

A twinkle sparkled in her eye—amusement.

It quickly died, the embers casting spots in Sima's visions as she woefully watched her expression change.

There was something here she had planned to show her. She didn't bring her here just to inform her of her reassignment. The Rani's wings fluttered in a gentle rhythm behind her, a nervous tick, Yadira unable to control her muscles enough to keep them from moving.

Sima swallowed hard.

Cumbersome iron nails fashioned shut the crates beside them. Yadira simply grabbed a corner, wedging her fingertips beneath the wood, and wrenched it open. Dust particles misted them, the art becoming clearer as it settled.

"This is the truth, whether the King admits it to Aeria, to the Goddess… This lies Below."

A gasp escaped Sima's mouth, her hands flying up to contain any other verbal expressions of her horror. The painting—*paintings,* Sima realized—had excruciatingly accurate detail. The images were more lifelike than any drawing or enchanted hologram she had ever seen.

Monsters. The word fell flat. *Demons?* Even that could not accurately describe the otherworldly horror before them. They were not just monsters slipping through the veil, they were enormous, mangled globs of muscle and flesh. A humanoid figure only dreamable through drugs as heavy as the ones fed to her by Aurelio. Multiple arms extruded from the body, something about it so insect-like in nature, as if the extra appendages were some sort of advantage for mobility.

The face—what Sima thought might be the face—was mostly teeth. A mouth, dripping in poisonous goo, teeth like a pit of needles, and three eyes. Two unsettlingly human-like eyes— depicted so well it was almost as if Sima could taste his fear—sat beneath another eye so large it took up nearly the entire head of the beast. A chill found her, as if the creature in the painting might blink and jut to life.

As they reluctantly sorted through the paintings, the images only grew more distressing. Some showed dragon-like beasts with large, congealed flaps of translucent flesh. Ripped skin exposed strange organs beneath. Some of the depicted creatures bore a striking similarity to the Viipir shifters, except their wings—once slender, black, and crimson, wings that spoke of elegance and agility—were in broken shards. The bones pierced delicate tissue, drowning all color in matted patches of blood.

"Who painted these?" Sima said, finally breaking the silence that fell over them in their shared shock.

"A human man, I believe, named Simon. That is all I know. The Rani Guardian who discovered these risked his life trying to smuggle them into Aeria. It would have taken just one look by another Guardian or Messenger Ambrosi for him to be sentenced to death. Any artwork or literature that goes against Aurelio's regime, Guardians immediately destroy. These paintings are the only images we have of what is occurring there."

Sima was going to be sick. "How is this happening to our people? The people of Haelos are watching each other die at the hands of these *things*?"

"The beasts are coming from the veil itself or from within Ombra. That is as much as we have been able to uncover. The Rani Guardians in the Shadow District that have joined the rebellion must be careful to keep their alliance hidden, so investigation is at a slow crawl. Until I get there, that is."

"What is this?" Cosima asked, pointing to a strange painting, unlike the others. The monster depicted in this one appeared to be sprouting plant-like limbs and leaves. Mushrooms encapsulated the creature's face.

"The beasts are becoming, for lack of a better word, infected with that fungal mass. I wish I knew more."

"He is leaving those people to die," Sima said slowly. "When I left my rooms this morning, I never expected to find myself faced with pure cruelty. He abandoned them! He is there, right now, in the Ombra District. I wish I had it in me to believe he is there to help. In reality, he is covering up his crimes."

"What does he gain by putting our planet at risk?" Yadira

asked, more to herself than to Sima.

Sima paled. "The King has always spoken harshly of the Goddess, Ehses. One minute he is praising her for all she has done, and then the next, he is moody and critical of her decisions. He has threatened to wipe out the people Below for a long time, though perhaps I was a fool to believe he wouldn't actually do it. Aurelio cares so little for them. I am sure his negligence benefits him only in not having to do it himself."

"Why lie to the Ambrosi?" Yadira asked.

"I think it is easier to do as he wishes if he can keep them in line in other ways. The King enjoys the way the elites kiss up to him. His desire to win works in tandem with his ego. His compulsory need for attention drives every decision. I have allowed my power to wilt within my hands, and now I am unsure if I am strong enough to stop Aurelio. There is not time for me to learn how to master them." A tear slid down Sima's cheek. "What if Ehses choosing me damns our planet to the mercy of enraged deities for the crimes Aurelio committed?"

"Your power belongs to you, my friend. There is nothing that can truly get between you and the gifts Ehses gave you. Is it burdensome? Indeed. Is it cumbersome? With absolute certainty. Still, the power has found itself within your vessel, and the Goddess makes no mistakes. I see the fire burning in you, even if you lost your ability to wield your magic properly."

"How do you know what the right answer is when everything is going wrong?"

"There is a calling in my soul. There has always been. To be something great. To be what the Goddesses envisioned when the first Rani fell from the womb. To be a direct defense against evil. When I took my oath to Ehses, I swore to defend Haelos with my life." Yadira slipped her hand into Sima's, squeezing it gently.

A tear tugged at Sima's eyes. To live immortal, forever enjoying the fruits of this world—or to release their tether to this existence, and float free amongst the fabric of the universe until a tide would wash them home again. There were millions whose time to return had still not come.

"In my heart, I know the Emblems assigned me to go to Ombra to defend the people of Haelos with my blade, and to uncover what has caused this to happen."

Yadira released Sima's hand, reaching for the lid to the crate, before sealing the nails shut with a hammering of her fist.

"The whispers in the wind, Cosima," her friend's eyes blazed, "I hear them calling me, guiding me to where I am supposed to be in this life, what I am supposed to do. Have you heard yours, or have you not been listening?"

Chapter 9

"A caged bird will sing loudest the times it longs for freedom the most," Sima read aloud. Ivo left behind novels filled with fictional stories of women breaking free from their confounds. Sima shook her head as she imagined ocean-eyed Ivo smuggling novels in the base of her cleaning buckets.

The King appeared to be unaware of Cosima's absence. With Yadira's help, she had returned to her cage, not a feather out of place. After waving off her friend, Cosima stood on the balcony for a long while, watching the sunset in the distance. Whether Aurelio was within the walls of the Palace, or miles below in the Ombra District, it made no difference to her.

The taste of unrestricted decisions foamed along her taste buds as her soul grumbled for more. She yearned for freedom, ached for the deliverance only more of it could offer her. Her bravery battled beside curiosity, mind racing with options.

A knock at her room chambers sent books flying, Sima snatching them quickly and hiding them beneath the green down comforter. Ivo's face peeked out behind the door, the tiny taps of her black shoes sounding across the rose quartz slabs beneath her feet.

"Queen Aphelion?" Ivo asked quietly, eyes hidden beneath straight midnight-colored bangs. "I have brought you dinner. Our Majesty is otherwise occupied."

Sima smiled. "Please, come in Ivo."

Ivo returned the expression, pulling in a rolling wooden cart. Sima stood, following her to the small dining area within her chambers. Clear glass bowls clattered atop thin Selenite plates. A spicy cabbage soup steamed within it.

Red broth left a colorful splatter on Ivo's pale skin. Sima reached for a napkin from a stack on the cart and wiped the food from her friend's arm. Ivo looked at her suspiciously before laughing.

"Enough, Sima," Ivo said, returning to her informal way of speaking now that they were out of earshot of the Guardians at her door. "You know how disgusting my clothes get throughout the day? Burn that napkin."

Cosima laughed as she took a seat, dramatically laying out the napkin across her lap. "I will survive."

Ivo placed the glass bowl of soup in front of Sima before reaching for two slender saucers. Heaps of fluffy white rice and spicy fermented vegetables overflowed the dishes. Another bowl of soup found its way across from Cosima. Ivo sighed as she slipped into the chair.

"Imagine my excitement when I was told the Captor would not be returning this evening," Ivo said, her bright eyes wide as she funneled food into her mouth.

Sima blew on the soup, delighting in the way it warmed her. The aroma tickled her nose as she took slow sips of the broth. "I love to share my meals with you," Sima said between bites of cabbage, beef, and green onions, drips of broth colliding with the tabletop. "Especially when you come bearing delicious gifts."

Ivo's head tilted to the side. "I know it's been a while since we've had food like this. The King disapproves of spicy food. I cannot believe a man fearful of peppers enslaved my people."

"Fortune laughs in our faces," Sima replied.

"Indeed, though, we are on the upswing. The mighty Wheel of Fortune rotates again, my friend."

"What brings about the confidence?"

Ivo reached into her pocket, retrieving yet another letter. Sima frowned as she recognized it as another letter from the desk of the King. Ivo handed it to her. Sima squinted at the text as she read.

"Aurelio is not waiting on the Astral Atheneum any longer. Everything within is at risk if he hasn't already begun destroying it." Ivo chewed the inside of her cheek.

The King went to great lengths to destroy the culture and customs of those Below the Aeria Archipelago. However, the Astral Atheneum had remained untouched—until now.

"The first stage," Cosima read aloud, "is refortifying the enchantments upon the library." She put the letter on the table. "Another building of Aeria to be broken, its former walls inhabited by cold, glimmering stone."

"How is he able to do this? I thought the wards on the Atheneum were strong enough to withstand tampering," Ivo said, reaching for another scoop of rice.

"By everyone except for the reigning family," Cosima said quietly. Sima chewed her thumbnail. "Yet another thing handed to him by my blind mistakes. If only I had seen the monster before it was too late."

"You can only blame yourself for that for so long. Eventually, you must decide to release the guilt and shame. All they do is weigh you down."

"How can I release the pieces of me built from the guilt? My love for Aurelio allowed him to infiltrate our kingdom."

"He would have taken Aeria, and Haelos, regardless."

Sima blinked. "I suppose, but—"

Ivo waved her hand. "No," she said. "No more blaming yourself. It is not your fault you were the chosen victim of an abuser. Aurelio is evil incarnate. He did not need to romance you first. He was always going to force you to marry him. You are the one who has outlasted his treachery, and you will continue to do so."

Sima stared into her soup, aimlessly pushing around vegetables. "Every time I denied him, he threatened the lives of the Hexia girls. You, as well as the others. I learned to stay in line, telling myself I would remain dormant, waiting until the right time to attack. I have yet to find such a moment. If I fail, he will begin slaughtering people."

The sound of paper sliding across the table caught Sima's attention. It was not from Aurelio's desk. It was a hand-written letter in some kind of coded language.

"I told you about my traversing of the servants' passageways. I have found passages that lead to each of the three islands. I have been rescuing the stolen items from my people, storing them. That paper is a list of different access points across the Archipelago."

"Why are you showing me this?"

"I have no choice but to search for them. I think I am getting closer."

"Closer to what, Ivo?" Sima's mind swam within her skull.

"I told you I have my way around the King's restriction of our magic. I have been tampering with the Light Reserve and the Temple."

"The *Light Reserve*—have you truly called for death so callously? That holds all the magic given up by the Ambrosi during the Giving. The magic that powers all three islands. Messing with it could have disastrous effects."

"Relax," Ivo said, shoving her bowl away from her. "I live not in fear. The Light Reserve has channels and strange stones that funnel the Ambrosi power. If I blocked the channels toward Aurelio's office, my sisters and I would have a stronger recall of our powers. I believe whatever he is using to keep this hold over us is within his office, but I cannot find it."

"What are you needing from me?"

"I need to get into his office. We can work on a distraction. You know him the best, Cosima. I know you cannot alter Aurelio's Fate, so it won't be easy, but—" The sounds of footsteps within her chambers interrupted Ivo. Caelian walked into the room.

"It is time for you to go," Caelian said tightly to Ivo. "You know better than to be dining with the help, Queen Aphelion."

"I can do as I please, Caelian," Sima said as Ivo placed the empty dishes on the cart and rolled away, leaving her alone with the Guardian.

"The King will begin his ascent to the Archipelago from the Ombra District within the next five hours," he said, walking until he stood behind her. He whispered in her ear, "You're lucky I don't plan on telling him what I saw today."

Sima swallowed hard. "Where?"

"The Square, eating treats with Yadira. If Yadira wasn't already being thrown to the wolves by going to Ombra, I would've ratted on you both. However," he said, straightening, "I gain more from keeping this a secret between the two of us."

"Don't want to interrupt your chances of being accepted into the Emblems?" Sima guessed. Caelian had been pawning for the position for several years, hoping to be chosen above Eugenio. She considered them both depraved individuals. Cosima shifted in her seat.

"You know how the King is very touchy when it comes to you. In exchange for keeping your secret," he said, inspecting a minor cut on his hand, "you be on your best behavior. Whatever the King wants, give it to him. Ambrosi treat anyone accepted into the Emblems with riches, fine women, and delicious foods. I'll never work another day in my life."

Sima clenched her teeth. She forced a smile and said, "Deal."

With a satisfied grin, Caelian turned and left. Once she was sure he was gone, she stormed into her bedroom to change. Her rage flickered on and off, one minute furious about being instructed to behave, as if she were a pet, and not a person, the next terrified of her husband learning of her adventures.

Before her eyes could adjust to the sudden light, Sima was halfway down the hall, tugged along by two Guardians. Cosima wrapped her robe tighter against her body, its blue fabric long enough to cover her knees. Fear prickled along her extremities. She wondered if Caelian had decided it better to come clean to the King or if she was being dragged to his office for another reason.

She had tried to escape only once, right after the coup. He dragged her back by her hair, in front of everyone. Scabs that bled on and off for days littered her scalp and brushing it had been unbearable. As they walked in the present moment, Sima's hands clutched her hair, the length and fullness of it proof that she had survived. Resolution swelled in her gut. She would survive this, too.

It was dark inside his office, save for the light illuminating the war table from below, the topography casting the scaled shadow mountains of Ombra across the back wall. He decorated his office well. Fine art hung as if it were a private gallery, and not the room where he plotted the further demise of their world. The Emblems and Captains were more acquainted with this room than Sima. Even Caelian had more of a place here than she did.

The King's chair sat turned away, his back muscles tense as he leaned over his tactical map, a brooding wave overpowering the air in the room—or Sima was just so scared she could hardly breathe. She lowered herself into the chair opposite him, unable to see his face.

"What was Aeria before me?"

"I'm sorry?" Sima asked, her voice nearly daring to crack at the end.

"What. Was. Aeria. Before. Me?" he bit out, the grip on his pen tightening, snapping it in two.

Sima lowered her head. They had had this conversation before. She knew what he wanted to hear.

"It was weak."

"It was downright pitiful," he shouted, violently standing up from his chair.

Sima flinched.

He turned to her then, the eyes of a man gone mad.

"The Rani were skin and bones, so focused on protection, they didn't stop to eat. Your father took no qualms watching his soldiers starve for *his benefit*. Aeria did not know peace before me, no matter what the pernicious rebels claim. Rather than beg our Goddess for more soldiers, I turned Haelos into a fortress. I did it, all of it, without crafting prisons. I have replaced anxious preparing with blissful restoration."

He hunched over, retrieving a cigar from a hidden cavity on the table. "All this magic, all this power, it was going to waste. When I took the crown from your father, I could feel the hum of gratitude coming from it. It was thanking me for getting it off that sad excuse for a man and bringing it to a proper king."

He turned then, his muscles flexed tightly beneath his shirt as he shivered, the anger building with more momentum. "It was me," he rasped, the flames in his gut nearly staving off his air. "It was me that turned this floating hunk of garbage into the beauty that it is today."

He slithered to her side, his gaze burning holes in what bravery she had mustered during her escape. He searched her eyes—a chaotic, desperate search. For what? Sima didn't know.

"There are *rebels* inside Aeria," he spat, hand sweeping across the table, knocking over the small figurines across Aeria's map. Sima winced as he continued, "They are trying to start a movement against *me*. I thought I was successful at mitigating this little group of theirs, but apparently not."

Sima's eyes widened before she could stop them. This wasn't about her sneaking out. This wasn't about her at all.

"They have infiltrated Perpetuo," he said, resting his hand on the edge of the war table beside them. "The Guardians reported droves of Rebels attempting to land on the island, forcing me to return early."

The third island of Aeria lay directly above Ombra, and the Devout Rising rebels had infiltrated it. Her mind sped through a hundred thoughts.

How could something like this have happened—and so quickly? she thought.

"They say I am not fit to lead Aeria any longer. They demand I let their grimy little hands all over my work, to prove that I uphold my duties. Of course I uphold them! The worthless magic types, and small humans, all live in Haelos. We keep them from famine, from war. Yet, they shame us for not curing all of life's ailments.

The Spirit Goddess wants their souls to be molded. It is impossible without fire! A bit of hardship is *good* for them."

It was true, people from Sotto il Cielo often complained to the Ambrosi, their prayers falling on deaf ears. Ambrosi dedicated entire streets of Perpetuo to managing the prayers and complaints from Below. Ambrosi casually called it the Complaint's Block. The residents of Sotto il Cielo wished for luxury and freedom, believing themselves to be owed the same life as the Ambrosi. Yet Ambrosi were not capable of changing the tides of Fate, nor could they solve every problem. However, there truly was no reason anyone should have to go without necessities at this point, as they were rumored to be now. It was part of what she hated about him the most, the piss-poor job he did of running Haelos.

"*Rebels*," he spat again. "They dare to speak against me. The Devout Rising leaders believe themselves more fit to lead, do they? They know nothing of sacrifice. How could they comprehend the weight upon a king? I must carry my rule, no matter the pressure from my own subjects."

He paced back and forth across the room, murmuring plans to gut the perpetrators. He slowed, coming to a stop beside her.

"Someone crossed me, and I do not know who." He grabbed her face, his fingers pressed to her jugular as he tugged her chin just inches from his. "But I will find out."

"Did you see them? Did you see the beasts?" Sima whispered as her body trembled.

His eyes were wild, and it was enough to have her nearly collapsing, her body feeling too weak to move. She begged herself to do something, to break free, to get away from whatever sadistic way he planned to take his anger out on her. Yet, her body betrayed her, refusing to even shut her eyes and shield her from what was to come.

All she could do was stare and stare as he glared back.

The grip on her chin tightened, a yelp of pain never finding its way out of her throat. A rough kiss scratched along the top of her head. He looked at her with delirious madness, like a greedy feline, belly full yet still toying with its prey.

She almost tipped out of her chair when he released her as a knock sounded on the door. She corrected herself, smoothing out her long hair as Aurelio opened the door. His refusal to answer her question told her everything she needed to know. There was no doubt in Sima's mind the beasts existed.

"King." The Rani Guardian she could see behind her husband briefly folded in half with respect. "Ermete reports activity in Iridicenza. It is spreading"

"You idiots! Did I not order you an hour ago to get the hell over there and secure it?"

"My King," another Guardian said, a woman, "Ulrico and I couldn't make it. Our hands were full here. We have taken a couple of hostages and killed the rest. Those Below report more coming, some apparently on the back of Vipus."

Vipus? Sima's curiosity piqued. They were massive, winged beasts. A much smaller cousin to Dragos, Ambrosi occasionally rode them for brief trips to the surface. Few Ambrosi felt motivated enough to use them lately, however.

"To Perpetuo?"

"No, my King. The bubble around Innamorati is faltering. The Devout Rising are reportedly carrying explosives as well," the woman said. Sima detected fear in her tone, something they usually went to great lengths to hide.

Sima peered around her chair at them.

The bubble. The childish name for the invisible borders surrounding Aeria. It was accurate, but the terminology always implied the possibility that it might *pop*. Without the shields, and with explosives in the hands of rebels, they stood a chance at toppling what Aurelio had built here. Aurelio touted a narrative that the bubble was impenetrable, yet the Devout Rising rebels had found their way through it.

The woman was Lucrezia, another Rani who was quite kind to Sima, though she had mostly kept her distance. Sima glanced at her companion, Ulrico. Both had sleek, short red-black hair, though Ulrico's face was full of harsher lines than the woman's. Lucrezia, in place of hard angles, had softer features. It did nothing to make her seem less threatening. She was still a Guardian, the wings of both guards casting deep, feathered shadows into the office.

"Here?" Aurelio said, his voice suddenly hushed. "The enchantments should be stronger here. How did they—?"

"Over half of the enchantments for Aeria are no longer working. We got reports as we were on our way here. It is pandemonium out there, King. What should we do?"

"Which ones are down above Ombra?" he demanded, deep within the throes of his own madness, not understanding that *all* of Haelos, Aeria included, was now under siege. Yet Sima understood, her heart pounding so loudly she had to strain to hear the rest.

Lucrezia tried again. "All protective border enchantments are faulty, a few spots are still holding strong, but information is changing by the second. I sourced servants who once functioned as enchantresses that live here in Via del Profeta. As for the other islands…they might be down completely by the time we get to them. They have access to Light energy from the Reserves for now, which should sustain any citizens until evacuations can begin. However…"

Aurelio waved a hand. "However, they are vulnerable to Vipus attacks."

The Rani lowered their heads, both of them unaware of Sima listening nearby. Winged beasts meant a greater chance of bringing down Aeria, avoiding the built-in safety net that came from being thousands of miles above the surface. Every single person who had built a life here—the population which had been growing over thousands of years—was now at risk.

"Then we will fight with fire. Send our own Vipus on their trails. They will regret their resistance, and their blood will be proof of it." Her husband reached near the door for his sword.

"I have sent a team of reinforcements to Ermete in Iridicenza, but Perpetuo will have to be guarded from the ground and the sky. We can begin evacuations once the Guardians in Ombra and Prisma return. Eternita is still unresponsive to all communication," Ulrico said.

"You will round up the Hexia, starting with Costanza." Sima

swallowed harshly. Costanza was her mother, a Hexia woman. "She is skilled at repairing enchantments like the bubble. Let her choose her assistants and make sure they seal us off again within the hour." He spoke as a king, with an empty heart. "The Goddess gave this power to me, and I will not let those beneath tell me how to wield it."

Lucrezia spoke, "For now, my King, we would advise you to shelter somewhere safe. Perhaps leave Aeria completely."

"Plans are already in motion."

Her husband pushed over the two Guardians, intent on protecting himself before he put any effort into saving the others. In some of his ramblings to Sima, he had admitted his disdain for the prying eyes of the other nobility in Innamorati. It would surprise her none if Aurelio left them to defend themselves.

The door shut as the Rani Guardians stormed after Aurelio, leaving her sitting quietly in the dark. Alone, for the first time, in Aurelio's office. The *King's* office.

Chapter 10

Time, a perfectly stocked war room, and a disgruntled wife.

She dragged her hand along the well-adorned wall of accolades, her fingers making routes around the framed memorabilia and awards. The merit, for some, deserved. The merit for others, apparently, delusion.

If you create the military, it's a little strange to go to desperate lengths to signify your own authority over it, Sima thought. Her blood felt cold beneath her skin. The King was beginning his destruction of every important piece of history their planet bore, and Sima could no longer submit to him. The safety she gained by following orders did not outweigh the lives at risk.

Cosima stared up at the wall of ribbons and flags. He stole the idea from the humans, or so she had heard. Ambrosi lived forever, and some found themselves interested more in novelty than sentiment. Humans, however, needed all the extra showcases of their accomplishments, with so little time to prove themselves, so little time for mastery.

Aurelio maintained a deep devotion to the image others had of him. Outwardly fearless, inwardly cowardly. The King had carved his office into his own personal museum exhibit, everything in just the right place. He had perfectly planned every square inch for the prying eyes of those with high enough status to sit in it or at least be offered a tour.

He hadn't planned on it being for Sima's eyes, however. Especially not left to her own devices. Working quickly would be advantageous, though she found no reason to rush. He wouldn't be back, not until he had at least arranged further reinforcements for their neighboring islands, she figured. It was more likely he had forgotten entirely that she was in his office. He cared more about being protected from attacks than actually being a leader.

Ivo had mentioned to Cosima over their dinner that she suspected Aurelio's method of control over the Hexia's magic lay within his office. It took some digging, but one-by-one, she popped open the hidden compartments within his desk. He had opened a concealed drawer on the war table earlier. Sima had become somewhat of a caged animal, learning the habits of her captor for safety. This practice had become valuable. No one knew him better than she did because no one was as afraid.

The mechanism was fairly simple, and once she figured out the first, the other five slipped open with minimal effort. Sima's eyes hesitated on the contents of the first drawer.

Dozens of packages lined the inside, and where Sima punctured, black capsules spilled. *Mortoid*, Sima knew instantly. Her hands were slippery with sweat, her mind blank. Every bit of confidence she had slipped away like sand between her fingers.

"What would possess him to hoard this many packages?" Sima said aloud. Her fingers tore through another, confirming it, too, contained the psychedelic drug the King implemented to force Sima into accessing her powers.

A few packages contained rose pink and lilac capsules Sima did not recognize. She hissed under her breath, frantically searching for something she could shove the packages into.

"I told you, *King*," Sima whispered, "I am done following every order."

This was all meant for her, at one time or another. The King was stockpiling drugs to use against her, preparing for centuries of torment. It made her head hurt. She tore open a nearby cupboard, thankful to find a black luggage case, no taller than her knees.

She opened the latch to the case and began frantically throwing the packages inside, careful to grab every single one. If he came back and realized they were gone, at least it would take some time before he could restock.

She gulped.

Hopefully.

Ice filled her veins as bag after bag passed through her hands, her eyes blurring with tears. Sima shoved aside her inconvenient emotions as she remembered why she was here.

Ivo.

Sima was on the prowl again, hands sliding across every surface in the room, within cabinets, beneath paintings on the wall. Determined to locate the mechanism by which he maintained control over the *Hexia*, Sima tore apart the office.

When the search revealed nothing, Sima trashed his mantle of self-importance, beginning with the accolades. Glass smashed against the floor, broken wooden frames cascading across his desk chaotically.

Tears persistently streamed down her face. As the rage tempered, her chest rising quickly to keep up with her demands for air, Sima slammed a fist on the illuminated war table. It went through the thin layer of painted glass that displayed their world.

Sima pulled a bloody hand back, glancing into the hole she had created while cradling her injury. Within it lay three gray stones. However, when light from above caught the stones at a certain angle, they flashed blue. Sima moved her body back and forth, observing the way the crystals glinted. Each lay within a strange iron casing, the strands of metal mimicking vines.

She reached in, pulling out one of the three shiny obelisks. The one in her hand was slightly larger than her palm. Sima admired the flashes of gold, blue, and green as she inspected them beneath the light. As her healing took over, bits of glass clattered to the ground, shoved outward from her skin.

All three of the obelisks composed of mysterious crystal found their way into the luggage. Sima stared back at the sizable hole in the table. She struggled to understand why he had hidden them beneath the glass. Though nothing outwardly confirmed it, Sima was sure something had changed in the atmosphere once she clasped the latch on the bag.

Her teeth clenched as she hoisted the luggage up by its handle, the weight of it pulling painfully at her skin. She paused before leaving his office. Doubt nipped at her heels once again. The glaring evidence of her outburst lay tattered across his war room. Sima cringed, ashamed of letting her emotions get the best of her. Then, she remembered her home, her friends, the library he was soon to destroy.

Sounds echoed through the hallways. Sima leaned closer to the door to hear them better. Ecstatic voices surprised her, causing Sima to peek around the door. Hexia girls ran by, dropping laundry and trays full of food behind them as they ran.

Had she done it?

Disbelief swamped her body as she tiptoed through the hallway, the luggage still in tow. Beyond the windows of the Palace, dozens of Vipus flew above them in the sky. Sima gasped, realizing the rebel attacks were closing in on them.

"Come this way," a girl shouted from behind her. "Queen Aphelion, please."

Sima turned to find two Hexia girls. The ones Sima had saved from the angry Ambrosi couple in the gallery. They motioned for her to follow them. Before Sima could take a step, a hand wrapped around her wrist and fear coated her insides.

Life was rather cruel, Sima reasoned, as she stared up into Aurelio's crazed eyes.

His well-groomed near-white, blond locks were loose from their usual restrained hairstyle, a mess of frizz, as though he had been sweating. Her mind twitched at the scent of something, something like iron. He released her wrist as he took a staggering step forward.

"They attacked me," he rasped, eyes still frantic but glazed over, seeing far past Cosima. Only then did her tunnel vision open up enough to realize that blood coated Aurelio. The frizz in his hair was accompanied by flecks of crimson, stemming from the larger spray of blood across his neck and ear. "And I gutted every single fucking one of them."

The crazed look Sima understood. Bloodlust. An angry man with a chance to be an angry man. Sima, remembering what she was stealing, adjusted herself quickly, hiding as much of the case behind her body as she could manage.

Sima reflexively took a step backward as he stumbled forward. The wince on his face told her the rebels had injured Aurelio, the blood pooling around his left shoe told her where. She glanced behind her, the two girls still watching, unsure how to respond. They, too, feared the King.

"Go," she mouthed, before facing him once again.

He erupted into laughter—manic, bone-chilling laughter—steadying himself on the archway beside them.

"They thought they could take *me*? They thought I had grown weak, fattened with the spoils of the seeds I have sowed? Oh, how I wish you could have watched the way their blood coated my fucking teeth, *Yin*. I was the one who took Aeria with my bare hands. The Rani respect me because even they could not stop me."

Another laugh, another step backward.

Breath caught somewhere deep.

"Do you know how much Rani love the sky? They thought their city belonged to them, like Ehses built it to be a birdhouse. Now it belongs to me." He rolled his head backward, cracking his neck, before his raging eyes were on her again. "They remember the way I cut the wings off survivors who refused to obey. The way their brothers and sisters writhed in agony, their muscles still jutting with the electricity—the instinct to fly too great—as I pushed them off the edge of the city. The pathetic creatures still tried to save themselves, even as I burned their wings in the center of Innamorati. Every Ambrosi here heard the cracking of their skulls as they collided with the dirt of Sotto il Cielo."

Sima was going to be sick.

The Guardians. Immortal, similar to Ambrosi, but only possible to kill after removal of both wings—the source of their power. Sima still remembered the smell of burned flesh and feathers, how it tainted her city for months, the winds of spring not strong enough to wash it away.

"I have been thinking of how to solve this," he said, cocking his head to one side, "and every idea I come up with leads back to you."

A sudden explosion in the distance had them both steadying against the wall, bracing for waves of aftershocks. Screaming rang alongside shrieks from Vipus as they tore through the sky.

"Look what you've done Sima," he shouted above the chaos. "Look at what you've done to Aeria, because you failed to do as I said."

"Stop it!" she shouted, her grip tightening on the suitcase, desperate to never do this again, to never be a victim again. To never be locked up again. To never be forced fed drugs, and touched too roughly, and never treated with care. "Enough!" she cried. She glanced back, shocked to see the two girls still waiting for her.

"Come," the one with glasses mouthed. "Come here."

Her head felt clouded with thoughts. Sima wasn't strong enough for what he had put her through, but she had to be.

"I never wanted to be like this, Aurelio," Sima said through her teeth, biting back tears. "I never wanted to know all these sides of myself, all the ones that are so fucking scared. But you made me. You made me learn how to survive you."

"Come," he said, grabbing her wrist free of the wall. "We have work to do. I'll deal with your poor attitude later."

"No!" Sima shouted back, tugging at the precise moment another explosion hit, the extra force freeing her.

Another hysterical laugh escaped her husband, dragging his now-useless leg behind him. He had been losing blood the entire time, Sima realized. He was so caught up in the adrenaline of it all, he had barely noticed himself how extensive his wounds were.

A round of explosions rocked them once again. His injured leg left him unsteady, causing him to fall and collide with the floor. Without thinking, Sima kicked him directly in the groin.

"You will never control me again, Aurelio," she said. Though terror coursed through her at her own actions, Sima turned on her heels and ran toward the girls.

Salvation found her quickly. The three of them ran, not daring a look back. Once within the servants' passageways, a slender arm emerged from the darkness, pulling her closer.

Ivo.

"They called for me—Cosima, you did it!"

Sima hardly registered the words. "I have the *Mortoid* he used, Ivo. We need to go," she choked out, hot tears flooding her face.

Her friend's eyes widened, but she turned, grabbing Sima, and ran. The suitcase clumsily thumped against her side as they bolted, her muscles burning from supporting its weight this long already.

Ivo had told her she knew her way around the Palace without being seen, but Sima had never imagined the servant's corridors to be so complex. Hallways, doorways, and other servants flew past her vision. Many were escaping, cries from scared girls echoing through the stone passageways, but Ivo had them running down a different path.

"Where are we going, Ivo?" Sima readjusted, placing the suitcase in her opposite hand for relief.

Her friend didn't slow, instead reaching a hand out behind her, and wrapping her fingers through Sima's, tugging her along faster.

"The Rani girl, the one who is nice to you, not like the nitwits the King stashes at your doors. I saw her when the explosions began. She looked at me, and it was as if we silently agreed that I would go for you, to get you out while she fought. I have never spoken to her, but I can tell she has a pure heart. She reminds me of what they promised us the Rani would be for Aeria."

"You want me to leave Aeria?" Sima asked, not understanding.

More explosions rang, causing the girls to bump into each other and nearly collapse to the floor. Aftershock had them scrambling again, but Ivo held strong to Sima and kept pulling her forward even on the unsteady ground.

"We must hurry. I fear your Rani cannot wait much longer."

A set of stairs and one more doorway and finally, their shoes touched grass. Cosima realized they were on the southern end of the Palace. The southern end had nothing behind it, just an endless open sky. Just as she feared that Yadira had already left, a winged figure appeared, flying above the railings marking the end of Aeria's turf.

Momentum found the girls then, as if seeing Yadira had given them a boost of energy. Sima hardly felt the weight of the luggage as her feet dug into the ground, determined to go faster.

As the wind tore at Sima's face, she thought about what all of this would mean. She had been careful to avoid looking at Aeria, to avoid seeing the devastation and destruction that had taken place today. A city born a millennium ago had come alive fifty years ago and threatened to fall today. What would Aurelio do when he learned she had fled? Would he send Rani to find her? Would they bring her to him alive, or would he finally decide to end her for her betrayal?

Though her mind was a storm of thoughts, she focused on Yadira as the distance between them closed. Yadira's spear glistened in the sunlight, a beacon welcoming them, still dripping with blood.

As they approached, Yadira shot Sima a quizzical look. Yadira restrained her tightly coiled hair beneath a scarf. Her hair's auburn color was a similar scene to Aurelio, splattered with evidence of her bloody run-ins.

"Queen," Yadira called.

Yadira gave a small nod to Ivo, the Hexia girl returning one, a shared, silent respect in the air between the two of them. As if they saw the same dedication to Sima, and to Aeria, in each other's eyes.

Behind them the rampage of screaming and chaos continued. Sima imagined the townspeople were still in shock, even if the explosions had come to a stop.

"Whatever you did in his office…" Ivo said, water spilling from the lake in her eyes. "We have our power back, Cosima. Do you understand what you've done for us? We can fight back, we can flee. With the mayhem around the Archipelago, my sisters and I finally can break free."

Yadira's full lips pressed into a firm line.

"We must go," Yadira said, reaching for the case before

offering her free hand to Sima. "If this is true, then Aeria is no longer safe for you, for more reason than one. Tell me where you wish to go, and I will take you there."

"What about you, Ivo? Shouldn't I stay to help?"

Ivo smiled, wiping a tear. She took Sima's hands in hers. "We can fend for ourselves, especially with our magic back. I will make sure as many of us escape as possible."

Sima shook her head, unwilling to leave Ivo behind.

"Go, Cosima," Ivo urged, "Go, and don't come back until he can't hurt you anymore. Don't waste this chance at freedom."

The words stung.

Freedom.

Her mind flitted back to all she had seen in Aurelio's office.

With all the fear in the world, as well as all the bravery, Sima said, "Take me Below."

The Afterlife

In the vast sprawling of the universe, realms of infinite potential exist. All much the same, all nothing alike.

The children question it—often—in their prayers, their judgments.

How did we get here?

Why do we exist?

"You have always been here," she says, "you exist because you must."

Why must they writhe against the breath in their veins, the stardust in their eyes?

You were not, and then you were.

Chapter 11

The chaos of the falling pieces of their city accompanied the onslaught of bodies—Aeria citizens and rebels alike. Yadira was unfazed weaving through the gore, as if it were rain and not blood falling upon them. She clung to Cosima as the two made their way towards a new beginning.

Legends common amongst immortals mentioned times like this. Some called it *Torre* or tower moments—complete and utter destruction, for the chance at renewal. Voices shouted indiscernible commands above them, nearly drowned out by harrowing screams of pain.

Feathers hovered in the air, cascading downward in dawdling swoops. Limbs, weapons, and wings cleaved from Guardians were destined for the dirt, falling helplessly by.

Cosima squinted amongst the flurry, daring a last peek at her home. The main island, Innamorati, stood, the Palace still visible. Flames erupted from Iridicenza, and pieces of Perpetuo found their final resting place on the surface of Haelos. The Archipelago had seen its fair cycles of destruction and renewal, but this day, they witnessed unprecedented destruction.

Cosima's heart ached for Ivo, her mind full of worries. She wondered if returning their power had been enough to fully free the Hexia. If fleeing was the cowardly thing for her to do. Yadira strapped the case to her side, refusing to occupy her hands should she need her weapon. She wondered if it was as heavy for the Guardian as it was for her.

Then she saw them—the beasts.

Her jaw fell open, fingers clutching tighter to her Guardian friend as the monsters launched indiscriminately at those nearby. Rani paused their attacks against rebels to slaughter creatures, but the plentiful display of otherworldly terror was overwhelming. The ground quickly approached, and for the first time, Sima stepped foot somewhere other than her city in the sky.

Yadira's hand latched tightly onto Sima, dragging her toward the city. Cacti littered the open desert beyond the walls of the town, dirt blowing wildly. To avoid getting sand in her eyes, Cosima used her free hand to shield her eyes, trusting her feet to bring her to safety.

A snarling mass of fungus thundered toward them. The gnarled skin of the creature gave the impression it was bruising that caused the deep purple patchy hues. Yadira showed no sign of fear as she pulled her weapon from its holster on her hip. The metal sword, adorned with black tourmaline deposits, three to a side, slid cleanly through dreadful flesh. Sand and blood clumped beneath their feet. The two twirled together, Cosima following Yadira's lead as they spun.

Heads with too many teeth and frightful eyes flew by Sima's eyes as Yadira brought the creatures swift deaths. A startling number of them were three times their size. Guardians sliced limbs from beneath the gigantic beings to ground them.

"Yadira, look out!" Sima screamed as one barreled toward them, dragging two snapping heads behind it. The red and orange scaled demon ran on all fours, claws leaving deep indents in the dirt. Yadira grabbed Cosima and launched the two of them into the air with her wings, narrowly evading the creature's intimidating jaws.

Hollering from Rani Guardians scattered around Ombra warned others that only minutes remained, the enchantresses on the final stages of their work. The people of Haelos ran for their lives, some carrying children or pets. A few dozen citizens joined Rani in the rescue attempts of their citizens, sharp swords and elongated fangs in plentiful display.

A vibrant variety of magic types cohabitated within Ombra alone, but the impressive legends of the Viipir claimed they were the most formidable. Her eyes widened at the brave vampires, armed with weapons of all types, dropping from the sky. They shifted into bats mid-air, landing on beasts, savagely hacking off their heads, before shifting again as severed corpses hit the ground.

They found their way into the city walls just as the enchantment took hold, the bubble slicing anyone, and anything, in its path in half. A wave of invisible electricity signaled the first stage of the protection. Next came the seal. A shadow overtook them, briefly dropping them all into utter darkness. A buzz snapped through the air before the bubble cleared, revealing the fighting still taking place in the sky for those who either did not make it inside the enchantment, or were still needed in Aeria.

Complete seals like the one the Hexia enchantresses formed were rare, taking a considerable amount of magic to hold.

"This is Senz'acqua, the most populated city in the District. That's its official title, at least. The Ambrosi gave that name. It means *'without water'*. The residents prefer Speranza—*hope*." Yadira led the way, her body moving seamlessly through the crowd. Only now, with the enchantment in place holding out the violence, did Sima drink in her surroundings.

They had not crafted the city from large stone slabs or expert architecture, yet it was still beautiful. The stress of recent events was not enough to wash the elegance from Speranza, its charm distinctly homey in feel. Though exhaustion tainted the air, a hint of relief hung there, too. The people began lively greeting each other, congratulating one another on a battle well fought. Even those she had seen frantically carrying their children seemed to adjust quickly to the change, letting their babes run free as they hugged loved ones.

The architecture was darker in nature, a painter's collection of grays, blacks, burgundy. Thoughtfully placed along the streets were orbs of light, giving way to cobblestone pathways. Several magic types from Ombra could fly, and Sima noted the unique solution the city had implemented to accommodate all—dual entrances atop roofs, their twins below on the street. Bridges sprawled between buildings, connecting the entire city intimately.

Signs illuminated the names of businesses and housing complexes, the enchantments within glowing hues of red, purple, or gold.

"Yadira, why do they not keep a constant bubble around this city, like in Aeria, to keep the people of Ombra safe?"

"It burns a considerable number of resources. The enchantresses will be out of commission for days. How Aeria maintains its bubble consistently is unknown to us. Aurelio did not extend his ability to protect Aeria to Ombra." Yadira motioned for Sima to follow her down a small alleyway. "The people of this District are being mauled by those *things* and the King has done nothing."

They ducked into a small restaurant as it filled with displaced people coming in from nearby cities. Yadira's wings folded compactly against her back within the tighter quarters, and she strutted straight through two double doors marking the entrance to the kitchen.

There, raiding through a black wooden icebox, was another Rani Guardian.

His wings were bone white, delicately adorned with streams of black along the outer edges that met at the tips. His hair was split down the middle, half the same bone white of his feathers, half the same midnight black accent, traces of his brushed-out curls adding to the mess. Wisps of his hair concealed the rest of the large scar spanning from below his ear and up the length of his face. He was handsome—divinely so.

He wiped a bit of food on his leathers before rushing to hug Yadira.

"My friend," he said, voice low and warm.

"Vincenzo," Yadira said, clasping her arm around him in a hug. "This is Cosima—"

Before she could finish the introduction, Vincenzo interrupted, "Do not think I don't recognize our Queen." He offered Sima a gentle smile, as if to say he knew exactly why she was escaping. His eyes were an emerald green similar to the Drago from the in-between. She must have frowned because Vincenzo's expression changed.

"Right," he said, sheepishly rubbing a hand behind his head, "no discussion of royalty, then."

"I don't know how to be a proper queen," Sima said, hoping to convince him somehow that she hadn't intended to be rude. "I think I did once, but it's been quite a while since I have had a say in my kingdom."

"You have done your best," Yadira said, her smile earnest.

"It is good to see you here, Yadira," Vincenzo said, continuing to take food out of various pots along the cooktop. He put his pristine black and gold armor at risk of staining as he stuffed a chicken leg into his mouth, his arms full of various jars. "I thought I had seen the last of you when I finished training." He turned to Sima to explain. "Yadira helped me become acquainted with Haelos when I arrived through the veil." Bits of food fell in a slurry as he ate.

"He was in the last shipment of Guardians from the Eternal Kingdom," Yadira said.

"How often do Guardians come through?" Sima asked, peering into a pot. She smiled as she inhaled. It was a heaping pot of Sima's favorite spicy soup.

"Not frequently, perhaps every hundred years or so," Vincenzo said, dropping everything in his arms. Sima startled at the sound of jars and containers colliding with the tabletop. However, when he placed a warm bowl of soup in her hands, she felt grateful. "I can see you have good taste in food," he said. "Let's eat something, and then I can show you to your rooms."

Sima followed him to the dining area, where the songs of conversation reached every corner. As hungry as she was, Sima yearned equally for quiet. The loud interior of the dining room made her head pound, and an anxious leech rooted itself in the pit of her stomach.

"Actually, Cosima," Vincenzo said gently. "I know a better spot for us."

He reached for her bowl, carefully scooping it from her hand, and led Yadira and Sima to a quieter back room where a small wooden table and four chairs sat.

Vincenzo and Yadira turned their chairs backwards to accommodate their wings before sitting. Sima slid into her seat, eyes latched onto her bowl. At last, she sipped the broth and sighed with relief.

"You like it?" Vincenzo asked.

"Yes, very much so," Sima replied with a smile.

"Vincenzo is an excellent cook," Yadira said, taking a sip from her bowl.

"You made this?"

"It's my favorite," he said, grinning. "I had a feeling soup would come in handy today."

Both Guardians relaxed their wings, the feathers fanning out on the floor. Sima gathered the sense that Yadira truly trusted this man.

"So, what does our very normal, everyday citizen know about her new home?" Vincenzo asked.

"Not much," Yadira said, scratching her brow. "He kept her in the dark for a long time. The good thing is, Cosima, Enzo here knows the workings of Ombra better than anybody. He practically runs this District."

"Oh, please," he said, cheeks growing a touch pink, "it is a joint effort, I promise. The reason people come to me is because I have made myself quite resourceful in my time. When I got my assignment, I circled the skies for seven days straight. I learned all I could about the movements of wildlife, the topography, water sources, potential weaknesses. I also mapped out where our boundaries with Eternita are, in hopes of us being able to reopen trade soon. We have stockpiled supplies, but we have taken on many more heads."

"Four thousand, if the latest talk is true," Yadira said.

Four thousand people, now the responsibility of the Rani here. Sima shook her head.

"How long will you stay?" Enzo asked.

"Not long, I was going to ask…" Yadira shared a quiet look with Vincenzo.

"No need," he said, waving a hand before his face. "I will gladly do it."

"Do what?" Sima inquired.

Yadira looked at her with a wariness she wasn't used to seeing.

"They will open a temporary gateway through the bubble sealing Speranza. It's the last chance for anyone to get in or out without putting everyone already inside at risk," Yadira said carefully, her back muscles tensing, raising her feathers from the floor. "I must return to the Palace in Profeta."

"You can't go."

"I have to go," she said, shaking her head.

"Cosima, if I may, I'd like to offer some perspective," Vincenzo interjected. "You freed the power of the Hexia witches on the Archipelago. They will need help to return to Ombra, and Yadira is a vital piece to that plan."

Witches.

Sima had forgotten that Ombra was also home to the largest covens of Hexia, except they didn't call them that here. Sima wondered if Ivo's family lived here, or if Aeria had enslaved them, too.

"Your friend will need me, as well," Yadira added.

"Ivo," Sima said quietly. She met Yadira's eyes. "I understand. I want nothing more than to help them."

"You will stick with me, and I will teach you the ins and outs of this District. You will know more than any leader before you," Vincenzo said, eyeing the luggage case as Yadira removed it from her body and handed it to Cosima. "That reminds me," he said, tossing a case similar to the one in Cosima's hands onto the table. "A skilled enchantress gave me these."

He pulled a large black cloak out. Once the light struck it, Sima realized the cloak was actually a deep, velvet green.

"You don't need the hood up, or anything. The enchantress is skilled at glamor clothing, but don't tell anyone you have it, obviously. This kind of magic preys on natural inattentiveness and suspension of belief. Once they know you are not who you say you are, the magic will no longer work on them. The illusion will fall apart."

He held it out, motioning for her to put it on.

She shot Yadira a wary look before stepping into it, shuffling the case from one hand to another as she slipped her arms through. It was soft, yet weightless. There was a certain comfort to it, the glamor laced in its threads. There was something familiar about it, the smell or the fabric against her skin, she didn't know.

She shuddered, the sudden wave of emotion surprising her.

"We will always know it's you. You won't look any different to us. This isn't a sure thing, but it is the best method we have for shielding you. It should be enough to get us by should we need to move you." Yadira fastened the small golden clasp, securing the cloak.

"You're safe inside the city for now," Vincenzo said. "Yadira and a few others will be the last ones out, then we're completely walled off."

"How long does it last?" Sima couldn't help but still feel on guard even if they said she would be safe here.

"Twelve days," Vincenzo said, slipping on an emerald ring before handing the identical one to Sima. "This will help keep us tethered should we get separated. It will glow when I am near you. The stronger the light, the closer I am. As for the enchantments, no matter what happens, the magic will fail on the Day of Return. It is unfortunate, but no magic is stronger than the will of the veil. That zap of power is necessary for the souls to pass through."

Yadira pulled Sima into a hug, sliding the case from her hands, and slipping it to Vincenzo so they could properly embrace.

"He will take care of those," Yadira assured.

"I need them," she replied, desperation painfully exposed on her face. "It's the only way I know how to fully access my powers at this point."

"*Mortoid,*" Vincenzo said, peering into the case, face grim. "What do you mean, this is how you access your power?"

Yadira shot him a warning look, which he heeded, engaging the closing mechanism again.

"There is no safe way to use them," Yadira said. "We may be teeming with witch healers here, but I can't afford to lose you."

"*Haelos* cannot afford to lose you," Vincenzo interjected. "You are the rightful Queen of Aeria, and I suspect you desire to lead once Aurelio releases his tether to this world. There is no one more fit for the job."

The double doors swung open. A Guardian made her way through, immediately locking eyes with Yadira.

"They have secured the hatch. The spells were double-checked for reliability. Yadira, if you plan to return, it must be now. This may be the only time the witches can perform the spell."

The Guardian's voice was smooth and light. She tucked a lock of black-red hair behind her ear, whispering something too quiet for everyone to hear to the Guardian who stepped in behind her. He stared back, unrelenting, but revealed nothing.

Sima shifted on her feet as Yadira waved goodbye and departed. Vincenzo and Sima walked briskly through the night air, taking a series of alleyways until they reached one that gave way to an empty, sand-filled square. Vincenzo raised his hand as a beam of pure darkness sprinkled with starlight erupted from his palm.

The Rani Guardians all possessed starlight, and the display always dazzled Sima. Space itself flooded from their extremities, the uses for it bountiful. In this case, it activated a mechanism beneath the sand, sediment pouring from the center of the square.

"May I?" Vincenzo asked, motioning his request to pick her up.

She nodded and allowed him to scoop her into his arms. Her body was tense at first, rigid in remembrance of her time with Aurelio. Sima dared a look at him, and he met her gaze with gentle green eyes staring right back.

His smile blanketed every anxious thought for a heavenly moment as he flew them underground.

Chapter 12

"Cosima, we have our first assignment," Vincenzo said, beaming at her. "Since you will tag along with me, our primary order of business is attending to all the ghastly things Ombra keeps hidden in the Depths."

Sima rubbed her eyes, adjusting to the light from the hallway as she rested on the wooden door frame beside her. Vincenzo wore black and gold armor, his large wings towering above them both. The night before was a haze, and she vaguely recalled being shown to an available room near Vincenzo's in the underground city, before diving face first into the bed to sleep off her tumultuous day.

"I came to bring you some clothing, as well as breakfast."

Her head tilted downward as her nose caught the scent of warm rice and charred meat. Vincenzo's hands held a tray littered with small vegetable side dishes. Several outfits lay draped over his arm, and he looked impossibly refreshed for the early hour.

"Thank you," she murmured, stepping aside to let him in.

"How did you sleep?" he asked, laying the tray on the desk in the room.

Sima glanced at the bed. It was smaller than the one from Aeria, with no fluffed comforters or mountains of pillows. Instead, it had two plush pillows, a warm quilted blanket, and soft sheets. Sima found she quite liked it.

"I thought my mind would keep me up all night," she admitted. "Instead, I fell asleep before my head hit the pillow. I think for the first time in years, I felt safe enough to rest."

Vincenzo seemed pleased by her answer, nodding as if he understood. "You are safe here. I will do whatever it takes to keep him away from you," he said. "Please, eat, and get dressed. I will come back for you in about an hour. I have some loose ends to tie up, and then we will begin our tour of the Depths."

Sima sat, taking a small bite of the meat. She sighed, embracing the taste as she reached for another bite, this time with a sliver of spicy chili paste and seasoned fermented vegetables.

"I don't know if I will ever tire of seeing you enjoy the food I've made," he said, clasping his hands together. "Makes the effort worth it."

Sima's cheeks grew hot, but it was true. Vincenzo was an incredible chef. His food felt authentic, and not replicated like the food of Aeria tasted.

"I will be back in about an hour," he reminded, making for the door.

Once it clicked behind him, Sima walked over to the door and locked it. A lock would not stop Aurelio if he felt motivated enough to come looking for Cosima, but the thought of leaving it open was more than she could handle.

She resumed eating, hungrily devouring every bite. While she ate, Cosima repeatedly fought off the creeping thoughts, each more dreadful than the one before it.

He's coming for me… he'll kill everyone who's helped me and drag me back. I won't be free, I won't be able to escape.

She placed a shivering hand across her chest, hissing slightly from the chill of her fingertips. Goosebumps raced along her skin, kissing every inch of her body. Hair stood on edge, her eyes laid closed as shaky breaths wound themselves in and out of her lungs.

I am free, and I won't go back.

The words echoed throughout her mind, strength building somewhere in her core. Sima made her way to the tiled bathroom, breathing through her nose in measured inhales. Cool sink water ran across her wrists as she attempted to pull herself back from the brink of panic.

Sima had dealt with anxious whirlwinds daily due to the torment she endured behind closed doors. She taught herself with time how to withstand the attacks, prioritizing her sanity, even when it seemed unobtainable.

Now, she studied herself in the mirror. Her hooded eyes swelled from fatigue, though her skin was paler than usual. She splashed cool water on her face, imagining it was washing the remnants of Aurelio down the drain.

"I am strong," she whispered to her reflection. "Even when I did not want to, I remained strong. I am alive today because of *me*. I am going to survive this."

The pile of clothes left by Vincenzo included two long dresses, similar to the ornate fashion of the Archipelago Above, and two sets of utility-minded pants with matching black tops.

As she pulled on the pair of pants she had selected, Sima took stock of the various pockets and hidden weapon holsters lining the pantlegs as well as the reinforced waistband designed to hold heavier items. It was certainly different from what she was used to wearing, but she found it suitable.

Fully dressed, Sima combed her hair with her fingers and water as she waited for Vincenzo. A knock on the door made her heart skip a beat. Fear dissipated as the ring Vincenzo gave her illuminated on her finger. Sima walked to the door and unlocked it.

"Hi," he said. He glanced at her pants. "We will have to fetch you some weapons to fill those."

She looked away. "It's been a while since I've worn anything beyond what Aurelio has picked out for me. I enjoyed the opportunity to select for myself."

"Ah," he replied. "You will be pleased when we reach the armory later today. You can select any weapons that call to you, and I will keep my mouth shut, too, if you like."

Sima laughed. "The silence of a man can be the greatest gift."

He smiled, nodding in agreement as he pretended to seal his lips with his fingers. Sima laughed again as she slipped her arm through his. He led her down deep, black stone passageways, all incredibly cluttered with people. The Depths weren't nearly as ominous as he had made them sound. In fact, Sima found them hypnotizing.

As bodies pushed past them carrying heavy crates full of supplies, Cosima and Vincenzo made their way further down a stone passageway. Small strips of fabric lined the steps to prevent slipping, light orbs hung from the ceiling, and there was not a cobweb in sight.

Sima could barely tell this passage went miles deep beneath the city.

"This place has been in the works by the people of Ombra for a couple of decades. They started on their own," he said, flattening against the wall, Sima following suit, as a few Viipir squeezed by, large bags of rice and beans in their arms. "But once we got stationed here, we realized we could finish it within a matter of months. The city above is nothing compared to the truth that lies below."

Sima realized this underground sanctuary must be the reason so many Guardians tried to bring survivors here. They had not just made a way of traveling all around the city with multiple access points and reinforced doors. They had created a masterpiece—innovation beyond what Sima thought capable of a city forced to become warriors.

"You will find the people of Ombra are not air-headed fighters. It takes dedicated practice and skill to do what they do. I respect the citizens for stepping up, for not allowing themselves to become victims to the beasts pouring through the veil."

"If I am being honest, I am not sure what of Ombra is real and what is fiction. The King did not speak well of this place, much of it the furthest thing from the truth. I want to know everything."

He smiled warmly as he stopped before a door and opened it for her. "In time, you'll pick it up. The citizens of Ombra are a magnetic bunch. No way you'll make it out of here without hearing at least a portion of the history from someone. Besides, we're lucky we can interact with the citizens. There are planets that can't speak directly with the inhabitants."

"How do they help?"

"In those places, Guardians and Ambrosi are myths. Their people call our kind angels," Vincenzo said, flexing his wings. "The immortals shield their Archipelago, hiding from the people of their planets. Their help is unseen and mystical."

They stood inside the pantry holding canned vegetables and different types of nut butter. Pantry seemed like a silly word. This was more akin to a storehouse. The square footage alone hinted that the underground sprawl was vast. So many divisions, so many preparations.

"I have taken a lot of time to study on other realms, more than most," he said, passing boxes to volunteers fluttering in and out, showing up empty-handed and leaving straining their muscles.

Sima took note and began handing out boxes, her heart warming to the frequent kind smiles she saw. This was not how Aurelio spoke of Ombra. She had heard every insult he could hurl against this District. His long-winded, drunken ramblings had depicted his hatred for the magic types, regarding them wholly as demons.

Odilia and Grimaldo, the two odd Guardians she had met when Yadira left, returned. More conventional dispositions substituted their once-strange demeanors, a smile emanating from both of them. Odilia was kind, rambling about what it was like being a Guardian. She told Sima about the closeness of the bond between her and Grimaldo, and how all Guardians were close. Something about it bothered Grimaldo, and he stood grimacing fiercely.

"What is it, Grim?" Vincenzo asked.

"They separate us, you know? When we are born, they take us from our mothers and raise us with our brothers and sisters. Guardians learn only how to depend on each other. We fight together, bleed together, cry together. We form unbreakable bonds, not just to our cause, but to each other. In every realm, whether they regard us as angels or demons, we are subservient—bred for war and taking commands," Grimaldo said. "Don't give her the wrong idea about it, Odilia."

The Rani Guardians who walked in bowed their head at the conversation, adding the same warm smile she got from the others, before retreating. The Guardians in Ombra were mellow, nonchalant. It stood in stark contrast to the uptight nature of the Guardians in Aeria.

Vincenzo motioned for her to follow him to the next room, as he called out commands to the others.

"Once we reach half stock, seal the room. Odilia, Grimaldo! Grains next," he said, pointing to two guards Cosima could only see by the tips of their wings extending over the crowd of bodies.

"Now I have something really fun to show you," he said, a mischievous grin on his face. She found him quite handsome, though strangely, it made her feel sad.

You're just looking for comfort, she thought.

Vincenzo led her through a hallway not lit by orbs, but by the sun. Stained-glass windows lined the entire hallway, including the ceiling. Whirlwinds of color fought for attention from her eyes, but ultimately she settled on four gigantic figures depicted in the art. Animals surrounded the figures, the kinds Sima had read about in the library.

"The people here dedicated themselves to the different magic types that founded Ombra. These four are the founding types. All magic types in this district can lead their origins back to one of these original distinctions. They are the Viipir," he pointed to a fanged woman brandishing a dagger, "the witches," finger sliding to a mystic woman with glowing eyes, "shadow-born—though few remain," a man stitched of clouded shadows and deep red eyes, "and the Echos." He pointed to the figure directly above them.

Sima craned her neck, taking in the humanoid figure. He looked similar to humans and Ambrosi, with no significant defining features or symbols.

Then the stained-glass mural moved.

The mural shape-shifted and bent light. Animals transformed, rearranging their bodies as their real counterparts could, into humanoid bodies more like her own. The figure itself transformed into a hawk. Sima gasped, eyes alight with wonder.

"The hawk is a form that every Echo can conjure. It is said that they descended from birds of prey, mixing their blood with other creations from the Goddess, though that part is pretty debated depending on who you ask. The Viipir were once all over this continent until your father split them into Districts to ease disputes. Tensions continued to mount between Shadow-types, the Faeries, and the humans."

They walked beneath the colorful light as Sima grinned, admiring her palms as they changed under the light from blue to green, green to yellow.

"Humans were progressing quickly with technology. After relinquishing their weapons, they continued advancing their society. Trade began between Ombra and Prisma. Viipir were not capable of basking in the sunlight as they do today. Their ancestors lived in caves, their grandparents in coffins, and their children, well, they know the Day."

"What changed?"

"The humans and Viipir collaborated to create a treatment. The Viipir and humans have a long-standing truce which forbids them from feeding on humans. They are required to source their blood from animals and have stuck closely to that. As a result, the humans used their medical advancements to study what caused the reaction to the sunlight by the Viipir. It has been thirty beautiful years of relief for their kind."

"Incredible. Is the solution permanent?"

"No, though I hear they are working on a way to extend the effectiveness of the remedy. The reason I tell you this is because Aurelio has the wrong idea about the people from Ombra. He believes they are devils, but I have been here nearly all fifty years of my time in Aeria. They are a phenomenal set of people, and we should celebrate their abilities, not destroy them. Eternita sealed their District, not just from Aeria, but from Ombra and Prisma as well. This means they cut the people here off from Prisma entirely, and as such, they have been suffering."

"Why has Eternita sealed themselves off?"

"Some say it is to protect their citizens from the beasts pouring from the veil, but that leaves the question of why they did not help Ombra instead of abandoning all who live here. It forced people underground."

"I see," Sima said, taken aback. "I never realized Aurelio's ruling caused all of this. The people here have been suffering for decades, and no one in Aeria knows. How has he kept it all a secret?"

Vincenzo frowned. "Too many people willing to look the other way, and a man who will do anything to maintain control. I hope you enjoyed the display. I thought that might prepare you," he said, opening the door, letting an explosion of merriment and chatter wave through the once secluded hallway, "for this."

As they maneuvered through what Sima would now classify as an underground empire, she saw wolves and trolls, and Phoenix's with for-sale signs forged of fireproof materials dangling around their necks. She saw tigers large enough to eclipse seven-foot Orcs, and rainbow-colored cats chasing each other through the crowds.

"Do—do people live down here all the time?"

"Did we forget to mention that? Oh, it's probably because none of Aeria knows about it. Only the Rani Guardians in Ombra who swear to keep it a secret. It isn't hard to convince them when they see what could be, what could be possible for them, too."

Elation lit every inch of Sima's face, the smells of food of all kinds sweeping her senses. She watched baby witches have their footprints stamped in spell-books, teenage shadow-borns dancing as a band played instruments she had never seen. A man with the eyes of a serpent flicked his split tongue at her, before shooting Vincenzo a smile.

It was nearly too much.

She felt as though Vincenzo had transported her to another realm. The surface city had become a decoy, disguising the people below to ensure their safety. It was brilliant. She wished she could hide down here forever.

Perhaps she would befriend the Echos. Aurelio would think twice about coming for her if she had a giant tiger to help her. Her attempt to make herself feel brave didn't land, but she still drank in the surrounding beauty.

"They are preparing for the Day of Return," he said, plopping a coin into the hand of a vendor. He handed Sima a fried bread and meat sandwich. She took a bite as she eyed the decorations being hung by Viipir. The Rani moved supplies, she realized, to the kitchen to prepare for the celebration. "It is especially important to the people here. Their claim on this land is one made in blood. They have given their lives to protect Eternita and Prisma from this. The human district would never survive these kinds of attacks."

"Ambrosi took holidays like the Day of Return from their people, morphed it into cheap replicas and expected to turn a profit instead of upholding their beliefs. In Aeria, there are mockeries of ancient traditions that contain none of the meaning. Here, they regard the Day of Return as the end of the harvest, the beginning of a quiet winter after the souls have passed. If you are interested, I can take you to Calix. She has studied the veil diligently, each harvest season. A majority of what we know is from her."

Sima smiled. Aurelio had never been forthcoming, giving her information only for his own amusement or to toy with her. Vincenzo had a light in him, something so gracious, so similar to Yadira, yet more pure.

"I would like that," she said.

As they made their way through more hallways in the maze underground, people everywhere seemed to have something to say to Vincenzo. Some brought concerns or questions about problems arising in the city, others offered a friendly *hello* and a *thank you*.

He had become quite important here since his arrival to the District. Rani Guardians came in batches from the Eternal Kingdom when requested, and Vincenzo had arrived with one of the last. Ombra lacked freedom beneath Aurelio, so the people took matters into their own hands. And with the aid of other castaway Guardians, they had advanced greatly.

"We seal all entrances to the underground during the Day of Return. It protects the people here should beasts flood the city, so the monsters cannot access those below," Vincenzo said.

"The celebration will still take place, despite the beasts pouring from the veil?" Sima asked.

He slowed to a stop, turning to her. A spark of electricity jolted her as their eyes met.

"They need this. To celebrate their heritage and remember why they fight the good fight. Why it is them before the monsters of worlds beyond, and not the innocents. Come, I think I know exactly where we can find Calix."

Chapter 13

Candles were deposited throughout the main dining room, spreading across the lengthy dining tables like stars in the sky. The obsidian tables sat atop cherry wooden legs, chairs upholstered with fabric to match the stone. Certain tables were roped off, place settings featuring neatly folded cards upon fine plates.

At the end of the substantial room sat a dais, with two tables facing the flesh of the room. Three people lounged in the chairs, immensely more at ease than the fine decorating would have suggested. Each wore green and gold armored sets, similar to Vincenzo's, with enormous swords at their sides.

Sima's heartbeat echoed in her mind as she ascended the dais with Vincenzo leading. Some animalistic instinct told her to flee. The mere idea of sitting up on display triggered a nasty fear.

"Calix," Vincenzo said, the heads of the trio snapping towards them. "I want to you introduce you to somebody." He motioned to Sima. "This is—"

"Queen Cosima Aphelion, of Aeria," one woman said, breathless. She tucked a lock of bright, blossoming red hair behind her ear. The woman's fawn skin and blue eyes reminded Sima of Ivo. She had adorned her slender nose and ears with jewels and piercings.

Sima blushed, unsure of how to respond to the adoration in the woman's eyes.

"This is Calix," Vincenzo said.

"I was barely walking when King Aurelio took Aeria," Calix said. "My parents both attempted to help, but…they didn't make it. My mother was a witch. My father, Viipir. I remember a little. I remember the chaos in Haelos when the coup happened. People were desperate to do anything to get the carnage to stop."

A lump rose in Sima's throat. She averted her gaze as she spotted the tears welling in the woman's eyes.

"I am sorry," Sima said. Worry flooded her gut for those still in Aeria while she hid with Vincenzo and the citizens of Ombra.

"Don't be." Calix stood up, the table in front of her vibrating from the abrupt move. Sima flinched, Vincenzo placing a steady hand on her shoulder.

"The reason we know your name is there were rumors in Ombra about you. They say it took hours for the wounds you left on his face to dissipate. The people here couldn't believe how brave you were to stand up to someone as strong as the King. It is an honor to meet—"

One of the Viipir women sitting next to Calix cleared her throat, causing Calix to clamp her mouth shut, ending the spillage.

Sima blushed, uncomfortable with reminders of Aurelio's crimes. When she had realized her home was under siege during the coup, she attacked Aurelio, clawing away at his face with her nails. That moment had been one of thousands of attempts to fight back—until it became clear she would not be successful.

Sensing her overwhelm, Vincenzo spoke up. "I think Cosima deserves a bit of time to process everything that has happened. Calix and Alma mean only love, I promise."

The one who had stopped the onslaught, Alma, eased Calix back into her seat.

"By now, she must know?"

"Calix," Vincenzo warned. "Later."

"What brings you two to us?" The third figure, a male, questioned. His smile caused his lip to slide over his fangs. His eyes flickered red for a moment before returning to their original brown. Deep hazel hair flooded his shoulders, paired with sharp eyebrows and smooth terracotta skin.

"Cosima is interested in learning about the Day of Return, as well as the veil," Vincenzo said.

At that, all three went stick straight.

"I like her already!" Calix laughed.

"Calix is half-witch," Alma said, sticking a thumb at the Viipir beside her, "other half being just like Monte Viipir. I'm an Echo." Alma had golden-brown skin, eyes like honey, and impossibly elegant braids down to her waist. She held her hand up, soaking in Sima's shock as Alma morphed her appendage into a cat's paw.

"Our people have celebrated the Day of Return since our creation on this planet. Even the other Districts have celebrations," Calix said.

"None are as grand as those in Ombra, of course," Monte said.

"True," Alma said, clapping her hands together lightly, "Ombra has some unique traditions."

The trio took turns excitedly telling her about the holiday. Sima learned ropes barricaded tables for those without a living family. The tradition included setting out a place mat during a meal and inviting their passed loved ones to dine with them.

"Parties will continue for several days after the Day of Return, though my favorite tradition is the Electric Parade," Monte said.

"Electric Parade?" Sima asked, eyes glowing with excitement.

"Yes," Calix said, mirroring Sima with an equally enthused smile. "Enchantresses cast powerful spells in an ample array of shapes. They guide the souls to the veil, but they are incredible to behold."

"Wow, I never knew how Ombra celebrated," Sima said. "On the Archipelago, there is no tradition other than drinking wine and putting off work."

"Did you know other worlds celebrate this event too? Even if we cannot be together in this life, we know there are others like us who pay honor as we do. It has always been in us," Calix said.

"How have you adapted to the loss of your parents?" Cosima asked.

"It was hard at first since I am half-witch and Viipir. In our community years ago, people couldn't decide which side of me they saw, and if they didn't like one half of me, they didn't like all of me. My parents being gone meant I never got exposed to the culture of my heritage."

"Until recently," Monte interjected, reaching for Calix's hand, and brushing a reassuring touch across her. "We are all working to revive what war and ego have taken from us."

"That is beautiful," Sima said. She could hardly recall being able to experience a companionship that didn't have to be hidden. Sima never wanted to add more fire for her husband to use against her. "You honor your loved ones and ancestors, and you continue to do so no matter the surrounding conditions."

Calix nodded. "With hopes they will return to us when their souls are ready. Through friends, through children."

"Through every lifetime," Alma said, beaming at her two friends.

"The witches in Ombra have a lineage that dates back to the Founding of Aeria," Calix said, fingers aimlessly twirling the rich, wine-red hair tucked behind her ear. "We were one of the first creations in Haelos. Next came Viipir, and then the Fae. Witches have long since lived in the District we know today to be Ombra, however, some covens were once along the Eastern border of our continent. Depraved others wiped them out or forced them to find refuge in our District."

"When did this happen?" Sima asked.

"It's hard to say exactly when it fell apart completely, but things only worsened when Aurelio took over Aeria. While he was busy attending to controlling the Archipelago, the people here were suddenly finding themselves within the jaws of demonic creatures," Monte sighed.

"The confusion allowed Eternita to close their doors, slay prisoners, force our people into cruel experiments," Alma said. "Fae have not always coexisted well with any Shadow-type. They believe we are their 'dark opposite', yet no coven here believes that. We believe they are just as welcome here as we."

Vincenzo coughed. "Eternita banned all from Ombra. They are

between us and Prisma, and it is impossible for us to reach the humans."

"To be fair," Calix said, "it is so difficult because we are too busy murdering cosmic creatures slithering into our home to argue with Eternita. Who knows what they're up to in their pretty forests?"

"Calix," Sima said, "do you know much about the Hexia girls on Aeria?"

She nodded. "They are all of one coven, enslaved by Aurelio at the same time he took Aeria. Other covens are scattered around Ombra, lucky to have escaped before he captured them. Why do you ask?"

"I have a friend. Her name is Ivo. She is from that coven. The girls there all wear a pin with a Viper on it."

"They represent the Vipus bred by the witches. They were the only coven to possess them."

"Now, the Ambrosi use them for joy rides," Vincenzo said, with a strange tone.

"That makes me sick," Alma said, fuming. "The Vipus are warrior creatures. They shouldn't be chained up. Their coven never wanted them to be misused like that. They are meant to be ridden into battles as trusted companions, fighting alongside their coven."

Sima inspected the three in front of her, the answer to an internal question she had posed now becoming more obvious. *Are they involved in the rebellion?*

"Are there any updates on the Archipelago?" Sima asked.

"The attacks ceased around thirty hours after they began. Aeria is in the process of damage control," Vincenzo replied. He gave Sima a half-smile. "Yadira and other Guardians have been helping the Hexia witches flee. I won't know much else until a Guardian reports back with more information."

"Is Ivo safe?"

"As far as I know, yes, but she is still on the Archipelago."

"Who rules over this District?" Sima asked.

The Viipir man slipped a knife from his side. Monte cocked his head to the side, the dagger now spinning atop the table. "We take care of ourselves. We have enchantresses and builders working together to keep our city safe, to keep our people fed. If they cannot fight, they will teach, they will create, they will be a village for those who do. This means we are strong, but only when we work together. We can do nothing if it is not from the heart of all of us."

"Where do the rebels come from?"

All four of them shrunk away from Sima, uncomfortable with her question.

"All over this District," Vincenzo said at last. "There is a separate movement in Eternita. At least that's the latest rumor. The Devout Rising are well known, but people do not speak freely of them. To protect the identities of those involved, you see."

"The rebels are not evil maniacs interested in harming the King. They are people who demand the world Above pay attention. The rebels are our brothers, our aunts, our cousins. They are people we know, whose hearts we understand intimately," Monte said, sliding his tongue across one fang.

"Which is why we are thankful for the help of the few special Rani Guardians who are risking their lives to care for us. Aeria has not heard our prayers, but they have."

"It's our job," Vincenzo said, nodding his head.

"Don't let him fool you," Calix said, a laugh simmering in her eyes. "He is humble, but he has done more for Ombra than any other. He sees what we have here."

"Of course I do," he replied. "When the Fae sealed themselves off, it made the land here barren. They are nature's protectors, yet they had no problem leaving children here to starve. We have gotten around it, learning with time from the witches how to nourish the soil, how to call in nature."

"All his ideas," Monte added. "Imagine our surprise when in comes this recruit, nothing like the fierce warriors we had seen in the past. Softer." The group chuckled.

Alma jumped in. "Soft in the ways he should be. Brave as iron is strong."

"Enough, enough," Vincenzo said, though Sima could see what

their words meant to him.

"Queen Cosima," Monte said, drawing her attention.

"Cosima, just Cosima," she said, waving her hand.

He smiled. "Just Cosima, then. How are you adjusting to being in Ombra? I know it must be scary to not know what is happening in your kingdom."

"It is hard, but I am relieved to be away. I have been yearning for novelty, something other than the walls of my room. Being here with you all is better than any book from the library, or any day sat beside the King." Sima smoothed her hair, reassuring herself. "Being here with you all has made me realize how badly I wish to fight back. If I regain control over my power, perhaps I will do something about Aurelio."

The next sound was of metal scraping the table.

Monte's dagger.

Affixed to the hilt was a piece of moonstone, the crafter embedding the stone so it lay flush when held. The blade was smooth, the metal unblemished. She recognized the silent offer.

Fight back.

"We will help you, so long as this is what you want," Monte reassured.

Sima stared at the weapon. "It is," she said, accepting the dagger as her fingers curled around it.

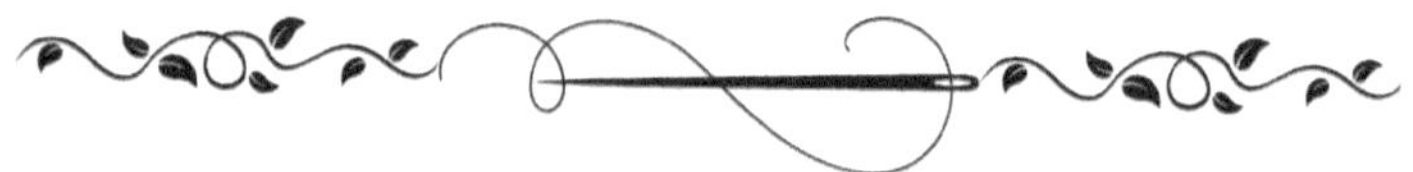

Vincenzo made her stay in the Depths as easy as it could be. Following up on Sima's desire to choose things for herself, he arranged for two local seamstresses to visit with fabric scraps. After careful contemplation, she selected an assortment of green, blue, and black outfits, and they were off, preparing what she would wear beneath her enchanted cloak. She would not need to wear the garment underground, but any time they ventured to the surface, it would be necessary for keeping her hidden.

The anxiety was overwhelming. The first two days, shock had stalled all emotion, but now the dam was falling. It had been fifty years since she was last free of him. Fifty years in which she went from being a girl barely touching adulthood to a woman with unthinkable hidden scars. But there was no time to dwell on who she was. She was here, surrounded by dignified, powerful people, and not one of them shied away from a challenge. She needed to be stronger, needed to learn more.

The guilt ate at her, the "what-ifs" allowing her no peace as she broke down in the warm water of her shower. She had told Monte she wanted to fight back, but nausea knocked her down each time she touched the blade he had given her. She was aware that her aid to the King's plans had further perpetuated the torment endured by the people of this District.

Warm water dribbled across her face, combining with tears as she contemplated her powers. Suddenly, Sima was back in the Palace, receiving harsh criticisms from those closest to her.

Miserable gifts, her mother had said, *evil beyond measure.*

Altering what is not yours to change, her father had lamented.

Sima's lip quivered. She could not fully comprehend the full extent of her alterations. It was only a matter of time before she learned of the disastrous outcomes of her choices. The Drago had warned her Kismet would seek to balance her changes. The red-tiled shower was cool against her back as she sank to the floor, letting water pour over her head.

"Why did I not push further? Why have I let myself become useless? I spent fifty years with him." Sima's palms pressed harshly against her closed eyes. "And wasted all of it. My control over my powers is weak, especially without the stupid drugs."

A flame ignited somewhere in her core.

"No," she said, wrapping trembling arms around her knees. "No more sitting in the pit. I have spent my share of time in the grips of self-doubt but I will learn now. I will make my stand now."

This was Sima's second chance, her opportunity to show her love and devotion to all of Haelos. Sima stood, turning off the shower and reaching for a towel. As she dried off, her mind raced with ideas for mastering her power.

Vincenzo had told her he would come by to pick her up in the afternoon. He was on the above-ground level of the city, Speranza. Each Guardian was required to return to the surface to maintain appearances should their brothers from Aeria come to inspect through exterior the shielding. The enchantments would be in place for a few more days.

In fresh clothes, Sima sat on the edge of her bed. She tucked the suitcase—which Vincenzo had mercifully placed, untouched, in her room—underneath the bed for safekeeping. She was not yet brave enough to open it. Removing the crystals had freed the Hexia's powers, but Sima could not understand how.

She questioned destroying them, throwing them away, or giving them to Vincenzo. If what Aurelio had said was true, and the crystals could kill the wielder, Sima felt dissuaded from freely giving them to others.

Against her better judgment, Sima reached for the case and opened it cautiously. The three large blue and gray stones flashed brilliantly when the light hit. Beneath them lay the packages stuffed to the brim with drug capsules.

Sima picked up one capsule that escaped from its package and held it between her fingers. She could only manage minor changes to Fate without the *Mortoid*, and yet Sima was reluctant to use the drugs ever again. She placed the capsule back in the luggage before selecting one crystal.

It was heavy in her hand, and each side reacted differently to the light. One side gave a lengthy, full display of color, while another gave scattered shimmers like scales on a fish.

"Are you as dangerous as he says?" Sima knew it was silly to speak to the stone, and she shook her head at herself as she returned it to the case.

Sima's ring began glowing, faintly at first, but it grew brighter within moments. Vincenzo had returned from the surface, coming to retrieve her from her rooms. A knock at the door and a blaring glow confirmed his presence.

"Vincenzo," she said as she opened the door.

Today, sapphire blue and silver armor lay across him. His emerald eyes crinkled with happiness when they met hers. "Hello, Cosima."

A bolt of electricity raked through her at the way he said her name. She smiled, accepting his arm by intertwining it with her own, and followed him down the hall.

"We are heading to the armory. I know Monte gave you a dagger, but you have space for more pieces of equipment."

"Will you teach me how to wield them?" she asked shyly.

"It would be my pleasure."

Two blond Guardians guarded the armory, but it was also protected by thick iron bars and locks. The men greeted Vincenzo, opening the door, and waving the two of them through. Vincenzo nodded his head and led Sima inside.

Sima's eyes dragged along the wall, unable to believe how considerable the weapon selection was. An assortment of metal bows and arrows sat beside hundreds of knives in every size. The smallest was the length of Sima's hand, the largest as long as her arm.

"Which one speaks to you?" he asked. He stood near an array of swords and staffs, the collection fit for an army.

"This one," she said, reaching for a sword with a deep forest green ribbon wrapped around its light gold hilt. The blade was thin, and along the handguards, carved into the metal, were wings, similar to those held by Rani Guardians. At the center lay a triangle carved of emerald, like the color of Vincenzo's eyes.

"That's a beautiful one. It is double-edged, so be careful with it." He reached for a matching sheath and slid the sword within. "Any others?"

"What's that one?" Cosima pointed to a sword with a nearly translucent blade. "It's marvelous."

"It's a newer type of weapon we have been experimenting with. It is thought that the fluorite you see here helps with focus, allowing the blade to siphon the user's energy." He reached for it, and once it connected with his skin, a deep mossy green illuminated the blade. Delicate streams of metal swirled around the guard, like a ribbon being tossed with the wind. Rose gold held purple-green fluorite teardrops.

"Are the stones… dangerous?" Sima asked. "Will it hurt me to use it? Your weapons are all made from the same material."

"These are safe, I promise. You are immortal and your tolerance far exceeds humans."

Vincenzo handed Sima the blade. The green faded as it met her hands. Instead, the glow from Sima was opalescent.

"Magnificent," Vincenzo breathed. "I haven't seen that color combination yet. It suits you."

Sima blushed as she held the sword at her side. "Maybe it's too much."

"Nonsense. Only someone as worthy as you can do this blade justice."

Sima couldn't stop the smile from spreading across her face. "Thank you," she breathed.

"You asked me to teach you, and I would love nothing more. We can get started today if you like. I have already surfaced for the time being, but with Aeria in shambles and the enchantments in place for another couple of days, it seems like we have found ourselves the perfect opportunity to train."

"I would like that," she said, studying the blade in her hand.

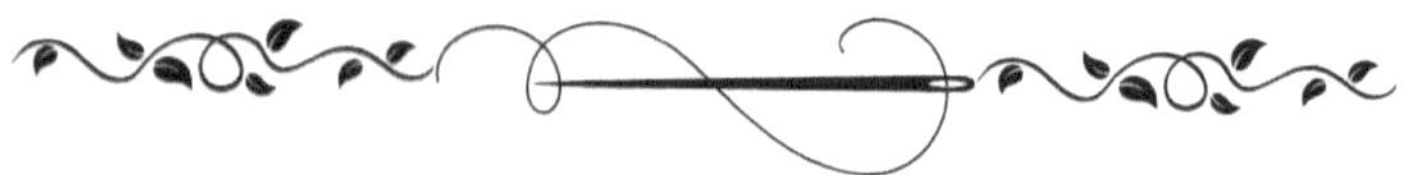

The training room held six punching bags, armor, and an array of body padding which varied to accommodate diverse methods of practice. Vincenzo selected a few pieces of equipment for the two of them, as he told her about the latest news from the Archipelago.

"The main island, Innamorati, has resumed normal functions. The damage sustained in Perpetuo will take several months to repair. As for Iridicenza, attacks halted all construction, and from what I hear, it has led to immortals all across the island being displaced to Innamorati. The overflow of scared people has the

King on edge, though my source says he hardly makes appearances."

"Do you think he'll find me?"

"Not if I can help it, Cosima." He held up a piece of silver armor. "This will make sure you don't hurt me or yourself when you're learning how to wield the swords you picked out." He slid it over her head and fastened it around her. Sima held her breath the nearer he got, but soon, they were both suited up.

Vincenzo pulled two dummies adorned with metal in front of them.

"I want to begin with you first getting a feel for the weapon. Adjust your hand position on the hilt so that you maintain a comfortable but firm grip on it. From here, practice slicing diagonally, starting by raising and bringing it down at an angle."

Sima did as he instructed, trying to not cringe at how deftly out of place she felt as she removed the green-wrapped blade with jade from her left side. On her right, the sword capable of glowing stayed neatly tucked away. After a series of practice swings and suggestions from Vincenzo, Sima grew more confident.

"You're getting the hang of it. Let's practice together," he said, withdrawing his own weapon. Orange and black ribbon wrapped around the hilt, revealing a triangular pattern along the length of it. "Timing is incredibly important when using a blade. Not only do you need to practice defense and block incoming swipes, but you must also be on the offensive, striking when the opportunity presents itself."

Sima mimicked his movements, practicing blocking overhead attacks by turning her blade parallel to the ground as she held it above her. She learned cross-body movements, and how to defend against low attacks by pointing the blade downward to block.

After two hours, the two of them sat sweaty and out of breath, sharing a cup of water after Sima finished hers, and laid claim to his as well.

"We can practice a bit every day," Enzo said, wiping his brow. "I know exercise helps me when I'm nervous, and maybe it will help you, too. You'll be a symbol of hope to people everywhere."

"What does being a 'symbol of hope' entail, exactly?" Sima asked.

"Foremost, it means learning to control your power *without* the drugs. Then, a delicious variety of dreary, tedious work like returning Aeria to its former glory through massive systemic changes, while reassuring your people that you strive for the greatest good."

She glared at him.

"I am being serious, and it just so happens on a completely unrelated note, I know a real-life wizard. A wizard who, a time or two, dabbled in teaching mastery of the arts."

"Wizard? Is that what Calix was on about? You know a sorcerer capable of using spells?"

"He prefers *wizard*," he said, rolling his eyes.

"Yeah? He told you this?"

"Yep, told me straight in my face."

"That face?" Sima asked, pointing a finger an inch from his nose.

He smiled. "This one, exactly."

"That's probably because you have fool written across you in invisible ink."

"I may very well, but since you can't use your power, I highly doubt you'd be able to tell."

She scowled. "What do I have to learn from a sorcerer?"

"Wizard," he corrected, "whose name, by the way, is Ostrum."

"Ostrum?"

"Ostrum von Toadsage."

"Now you're joking with me."

"He would be disappointed to hear you jest at the beautiful name given to him by his mother. Or father. Not really sure which. The wizard naming be damned, will you stop being miserable and angry at *me*, and go be miserable and angry productively? Through fight club."

"Wizard fight club?"

"Shame you have no sense of imagination. Ombra is not all that meets the eye. Haven't you learned that yet?"

Chapter 14

Three days remained until the Day of Return festival, and Sima was putting on ridiculous clothes to join in a wizard fight club. It was actually called The Reckoning by the others, but it was real, and if the outfit predicted anything, it was going to be ridiculous.

She frowned at herself in the mirror. She wore a support bra and athletic shorts, both in velvet purple with golden swirls and stars drawing patterns of constellations. Then, an oversized cloak, a matching velvet purple, but with *Intermediate* branded across the back tail. Ostrum had given her pale golden gloves, which she learned was something the wizard had stolen from Gaia during his trips through the veil.

"How can he go through the veil?" Sima questioned Vincenzo. "I thought he was an alchemist."

"I told you he is not an alchemist, but you won't listen to me," Vincenzo had said. "Few can travel through the veil, but Ostrum is not just anybody."

She frowned again, then placed in a mouth guard to protect her teeth. Part of her wanted to believe this was dumb, because, well— it *was*—but also she wanted to believe it was dumb so she could stay in denial about the fact that every sign seemed to point to the necessity of physical violence.

Sima was not a fan of using her body as a weapon unless she had no other choice. Sparring with swords for four days hardly seemed adequate in putting up a proper fight against those more skilled.

As she exited her room, she lamented the smile that Vincenzo wore.

He, too, donned athletic shorts and a cloak.

By the Spirit.

He was shirtless. She wondered if the surface of skin was cool like the carved statues they keep roped off in museums, or warm like her. She immediately scolded herself, wrapping her cloak around her exposed midsection.

Just like the museum, he is not for touching. Perhaps just looking.

"You're looking mighty fierce," he laughed. "Check this."

He swirled, showing off *Expert* on the back tail of his cloak. Sima rolled her eyes, making a show of trying to stomp on it with her shoe.

"Hey," he said, pulling it before her foot landed, "at least they didn't put *Novice* on yours. He makes those guys go first."

It didn't take long walking through the town center beneath the city to reach where they were going. Large signs pointed directions to the *Arena of Divine Retribution,* and Cosima grew suspicious of how much chatter and noise she heard coming from behind the double doors before them.

"Calix!" Vincenzo said, greeting his friend with a clasp on her shoulder. She was dressed similarly to them. However, her cloak was black, with reddened stars.

"Checking me out?" Calix grinned. "I'm a big deal, but only when Ostrum's around."

Sima couldn't help but mirror the girl's mood and smiled back. "I am worried about what Vincenzo has talked me into. I don't know what to expect."

"There's no way for anyone to explain it to you sufficiently—you need to see it for yourself. Good luck, I won't be joining until later." She hugged Sima, brushing a quick kiss across her cheek before running down the hall to another set of doors, and disappearing. "I'll find you later, Sima!"

"Ready?"

"As I'll ever be," Sima murmured.

They were right. There was no way to explain what Sima was seeing. There were over fifty rings. Sima's eyes blinked rapidly, as if the mirage would end. She stared around, disbelief overtaking her at the arena full of people who came to watch.

"They're not real," he whispered in her ear, "well, they are. They're here watching from other worlds, and the wizard does a little fancy magic to connect them to us. He calls them Hologram Mists, something about light and refraction. Listen, the guy is a nut, but *the* most impressive stuff happens here, so you've got to just roll with it."

She laughed, the sound jarring. It had been a long time since she heard herself laugh. *You're just a little nervous*, she told herself.

He moved around her, holding out a hand.

"The rest of the competitors will join soon. Let's pick a ring now. A few rings have high viewers, and that's not my style today. I know a neglected few that would perfect for us."

She accepted the touch of his hand, sending little streams of electricity through her fingertips, numbing the anxiety that jumped into her stomach at the word *viewers*.

He led her near the outer edges, the middle of the room suddenly filling in massive waves. Jungle cats, birds, walking tree monsters and more brushed by them. Echos were people capable of morphing into animals, but Sima had recently learned they practiced nature-based transformations, mimicking plants as well.

Vincenzo snagged a rope from his selected ring, pulling it to create space for her to step through. He still held her hand and used his grasp on her to keep her steady as she climbed in. He followed suit, clapping his hands together, causing lights to illuminate from above. The bright lights fixed to the ceiling cast a shadow on his wings, making them appear twice as large.

She swallowed.

Surrounding rings were filling quickly, with six to each. The four who joined them were two Viipir, an Echo as a lioness, and an Orc. The Orc was taller than Vincenzo, towering above them all. He smiled a toothy grin, cracking the joints in his gigantic hands.

Vincenzo smiled up at him, a picture of ease. He flexed his wings a bit as a jest, but the Orc stared only at Sima. All four opponents focused on her.

They think I'm an easy target. She scowled. *How did this become a competition with no wizards and no teaching?*

As if her doubt of him caused him to manifest, a bearded man appeared inches from her face, eyes wild. His velvet cloak quivered as he floated above the ground.

As she jumped back, he laughed, disappearing again. Sima glanced around, but he was gone. The others merely kept staring at her, and Vincenzo kept trying to size up the Orc. Those in other rings had begun throwing fists, beams of magic and electricity, or withdrawing weapons from holsters.

Cheers from the crowd disoriented her as a bell dinged, the Viipir women drawing their blades. The lioness stalked around her with her teeth bared.

Vincenzo finally decided he'd had enough of the Orc and knocked him unconscious with a swift punch to his throat, and shouted, "Ostrum!"

Ostrum von Toadsage appeared before them, now wearing comically small glasses on the top of his nose. His aura was wholly impatient, a wand in one hand, a long velvet hat in the other.

"*What?*"

"She can't do magic," Vincenzo said, pointing at Sima.

Subtle, she growled to herself. Way to tell the others in the ring, who gazed hungrily at her like meat, and she was, that she had no defense.

Ostrum's bushy eyebrows met his hairline.

"What are you?"

"I-I…" she didn't know what to say. "Ambrosi and Hexia."

"Unlikely," he replied.

The world stopped, everything around them ceasing to exist. The darkness of the void filled her eyes. It was her, and Ostrum, in the ring, and no one else.

Quiet befell them, Ostrum studying her as if he were solving a great mystery.

"I'll admit," Ostrum said, cocking his head to the side, "I have not met one of you, either, my dear, though I doubt you are born of Haelos. I can smell the veil on you, like the universe melded you of the cosmic roadways."

His nose crinkled.

"What are you capable of?"

"Well, I—"

"Out with it!"

"With drugs I can sometimes go to a place, I think, called the in-between."

"With drugs, many of us can go many places," he said, bored.

"I change Fate."

That had piqued his interest, a network of puzzle solving firing off in his brain once more. "How? I want you to show me."

"I can't without the drugs," she said.

"Why?"

She was growing frustrated. He was supposed to teach her.

Doesn't he have a way of unlocking my true potential, or something like that?

"I don't know," she replied. "I've tried, but it doesn't come."

"Oh, you've tried. Well then, that solves it."

He clapped, jutting them back into the arena once again.

Before Sima could react, the lioness pinned her to the floor, claws drawing blood along her stomach.

She searched for Vincenzo, sure he would save her from the attack. When she found him, he merely held a thumbs up and shouted, "You've got it!"

She wanted to scream, her hands straining to keep their grip on the lioness' head, her hot breath nauseating as the pain was setting in.

Then it was all gone again.

Behind Sima's eyelids a scene played out, a little girl playing with a stuffed lioness, practicing morphing her hands into paws.

Sima pulled her hands back, and the image faded.

The lioness lunged for her again, as if she didn't notice what had happened. Her jaws snapped, Sima moving her face just in time. The weight of her competitor crushed the air from her lungs, her bite snagging on Sima's wrist.

Behind them, Vincenzo had knocked out one Viipir, and was going toe-to-toe with the other. As the Viipir's fist landed on Vincenzo's face, time warped again. She was going to be sick.

The moment sped backwards, then forward again.

There.

She'd done it. Even if it was only for a moment, she had altered the surrounding time.

The void appearing again made her question if she were going mad, but Ostrum simply stood there, hunched over. He stared at her from where she lay trapped on the floor. The lioness was paralyzed, as unmoving as ice.

"How did you do that?"

"I don't know!" Cosima shouted, irritated.

"You said you change Fate. You didn't tell me about the time-warping." He frowned and had the gall to appear disappointed. "Wizards can touch the Weave. Do you know this? The Weave is the origination point for every tether of Fate. You are not casting spells, but you are touching magic just the same." He pulled a large, dusty spell book from behind his cloak and began thumbing through it.

"The time what? I barely know anything about what I can do. I was bound to leave things out."

"I suppose they would intermingle, not that I would put Fate down to the second," he said, stroking his beard, murmuring as if he weren't even actually speaking to her, "but I can see how it makes sense. Have you considered you are a time mage of some sort?"

"I haven't considered what I am. There is only so much I know how to do."

"A diviner, an evocation-mage, and an illusionist walk into a bar. None of them are your father," he laughed, sputtering breath escaping his chapped lips as he made a show of slapping his knee. "No? Okay, I'll tell you what. You describe to me how you use the Fate, and I'll do a little digging. Tell you if I come back with anything. You take the drugs, and then?"

"I usually find a door. Behind it lies a memory I can access. I believe it's random, but occasionally they're highly specific to what I am there for." She racked her brain. "Sometimes, I find the people as babies, but it can be anywhere in their life. More often, it is the past, almost never the future."

"Future is harder to make concrete, I'd imagine," he said, stroking his beard. "Do you have some idea of what you are changing? Are there threads?"

"Yes, and it feels like finding the path of least resistance. I think about what I want to change, and I let my senses find the way. It doesn't always work. Frequently, the changes I make fail and snap."

"I'd wager those are pathways that would not occur, even with the hand of magic guiding the outcome. So, you cannot make anyone do what they wouldn't already?"

"No, I have to get more creative. When I get glimpses—"

"*Glimpses?*" he spat. "Of what?"

"Sometimes touching someone's skin gives me a vision from their past, usually relevant to the moment in time we are in when I touch them."

"Show me," he said, disappearing.

The bite from her opponent let up, the lioness fading to reveal a woman with black coiled hair, matching the one she saw in her vision. She launched a punch at her, but Sima rolled, narrowly evading the attack.

Sima growled. She kicked her body upward and got to her feet as blood pumped loudly in her ears. She held her fists up, growing stronger as the shallow wounds healed along her wrist and abdomen. The extra pumping of her blood brought more than adrenaline, it flooded her with fury. As the woman launched herself toward her, Sima reached for the Echo and wrapped her hands around her wrists.

The glimpse revealed a previous injury to her knee, and Cosima realized the girl switched forms to avoid persistent, lingering pain. Just moments prior, Sima's opponent had swapped into her normal form, meaning Sima could now exploit her weakness.

As Cosima returned to the present, she enacted her plan by first dodging the incoming attack, rolling as she hit the ground. Hungrier than ever, Sima kicked, her shin bone colliding with the woman's knee, sending her howling to the ground. The woman morphed into a lioness, a single tear dripping on her golden fur.

Sima turned to find Ostrum beside her, time frozen again.

"Your power intrigues me," he said, stroking his beard. "It would be interesting to see what you'd be capable of with a proper hold on your powers. You are not stunted, my dear. I believe your restrictions to be self-imposed."

He snapped, vanishing. Sima re-entered the dance with her opponent, once again brainstorming ways to fend off her attacks as they circled the ring. Sima noticed the woman's lion form now walked with a limp. Cosima might have felt guilty if it weren't for the razor-sharp teeth snapping inches from her face as she advanced. Sima spiraled, diving for the injured leg with no mercy, and pulled it out from underneath her opponent.

Cosima's lion and Vincenzo's Viipir hit the mat simultaneously.

Vincenzo gave a celebratory yell and picked Sima up in an enormous hug before dropping her and yelling out for the wizard once more.

Ostrum appeared with another irritated look on his face.

"You know this entire show takes quite a lot of magic, don't you? I can't be here for you all day. You said she doesn't know how to use her magic. She showed you she does."

"I don't know how to control it," Sima remarked.

He rolled his eyes. "More personal journey, less ancient mystical wizard territory. Bring her back when she has a grip." He smiled at her then. "She'll be fun to put bets on."

He winked and was gone.

Chapter 15

Applause erupted from the real-but-not-real people in the stands. Losers left conscious waved as they strolled from the rings. Cosima blushed as others cheered, realizing they classified her as a winner. She let the feeling of pride flourish and take root inside of her. She had unlocked a distant ability, one she thought lost to time, and for the first time in decades, her self-doubt was quiet.

"You did a fantastic job, especially for your first fight," Vincenzo said, tucking her into a small embrace. Goosebumps, from the adrenaline or his touch, sprouted along her arms. His feathers were soft against her skin. She was surprised to find the sensation of it didn't bother her.

"Thank you," she replied. "I am still in shock that I survived, if I am honest."

"I'm not," he said. "I knew you could do it. You are stronger than you think."

Vincenzo guided Cosima to a sitting area nearby where they could watch the last performances. He handed her a cup of water before sitting on the gray metal bench. She took the spot beside him, gulping the water he offered. The lights dimmed, all but those above the largest ring in the center of the room. Sima rubbed her eyes, unsure if what she was seeing was there in reality, or if optical illusions were normal for this District.

Calix was among those performing, showcasing mastery of her

chosen form of combat. Shimmering red hair dazzled as it swished alongside Calix's face and down her back. The Ombra District consistently amazed Sima, and after utilizing her power and securing a win, she was more than content to lay witness to the display.

Each performer took a bow as an announcer introduced them. The two Viipir women with jet black bobs and red eyes impressed Cosima as they shifted to reveal their wings. Remarkably bat-like, their wings were smaller than those of the Rani Guardians, and the skin covering them was thin and semi-translucent. Three witches took the space to the left of the vampires, each wearing moonless night cloaks, faces hidden beneath hoods. Finally, an Echo as a Panda strutted out, the vibration of his roar tickled the inside of Sima's eardrums and chest cavity.

Calix and the three witches were first. Calix armed herself with a wooden staff twice the size of her body, first swirling it around her in swift movements, then charging at the others. One pulled back her hood, revealing fine pale-yellow hair and brown eyes. Her hand rose, purple dust spilling from her palm. The particles spread with an invisible force, creating a barrier Calix's staff could not penetrate.

Unfazed, she continued her flurry until the dust exploded and plummeted to the ground, breaking the shield. The witch dodged out of the way of the wooden weapon, tumbling to the ground.

"*Freccia di luce!*" shouted another witch, her hood revealing a short brown hair cut, and fierce yellow eyes, as the fabric toppled around her shoulders.

Calix yelled as she launched another attack, aiming for the second witch. The brown-haired woman lifted her hand as ribbons of magenta light sprouted from it. The light spiraled toward Calix with precision, following her movements even as she tried to evade. Sima was on the edge of her seat as the witch's light disappeared when Calix's staff struck her.

Only two remained. Determination littered Calix's face as she planted her feet on the stick and created a bend to propel herself higher into the air. She pulled the weapon up with her before bringing it down in a swirl on her opponents.

Another shield knitted together, blocking her advances as the third witch shouted: "*Cane demone!*"

Two tremendous black canines emerged from behind dark smoke, sending saliva sloshing as they snapped their jaws. Harrowing red eyes, sharp claws, and pearl white incisors aimed at Calix, the metal tips of her staff colliding with teeth and bone as she fought.

"Not fair," Vincenzo said. "I didn't know the Aura Sisters could summon demonic canines. I would have bet differently."

Sima shook her head, but her eyes remained locked on the ring.

Calix kept the canines at bay but found herself no closer to victory. Her movements transformed into defensive blocks, no longer the aggressive pursuer. The women Vincenzo referred to as the Aura Sisters huddled together as the blond maintained the shield before them. Calix ran directly at them, using her staff to vault herself into the air, her body flying over their heads. Once behind them, a steady swipe of her weapon toppled all three to the floor, cementing her win. The demonic canines vanished within seconds.

Sima stood and cheered, clapping with delight.

"Did you see that?" Sima said, eyes wide. "She's incredible. You should teach me moves like hers!"

"Easy now," Vincenzo said, smiling as he stared at Sima. "You just learned how to hold a sword this week."

"Right," she said, cheeks turning pink.

"Don't worry, before you know it, you'll be showing Calix a whole new world. Your predictive abilities are impressive, and with a little work, there won't be a fight you can't win." Vincenzo's eyes softened as she smiled up at him, and Sima blushed again, turning back toward the ring.

The performances lasted another hour, showcasing all that Ombra could offer. The unique blend of physical force and magical ability in the District surprised Cosima. A handful of fighters relied heavily on their magic. The others were proficient in bodily strength and physical talent alone.

Walking back with Vincenzo to her rooms was another whirlwind as Echoes filled the halls in a variety of forms. Birds taller than people flew above them, and the howling of wolves reverberated even above the noise. Vincenzo and Sima walked arm-in-arm as she recounted her fight with the lioness. Vincenzo laughed, amused by her descriptions of Ostrum.

"I thought the inter-dimensional wizard would teach me how to access my power, not just question me while stroking his weird beard."

"He's right, though. You only needed a small push. Your abilities will only get stronger with time. Your powers are surprising though, to say the least."

"Having one night where I can use my powers is invigorating. I won't lie, I am worried about my ability to maintain this control. I was under a great deal of pressure inside the ring. What if I can't replicate it again?"

He pondered her question for a moment as he held open a door, quiet sprawled through the halls the moment they stepped foot outside of the Arena of Divine Retribution. "You must figure out what exactly causes your powers to surface and replicate that yourself. Whatever triggers your magic is likely doing so consistently."

"Fear," she said softly, "it's probably fear."

"That's alright," he said, resting his hand on the arm she had looped through his. "Bravery is being afraid and charging forward regardless."

Sima's lips curled into a small smile. "I like that."

The soft keys of a piano played music, the notes making their way into Sima's ears from an unknown source. A rush of energy tore through her as the hallway opened into another room with stained-glass ceilings. Hawks, snakes, and green herbs were the focus of the colorful mural. Moonlight dribbled through the glass, illuminating the floor in a bewitching arrangement of light.

At the center of the room lay a massive water fountain, two sculptures protruding from the base. Carved from white marble, a Viipir woman stood seductively with a single fang balanced on the pad of her thumb. Composed of black marble, the Shadow-born kneeled at the vampire's feet, gazing up in admiration.

Cosima released her hold on Vincenzo's arm, approaching the fountain. The music continued to float through the room, and Sima spun to the song as colors fluttered across her closed eyelids.

"The only time I got to listen to music was at parties thrown by the King."

A hand lightly grasped her arm just below the shoulder. She opened her eyes to find Vincenzo's green eyes on hers. "I would learn to play any instrument you commanded if it meant seeing you happy. You would never know a day without music."

The breath left Sima's lungs as his words settled across her skin.

"What if you ran out of compositions to play?" she asked, voice hushed.

He shrugged, gently releasing her arm. His hand pushed a lock of her dark hair from her face. "I wouldn't rest until I composed a symphony for you, Cosima."

Sima glanced away as her cheeks grew hot. Her mind, which normally raced with endless contemplations, was empty and silent. The only emotion that prickled along her body was a twisted fear she was undeserving of such treatment, muddled with desperate hopes she wasn't a lost cause.

"Why did you bring me here?" Sima asked, taking a seat at the edge of the fountain. She placed distance between her and the Guardian, though a piece of her longed for the opposite.

Vincenzo walked around, his cloak from their time at the Arena dragged behind him. "It's one of my favorite places. We're right beside the music room where musicians practice. Before Ombra became overrun by beasts from the veil, the people here enjoyed weekly performances. Only with the enchantments in place do the people feel safe enough to resume."

"Why were you assigned to this District when you arrived to Haelos?"

"The King was removing all forces in place when your father held the crown, when I, and a group of other young Guardians, made our way from the Eternal Kingdom to planet Haelos. I think he sent us here so he would not have to deal with us. Out of sight, out of mind."

"How much of the Archipelago have you seen?"

"Not much," he said with a frown. "I have spent almost all fifty years here. I'm unsure if the King even remembers I exist, though I have no qualms with that. My duties are easier to uphold without his watchful eye."

Sima swallowed hard at the mention of Aurelio. He had not crossed her mind once since they first entered the Arena, and the brief respite was not long enough for her.

"I want to be more involved," Sima said. "My ability to alter Fate is not one that comes without consequences. I am changing the balance put forth by Kismet, and the use of it calls for balance to be restored. If I become more involved with aiding this District, I can apply my power more acutely."

"I see," he said as he wandered around the room, "your powers are vast, and yet it is limited by how adeptly you employ them. Your powers vex me. How have they been hidden so well?"

Sima gave a soft sigh. "I haven't explored my abilities fully, for one reason or another. I need guidance. If I understand the ins and outs of Ombra, I will know what I am looking for, should I need to change Fate. I can work to discover what I need, but it wastes both time and energy. Altering the threads of Fate takes a considerable amount of magic compared to glimpses or time manipulations."

"We have two days until the Day of Return. Getting you comfortable with your weapons is our focus, should there arise a need for you to use them. The opening of the veil is dangerous, and without the enchantment to protect this place, we will need all the hands we can get."

Sima brightened at his response.

"You really think I can be of some use on the Day of Return? When I was young, I would watch the Guardians train in the early mornings, and at night, I would dream of flying and fighting."

Vincenzo laughed. "You are the Queen of Aeria, and there is no one more fit for the title. Though the world would need to prepare should you sprout wings."

"I would never leave the sky," she said, standing and twirling to the music once again. "They'd have to lure me in with chocolates and books, or I may never return."

Sima gasped as Vincenzo's powerful arms wrapped around her, hoisting her into the air as his wings pushed them off the ground. Laughter erupted from her freely as the rainbow of colors from the ceiling became a blur around them.

He carefully placed her back on the floor. "Chocolates and books. I will keep that in mind should the citizens of Aeria need you." He halted, his face blank. He pressed a finger to his temple. "Sorry, the tele-bond," he said, a smile returning to his face.

"Tele-bond?" Sima asked. The tele-bond allowed Guardians to communicate telepathically with one another. "The Guardian who watched me when I was a young princess told me all about it. Is it true you can feel the emotions of others as well?"

"Yes, though only those you are close with. The connection strengthens with frequent use and deep bonds."

"Do you hear everyone all the time?"

"No," he chuckled, rubbing a hand behind his head. "There are ways to send a message to any Rani within a certain distance, but I can tune out most unwanted broadcasts."

"Can they hear your thoughts?"

"If you're not careful. It is the same as accidentally saying your thoughts out loud in front of others."

Sima shook her head. "I don't know if I'd like being able to hear my friends inside my head."

"Got too many skeletons in the closet?"

"Something like that," she said, sighing. "I think I used to be a cheerful person before I met Aurelio."

Rage flickered across his face, and if Sima were not so used to studying the emotions of others, she might have missed it. Vincenzo gazed at her with a softness she was unaccustomed to, reigning in his anger and replacing it with compassion.

"You are still that person, Cosima. Beneath what happened to you is the person you have always been. He cannot take that away from you. After fifty years in his grasp, when the opportunity presented itself, you freed the Hexia he enslaved and escaped."

"It all happened so fast, I wasn't sure I'd actually done it. My friend, Ivo, is the one who realized his lock on their power rested somewhere within his office. He left me behind by mistake, and…" Her voice trembled. "I found the *Mortoid* you saw in my bag. Resentment blinded me and I destroyed his office. That's how I found them."

"Found what?"

"The crystals."

Vincenzo's normally vibrant tan skin blanched of color.

"What crystals?" he asked slowly. "There were crystals in your bag?"

"Yes," she said, placing a hand across her chest. "Why?"

"Cosima, I'm sorry, but I need you to give them to me immediately."

Sima thought back to what Aurelio told her about the mysterious properties of the stones. "It's true, oh Spirit, it's true." Her heart pounded in her chest.

"It's going to be all right, I know how to handle them. Have you told anyone else about them?"

"No, I've been with you almost nonstop since Yadira left. What are you going to do with them?"

"I am going to destroy them. If those crystals captured the power of the Hexia, returning them to their reservoir will activate the lock again. The only way to ensure their safety is by destroying them entirely."

Sima nodded, and they rushed back to her rooms as she silently reprimanded herself for not telling him sooner.

Chapter 16

Vincenzo did not reveal how he destroyed the three crystals Cosima removed from Aeria. All she knew was that by taking them from their place within Aurelio's war table, she freed the power of the Hexia. Breaking the obelisks was the only way to keep them safe.

He disappeared immediately after retrieving the crystals and told her only the name of the stone's composition—labradorite. According to Vincenzo, labradorite, as well as other gems, were being studied by someone within the Ombra District.

In the two days leading up to the Day of Return, Vincenzo conducted the training he had promised her, and Sima's confidence using Monte's gifted dagger grew. The light blade was easier to wield than her cumbersome sword, though Sima managed occasional practice with it, too.

Otherworldly beasts and crystals aside, Sima enjoyed her time in Ombra. The people were content with what they had, and whatever they went without, a neighbor gladly supplied.

Their shun from Eternita was strange, but other travesties, such as a lack of food, clean water, and education for the children, were more pressing as beasts shoved citizens deeper into the District. The city they were in, Speranza, was the last city in Ombra before reaching the border with Eternita. There was nowhere else to hide.

Before she knew it, it was the Day of Return, and Cosima

agreed to assist Vincenzo, even if it meant surfacing from the Depths. They sealed the underground at every access point to prevent creatures from harming people. A group of Guardians working outside of the enchantment near the Star Realm Portal had located a family of twelve hiding away. When the protective barrier failed, they would escort the group to safety.

Vincenzo instructed her to get her cloak and prepare to walk to the surface. Her hand reflexively shifted to the dagger at her side. Monte insisted she keep it, and now there were few places she went without it. Something about the air in Ombra made her not want to give up. She had fifty years to make up for, and she wasn't keen on ending up victim to another abuser again.

Her ring illuminated as Vincenzo neared, and Sima was out the door before he could reach it.

"Hi," she said, closing the door behind her. "I'm ready."

"Good," he replied with a warm smile. "We are going to have to be quick. The enchantments are failing faster than we expected. This family needs us. They won't survive on their own out there."

"Why are some of the safe houses on the surface?"

"Each is stocked with those capable of healing anyone fighting outside. These locations are vital for those who need to seek safety."

Sima followed him up the stairs and to the surface for the first time since her escape. Dry air from the desert surrounding them sucked the moisture from her lips. Sima's heart pounded, and she grappled with her desire to become more than a victim, despite feeling terrified. The only sounds were their footsteps as they walked the empty streets.

"Over here," Vincenzo mumbled.

The edges of the city were barren and silent. Mounds of sand as far as the eye could see greeted them. She tugged on the cloak, double-checking her concealment. A Guardian stepped from an alleyway and quickly greeted Vincenzo with a nod. He pointed.

Before them stood a family of twelve. The adults of the group wore tattered, dirty clothing. Scrapes and dried blood littered their skin. Exhaustion hung in the air. Cosima swallowed harshly, examining the people in her care, people she needed to escort unharmed to the designated location.

"Come with us," Vincenzo said. His voice was soft and reassuring.

Just two blocks from the safe house, alarms sounded. Those at the front lines were warning the city of an incoming attack, the blaring tones signifying that it was a sizable one. They picked up the pace, Vincenzo biting his lip like he had half a mind to pick her up and fly her the rest of the way.

They both knew he couldn't. There were others in their group. Singling her out would be unfair and risky.

"There are Guardians from Aeria here," he shouted, pressing a finger to his temple. "We must go now. Everyone, let's move faster."

"Did he send the Guardians for me?" Sima whispered.

"Maybe he is still unaware you are in Ombra. As much as I don't want the extra oversight from my brothers," Vincenzo said, as the blaring ceased, "It will be good to have the extra hands. Usually Aurelio is sparse with his assignments, but I suspect the Day of Return and a missing queen have something to do with his persistence today."

The safe-house was within sight, and though they were on the front lines, she scanned for Calix, Alma, and Monte. Yadira, too, but Sima had a habit of looking out for her everywhere. A blast sent several in the group to the hard ground, cries escaping from the children. Vincenzo used his wings to shield the crowd as Sima pulled them back to standing.

They were running out of time.

Pieces of the bubble gave way, and a siege of winged demons carrying boulders emerged. Pieces of jagged rock flew in all directions as dust filled the air.

"Go!" Vincenzo cried. "Take them inside."

She hesitated, and she could have sworn he did, too.

"I will find you, Cosima." His eyes flicked toward the safe-house, reminding her of her orders.

Sima nodded, rushing slightly ahead of the group, pulling a

small boy behind her. She focused her sight on the door, making herself an unstoppable force. Vincenzo trusted her to save them, and she would. The group included four children. The adults, to their credit, did not falter. They picked each other up and kept pace behind her.

Cries of battle echoed through the empty city streets as floods of monsters began making their way in. She heard the distant ring of metal being drawn from sheaths.

Steps away. She was only steps away.

Her sweaty palm nearly slipped off the knob, but she threw the door open, everyone piling in behind them. Quickly, her eyes scanned and counted... *eight, nine, ten...*

Eleven and twelve.

Where were eleven and twelve?

She turned back, a nightmare coming to life, as she realized a young girl and her mother were being cornered by a mutant beast with plant-like stalks in place of limbs, fungus and pollen in place of facial features. Bursting from its chest, a chlorophyll green mouth unhinged its jaw, leering right for the small brown-haired girl.

Without thinking, Sima slammed the door behind her and ran for them, unsheathing her dagger. She held a hand out in front of her, and begged her body to obey, to stop time, even for just a second. It refused her desperate requests. Worried she was too far, her legs pushed until her muscles screamed beneath her.

Her breath burned in her lungs, and something like fear itched at the back of her mind, but her legs propelled her forward. She raised her dagger and lunged, the two-headed beast unaware of her ascent.

The feeling of the blade meeting the beast's neck was distressing, too much like flesh, and not enough like the plant it was. Or the plant it was now? Some parts of it bore a resemblance to the bodies of people, all lost under pounds of heavy foliage. The sound of thousands of miniature shrieks escaped the creature, threatening to barrel a hole through her eardrums.

It took everything to keep her hands focused, and she was

straining to maintain her grasp and not cover her ears. Cosima's arms did not rest. She hacked and hacked, even as the beast's vines twirled around her, trying to pull her off. Her grip did not loosen, even as the beast's small, mutant head rolled, revealing a caustic web of parasitic infection.

If it were a person before this, then Sima considered it an act of mercy as she sawed the remaining fungus-ridden head off its body, green ooze slithering out of its veins and not blood. It hit the ground with a wet thud, the screaming finally ceased.

The breath heaving her chest in and out was now the only sound. She glanced down at the little girl, her mother shielding her from the attack. They peered up with gratitude.

"C-come," Sima stumbled, limbs shaking as she strained to replace her blade. She helped them rise, the little girl's eyes like moons as she took in the sight before them. She placed a hand on the trembling girl's shoulder.

The safe-house door opened briefly, and the mother and child ran to the sanctuary. Sima would have ran, but she was exhausted, the adrenaline wearing off already, leaving her sick to her stomach.

"Close it, I'll be right there," she said. The woman at the door gave her a wary look before slowly shutting it..

She paused, resting her sweaty forehead on the cool brick of the building before she emptied her stomach. She didn't know who she had become, but she wouldn't have guessed she was the type of person who could do something like that, even without a grip on her magic.

As she heaved again, she thought not of the acid burning her throat, but of the pride rooted firmly in her gut, not to be misplaced by any kind of sickness. She had come a long way from the submissive girl she once was. She peered back at the creature, feeling dizzy again. *Why are the streets so quiet?* She looked to the skies, seeing no monsters. She strained but heard no fighting or yelling. Her head turned toward the safe-house, the door closed tightly.

Good, she thought, *at least whatever shit is about to go down won't be on them.*

Her breath became more rattled as fear took her. A chilled wind had her reaching for her cloak, only her fingers grazed skin instead of the neckline of the garment. She gasped. The creature had torn it off.

She ran for the cloak, attempting to tug it from beneath the colossal corpse with exhausted muscles. As much as she pulled, it would not budge. Realizing she was now a very obvious target, she hurtled herself toward the safe-house, feet slipping across the dirt, when she spotted another monster.

Sima darted down the opposing path the moment the beast clocked her, afraid of giving away the location of the safe-house. It ran on all fours, its head a disgusting glob of weeping fungus. Nausea sullied her gut again just at the sight of the mangled body of the beast. It almost looked like a wolf, except the ribs along the left side of it revealed not organs and flesh, but more overgrown fungus and rotted tissue.

"What the hell are these things?" she shrieked, sliding around a corner, and making a dash for the second safe-house she knew of. Besides this one, there was only one more, and it was on the opposite side of the city. She begged the universe, Spirit, anybody, for just one person who knew what they were doing. Sima was immensely in over her head.

The wolf was gaining on her, its intestines falling out and trailing behind them like a canine dragging a leash. Fright could not describe what she was feeling, especially as she noted the wolf was watching her with one horribly milky white eye. The dark iris floated beneath the surface, and the rest of its face was a living mask of fungi.

A thread, seemingly out of nowhere, appeared, her consciousness sliding over it like a tongue over teeth. She tugged, and a flurry of outcomes hurtled in front of her eyes, making it harder to see where she was going. Then she found it. A clear path, the multitude of outcomes solidifying into one reality.

Cosima took another hard corner, overshooting the corridor that would lead to the second safe-house, and instead made a break for a sign jutting from over the door of a tavern, just as she had seen in her vision. The placard was gone, but the iron pole remained. Her feet sped across the terrain, her hands opening in preparation. She spotted a piece of rubble and gained extra height by pushing off it. Her hands narrowly wrapped around the smooth metal.

The momentum sent her swinging forward as her abs screamed. She tucked her legs in tight, and the wolf ran directly beneath her and forward down the street. He stopped, as if he knew he had lost her.

The blindness obstructed enough of his view, he could only see shifts in light. His one-pointed ear stuck out above the fungi, scanning for sounds of her running. A growl shook the ground as Sima wrapped her body around the pole, relieving her abs of their strain.

She needed him to come back her way, right beneath her again.

She whistled once, nearly regretting her decision with the way the wolf turned, stalking toward her. As he neared, Sima unsheathed her dagger, ignoring the flutters of self-doubt that swam against her insides. She could practically hear Aurelio mocking her for the way she held the dagger.

No.

She couldn't do that to herself.

Cosima deserved more than to have come this far, just to get eaten by a half-alive wolf.

It stood directly beneath her now, his hot breath coming out in snorts from the infection's obstructive attachment to his muzzle. The eye scanned, and for a moment, Sima felt small, powerless. Until her fingers tightened on the blade. Then she felt strong, unstoppable.

She angled herself before dropping the weight of her body on top of the knife, driving it straight into the eye of the wolf. Her blade met the bone inside his skull cavity, and Cosima knew he was dead.

Cosima's hands shook as it set in. She had killed *two* beasts on her own in one night.

Her eyes drifted to the darkening sky above her and the corpse.

Thousands of winged beasts lit the sky.

Sima tugged on the wedged dagger vehemently, tears streaking her face by the time it came free. Her feet loyally dredged toward the second safe-house.

Her knuckles communicated the code against the door. It opened, and sanctuary laid within. She joined the others huddling around, telling stories, and drinking spiced wine. She smiled to herself, snuggling within the warm cloak an Echo woman lent her.

Cosima was not a victim.

Today, she was a killer.

Chapter 17

A banging on the door interrupted the flow of conversations. Inside the modest maroon and olive room, people gathered. The group she joined here cooked in the kitchen, delicious smells wafting her way. Clatters of knives and dishes followed the incessant banging. Everyone glanced around, unsure of what to do next.

The wards on the outside of the safe house kept out monsters, but only because they masked them entirely, down to their scents and heartbeats. A knock meant someone was here, but not that it was safe.

An elder Viipir man stood, nodding to another who sat, arm cradled around his sleeping son. Two others joined, weapons at the ready. The door opened to reveal the opposite of a threat.

Vincenzo and Yadira.

"Oh, by the Spirit," Yadira said. She threw her arms around Sima for a painfully tight hug. "We went to the first safe house, and they told us about how you had decapitated a beast and before you could make it back in, you ran from another one. We thought the worst when we couldn't find you."

She released her, resuming her stoic nature within moments, a gentle cough escaping her throat.

A shadow loomed over Vincenzo's face. Sima feared he was angry with her.

"What were you thinking?" Yadira asked, shaking her head. "Though, you have inspired many tonight. The girls in the safe house called you a hero." She laughed then, disbelief on her breath. "I think Aurelio hid more about you than we thought. You are braver than you look."

Sima blushed and glanced at Vincenzo. That shadow grew harsher over his face, and steam threatened to tumble from his ears.

"Can I talk to you alone?" Vincenzo asked, pushing past Sima and into the safe-house. Before Yadira shut the door, Sima got a glimpse of the fighting outside. Stacks of corpses lay in the streets where they had not before. She clamped down on her desire to vomit again, following Vincenzo to the empty kitchen.

"Are you hurt?" he asked, voice low.

"No, I got really lucky," she said. She was expecting him to be angry with her. She knew she had done something risky that could have ended poorly. "I know I should have run inside with the others, instead of through the streets." She swallowed.

"There are Rani here, more than we thought. I watched them doing their patrols. Aeria may have sent us aid for the battle, but there are two Guardians who have not engaged in combat yet are approaching every home."

"The underground," Sima said with a gasp.

"They sealed it—so well, in fact, that I can't even find the entrances now. The hallways move, the doorways lead you through to dead ends. It's good magic, and it should hold."

"What is it that has you so worried, then?" Sima asked, wishing to get her reprimanding over with.

"I thought the beasts hurt you. Guilt is drowning me. I didn't come back for you. I didn't even make sure you had gotten in all right."

"A lot of lives rested in your hands," Cosima said.

"I was caught up helping others, yes, but it got quiet. It got so quiet, I thought it meant you had made it, that the beasts were prowling, but that *you* were safe."

He turned away from her, a hand braced across his forehead.

"When I saw the extra men, the Rani searching, I knew they were searching for *you*. Eventually, they'd stumble upon the safe-houses, and we couldn't get them enchanted the same way as the underground and still be able to go in and out. I-I thought," he paused, taking a steadying breath. "When the people at the first safe-house said you had killed a beast, I thought I was going to be sick."

"I was actually quite sick," she said shyly. "Part of why I didn't make it to the safe-house. I just needed a breath, a moment to pull myself back together. Eventually, I'll harden up to this kind of thing."

He looked at her deeply then, sadness pooling in his emerald eyes.

"No," he said, "you shouldn't. Perhaps the vomiting should cease, yes. But the way it tears you up inside, you can *never* lose that. The feeling keeps you who you are. It reminds you of why you do this. It is beasts now, but should it ever be another person, you will want to know you don't take life easily."

She nodded, understanding coating her in a wave of calm. That part of her she kept alive, the small fire she stoked night and day to keep burning, was her compassion, her love, her hope. When her cup ran dry and sobbing prayers went unanswered, it was only her dreams of something better that had gotten her here.

"They might come here," he said, hands balling into fists. His massive wings fluttered with the statement, as if he were struggling. "Where is your cloak?"

Sima blinked.

"I don't have it," she said.

"Where is it?" he asked slowly.

"Beneath a body, by the first safe house. The one without the head."

"Damn it," he whispered.

A knock at the door caused him to shoot from the kitchen so fast the wind blew her hair back. Within a second he was back, the unnatural speed casting Sima's eyes wide.

"Fuck, we are out of time. There are two guards here. It seems like they have split into smaller groups. We can try to hide you. Maybe you can crawl into the attic, or beneath a bed…"

He trailed off as he paced frantically in front of her.

"I won't let them take me back," Sima said.

He looked up from his spiral at her, eyes clear.

"They will *never* take you anywhere you don't want to go. I will die for your freedom, I swear to you that."

Panicked problem-solving resumed as he scanned the safehouse, the knocks on the door becoming more persistent.

Sima looked down at the cloak she was wearing from the Echo woman.

"I have an idea," she said, taking a step back as he fluttered in front of her. "Go open the door."

Vincenzo was wary at first, but when Sima asked him to trust her, he agreed with her plan. Sima assured him it would work, and to his credit, he trusted her.

It will work, she told herself.

It had to.

As the door creaked open, Sima sat along the wall with the others, light conversations still taking place for the façade of normalcy. She pulled her hood up, the fabric enveloping her features in the darkness.

"How can I help you two?" Vincenzo asked, voice merry.

"We are here to look for her."

"For who?"

At that, one of the Rani growled. She couldn't see their faces, but she didn't recognize their voices. She wondered where in Aeria Aurelio had stationed them.

"Move aside so I can get the traitorous bitch and get back home," the Rani grumbled.

She couldn't see Vincenzo, yet she knew he had tensed at the way the Guardian spoke of her.

"No traitors here," Vincenzo said simply.

"I will look for myself. You know how rats are, making nests where they aren't welcome. She could very well be trying to hole up in the garbage that is the Ombra District."

Sima stewed but willed her muscles to remain relaxed to avoid any sudden movements.

"That won't be necessary," Vincenzo said. "I am the lead here, chosen by our King himself."

"Cute," the other Rani responded. "The King told *us* we outrank you. Move."

Vincenzo conceded, Sima watching his shadow bow dramatically where it was cast before her, motioning for them to come in. She stifled a laugh at his theatrics.

"Listen up," the first one said, his boots now standing atop Vincenzo's shadow, "We are in search of your Queen, Cosima Aphelion of Innamorati, Aeria. The King has declared her a deserter of the crown, making her a traitor to Aeria. As you very well know, you all have Aeria to thank for your lives, so we must compel you to comply."

A bead of sweat found its way down her forehead. Her nerves told her she was going to be given up immediately, that she could never carry out her plan before they captured her.

Yet no one said a thing.

"If that's the case, will everyone line up? We will check you all one-by-one. You are required to state your name, your magic type, and district of origin."

"Hey, man," one Viipir said coyly, "what do you suggest we do if our district of origin doesn't exist anymore? You know, because the Faeries occupy it now."

Sima's breath caught.

The boots moved, stopping just before the talking Viipir. It was the one who opened the door for Vincenzo and Yadira.

Yadira.

Sima silently cursed but prayed that wherever her friend had run off to, she would draw these men out if what happened next didn't work.

"I would suggest," he said tightly, "that you stop pretending you ever belonged in Eternita. Ombra is where you belong. Try that."

Her blood boiled, but calm breaths found their way in and out of her chest, settling the rage-filled magma in her. The people around her stood up.

"This won't take long," the other Rani said, now standing directly before her. Her face was hidden well behind the hood, but she dared a peek at him. Cosima didn't recognize him, but he had white hair, instead of red-black, and his wings were rose-gold. He was magnificent.

Pity, she thought coldly.

"You," he said, "remove the hood."

Cosima didn't move a muscle.

"I said, remove the hood."

Not an inch.

"Guy, listen, this isn't the fight you wanna pick."

Not a breath.

"That's it," he grumbled, reaching for her hood.

As his fingers grazed the fabric, Sima's hand jutted out from beneath the billowing sleeves, fingers coiled tightly around his wrists.

Thankfully, it came even easier than she'd hoped.

Luck was on her side. Instead of a useless memory, she viewed one of his training days. Ignoring her first glimpse at the Rani training institute, she focused on the conversation happening in his memory. He was speaking with a mentor of sorts, instructing the much younger Rani on overcoming his predictability.

"You go for the face first, every time. Try to switch it up."

It faded, but not before she witnessed a few jabs from the Rani on a dummy.

Thank the Spirit.

Cosima used all her force, and the surprise, to throw him to the ground. Like Vincenzo, he was unnaturally fast and was on his feet at once.

Yet she was half-Ambrosi. She could be fast, she could be strong.

Cosima smiled, truly smiled, and ducked.

His first punch flew right over her head.

"So predictable," she taunted. "Never really learned, did you?"

His face crumpled at that. He threw another punch, and another. She dodged them all like she was in a dance. His dedication to his comfort style was impressive, if not downright idiotic. She drew her fist back, feeling the power as her body twisted to land the impact on his jaw.

"What the fuck?" he said, baring his teeth and lunging for her again.

Vincenzo took no time to leap after she made her first move. The other Rani was fast, but Vincenzo was faster, stronger. He had trained with the Viipir, with the people who bred children to fight demons.

She let his energy fuel her own, continuing her antagonizing movements to invisible music. The small glimpse gave her everything she needed to know how to bring him down, and a selfish part of her was enjoying it too much.

It was almost sad how quickly he shrunk in size, deflating as she prayed upon his weaknesses. A thrill caught her, moments from bursting through her body. Laughter trickled from her lips as she continually bounced and dodged out of his way. Minor pauses in time were all she managed in terms of her power, but the small jumps aided her in staying one step ahead of him. Not one of his punches landed. Perhaps he was used to fighting various beasts, instead of nimble, past-reading girls.

She'd never taken a breath so clear, and as the air filled her lungs, her leg found a gruesome angle as she twirled. Her foot pummeled into his face and time slowed, but not because she needed to. Because she wanted to watch. She savored the way his jaw contorted at the impact, the singular ivory tooth floating free from his face followed by ribbons of blood. The way the blood in her veins screamed *never again*. She would not go back.

It was as if a piece of her had broken wide open after her first kill. The inner knowing overcame her, shielding her from fear of being hurt, shielding her from fear of not being able to access her magic. She knew now what she did not before: she did not have to be who she used to be, ever again.

Her leg ached with a tantalizing amount of pain, and she limped as she made her way over the unconscious Rani. Vincenzo appeared, touting the other Guardian across his shoulder.

"This one's out, too. I am almost insulted. The King sent us two weak men instead of his best. I'm sure he'll regret it when word gets back about how easily we got away."

After discarding their unconscious bodies down an empty alleyway, Vincenzo pressed a finger to his temple.

"Damn it," he said, pulling her down an alleyway. "Yadira is too far. I don't know where she went or why she left us. What is she thinking? The Electric Parade is going to begin within minutes, whether people are in safe-houses, guarding the gates to the city, or bent over spell books."

It wasn't until blinding flashes of magic and energy shot past her that Cosima realized what Electric Parade meant. The enchantresses upheld a tradition of creating temporary art with magic, and the light from the parade would lead lost souls toward the veil. It also deterred beasts, as the electricity from the magic was enough to make those within the city's walls have their hair stand up.

They timed their movements between the bursts of light, counting, before leaping hand-in-hand inside of one. Their feet pounded along the street as they ran, and wonder overtook her. Window blinds opened, revealing small eyes watching the parade.

The bursts of electricity caused the ground beneath their feet to shake as it morphed into differing shapes. It was serendipitous the way Sima ended up where she was, witnessing the electricity become butterflies fanning their wings. The current morphed into the crest of Ombra, and beside it, a panther ten stories tall sprayed bolts of lightning as it bared its glowing teeth.

Vincenzo grabbed her then, pulling her into his arms, running harder to keep pace. She peered over his shoulder to see an ominous onslaught of beasts flying above them, keeping track of them, but unable to get closer because of the beams of light.

"Where are we going?" she shouted above the deafening buzz.

"Where I should have taken you in the first place!" he shouted back.

The magic shifted the figures into ribbons, the swirls encapsulating them in a cage teeming with the capability of electrocuting them. Instead, Vincenzo, knowing something she didn't, gave a large push of his wings, making them airborne. The cage remained over them; the ribbons twirled as if composed of thread and not pure, harnessed energy.

He hovered only a foot or two above the ground, but they moved much faster with his wings. The beasts stayed back, watching, but never attempting to close the growing gap between them. The further they got from the parade, the more the glow faded, the energy returning to the pack.

Rani Guardians came out of various streets and flew beside them. Vincenzo didn't so much as flinch when they approached. The tele-bond allowed him to have silent conversations with others nearby and call for aid.

As they approached a park at the center of the city, Sima stretched to see where they would land. All of the Guardians held a hand out before them, bright streams of pure starlight pouring from their palms. The ground moved, soil pouring into the hole, as a massive Viipir statue descended beneath the surface. Vincenzo bowed his head, speeding up and throttling them straight into another underground passageway.

Chapter 18

Dirt dusted their heads like swords knighted men—with reverence.

The hatch sealed as the Viipir statue ascended, an angel bound to heaven, finding its way above. Quiet embodied them, concealing chaos mere feet above their heads. Souls desperate to find their way home and monsters hunting residents down in the streets no longer within sight.

Vincenzo stood before her, a Rani Guardian, her angel in this reality. She could understand why people in other realms thought Guardians were beautiful, the duet between day and night in the fibers of his hair especially captivating. They watched each other in silence as the absence of light slowly consumed them. Shock waves from the terror on the surface jilted them into stepping towards each other in unspoken dance, both a part to play.

Emerald eyes found her, slipping across the length of her body. She stood frozen, feeling herself thaw under his gaze. His feathers caught ripples of light from the orbs that flickered on, delicate black framing along a cloud-white canvas.

He was grace itself, the desire to worship at his feet overwhelming. More overpowering than that was the desire to see him kneel. His devotion was unfamiliar, and yet, parts of her heart long thought dead sang beneath his aura.

I will die for your freedom, echoed in her brain, colliding only with the impulsive wish to touch him.

She was delicate before, bruising under a too-rough touch. She was vulnerable before, chaos beating in a too-soft heart.

That was before she uncovered the truth. Beneath flesh lay iron, a heart unbreakable. Her resolve would become formidable, secure enough to withstand the uncertainties surrounding her.

Perhaps the answer lay not in becoming immune, but resilient instead. Others taught her to fear, to hate, to tuck away her powers, her anger, her light. She learned to show nothing, simply because it was safer. Yet with him, walls crumbled without her command, the edges of her soul reaching out for his.

She didn't want to be left numb, not with the way he looked at her, and the way she felt staring back.

He merely watched her, unaware of the way she was spiraling internally. He gave her a face that drove her mad, an unreadable mask. Doubt flickered. Duty, his loyalty to the cause, could explain his kindness away. She was his ticket to providing a pieced-together army, a beacon home.

Why did she feel her guidance led to him, and not her home?

She broke the stare then, finally absorbing their surroundings. A stone and mortar passageway, as usual, but this one led toward a strange room built of metal. Sima glanced once at Vincenzo, who had still not taken his eyes off her. He nodded toward the room.

"If you thought Ostrum was a nut, wait until you meet Doc Santoro. He looks and acts like a guy who fell through worlds and got stuck."

"Is that what happened?"

"You're a quick whip, you," he said, his usual playful smile returning.

It calmed something in her to see it. To see evidence of how he felt, instead of guessing.

"Where is he from? Another planet similar to Haelos?"

"Indeed. He and Ostrum share a mutual love for the enigmatic delicacies of the universe."

"Right," Sima said, biting at the skin around her nails. "Why did those creatures look…familiar? Underneath the heaping piles of foliage."

"Doc can explain."

"How is Aeria handling this? Are the Ambrosi not mortified?"

He shook his head, running a hand through his hair. "You know how convincing Aurelio can be."

She rolled her eyes, already growing tired of mention of her miserable husband.

Or is it ex-husband? she wondered.

Vincenzo aimed his palm, and beams of starry night speared through the wall. Another passageway opened, and he held out his arm for her in a silent request. As her hands wrapped around his muscular arm, Sima gazed up at him. His full lips tugged into a smile, and without thinking, she reached up and touched the scar that ran along his cheek and chin. Vincenzo shivered gently.

"What happened here? I thought Guardians could not scar?"

"I'm not like other Guardians," he replied quietly, leaning his head further into her hand. His eyes fluttered shut for a moment, a deep sigh filling the air between them. The scar was a streak of pale lightning across his tan skin.

Sima waited for guilt or fear to awaken and make her pull her hand back and claim it was all wrong. Yet, nothing came. Within her, she found only hushed calm, every loud thought mute, and relief coated her bones.

He was beautiful, artwork in a gallery she could never bring home. A visitor, a viewer, a wisher—that's all she knew how to be. Sima shook her head, reluctantly pulling her hand away from his warm skin.

His eyes opened. "I received it before coming to this planet. The Eternal Kingdom bred Guardians to be unstoppable, or so we say." His finger trailed the old injury. "My brother did this to me, but truthfully, I don't want to talk about my past."

"Oh," Sima said. "I'm sorry."

"No," he shook his head, "I mean, we have all the time in the world to talk about me. I want to get you fed and get you somewhere comfortable to rest."

Sima followed him down the passageway, the bulky gray stone blocks fading as red rock slabs and pillars unfolded. They were in another piece of the underground city, and empty hallways greeted them.

"They sealed this section, like all the others. Only Doc, Calix, me—and now you—have been here before. You'll need a good night's rest before you're prepared to meet him and see why that's the case."

He led her to the room where she would stay, and it was promisingly cozier than at first glance. A brown rug, stitched with illustrations of the desolate Ombra desert, lay beneath a thin, mahogany frame. Two sage green pillows and a sandstone blanket completed her bed, and a pile of books topped the desk beside it.

"This is it," he said, leaning against the door frame. "I'll see what I can throw together in the kitchen. If you'd like, there is a bathing chamber through the door on the left. On the right is the wardrobe, and there should be some clothes in there."

"If no one ever comes here, why is it stocked so well?"

He chuckled. "I get bored, and I thought I might need something more secure than a safe-house for you. You are royalty. It is the least I can do. In fact, I would have done more if I didn't think it would scare you away."

She lifted a brow. "You get bored? And what do you mean, scare me away?"

He shrugged, clicking his tongue against his teeth. "You don't need me to tell you what you're afraid of, but I am trying to make it very clear I am not him and will never be. Your safety, your comfort, they are the most important things to me."

Sima froze.

Vincenzo smiled. "I thought so. Don't worry, I am an exceedingly patient man, and I have all the time in the world for you. I'll be back in an hour with something to eat."

Sima stood for several full minutes after Vincenzo left, her mind entirely empty. When her brain regained control over her body, she found her way into the wardrobe, only to go blank again.

All the clothes were her size. Since arriving in Ombra, Sima had ditched dresses and skirts almost entirely, instead donning wrapped tunic tops and pants adorned with weapon sheaths. She pulled a set with mocha brown fabric and lilac flowers out of the wardrobe, as well as undergarments and a cloak.

Sima ran a washcloth full of a basil and blessed thistle-scented soap across her body, replaying the moment she had touched Vincenzo's face in her mind. Electricity with a magnitude comparable to the Parade simmered when their skin connected. Sima had endured their magnetic pull toward each other, acting like she was immune.

Yet, their adrenaline-fueled race to the escape hatch had withered her inhibitions, and she reached for him, the same way she did in her sleep at night. He had undergone an immense amount of effort to make her feel safe, to make her laugh.

Her hands found her face beneath the touch of the warm water flooding her senses.

The same thought stopped her each time her heart yearned: *Aurelio.*

The familiar lick of panic lapped at the back of her heels. She shivered, resting her head against the cool painted tiles of the bathing chambers. Freedom was once unobtainable, and yet, here she stood, in the land she'd known only from the edges of the sky.

When left with no other option, she had escaped from her confounds, embracing open air. An internal free-fall took over, interrupted only by the feathered wings of Vincenzo. She sighed.

Onyx locks of her hair dribbled clear water. Sima slipped on her clothing, and the ring Vincenzo gave her found its place again on her middle finger. The ring lit up almost immediately, causing her to gasp.

Vincenzo knocked on the door, opening it a crack after she called for him to come in. "My Queen," he bowed, smiling as she groaned. "I come bearing gifts from distant lands."

A bowl with noodles, scallions, and beef sat on a tray with a vibrant pink flower. Sima plucked it from the small cup and sniffed.

"It's a cactus flower," he said. Sima sat at the desk as Vincenzo slid the tray in front of her. "Do you know why they call this District Ombra?"

"The shadow cast by Aeria forces the District into darkness."

"Only pieces of it. The area near the veil has sunlight all day, making it the hottest place in all of Haelos. There are cacti there, and if you're lucky, you'll find these."

"How did you get this? I thought the Portale del Regno Stellare was on the other side of Ombra."

"It is. There are fruits harvested from the cacti as well. The kitchen had them, along with the flower." He scooped up a portion of the noodles, leaning toward Sima with a protective hand ready to catch anything that dropped. "Try this."

Sima arched a brow but took a bite of the food he offered. Her eyes closed as she chewed the perfectly cooked, savory meal.

"I knew you'd like it," he said, brushing a lock of her hair out of the way. "No way you were going to bed hungry."

"Thank you," she said, grasping another bite. "Though I am not tired."

He laughed. "I guess you will meet the Doc after all."

Gray brick covered with thin sheets of metal halfway up the walls surrounding them. Creatures with slender arms and massive claws floated upside down in yellow liquid, jars neatly placed throughout the room. A body lay on an operating table, strapped but obviously deceased. Obviously, because it was missing a head. Sima paled.

"Why is it here?" she asked, cringing.

"We collect the most preserved corpses for research," the Doc said. A metal and glass contraption sat anchored to the frame of his square glasses. He peered above them at her, briefly, before resuming his procedure. "Do you recognize this one?"

"I'm the one who put him in that state, I suppose," she said, shrugging tightly. She would never forget the feeling of the vines climbing over her skin, tugging like pythons choking the air out of prey. Despite her attempts to remain composed, she snapped her eyes shut tightly after peeking at it.

"Doc, was there a cloak of any kind brought in with this one? A magic-laced one?" Vincenzo asked.

"No, I don't have use for those things. I doubt any of the Rani on body retrieval would have snagged it. Check the street cleaners once the bubble is back up." One eyebrow arched, his slick black hair pooling around his neck. Sima avoided the incredulous look the Doc gave her by pretending to take in her surroundings.

"Why is she here?" the Doc asked, slicing pieces of the fungus in paper-thin sheets. He had a selection of glass slides prepped with tissue samples, each with a label of its location on the body. His lab was impeccable, not a swab out of place. His tone aired more on the side of curiosity. He likely did not get many visitors beyond Rani.

Vincenzo strolled by him, peering over his shoulder where drapes lay on a section of the chest cavity. Only then did Sima notice the disembodied plant-like head floating in a jar on the desk behind the Doc.

Yuck.

"She's the one who freed the Hexia, Doc," he said, squinting to get a better look. "Isn't that right, Cosima?"

They both eyed her then.

"Yes," she said, turning to the Doc. "I removed the labradorite crystals."

His gaze flicked to her, eyes riddled with invisible calculation.

"Ah." His knife slid into the corpse, retrieving another slice. "So, you are aware of their influence," he said. "What have you heard of the beasts?"

A shuddered breath escaped her. "I know they're terrifying. Why are some of them covered in fungus?"

"They are—were—people just like us. They have an infection," he said, motioning to the half-dissected mass of fungi. "I am studying why this happens. Mushrooms have not caused infections in the living, but they reanimate the dead."

Sima swallowed. "What about the vines? If they were people, how have some of them become—plant monsters?"

"It would seem the fungi, once it reaches the brain stem,

deteriorates enough for the bodies of Echo people to shift. Most manifestations are plant-like. The magic breeds a host of strange mutations, yet we have seen animals, too."

"We have not seen a single case in Ambrosi or Guardians," Vincenzo said, flipping through files to show her the data they had collected. The dates spanned back as late as a year and a half ago. "Though every type, including Faeries, is at risk. Perhaps the bodies of immortals do not make suitable hosts."

"Yes, that is the going theory," the Doc interjected. "The others remain in their original bodies. The mutations are more common in the Echos."

"What about the creatures coming through the veil?"

"They become infected, too, if they die. This is another reason the Guardians here collect corpses. We sever the brain stem in whatever demented beast that crawls through." The Doc laid tissue on more glass slides, green ooze lining his black slacks.

"Like I mentioned," Doc Santoro said, "most species of mushroom are not capable of this sort of disfigurement. I am collecting various tissue samples of both the fungi and the infected to pinpoint where the initial infection originates. I believe we are seeing later stages of the disease. This would all be much easier if the King hadn't gone on a sadistic rampage destroying valuable textbooks and documentation."

"I have a question." Sima chewed her lip. "The King mentioned the crystals to me, that they have power. Can you tell me more about them?"

He nodded, continuing his work as he spoke. "Each type of stone has a unique property. Some are harmless, such as amethyst, which can bring calm to the body of the user. Sinister crystals lie alongside innocuous ones, and those can kill even the Ambrosi."

Ambrosi were not impossible to kill, though it was as difficult to harm them as it was the Guardians. "If that falls into the wrong hands," Sima shook her head, "they could wipe out the Ambrosi of this planet."

"It is bigger than that, Cosima," Vincenzo said gravely. "Ambrosi and Guardians exist on every planet in every realm. Each realm contains a solar system, a planet capable of sustaining life, and us. If these crystals make it off of Haelos, there is no telling what could happen to the others."

"Aurelio has them. He recrafted all of Aeria from crystals." Her heart thundered in her chest. "The entire Archipelago—why?"

"I think he has crafted himself a fortress," Vincenzo's wings extended outward behind him. "He is keeping others out. Calculated resistance by the Devout Rising could not meaningfully breech Aeria enough to stop him."

The Doc laid his tools down, releasing a huff of breath. "He is paranoid. He has locked down the Archipelago, and he hoards all the Guardians for himself, except for those he sends to Ombra."

"We report them dead to the kingdom," Vincenzo said. "I am extremely protective over who knows what because there is so much at stake here. The ones who stay here know they cannot go back, or the King will kill them. It is how I recruit others to join in caring for this District."

"There's more," Doc Santoro said. "The humans in the Prisma District. They are in grave danger, as we believe Eternita has sealed their District completely, trapping everyone inside."

"The humans relinquished their weapons to the kingdom, to my father." Sima's mind raced.

"Precisely," Vincenzo walked over to her, placing a hand on her shoulder. "We think you can help, even if we can't reach them, by threading certain things into their Fates."

"I have to be careful with my powers. Whatever I change has consequences, much of which I cannot understand or predict."

"Calix and Vincenzo will help you," Doc said. "The Ambrosi and Rani in Aeria have not helped the people and will probably not sing your praises should your interference interrupt their luxury. If you help us, there is no telling what others will think."

"I do not lose sleep over what people who could not survive a day in my shoes think," Cosima said. "Truthfully, I have thought the very worst things about myself, yet I can look in the mirror and bare my teeth at the monster I find. Can they?"

Chapter 19

In sickly dreams, twisted fears came to light, smothering Sima as she fought for air. She sat up, hands sliding across her chest to search for the phantom wound. Sleep transported her backward in time, every forgone memory of her torment dancing behind her eyelids.

Her heart made a racket inside her chest, nearly as loud as the shaky breaths clambering passed her lips. She braced a hand on her forehead, aware of her surroundings once more.

After meeting the Doc, Vincenzo walked her to her rooms and left her for the evening. His absence became increasingly visceral the longer they spent together. For weeks, he had been the first and last person she saw every day. Sima reached for him yet again in her sleep, craving the safety that seemed to only exist in his presence.

Her heart was once empty, undetectable beneath the shell she had become to survive the King. Her hands covered her ears, but still, the memories came, crowding her mind with insults Aurelio hurled her way.

Worthless, sick-headed brat. The King's voice echoed in her brain. *Weak, so weak.*

"No," Sima pleaded, "no more. You're not here."

Are you going to cry about it? Let me see. I want to watch how you fall apart.

He was not with her physically, but a piece of him remained

embedded in her traumatized being. Steaming water coated every inch of the bathing chamber in a foggy layer of condensation. Clothes dropped beside her feet as she sought relief. Her body baked beneath the heat, her skeleton trembling under goosebump-littered skin. Focused inspirations flowed inward and out as she regained her control.

"No." She examined her skin, reddened from the temperature. "I know who I am. I know what I did to survive, what I did to make sure a piece of me held on. I am not the person you have made me believe I was."

Are you sure?

Emptiness tickled her gut.

"Yes." She shook her head. "No. I don't know."

"Cosima," Vincenzo called from outside the bathing chamber, "Cosima, are you alright?"

Sima hissed, leaping from the tub to dry herself off. "Yes, one moment," she yelled, throwing on a fresh outfit.

"Hi," she said a few moments later, emerging from the bathroom in raven black pants with a dozen pockets and a sleek moss-colored top. "I forgot we were meeting," she said.

He squinted at her. "Why is your skin red?"

"Well, the um," she jerked a thumb over her shoulder, "the water was hot. I honestly didn't notice until after I got out, so don't worry, I'm fine."

"Truthfully, I was wary when I knocked, and you didn't answer. I thought your ring would show you I was coming. I am sorry for barging in." He rubbed a hand behind his head.

Sima glanced down at the glowing band around her finger. "It's all right."

"If it's not all right, you know you can tell me, right?"

Sima met his gaze. "What do you mean?"

His eyes were a warmer shade of green than she'd yet seen. It made her heart skip. "I gave you the ring so you would always know when I am near. I want you to know in case you have need of me, but—" He broke eye contact. "I don't want you to be afraid of me and I thought if you had noticed, you could feel more comfortable. Then I barged in, and—"

"Vincenzo," she breathed.

His eyes snapped to her instantly. "Yes?" he mumbled.

"Thank you."

His tan skin warmed red along his cheekbones. "Anything I can do for you, I will. Are you up for training today? Even if we're stuck in this section of the underground until my brothers and the warriors above kill the beasts?"

Though her heart pounded, and Aurelio's voice licked the skin of her neck with vicious doubts, she nodded.

"Do you really believe I can help you and Doc with my power?"

"Only if you're comfortable with it."

"Interfering with the Fate of others was demanded of me, and with those drugs…I want to help, but I cannot yet change Fate without the use of those *Mortoid* capsules. Even more distressing, my twists have occasionally revealed extremely poor outcomes. I'm not confident I can thread without worsening the situation." She sighed, aimlessly braiding her dark hair. "I feel guilty for being free, and yet I feel like I can never be far enough away from him." Sima was unsure why she told him that and swallowed hard.

"You deserve the chance to live a life without him in it."

Sima titled her head to the side as she considered his statement. "I worry the stain of him is so deeply intertwined with me, I will pull his threads out of me until I die, and still more will remain."

Vincenzo shook his head, stepping toward her, finally closing the distance between them. "He is nothing more than a parasite. Your abilities granted him power he would never know otherwise. Whatever he convinced you of, whatever lies he's told you, they're not true, Cosima."

"I cannot tell where his lies end and my truth begins." She wrapped her arms around herself, unable to meet his eyes any longer. "He made me question my every thought, my every move, until I was so paralyzed, I couldn't decide for myself. It only got worse with time, and soon each individual piece of me became a target for his toxic ways. He is a wound in me that festers and never heals."

He stood only inches from her, gazing down at her with captivating gemstone eyes. "What do you dream of, Cosima?"

"What do I dream of?"

"When you endured him, what made you not give up?"

"I gave up for a long time." She swallowed hard.

"Someone who gave up wouldn't still care for others the way you do, Cosima. You have lives depending on you, and when it mattered, you rose to the occasion to free those enslaved by him. You should be proud of yourself."

"Why do I still feel I have done something wrong? Why does every piece of me always feel put back in the wrong place? I question what actions I took and equally lament the ones I did not. Still, I am no closer to the answer, to knowing what is right."

"It will take time. It will take as long as it takes, but on the other side waits a version of you so thankful you took the chance. What do you dream of?"

A love that doesn't hurt. "I dream of exploring the desert of Ombra, the forests of Eternita, and the mountains of Prisma. I dream of cleaning up Haelos and protecting these people the way they should always have been."

He smiled. "That, too, is what I dream of. I share your vision, and what is important to you is for me, as well. I would like to show you something. There is much hidden in this sector of the underground Depths because of how few come here."

He led her into a secluded roped-off room, drapes covering the hung artwork. He gave her a look that she could describe as apologetic as he tugged the fabric off an enormous piece.

She ground her teeth, staring up at an impossibly large portrait of herself, the artist even nailing the dead look in her eyes. Ornate gold-painted framing made with miraculous talent, all to exemplify her trauma.

Wonderful. Her knees were weak.

"What in Spirit's grace is this?"

"A commemoration, for you, essentially."

"*Why?*"

"We believed in you—well, they believed in you first. I was one of the last Guardians sent to Haelos, and by then, the capture had already happened. Only one other Guardian came along with me, and we knew the two of us would not be enough to take Aurelio on directly. We bid our time, deciding to aid the Ombra District to the best of our abilities, and that is when I learned of you."

He tilted his back to get a better look at the painting. "I have looked at this painting hundreds of times since I arrived. You inspired me, the way you inspired others. The rightful Queen of Aeria, hanging on like a promise to be delivered by the universe. I wondered what you were thinking, wondered if you were in pain. I thought of all my siblings in Aeria, of how they turned a blind eye. The Ambrosi, so distracted by riches, they allowed him to conceal your light."

Her hands trembled, though she didn't break when their eyes met, the air in her throat tight.

"I am no such fool," he said. "I would not waste a single opportunity to rescue you from the darkness. With every breath since I arrived, I have thought of you. No failure stopped me. I simply came here, looked in your eyes, and tried again."

"Failed attempts?" Her eyes searched his, finding sadness swimming in them.

"The day you escaped, Cosima. The others aimed to free Aeria. I aimed to free you."

"Me?" she asked softly. Her head turned toward the massive portrait again. "Why?"

"It pains me to think of how long you suffered, and yet I am unaware of the full extent of what you endured. Others overlooked it in the Archipelago, but not me. You are the Queen. You are how he could access the power of the sky islands. Rescuing you was the wise answer for a multitude of reasons."

She nodded. "I understand. You rescued me for the sake of the kingdom, but he still has access to the Light Reserve, even if I am away."

"Cosima," he said tensely, "I would have come for you one day, even if you did not run. I promised it on the very wind that carried me to Ombra. He will not take you back. My desire is for you to take it back yourself. You carried me through darkness without any indication I existed. Knowing you has only sowed a deeper seed of devotion."

He gazed down at her. Sima tilted her head back to meet his eyes, holding her breath as they locked onto each other. "As long as it takes, I will wait for you. I will be here, in whatever capacity you'll have me. I will take back Aeria, and return you to the throne, if that is what you wish. Your powers are unpredictable, but perhaps this means we learn to make informed decisions to mitigate the risks. There are ways, and you are strong enough."

A strange flutter in her chest made her blink harshly. It was a sensation Cosima was unfamiliar with.

"We can't." A piece of her recoiled as the words left her mouth. "I can't—I mean, with you. I don't know if I'll ever be able to…*be* with someone again."

Hurt flickered across his face, but still he smiled. "I apologize if I am too much. I respect your decisions. As I said, in any capacity. I can still aid you in harnessing your powers, if you would like."

Her smile was cold and wrong on her face. "I would, thank you." Inside, her soul screamed, begging her to take it back, to reach for him. She drowned the sounds of it beneath panicked thoughts that she was undeserving.

Unlovable. The word taunted her from the corners of her mind.

"I have more to show you," he said, all visible signs of sadness and disappointment suddenly vanishing beneath a smile. He stepped away from her, his wings concealing his face as he turned. "The Doc has uncovered more about the crystals, as well as more information on beasts in Prisma."

"How?"

"We have an extremely delicate line of trust with Eternita. The Fae use sprites in the faerie lands for monitoring and guarding. They have vast connections, using mushrooms and tree roots for communication. As you saw, some creatures have fungal infections."

"I saw a bird once. It fell off a statue, and I thought it died.

Later, I saw the same little thing, covered in fungus. I nearly forgot all about it in the chaos of everything."

"Yes, occasionally it occurs in animals. Because the Eternita District uses mushrooms, an informant told us what he knew to aid Doc's research. However, he was also willing to get his eyes on the human district. I will tell you what we know about Prisma first."

She followed as he exited the room; the passageway shifted before them to allow them access to a concealed area. A large iron door creaked as he unlocked it with starlight. The interior was of overwhelming proportions, continuing far into the horizon. There were dozens upon dozens of metal tables bearing black body bags. Sima cringed. They were too plump to be empty.

"What is this?"

He snapped his fingers, and the room was a quarter of the size, bringing the number of bodies around them closer to a hundred versus thousands. Sima shifted on her feet, unsure of what she had witnessed.

"Apologies. It is jarring, I know."

"Guardians can manipulate…space?"

He shook his head. "I can. I told you I am no regular Guardian."

"So, this entire time, all the shifting of the Depths has been you?"

He frowned. "You seem surprised. So little faith in me."

She scoffed, then laughed. "I must be dreaming. There is no way one man is capable of all of that. You are more like a God than a Guardian."

"I hardly think so," Vincenzo said, opening a body bag. "My powers are mysterious, primarily out of necessity."

Sima understood. Aurelio used her powers to further hold her captive. She could relate to desiring to hide them away. At times, she wished she had.

An elongated snout with four piercing canines made up the face of the bare-bone skull. Flesh remained below the neck, lined with meaty orange mushroom caps, stems jutting from the creature's body. Shadowy claws protruded from the mass of fungi.

"The infection spreads quickly after the creatures emerge. Doc's research strongly suggests the origin is the brain. The fungus works its way outward, advancing to the rest of the body. After death, the mushrooms break down and devour all that remains, beginning with the head."

"However," he opened another bag, revealing a red-scaled corpse with gray horns erupting from its scalp and lengthy tusks protruding from its lower jaw. The infection had sprouted from the beast's chest cavity. "As you can see, here it begins at the heart. The brain on this being is intact and unaffected."

She followed him as he approached a different table, the body inside the bag eerily similar to the Viipir. Vincenzo used a cloth to pull back the dead man's lip, revealing a fang. Red and purple fungi burst from his neck.

"The beasts contract it once they are on Haelos. The bigger issue is the creatures popping up in Prisma looked nothing like the ones crawling from the veil. They looked like this. It is not solely the otherworldly beasts, the dead warriors from Ombra also reanimate."

"So, somehow the dead people of this District are crossing through Eternita and into Prisma? The fungus is causing their bodies to…reanimate?"

"We are trying to learn more about how the humans are faring. They have ways to defend themselves."

"How? I thought they gave up their weapons?"

"Humans are inventive, intelligent. Brief lifespans mean nothing to their stubborn curiosity. It was only a matter of time before something drove them to invention once again."

"Oh," Sima whispered, relieved. "How can I help?"

"This information came this morning, so, as of right now, we are reassessing and pivoting. This is not as dire as we once thought. However, action will need to be taken soon. For now, we will focus on accessing your power without the drugs."

She nodded. She had spent the entirety of her morning flooded with doubt, and mention of the drugs threatened to submerge her. "Your last suggestion was the wizard. I'm curious what you've come up with now."

"You'll just have to wait and see."

Chapter 20

Fifty-two dead.

The number was staggering to Cosima, but Vincenzo expected higher, and the outcome pleased those in Ombra.

"It was one of the best years yet, with the lowest deaths. Last year, we nearly reached four hundred deaths. We are getting stronger, more adept at slaughtering beasts."

Enchantresses lifted the seals on the underground, allowing them access to the main areas of the Depths. The underground city was lively, gray stone blocks concealed behind red and gold banners for the continued celebrations. The souls had escaped through the veil and people had paid respects to their ancestors, meaning it was now time to celebrate life and the harvest season prior to the coming of winter.

"How long do the people here celebrate?" She ducked beneath his arm as he held open the door for her as they entered a small shop. Immediately, strong herbal scents accosted her. Too many for Sima to differentiate between them.

"Ah, could be up to a week, maybe more. This is the biggest holiday of the year for them."

Vincenzo needed to get her cloak replaced and the only place where he could find an enchantress willing to do this kind of spell-work was the shadow market. Luckily, the traveling merchant kept a successful shop in Ombra after the closure of Eternita.

The enchantress called out from the back room, telling them to look around while she finished her task. Surrounding them were eggplant walls and pristine shelves stocked with potions, clean animal bones, and packaged herbs. On the counter, incense smoke spiraled in the air, flowing from the nostrils of a mini Vipus. The creature was red with large snake-like eyes and an adorable smirk.

"She's going to charge me out the ass," Vincenzo said, "so don't be surprised when I have to haggle with her for a while."

"Are you good at that sort of thing?"

"Oh, you bet," he said, crossing his arms. "I'll have you know—I only fall for one in five scams."

"Those are impressive odds for you. Perhaps I have been underestimating you."

He smirked. "Indeed, there is much more to me than meets the eye. I'm not all muscle, you know? Occasionally, and I do mean occasionally, I can be smart."

She scoffed, rolling her eyes, but a smile found her, anyway. He did this frequently, trying to make her laugh. It was refreshing for her to feel free around somebody. Every action didn't have to be thoroughly thought-out and executed. She could laugh if she wanted, or scowl if it better fit her mood.

"Enzo," a woman crowed, voice shrill and sing-songy, "I didn't think to expect you to return so quickly. Superior quality has you coming back for more."

"Madame," Vincenzo said sweetly, "I was so impressed by the first cloak that I could not wait to return for a second."

Hair as dark as ravens tumbled down until it reached the woman's ankles. It was lustrous and full, split into two large braids. She narrowed her eyes, pointing one long, painted fingernail at him. "You lost it."

"Technically, I lost it," Sima piped up.

The dark-haired woman inspected her before arching a brow. "She is who you are trying to keep hidden? Vincenzo, my boy. I would have worked faster if you told me who it was for." She looked Sima up and down again carefully. "Perhaps the legends are true. Stay here. I will fetch something much better than a cloak."

She hobbled to the back room, slamming the door shut behind her.

"Oh, great," Vincenzo mumbled, reaching for the coin in his jacket pocket, "I am sure whatever it is, it is probably ten times what the cloak was going to cost me. You're lucky you're like a 'beacon of hope' or a 'symbol of a future to come' or whatever."

The corner of her lip twitched, but before she could respond, the woman returned. Sima wondered how old she was, her skin smooth and unmarred. Her brown eyes were aglow when she met Sima's gaze, holding a necklace with a crystal dangling from it.

"It's a special blend: black tourmaline, obsidian, and black jade," she said, adding a wicked smile, "plus a little spell-work, enhancing what nature gave us."

Vincenzo furrowed his brow.

"Grismelda," he said her name with warning laced tightly in his tone. "What are you thinking bringing these kinds of things out at a time like this?"

She jerked the necklace back, offended.

"Might as well call me a thief and a murderer, Enzo! You think these are synthetic? I would do no such thing. Mine are all ethically sourced. Proof being my own damn hands clawing it from the mountain ridges. You want the protection or not? The crystals can help keep evil spirits away and offer some minor protection, but you won't find spells like mine anywhere else. You will have no luck hiding her with a silly cloak. With this, she'll practically be invisible to anyone who means her harm. She's got so much power wafting off her. What makes you so sure you can hide her?"

She crossed her arms and stuck up her chin. Cosima looked at Vincenzo, who was clearly stewing, but merely asked how much it would be.

"For the Queen of Aeria," she said, bowing her head only briefly before sticking her nose up at Vincenzo again, "The Queen the prophet of Prisma preaches will liberate us? For that Queen, it is free."

The merchant thrust her hand forward, the necklace veering inches from Sima's face. Cosima reached up and took it, marveling at the way the three crystals were carved to intertwine with each other like a puzzle. She tugged it back. As it left Sima's hands, the woman shot Vincenzo a devilish look.

"For you, though, Enzo," Grismelda flicked her tongue across her teeth, "fifty gold, take it or leave it."

"Oh, come on," he grumbled, reaching for the money.

They thanked the merchant and strolled through the rest of the shadow market to return to the main plaza, where Calix would hopefully be waiting.

"What did she mean by synthetic?" Sima asked, holding onto Vincenzo's arm to avoid being swept away in the crowd. The necklace now hung around her neck, the crystal tucked beneath her shirt.

"There are two types. A natural form of these crystals appears all over our planet. The two areas of highest density are Eternita, along its northern border, and all the mountains of Prisma. Remember how I explained to you that the humans found weapons again?"

"They're using the crystals? Won't they die?"

"There is magic, ancient, within the soil of this planet. This energy existed long before our Spirit Goddess Ehses commandeered it for her creations. She crafted the people, controlled what was born here. She might still. However, this magic, it does not come from her, of that I am sure." He led her around a crowd of people with sticks that sparkled. Each of them bore brightly colored clothing, the shape-shifting Echos alternate animal forms just as equally adorned.

"If the humans get their hands on the natural forms of the crystals, it won't hurt them. The problem arises from the synthetic versions. The crystals tap into the source energy of the planet. A reservoir from the birth of Haelos, meant to supply life. It naturally creates deposits containing this magic. It is not life force, but it is pure magic. The stones themselves are merely vessels for energy, whether stolen or organic to the planet."

"Where does the extra energy come from?"

"Life force," he frowned as they walked.

"People can steal life force?" Her head spun at the thought of it, crawling over the scene she witnessed beside the Drago of Solara receiving her mother's life force. Sima fought the haze coming over her.

"Yes. The imitations became rampant in Eternita, the dark market flooded with them. Humans have no magic and were desperate to feel it. Synthetic stones, however, were unpredictable and to this day, are still incredibly unstable. The bodies piled, whether from those killed by magic or by the crystal itself."

"Aurelio is the one who first told me the crystals caused humans to die, that the power was more than their reserves could handle, and they'd..." Sima swallowed the lump in her throat. "During my last ever trip with Aurelio, he sent me after the Queen of Eternita. I watched her mother forfeit her own life force to the Queen."

"I believe what you witnessed proves what many in the rebel movement have been saying about Eternita. They shunned us from their lands for a reason. We believe that reason lies within these stones. The Fae are incredibly protective of their kin, especially before they are ready to give over the Crown. An assassination attempt left Solara's mother, Queen Cressida, widowed unexpectedly. Many questioned why she did not use her powers to stop the attacker, but it sounds like she had given them over to Solara."

"You're saying she couldn't protect her husband because she gave her power to her daughter? Why would she do that? No one knew she was powerless?"

He shook his head. "I'm not sure. We have a few very new—still very tense—relationships with some key contacts in the Fae kingdom. They give us bits of information, in exchange for some of ours. The rebel movement is not whatever you overheard from Aurelio. We are not solely seeking to dethrone the King; we also seek to make the crystals stable. If we cannot keep them from the surface, we can at least eliminate their lethal effects."

Sima blinked quickly in surprise. This was his first real admission about involvement with the rebellion.

"So, you—"

"Yes," he sighed. "This is where I tell you the uncomfortable truth about Doc."

Vincenzo led her into a quieter portion of the underground square, filled with people quietly reading books or watching others as they sipped warm drinks. They traveled down a dark alleyway, void of any light. She pressed her palms to the tight walls and followed behind, vaguely aware of his wings in front of her.

"The Doc is one of the few creatures to exist here since the beginning. He is not from our realm, and he is also not from the Eternal Kingdom."

"The birthplace of the first Ambrosi and where the Rani are trained before being assigned a realm and planet to protect," Sima said, remembering the stories of the ancestors. Neither could return to the Eternal Kingdom once they had left, but the Rani were the only ones who were new to Haelos, Vincenzo being one of the most recent.

"Yes," he said, his voice further ahead than she expected. She increased her pace. "He has a unique intelligence, but it comes with costs. Doc claims he spent his time here becoming obsessed with figuring out how the universe works. He wanted to know how the Eternal Kingdom created realms and how the veil allowed movement between them. The Doc studied the stars, he studied people, he studied *everything,* even if it meant traveling all his life between realms to see what others discovered, to complete his knowledge. That obsession got him stuck here. He can't figure out why, but he's locked here, unable to leave."

He slowed, the brush of his feathers tickling her skin, as he came to a stop.

Light illuminated a door as he used his starlight to unlock the enchantments. Constellations, stars, and planets were carved along the wood. The planets looked nothing like the ones that surrounded Haelos in their realm.

The door groaned as it slid open, disappearing into a recess in the wall.

Sima blinked and blinked again.

It was real.

Music played, violins sang alongside full drum beats. Above them was a breathtaking display of more constellations, similar to what Sima spied on the lock. It was as real as the sky above, the stars twinkling in heavenly rhythm—yet they were still inside.

"Thankfully, Doc being tethered here means we have one of the brightest minds alive today at our disposal. We have our own supply of natural crystals, and there are experiments being performed to enhance them with the replenishable magic of the Rani Guardians."

"Your starlight?" Sima asked, mouth agape.

"It is an almost unending supply. In the beginning phases, Doc successfully harnessed starlight into a gigantic crystal shard. However, we could not channel it into smaller stones. When I say we used a large one, I mean comically and impractically so."

"Does he believe the mushrooms have something to do with the crystals too, or is he just multifaceted like that?"

"His research on the fungi and his research on the crystals seem to lead back to each other. They are connected, so even though we are not the ones making them, we are the ones harboring magic-enhanced stones. Thousands of them. For study and to keep them out of the hands of others. I have done my best to keep that kind of filth out of Ombra, but it hasn't been easy. People, even good people, fall victim to promises of increased power. Truthfully, the search for more natural deposits led to some of the underground expansion. With great luck, we could replace the need for synthetic crystals."

She blinked, the information cascading over her. He was collaborating with Doc Santoro to create a safe alternative to the malignant copycat potentially responsible for Eternita closing its borders. It wasn't what she was expecting, that was for sure.

She covered her face in her hands, unable to stop herself. Vincenzo stepped closer, placing a hand on her shoulder. The warmth of his hand was comforting, but the tears only came out harder.

"You have been here, solving problems bigger than any one

person, and I have done nothing for my kingdom," she wept. "They build these monuments of me, but they don't even know me. Would they love me the same if they knew what I've done? *I* barely know what I've done. When he started giving me the drugs, a part of me stopped fighting it. Sure, some made me sick, but some made me feel good, or forget. It was bearable, and I didn't care that my kingdom was being run by a stranger who tortured me in his free time. I cared about the brief moments of relief from the fucked-up way I felt."

"Do you want to know what I remember from how my brothers and I were raised?"

She peered from behind her hands briefly, nodding cautiously. Grief pooled in his eyes, but he pressed his mouth into a line and spared a breath.

"They don't let anyone touch us. For any reason. We're babies when they take us from our mothers. They leave us in our beds to cry, saying we will learn to soothe ourselves. We learn to stop calling, we know no one will come. They don't pick us up when we stumble, and it is us who teach each other how to get up. No hugs, no affection. Grit, dedication, unrelenting loyalty. I was a shell for a long time, too, and I think most of my brothers are, whether they admit it or not. The things we have seen and done…they breed us deadly for a reason. We are unbreakable."

He let go of her shoulder then, his hand dropping limply at his side. Sima sniffled. He looked so regal, even as she watched the pain ripple through his face.

"I thought we were unbreakable. The reason we hide Ombra from those in Aeria is because we fear they are not like us. We fear those who live there will not stand for justice, that they will fall to a weak man like Aurelio and any horrible narrative he spews. You are not them, Cosima. They are bred for justice, and it escapes them. The Guardians could revolt, but they choose to be scared, or become too interested in the life he allows them. You were under his control for *fifty* years—nevertheless, you freed the Hexia."

"Fear kept me trapped," she said. "It made me go along with anything he wanted. It was blinding, how scared I was. I felt insane, but it was him manipulating me. Do you know how much effort it takes to make someone despise themselves so thoroughly? He was relentless, making me doubt myself until I abandoned me, too. He tormented me, leaving me in too much pain to fight back. There never seemed to be any rhyme or reason for the way he did things, so I never knew what to expect when I woke up. I thought he would kill me before I got away."

"And, yet here you are." The feathers of his wings slid across her shoulder and back as he stood beside her.

She peered up at the night sky above them. The trembling in her hands didn't stop, and her heart palpitations told her she was afraid, but something felt different, lighter. Part of her wished she could have met Vincenzo at another time, or in some other universe. One where she didn't have so much baggage and too many things to fix inside herself. She was still a married woman, and he was a rebel that her husband wouldn't hesitate to kill.

"Ivo is the one who figured out the source was in his office. She gave me the avenue to liberation. What you told me about your work on the crystals…you showed me there is hope, a chance for us to overcome the horrors the King has enacted. I am free, and it's time to do something about it. There has to be a way to revoke his access to the Light Reserve that powers the Archipelago."

"Sima," he said. The stars reflected light onto his delicate feathers. His wings were a symbol of the brutal strength of the Rani, inside and out, yet nothing made him look more picturesque, more delicate. His wings fanned, nervous energy sparking between them. "He is not my king, and I will not rest until that statement is true for everyone in Haelos." He placed her hand softly in his, his eyes crinkling slightly as he spoke. "I will release us from his stain, and I will stop at nothing until Aeria is reclaimed. I will do it for you, this day and the next, just as I have since the day I saw that painting. Say the word, I will tear the Palace down if it haunts you and build you a new one with my hands. I'll make it safe again, for all of us, and especially for you."

"I believe you," she whispered, eyes once again full of stars from the inexplicable night sky.

Chapter 21

"Calix," Vincenzo called.

The girl's fiery hair flipped over her shoulder as she turned. "Hey, you two. Did you get the supplies?"

Vincenzo reached into his pocket and revealed a small vial.

"What is that?" Sima asked.

"It's liquid black salt. Obsidian and sodium blended and added to just enough water to dissolve the salts." The inky potion swirled, the crystal specks shimmering as they caught the sunlight. "I've been holding onto it for Ostrum's assistant."

"Honestly, I don't appreciate being called his assistant." Calix frowned. "I do enough for Ostrum and Doc to be considered their equal. I shall accept Majesty, and no less."

Sima laughed. "I agree. It is a fitting name. You can have my crown if we make it back to Aeria."

Vincenzo shook his head as he handed it to Calix. "Don't inflate her ego, Cosima. She gets enough of it from Monte as is. Speaking of which, where is Monte? I thought he wanted in on the test."

"What test?" Sima asked, suspicion thick across her brow.

"The three of us figured out precisely how to help you learn to use your power," Calix beamed. "Enzo thinks you might need people to practice on, and here we are! Monte is otherwise occupied."

"Practice on? No, absolutely not. My control over them is uncertain at best, and the risk is higher if I am relearning how to access it on my own. Who knows what could happen?"

"We are willing participants." Vincenzo rubbed his hands together. "Besides, we trust you."

"I am glad you trust me, but you truly have no business doing so. Vincenzo, I could hurt you or wreak havoc with no way of reversing it."

"Wait, you can't change it back?" Calix grinned nervously.

"It depends," Vincenzo and Sima said at the same time.

"It depends," Sima repeated, "on what the outcome is. The larger the change, the more people and events it will affect. Those are impossible to undo. The smaller the change, the easier it is to find all the threads and alter them again."

"See." Calix clapped. "There's your answer. Minor changes it is." She spun on her heel and headed off, Vincenzo following quickly behind her.

"I—no, wait," Sima stuttered. She was wholly uninterested in meddling with the threads of her friend's Fate, and the very idea stoked the fiery apprehension boiling inside her. The effects were unpredictable, and the risk was high—yet curiosity flamed as well.

Could I do it for the first time with permission?

Her thoughts immediately went out the window.

Once Sima spotted Yadira, nothing could stop her from running to her friend and throwing her arms around her neck in an embrace.

"Yadira!" Sima gasped. "Where have you been? You returned for the first time since I left Aeria, just to disappear when those Guardians showed up. Why didn't you come and find me? How long have you been here?"

Her friend hugged her back tightly. "After I left you and returned to Aeria, the King captured me. I narrowly escaped, and I returned to Ombra. When I saw more Guardians from the Aeria Archipelago searching for you, I ran."

"Where have you been hiding this whole time?"

Yadira shook her head, motioning Sima to follow her. Sima

called out to Vincenzo and Calix, who eyed Yadira warily. The Guardian smiled and assured them they would not go far. They made their way near more storefronts and sat at an empty bench.

"I thought I couldn't face you again. But then Vincenzo called through the tele-bond and stated he couldn't find you and I immediately was frantic. I couldn't imagine you being left to die after all you have already endured," her friend cried, wide streams making their way across her rich brown skin. The gold and sapphire armor around her shoulders made her look elegant, even as she poured out her pain. Her feathers artfully lay across her back, as though she were the subject of an angelic portrait. "I found him, and we searched for you. Once I knew you were safe, I ran away again. Listen to me, the King..."

She trailed off, shaking her head in dismay.

"What did he do? Are you all right?"

"He questioned all of us. Your Guardians at the door, your servant, everyone."

Sima stilled at the mention of Ivo. "No, she was free. She was supposed to get away."

"She kept returning to help more flee. He put her in the Box."

"The Box?"

"It's a coffin, more than anything. It's dark and soundproof. Within a couple of minutes, I started hallucinating. I begged to be let out, and he refused. No one came. It's impossible to tell how much time passes down there."

Sima couldn't believe what she was hearing. She knew Aurelio had infinite dark ideas, but his depraved psychological torture never failed to shock her.

"I am so sorry, Yadira. I am so sorry everyone went through that because of me."

She could already feel the spiral that was building its way up, but her friend stopped crying and looked at her.

"This is more than just for you, Sima. This is a man who is out of control and cannot stand to see himself lose one ounce of it. Do not apologize. We all knew what could happen to us if we helped you, and we did it anyway. Ivo knew she was risking her life by choosing to rescue others. I commend her for that, and I promise you, I will get her out."

"Where is she?" Sima trembled.

Yadira softened, shaking her head. "Innamorati, still. Another Hexia has healed her wounds."

The words felt like a hot dagger through ice. All the confidence and good times she had gained here suddenly felt bitter and sad.

"All I did was pass my pain onto others. His rage is because I left, and now others must pay the price." Sima's magic prickled at her fingertips, a sensation she'd gone days without.

"I will retrieve her when I return to Aeria. I spoke to her, and she desired for me to relay a message. She wishes for me to tell you—" she paused, taking a breath through her nose, "that she loves you, and she is still happy you left. She said all of it was worth it to see you go."

Tears stung as they welled. Her heart was both empty and full.

"Are you sure you are all right, Yadira?"

"I am sure you have heard a bit about Aurelio's past. He and his eleven brothers are called the Sacred Twelve. They possess powers of realm-work far beyond what any Ambrosi could dream of. They do not show it. Harboring their true power as a secret is how they can maintain their parasitic relationships with the planets they steal." Yadira frowned. "I do not know why Ehses does nothing to stop them, but all of them are grimy men of war."

"Yes, I remember. Carmine was the only sibling Aurelio could never stop talking about. He is just as brutal from what I've heard. Imagining the other brothers makes me nervous." Her ring began glowing brighter. "Vincenzo is coming," Sima said.

"I will be fine, friend. At first, I was paranoid the King could track me, but I think I am in the clear. We will meet up again soon." Yadira stood up, and in a flash, was gone.

Vincenzo's wings blew back Cosima's hair as he arrived. "Are you all right? Where is Yadira?"

"She left." Sima pointed over her shoulder. "Vincenzo, she says the King captured Ivo, and he tortured the both of them." Her head fell into her hands. "We have to go back. I need to go back.

Ivo is in prison and Yadira is not all right even if she tells me she is."

"We will handle it. We will get Ivo out." He rested a hand on her shoulder, filling the empty spot Yadira left by her side.

"I felt my powers for a moment."

He placed a hand on his chin. "I think your emotions are key to using your powers. Yadira and Ivo brought pain, and that intensity helped you access them. Calix is waiting for us. We can discuss it with her."

Sima nodded. "I think you're right."

Once they met up with Calix, the trio entered the same training room where Vincenzo and Cosima had practiced prior to the Day of Return. Sima was uneasy, though quietly trying to summon courage as the three sat on a black mat in the center of the room.

"Start by telling me about some times when you felt your magic come easily, or without you trying." Calix sat with one arm draped across her knee, opposite from Cosima.

"It has come without my intention when I want to help someone. I am less likely to reach for it if I feel I could hurt them." Her head hung as she inspected her palms and picked at her nails. "I think I stopped reaching for it entirely when I felt like all I did was hurt others."

"I have an idea." Vincenzo stood abruptly, pulling Calix up with him. "Hit me, hard."

"Oh, with pleasure." Calix pulled her arm back and swung. The sound of her fist colliding with his jaw caused Sima to gasp. Vincenzo groaned, rubbing his face. "Too hard?"

Vincenzo turned to Sima. "Not hard enough. She barely believes you."

"Your plan is for Calix to beat you senseless, in hopes I find a way to stop you with my power?"

Calix launched another punch, this time sending Vincenzo tumbling backward a few feet. "Basically," he muttered. "Calix, where's your staff?"

"Stop it, Vincenzo, this isn't funny." Sima frowned. "I don't feel my magic coming to me at all. She's going to knock you out."

"I won't even fight back. Really lay them on me." He grunted as Calix's foot met his stomach. "What's stopping you, Cosima?"

"I don't know," Sima winced as Calix drew blood from his face as she pummeled him. "This is not your best idea. This is hopeless."

"I can do this all day," he said, crimson dribbling from his chin and gums. "Remember, you can jump in any time and help me."

"How can changing Fate even help right now?" she shouted, hands balled tightly. Though she refused to admit it, embers of her power engrossed her fingers.

Then it sputtered and blew out, as Cosima locked eyes with Aurelio.

The screaming was so loud, Cosima questioned whether it was coming from her or the others. It was happening everywhere, all around her. She clamped her hands around her ears, but it did nothing to muffle the sound.

Calix swung a training sword at his head, narrowly missing as the King ducked out of the way. Vincenzo launched toward Aurelio with a push of his wings, his preferred sword removed from its sheath and poised in his hand. Aurelio blocked his advance with his own golden blade, before raising a hand and blasting Vincenzo with the same starlight Guardians possessed. He flew backward, colliding with racks along the wall.

"There you are, *dove,*" he said, latching on to Calix and hurling her to the ground. He placed his foot on her neck. "Oh, how I've missed you."

"Stop it!" Sima shouted. Her heart beat wildly in her chest as she slid to the floor. "Leave her alone!"

Aurelio smiled, stepping over Calix.

A cool sweat washed her as she crawled backward from the door as quickly as she could. She scrambled, frantic for a way out, but she couldn't get her footing, eyes stuck on watching him walk towards her.

He strolled with an effortless grace, his shoulders stiff, his head held high as he looked down his nose at her. He scoffed, all that was needed to tell her what he was thinking. She looked pathetic to him.

"Time to come home." He drew every syllable out with precision. His voice was rough, but he looked pristine, even as he fended off Calix and Vincenzo. They could not slow him and the closer he got, the more her mind went blank. Goosebumps lined her skin, reminding her of the paper-thin barrier between the outside world and her inner flesh. Flesh that she could already feel being dug into.

She crumpled, wrapping her arms around her knees. He stopped before Sima, her eyes locked on his polished shoes. Instead of thoughts, she only found more rattled breaths and emptiness. The world around her faded, and the sound of her heartbeat drummed in her ears. She awaited the end.

She didn't know how long he stood there or if he spoke to her, but suddenly, the floor before her was empty, his shoes gone from her line of sight. The animal instinct in her begged her to look, to track him, but she couldn't move. Her own shame weighed her down, kept her brittle and weak.

Until she heard him cry out.

Her head snapped up, vision clearing to reveal Vincenzo atop Aurelio, landing a second punch. Starlight blasted from the King's hands, aimed directly at the Rani, casting him backward into the wall. He fell, debris collapsing atop him.

Vincenzo raised his palm, returning with his own starlight, burning Aurelio in the thigh. A roar escaped Aurelio as he sent a ray of burning heat at Vincenzo, the Rani tucking his wings as he barreled out of the way, leaping deeper into the room and further from Sima. He was drawing Aurelio away from her.

The Guardian tackled Aurelio to the floor again as Calix emerged with a staff. Her hands wrapped around the end, holding it like a bat and she directed force at the King's head. It collided with his scalp, creating a thin scratch. Aurelio yelled, and he grabbed the other end of Calix's staff and shot it toward her chest.

Calix hit the ground and stopped moving.

"Calix!" Sima scrambled for her, even if it drew her closer to the King.

"Run, Cosima!" Vincenzo shouted as he grappled on the floor with Aurelio. Both of their wings shook as they each fought for advantage over the other.

Red hair and blood poured across Sima's lap as she pulled Calix's unconscious body closer. She was injured, but breathing. Aurelio grabbed one of Vincenzo's wings, spearing it with his other hand as he viciously dragged the blade down. The gash leaked into puddles of blood, and Sima thought she would be sick.

Time slowed, the dust suspended in the air, illuminated by rays of sunlight through the windows along the ceiling. Aurelio bared his teeth, amber eyes glistening with unrelenting intensity. Vincenzo's eyes gave way to an equally perpetual sense of power— his hatred. Her heartbeat sounded farther and farther away, her eyelids heavy as Vincenzo and Aurelio faded into the abyss.

This time, monsters and beasts didn't cloud her vision. No hallucinations of terrors out of twisted fairy tales. Just silence. Her limbs cut through invisible clouds as she descended impossibly slowly. Her feet met the ground first, toes wiggling in her boots, surprised at her success.

A piece of her wanted to shut her eyes so she would not witness Aurelio kill Vincenzo, another piece of her was determined to save him. She allowed her eyes to close, and took three small, centering breaths. She collected all of her energy and reminded herself what she wanted to change.

Aurelio.

Sima filled her mind with thoughts of him. A piece of her recoiled, a combination of every part of her too terrified to fight back. Resistance to her power was rooted in resistance to the memories of his pain and her everlasting torment.

The ground before her rustled.

She opened her eyes to find a door illuminated by an invisible light. Her hands shook, but she reached for the doorknob, pulling it open. The portal within swirled with shimmering pinks and blues.

It was too much. She backed away from the door, just a step.

No. I will undo this.

Cosima had escaped him for a reason. She sought not only

freedom, but vengeance. A magnetic pull ushered her across the threshold. She balled her fists, accepting this was where she needed to go, and walked through, letting the door close behind her and seal her in.

Chapter 22

Her feet firmly planted on the opposite side of the reservoir while the memory formed before her. She tiptoed into the room, as if he would hear her—but she was not truly in the past. This was merely a rendition, a replayed encounter. A replication with a narrow view, subject to where the lens aimed.

As she reached for her power, searching the ether for the threads, she attempted to gain an understanding of how much of Aurelio's Fate would be accessible. Each painstaking attempt she had made prior to this had been met with miserable failure. As her magic skidded across her flesh, Sima understood that he limited her. His Fate was unchangeable, like her own. She thought of Vincenzo, and considered reaching for him next, when the King from time passed caught her attention.

Though she stood directly before him, his eyes looked right through her. The King's near white hair was sculpted cleanly to his scalp, a scorching red suit bearing images of the sun stitched in a magnetic arrangement clad his body, complete with polished black shoes. The tailored ensemble showed off his impressive muscular body and ferocious wings.

He smiled, a ghostly thing, watching her from the shadows as her past self carved clay in the garden. She had deemed herself unskilled, but it was something that gave her an excuse to use her hands.

Sima's heart tugged, unable to fend off waves of echoed emotion. It had been decades since Sima had made any kind of art. She wondered how long it had been since she had been able to create something, to feel life flow into something simply because she had willed it so. The brazen stain on this memory was one she couldn't remove, and it had subsequently drained her of motivation to craft art with her palms.

"Oh, I didn't see you there," Sima from the past said, smiling eagerly at Aurelio. She felt uniquely empty witnessing her former self wearing a light-flowing satin gown, her dark hair laying across the lace that decorated her breasts. Flecks of molding clay littered the ground, but her dress was still pristine.

"No worries, dove," Aurelio from the past said. He approached her confidently, the air of the king he would become surrounding him. Even this version of her was no longer naïve. He had not yet seized Aeria, but it would occur this very night as she slept.

His calm nature chilled her to her bones. In mere hours, the hands that trailed along her exposed shoulders—interrupted only by a flimsy strap—would be severing the wings of Rani she had known since birth. Rani who had devoted their lives to protecting the Princess of Innamorati, Future Heir to the Aeria Throne. All of them, gone, before the sun could expose the sins that happened in the dark.

He brushed a kiss across the small of her neck, staring down at the tiny figure she was crafting.

"What is that?" he murmured into her skin, as he breathed in her scent.

"It's a tiger," she replied, gesturing to the whiskers and pointed ears that had started to take shape.

"Why a tiger?"

"It's silly, but it is what I imagine my inner animal is," she laughed, setting down the clay and wiping her hands on a rag. "I haven't been allowed to go Below yet, but I read about the people there all the time. Father says I will be allowed to visit when I take the throne."

"Those are not actual tigers," Aurelio replied, amused. He

picked up her wad of clay, Sima hesitantly resisting the urge to snatch it back.

He smashed it, digging his fingers through all her hard work, clay snagging his skin. Both versions of her mirrored the same discomfort.

"Those were shifter *scum*."

He let the wad of clay flop onto the table before them, splattering a dastardly mess across her neat dress. She didn't move or react, but the fear wafting off past Sima's skin was a beacon of weakness.

Except—that wasn't how present Sima interpreted her behavior. It was not weakness she witnessed. Before her was someone young, who had met someone truly horrid and fought to survive. This former version of herself was naïve, yes, but Sima found that no self-criticism tore through her as this scene from the past unfolded.

I have changed so drastically, I hardly know who you are, yet you are me. We survive, she thought, *we survive this.*

Sima, from the past, swallowed her reaction and looked up at him with a bland smile.

"My mistake," she said, quietly, picking clay from beneath her nails in her lap.

"Hey, don't look so down. In three short days, we will be wed, and together, we will lead this kingdom. I can show you the worthy parts of Haelos, what little there is. As the Queen, you will be free to go wherever you desire."

"Yes, I suppose that is true."

"Do you know how powerful you will be? It is extremely rare for Ambrosi to be born with wings. I am the strongest of all my brothers. Our mother connected us, drew us into creation for a grand purpose—to rule the realms in totality. Here, I have chosen you and Haelos. Divinity has lain kisses upon you for such a fortune."

Sima smiled half-heartedly. "My father believes so, as well. He has always been doubtful of my ability to rule our kingdom here in Aeria."

"Yet now you have me. I have unparalleled expertise on traversing the veil, accessing its inner connections to explore what lay within. Together, we will make Aeria into a fortress."

"A fortress?"

"Don't tell me you're unaware? The Rani Guardians defend this planet from all who travel through the veil with ill will and evil on board. Yet, Aeria sits in the sky, secured in place with no way to evade threats. How can you be sure the Guardians below will be enough when the entity of their nightmare manifests and wreaks havoc on this world?"

"Why would anyone want to murder people in another realm?" Sima's dark eyes pooled, fearful for the planet she had grown to love as a spectator from Above.

He laughed, throwing his head back. "Boredom. Power. Ego. Take your pick, dove." He ran a finger gingerly beneath her chin, tipping it back to force her to look him in the eyes. A tear kissed her cheek before it fell into her onyx hair. "Shh, this is why you have me. To protect all of you, and to do a better job than your miserable father ever could. We will be unstoppable as long as we are together."

Present day Cosima's jaw clenched, unable to stomach watching her former self be so deluded, so poisoned. She turned, shielding herself from the moment the King would swap personas, the lethal variant clawing its way to the surface, desperate for air.

Aurelio's golden eyes lit with amusement as his fingertips bore into the skin along her chin. "Let's go. I've quite had enough of your silly hobbies for the evening. You are the future queen. Act like it." He threw her face as he released her, sending her toppling across the table, drenching herself in clay.

"Aurelio," she whimpered. "Why would you do that?"

"Emotional brat," he mocked her with the traces of a smile revealing his teeth. "Looks like you slipped. You expect the Archipelago to find you a convincing leader, and yet not even I am fooled. Toughen up, it's the best thing for the both of us."

Tears welled. "I don't know why I let you treat me this way."

"Because you know without me, everyone will realize what a

fraud you are." Smoke toiled above him as he lit a cigar. Void Vine clouds wafted over the three of them. "I have business to address, and I want you to wait in your rooms for me to finish."

"I want to stay here," her voice trembled.

"Have it your way," he said, snapping his fingers. Two Rani Guardians emerged, grabbing Sima's former self by her hands, and dragging her toward her rooms. Never before had her Guardians been so rough with her.

"Stop, stop!" she shrieked, kicking and pulling to free herself.

Every fiber of the present Sima's being recoiled, fists balling tightly at her sides.

You survive this. She repeated internally. *No matter how much it hurts right now, you make it out of this.*

Although she expected the memory to replay from the beginning, instead it continued onward. He sighed, brushing his golden hair back with his hands, smoothing it back into perfection. As his steps echoed through the hall, Sima followed behind him, her screaming cries waving behind them. The sounds of it were a symphony of the pain she harbored, a struggle that was keenly familiar.

Deep billows of smoke floated above the two of them. It painted hazy images of beings twirling to unheard music. Inside the fog, two figures embraced intimately. She blinked away a tear, imagining herself and Vincenzo—and not the King prowling within her gaze.

Sima reached for her power, deciding to curate a plan through Vincenzo's Fate if she would not be successful with Aurelio's. She hesitated as he marched straight into her father's office, the former king going pale once he realized who had interrupted his private time. He stammered, asking Aurelio what he could do for him.

"Your daughter is a spoiled brat," he spat. "If I didn't need her to gain access to the Archipelago, I would have ended her already." Another puff of smoke found its way to the ceiling.

"Yes," her father stammered, looking nothing like a king. "She can be…difficult. However, the Spirit Goddess brought her to us, a gift for wombs long empty. Matilde arrived by miracle a few short years after Cosima."

Aurelio scoffed, throwing himself backward into a lounge chair, ashing his cigar on the floor. "She was not of your wife's womb?" His tone left Sima with the sinking suspicion Aurelio was already aware of this fact, though he did well to play along. Hints of his deception crinkled around the corners of his eyes.

"We struggled for many years to conceive, as most of us do, but our struggles outlasted even the most patient of prayers. Then, Ehses appeared with Cosima, declared her the Heir and left, never giving an explanation."

"In what manner did she arrive?"

"She was young, still in immortal adolescence. The Goddess implanted memories within her, ones of this world—a manufactured childhood of sorts to bring her ease in a new home."

"Skilled, that Spirit Goddess is mighty skilled." He inhaled deeply. "She has no recollection of where she came from?"

Cosima's father shook his head.

Sima placed a cool hand against her forehead, unable to tear her eyes away from the scene before her. The contents of her stomach threatened to rebel, but she strained over the beating of her own heart in her ears to learn more.

"Did she show signs of worthiness for the throne?"

"Cosima is gifted far beyond what we could reasonably manage. She developed abilities quickly and passionately, mastering her hold over them. The Spirit Goddess did not warn us of the true extent of her power."

"Such as?"

"Such as…stopping time whenever the desire came over her. It was difficult to come to terms with the fact that we could not discern if she'd enacted her powers. If she did not tell us, we were none the wiser. There was no lying to her. She could grab a hold of you and see the truth, most of the time. Then, there was the Fate…"

"Go on, *father*," Cosima growled.

Unable to hear her, he continued along, "Outcomes of her alterations in Fate could be found in seemingly disconnected ways.

A painting would change, yet somewhere in a notebook, a sketch of the original bore evidence of the truth. Her powers, if harnessed incorrectly, have compounding effects that ripple far and wide. She has gotten people killed."

"Interesting," he said, drumming his fingers along the lounge chair. "Why does she not speak of these powers?"

"Her abilities grew faster than we could handle. Each day, we sat in fear of her trying to seize the throne before we were ready to step down, and though we never mentioned it, we struggled, knowing our true bloodline would not continue on the throne of the Archipelago. Our family has ruled for generations…" he trailed off, his melancholy smile distant. "We had her power contained."

"*Contained?*" Aurelio hissed, sitting up in the chair, ash piling on the floor beside him. A sharp smile carved into his cheeks.

The mouse in the king's garb winced, her father nodding once.

"The witch who did the enchantments removed memories of her power for a majority of instances. The memories she could not scrub—we let that be proof to her that her powers were weak and difficult to control. We discouraged her from reaching for it. I don't believe she even knows how to anymore."

It had been true. By this point in her history, magic had felt like the farthest thing from serenity. She had been discouraged; her parents had mocked and ridiculed her behind closed doors. This inability to utilize her powers led to the necessity of the *Mortoid* capsules. Sima pondered if that fear had tanked her potential. Only in moments of high stress could she override the patterned response that gripped her brain.

"These enchantments, they can be used for more than protection or illusion? I may begin to like the creatures of Haelos yet. I should like to speak with the witch who did the original spell. Maybe she will prove to be of continuing use." Aurelio twirled his cigar between his fingers as it burned, smoking, clouding his face as he blew out a large puff.

Another door appeared beside her, as if ushering toward the next memory. She turned back briefly, gaining one last look at Aeria before the coup, before the smell of burned wings and terror would seep into every crevice. Behind her father, the unobstructed window let her see the sun beginning to set. The magnetic hues of purple and pink flirted with the skyline. Tomorrow, when the sun would rise, there would only be hues of crimson as the streets ran with blood.

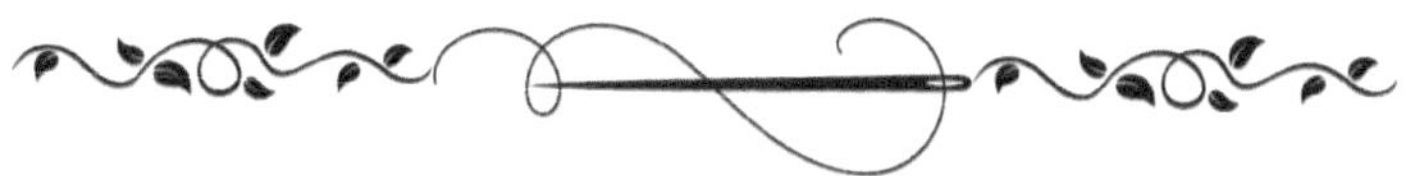

The next door was hard to open. If it hadn't popped up the way it did, Sima would've thought it wasn't meant for her. The memory began again behind her as she tugged the door open. The portal inside was grainy, as if the connection was being marred by something.

She reached a cautious hand through the murkiness, concealing her fingers from view. She peered back. Aurelio was crushing the tiger between his fingers again, a numb look on the face of her past self. The man she had brought inside the Palace would one day be the same man who would rip it from their hands and take it for himself. The man she thought she loved would hurt her in ways she didn't know were possible.

She stepped through the door, holding her breath and closing her eyes tightly, wary that whatever was swirling in the portal might stick to her. She slipped through the fabric of time once again, allowing one solitary moment dedicated to the searing rage within her. A moment of all the hatred and pain that had come to boil for a change. Tears spilled, speaking what her mouth could not.

Where do I belong? What was I made for?

Though a new line opened before her, Sima walled herself off, encasing herself in the emotions that rocked her. She had gone through extended periods without soothing the wounds covering her heart and soul, falling further and further from who she'd known herself to be. In order to survive, a version of herself she couldn't recognize had taken over her body. Pain rolled across her ribs, her chest tight with panic and unending anger.

For years, she had been trapped. Physically restrained to her nest—knowing it would not cease, no matter how she begged for mercy. The nightmare would continue, and a stranger would continue to operate her from the outside, a ghost of what lay at the core. Coping had meant learning how to stop dreaming of anything beyond her cage.

Cosima's hands trembled, and her body vibrated with the energy of all she dampened down, all she had shoved beneath the surface. She now felt alive, but in the type of way only people seconds from disaster could—knowing that they had mere moments before it was all taken away from them. She took large gulps of air, but all the breaths did was fan the fire, causing her panic to fester and spark until it was maddening. Moans of anguish left her mouth, hands clutched desperately at the skin atop her ribs, her eyes squeezed shut until flashes of colors formed behind closed eyelids.

It was overwhelming. She was going to burn right through her own skin, the anger transmuting from a suppressed emotion to an unstoppable force. She fought through the storm of whirling anger, willing herself to find some sort of grounding before she got too carried away.

Only one thought brought her home.

Revenge.

When her eyes opened, magma collected behind her irises, cooling into hard rock.

The scene she now saw her left her feeling grateful she had unleashed all of that anger instead of being crushed beneath the weight of it. It was Sima, but not of the past. Of the future. This was one she had seen hundreds of times in nightmares, as fitful sleep was a common burden to bear when living with a personified monster. It was not real. Sima realized she must have manifested the illusion with the fear she felt in her father's office.

Sima, of the non-existent future, brushed her hair gently in the mirror, smiling and humming a small tune. Her green dress accentuated her breasts, leaving their fullness on display, as her husband preferred it. A faint bruise marked her temple and the outer corners of her eye, though it was well on its way to healing. Her dress ran down until it collected at her bare feet. A dainty hand ran along her swollen abdomen.

Pregnancy was the only thing she thought could be more terrifying than being caught by Aurelio. Her choice to remain free from him in this one aspect came with hushed remedies from Ivo. She lived not in fear of how the baby might turn out, but in fear of her inability to protect it. Everything Sima did was to defend others, to shield them from the pain she experienced. She desired to encourage harmony, the divine balance Kismet was rumored to temper.

Though she no longer believed her world to be one rooted in justice, she knew staying away from Aurelio would at least allow her the chance to make sure this period would be no more than a hazy prediction, a recreation of deep paranoia.

No new door was present, but the image before her swirled away, the floor melting beneath her feet. *Perhaps now it is time for the hallucinations?* When the image pieced itself back together, and her eyes blinked away the last of the haze, she saw someone different.

Vincenzo.

He bore the same handsome face, but it was just a hair younger, his cheeks slim as if he had just met the other side of adolescence. It took little for her to realize he was in the Rani training camp. Thousands of wings surrounded him as they practiced a routine. A bead of sweat rolled from his hairline, diving off the tip of his chin onto the ground before them. She smiled to herself. The fury and anger she held onto stuttered when it became aware of his presence.

He was already becoming one of the few things that made her no longer want to be angry. But he was also one reason she *let* herself become angry.

A man called out Vicenzo's name, his armor marking him as a superior of some sort. Vincenzo broke from the line of trainees and jogged over, adding a small bow when he reached him. The man's hard expression changed little as he stared at the young Rani, his brows furrowed.

"You're leaving," he said, shoving a piece of blue paper into his hands. "Got word there's a world ready for you."

"Right now? I-I still have months left of training, I don't think—"

"You won't think anything if you don't accept. You want to be out there drifting in the void again, fine by me. They'll make more of you by dinner. Just because you got put on this fancy, investigative team and not with the rest of the brutes doesn't mean you're special."

Vincenzo swallowed hard, the evidence of the warrior he would become already enveloping him as he pulled himself together.

"Where am I being sent?" he asked, peering down at the piece of paper. The man didn't answer, instead tapping his foot impatiently. Sima looked the older man up and down before reading the blue slip at the same time Vincenzo did.

HAELOS, REALM 12,987
REQUEST TYPE: IMMEDIATE RESPONSE
INITIATION: DISPLACEMENT OF CROWN
OVERSEER: EHSES

"Displacement of crown?"

The man sighed, clearly aggravated by Vincenzo's questions instead of unfaltering acceptance. Rani were not meant to ask questions, he had told her that once. They were never allowed to question the orders they were given. Yet, the man looked at him sideways before shrugging.

"Someone took the nobility chosen by Ehses and threw 'em off the crown. You go there, you help fix it. Any more questions, princess, or can we get on with it?"

He nodded, running off to grab his things. Sima marveled at the sweet confusion upon his brow, the determination propping his chin high. He believed he would truly change things. Before the memory ended, Sima watched as another recruit approached him, holding a blue slip as well.

"They're sending us to Haelos," he said, voice grim.

"Yes," Vincenzo said, rubbing a hand behind his head. "Do you think that means they have narrowed it down? Do you think she could be in Haelos?"

"Only one way to find out. They say it's displacement of the crown, so it could be. They've been pinpointing the location of the last beacon before it was destroyed. That has to leave only a couple hundred realms where she could be. If we're lucky, it's Haelos."

"If we're lucky," Vincenzo said icily, "we find her *and* bring her home."

His companion shrugged, "Us or the next, brother. Finding her is all we need to worry about now."

Vincenzo's expression quickly soured.

"Hey, sorry, man. I forgot you knew this one. She's the whole reason you tried out for this squad anyway, isn't it? Is it love or lust forcing your hand?" his companion asked, adding a laugh.

Sima's breath caught unnaturally in her throat. This was a memory from the Eternal Kingdom, and a twinge of jealousy awakened at the thought of Vincenzo with someone else.

Vincenzo rolled his eyes. "You wouldn't understand."

"Love, then." He slapped a hand on Vincenzo's shoulder before packing up his belongings, as well. Vincenzo hesitated, then reached into the drawer beside his bunk, pulling out a small slip of paper, creased from being folded and unfolded frequently.

Sima walked closer, peering around his shoulder at the memento he held.

She was thankful they could not hear her when she viewed the memories. The noise that escaped her lips was one of grief and confusion. The drawn image beneath the word MISSING left nothing to mystery. It was a picture of her, except she wore a smile of delicate ease, her cheeks flushed with life, and no paranoia loomed in the whites of her eyes. Vincenzo had known Cosima, uncovering her true home—the Eternal Kingdom. A tether between the two had existed, all without her ever knowing.

"I am going to find you," he said to her picture, "and I will bring you home."

3

The Reincarnation

Surrender, the wind whispers, *be consumed to become whole.*
Accepting uncertainty eases the path, the soul craves growth.
There is no loss if there is no retreat.

The unknown cradles depths of night and heights of day in tender palms.
None can predict how favor is apportioned, its decisions shrouded in
mystery.
Yet there are no souls the unknown loves more than the ones brave
enough to endure.
Fortune favors shaky hands as much as steady ones.

Chapter 23

Paralyzed muscles screamed for freedom, but Sima could not move.

She willed her toes to relent a single minuscule wiggle, yet nothing came. The surrounding room was flush with darkness—or, Sima reasoned, she must have gone blind. The more she blinked, the more she believed she saw *something*.

She lay on her left side, face against the frigid floor. It did not resemble the Ombra District. The glossy quartz floor below her cheek was evidence they had been returned to the Aeria Archipelago.

Sima half-expected this outcome, considering the overpowering strength the King possessed. Her last images of her husband tangled with her last images of Vincenzo, the two of them locked in a fight to the death.

Fear lurked within her bones, unsure if she would find that Aurelio had killed Vincenzo. With luck, she could keep herself from hearing the gruesome details. The darkness kept her from uncovering the truth about him. Pain stung the tattered edges of her heart.

The world around her was quiet, but not empty. The presence of someone else lingered nearby. Sima assumed it was a Rani Guardian guarding whatever cell she lay inside. She could not discern any physically painful sensations beneath the weight of whatever paralytic drug thumped within her veins.

The sound of a man clearing his throat echoed from a distance. Her heart thundered rapidly in her chest. No footsteps followed, her ears straining to locate information about her surroundings. A gentle moan, as if someone were awakening, and a gurgle, as if gravely injured, came from the opposite direction that her head lay.

She was aware immediately it was Vincenzo. She fought against the paralysis in her body as a light illuminated the long hallway and the prison cell Aurelio locked her in. Her eyes darted frantically, attempting to read shadows and see through her ears.

The gurgling grew more strained, as if he realized then, too, that she was there. He could see her, but she couldn't turn to him. Heavy chains scraped weakly against the ground. A tear dripped across the bridge of her nose, but her body did not relent.

Sima's surprise at learning a piece of their conjoined history meant she had squandered the opportunity to utilize her magic and protect them both. Guilt slithered down her throat as she choked out a small sob. Meaningless morsels of magic accumulated within her reserves, not nearly enough to be effective yet.

Her tears crashed harder, her body shivering ever so slightly. She wondered if she had dreamed it. Her mind stilled. She took a slow breath through her nose, then tried again to wiggle her toes. To her surprise, and then dismay, a few moved, but not enough. Her vision blurred behind tears.

I don't want to listen to you die. Please not like this.

Pure wrath forced signals to her muscles to obey. Aurelio had hand-crafted this entire experience to torment her, she was sure of it. Her head turned away, a careful detail to keep her from seeing Vincenzo with her own eyes for the last time.

Another wave of stinging rage surfaced alongside more mental commands to her limbs. If he died now, he would be unaware of how impactful his kindness had been on her. Vincenzo alone had unlocked something within her. The darkness no longer equated to evil, but to a gentleness, too. Her heel slid an inch to the side.

You made me hope. You made me believe there was a world where I belonged.

Pins and needles nipped at her ankles, the slow wave working upward across her body. Likewise, she twitched as the tingling sensation bombarded her hands. Her fingertips trembled against the floor.

Whoever illuminated the hallway remained at a distance. Attempts at speech failed. The most she could manage was loud puffs of air from her nose, involuntary mostly because of the crying she was still heavily in the throes of.

Then the gargling slowed.

No, she shouted internally, *not yet. Please not yet, I am so close. I am right here.*

You're not alone, you won't die alone.

She heard it then, somewhere distant in the back of her mind.

I just found you.

Either she had pushed her brain to actual insanity, or his voice had sounded in her mind. She listened, but nothing came. Her feet began scraping at the floor, her hands pawing into the unforgiving stone. The pins found their way as high as her left elbow and mid-calves but moving them was like dragging heavy bags of sand. With every ounce of strength she had, she fought for a chance to look at him.

His face echoed in her mind, the weight of her own body the only thing keeping her from seeing it with her eyes. Occasionally, broken rasps of breath escaped him, but he was mostly silent. An anguished moan escaped her mouth, the side of her face was cold and drenched in tears as it slowly departed from the floor. Gravity got her the rest of the way onto her back, her limbs hitting the ground with a thud.

She strained to turn her neck the rest of the way, eyes digging holes in the edges of their sockets. Still, shattered breaths came from him.

I just found you again.

Her cheek fell against the floor. Sima gasped.

Aurelio had battered Vincenzo to the point that she hardly recognized him. He lay on his side, as she had. Forced to watch her. His eyes were closed now, but his brow twitched with movement. Each bone-white feather of his wings hung at a strange angle, soaked in blood. The only way to kill a Rani, was to cut off their wings. The King had left just enough of them attached to draw out Vincenzo's death.

Rage filled her again as she took in his purple-and-blue face, the marks upon his body, the chains around his broken wrists. A sound came from her again, this time, it was almost his name. Her fingers strained, finding herself inches from him. As more of her body gained feeling, the more she fought to drag the dead weight closer to him.

Their fingertips brushed, his wings rustling in response.

"En—Enzo," she rasped, "Enzo. Enzo."

She repeated it over and over, her lashes blinking madly to remove tears that made the image of him hazy. He was still beautiful, even like this. Sima vowed silently she would make Aurelio pay.

"Enzo."

Her hand grasped wildly at his forearm as she got closer, now dragging herself by her elbows, feet scrambling for better traction. She pulled herself up beside him, too scared to tip him back and hurt his wings further. She resisted the urge to touch his face, instead attempting to assess the damage. Clotted blood told her it had at least stopped bleeding. He was still breathing.

Fuck, she screamed internally, *please!*

A deeper breath shook his body, his eye flicking open for a fraction of a second. She laid herself next to him, cupping his face in her hands. She reached for her magic and refused to give up even as she came up short.

And then it came.

Small sparks at first, but a small reservoir accumulated, coming to her much quicker, she realized, when he had left her uninjured. Careful to not drain herself completely again, she ran a finger over his tattered brow, and saw.

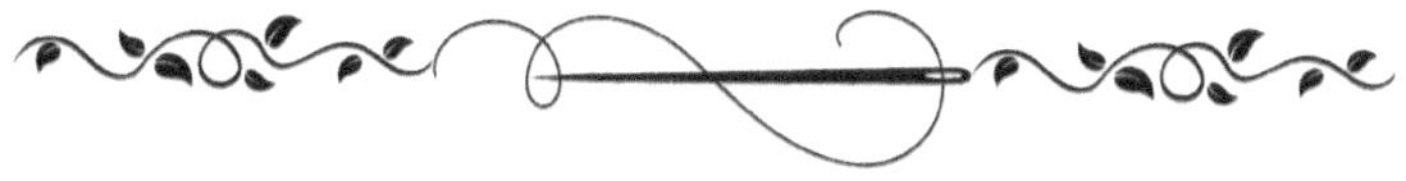

Nausea ravaged her senses. It was the only sensation she couldn't block out, as if her body were communicating to her spirit that her body still remembered, it still witnessed what was happening to Vincenzo. It reminded her of what was at stake.

Vincenzo stood in formation before thirty Guardian students. Stoic, blank faces leveled only by the deathly determination in their eyes. It was an expression Sima knew well, having spent so much time around Guardians in Aeria. She tore herself away, searching for the threads, refusing to let the opportunity go to waste.

The thread snaked across her fingertips, finding her before she'd reached for it. Sima tugged, following the opening and combing through endless possibility and uncertain probabilities. Her intuition stalled across those most likely to come to fruition. Her inner-knowing was louder than Sima had ever heard before.

Fingers plucked threads, weaving them with her hands through Vincenzo's ties. Though she could not see the fibers with her eyes, her flesh felt them innately. Options were limited, but not impossible. The path was obscure, but Sima was determined. What she could not see, she navigated around. Even as doubt hollered beside her, she slowed a little, opting for two routes.

No line allowed for an undoing of Aurelio's arrival and Vincenzo's injuries. Instead, Sima knew there were servants' passageways that let out near the prison cells, allowing the girls to clean the empty ones in the mornings. Prior to Sima and Vincenzo's arrival, the same had been done with their cage. Sima aimed to usher a forgetful Hexia out, leaving behind extra cloths and rags, by stringing together a series of chain reactions.

First, Cosima slipped through the servant's Fate, disrupting her day and putting her behind schedule with tiny mishaps. The smaller the changes, the stronger they held, and the less magic it took to enact. The Hexia girl rushed to the prison cells to begin her tasks, only to be interrupted by a Guardian. Sima tip-toed along his Fate, angering him with spilled drinks and burned bread for breakfast. Satisfied, she returned to Vincenzo's line.

Sima examined the possibilities, selecting to alter his actions while in the training room with her and Calix. Only one was promising. By delaying the start of Calix's attacks on Vincenzo, Sima hoped to eliminate the strain their fight put on him. If all went according to plan, perhaps Vincenzo would retain strength, pulled back from the edge. The rippled outcome of her changes would only be determined upon resurfacing.

The last bit of thread escaped her hands, now settling amongst the others seamlessly.

Sima let destiny run its course.

Sima's hand fell away from Vincenzo's brow, her eyes opening as she unintentionally tensed her muscles. They were still on the prison floors, but he was breathing. *Shit*. She realized he was speaking to her.

"What?"

"Please help me," he hissed through his teeth. Cosima stuffed clean rags into the gaping wounds between his shoulder and wings. One hand remained crossed over him, holding it in place to keep him from bleeding out. "You were talking to me a second ago, then you just zoned out. Did you—did you do it? You changed something?"

"You gathered that from me zoning out? Do you remember anything?" She reached for the rags and tied them together to create a sling. Sima tied the cloth together, running the fabric beneath the base of his wings, and hoisted them up. She secured it across his chest and abdomen.

"No, like I said, you were here helping me, then you went silent for a moment." He gasped and tensed as his wings were once again flush with his body.

Sima grimaced, glancing down at her blood-covered hands.

"Hey," he groaned, "come on, my reserves, they'll start filling again soon." He coughed, covering his mouth with his elbow. Despite his best efforts, he couldn't hide the blood coating the inside of his arm. "Sima, hey, come on, focus. We can do this. Grab the last of the cloths. The stronger we attach them, the easier time my body will have healing the injuries."

Her hands trembled, shaken by the sure confidence, delusional or otherwise, that he was able to convey, even in the throes of pain. She ripped the fabric in a forceful pull, utilizing the weight of her still tingling foot to get it going. She was unsteady on her feet, but she knew she couldn't leave him like this. This was not the time to fall apart.

Once she angled his wings properly, relief washed his face. Afraid of hurting him more, she held them up with her hands for a few silent minutes, the two of them breathing beside each other's faces. Sweat marked his brow, and though her arms were gelatinous, she persisted. The focus on his face intensified as he channeled magic to speed the regeneration of tissue.

"How long will it take," she asked, voice wavering, "until you're out of the woods?" She added a nervous laugh, the extra breath so painfully obvious in the small space they shared.

"He—I—" He stopped, taking a breath, wincing. "I tried to keep him from you. Grismelda was right. The power emanating from you outweighed the protections. Although, I think the crystal kept you safe from injury. You were under Calix, and you dropped limp to the floor."

"Time passes when I change Fate," she breathed. "How is she?"

"Aurelio left her behind. He saw his chance to take you back to Aeria. I promised you," he said, the wavering in his voice matching hers, "I promised I would not let him take you back and I am sorry I failed you."

"How long?" she repeated, refusing to acknowledge the painful emotions piling so high they threatened to spill from her throat.

"Arms getting tired?"

She frowned, catching a weak smile from him in her peripheral.

"If you can hang in there for me, just five more minutes, I can hold them again without ripping the new skin. Rani bodies heal fast—especially our wings, since they are our biggest weakness. I thought it was over for me when he started cutting." He swallowed hard, head ducking ever so slightly. "He left them dangling there by the nerves. It was…"

"Please, Enzo," she gasped, "please forgive me for bringing you into this, I am sorry for whatever events crossed our paths and led you to this." Tears poured, and he moved, as if by instinct, forward, resting his head on her shoulder, and ushering her face against his. Her hands remained holding up his wings, but she didn't move her face either. She allowed herself to nuzzle into his too-cool skin, clammy as his body fought to undo the damage her husband had done to him.

"I don't regret it, Cosima," he said. "I would do it again, every fucking day if I had to, for you. Next time, I'll do a better job, though, because, Spirit, this was too close. How can I convince you to fall in love with me if I die on you?"

She pulled back, careful not to allow his wings to dip even a fraction, but enough to take in his face. He was slow to raise his head, to meet her gaze, but when he did, he looked at her in a way she'd never been before—with impenetrable faith, devotion. His emerald eyes were bright, despite the lack of color in his cheeks. They looked back and forth, searching hers, awaiting her reaction.

Whether her eyes gave evidence of how she felt, or not, she opened her mouth to find nothing came out. They shared the same breath, faces only inches apart. With the slightest angle to her head, she allowed her eyes to flutter closed, and as if he had always known her, had always been capable of reading her, his lips met hers.

He smelled like the morning breeze after the rain, relief encompassing her as she indulged in a once-suppressed desire. She could not deny its existence, the way it resembled free-falling, like coming home to open air. In the deep expanses of her mind, something banged against a lost wall. Memories begged to surface but found no way out. Kissing him relinquished the pain that clung to her. She was unaware it had existed until he took it away, just for this moment in time.

She felt his wings lift out of her hands, his body strong enough now to bear them. He wrapped his powerful arms around her back, pulling her tighter against him. She reached for his beautiful face once again, not able to get enough, wishing she could draw him closer, entangle him tighter to her. Her hands wove through his hair as he did the same.

He grew stronger with time, holding her tighter. Eventually, they tore themselves away, breathing heavily.

"I'm relieved you're all right," she said.

"You don't know how long I have been waiting to do that." Vincenzo smiled, adding a small peck to her cheek. "Though I would wait forever to do it again."

"Do you know me? From another time, I mean. I saw a memory of you getting assigned to Haelos."

"Yes," he whispered. "I didn't know the right time to tell you. I…"

His voice trailed off as their ears picked up the sound of footsteps.

"Shit," she whispered. "We need to get out of here. They're going to realize you're alive."

A bit of color was returning to him, his tan skin finding its usual hues as his body fought to piece itself back together. Sima ran beside him, peeking at his wings. He would be unable to fly. The wounds were sealing, but his body lay tattered in black and blue, and he was exhausted.

"Lay on the floor," she whispered. "I have an idea."

"I would love to be bait, thank you for asking," he grumbled, but added a fake smile, teeth still flecked with his own blood.

Chapter 24

A Guardian sauntered down the hall at the sounds of Sima's desperate pleas for help. She recognized him immediately as Eugenio, a Guardian favored by the Emblems and the King. She waited for her body to respond to him with fear. Instead, Sima realized she was being handed an opportunity for pure, unmitigated revenge.

Sima made sure her small cries echoed loudly, adding every layer necessary of theatrical emotion needed to portray her grief. As the footsteps stalled in front of her cell, she threw herself up, begging the Guardian for help.

"Do something, please," she cried, anguished to lose what her husband must think to be her lover. Perhaps he knew something about the two of them he had gone to great lengths to hide. She hid the anger, piling the eons of unrelenting sadness on top.

Might as well make it cathartic.

The Guardian sighed, unlocking the door. He steadied a hand on the hilt of the sword fastened to his belt. "He is dead, *Queen,*" he hissed. "This is who abandoned your kingdom for? I thought you didn't like fucking Guardians?"

"What?" Sima's voice was hushed, quiet behind tears.

"All those times you pretended you were too good for the Guardians, like every other Ambrosi, and yet here you are, slumming it with an Ombra cast-off. Every last bullshit Guardian the King rejects, he sends to the Shadow District."

Eugenio entered the cell, standing inches from Cosima, as Vincenzo lay motionless on the floor behind them. "Remember those times we had fun? Maybe I should take my chance for more before I bring you home to Aurelio now that your *lover* is dead. See if you like my feathers on you like his."

Sima stood, cocking her head to the side as the tears she conjured slipped down her face. "No," she said and threw herself at him, like the tiger she knew she was. Before he could stop her, she reached for the sword, the surprise catching him off guard enough for Sima to get it from the sheath.

It was not enough to stop him from knocking it out of her hand. They fell backward in the tumble, Sima kicking the sword away from his reaching hand. Vincenzo pounced, and though injured, he was taller and stronger than Eugenio.

Once Vincenzo pinned him to the wall, Sima was relentless with her punches, throwing herself at him repeatedly. The impact sent pain cascading through her flesh, but she couldn't stop if she wanted to.

"I said I was never coming back. I told him I was done." Sima bit out the words as she bloodied his face. Her chest heaved with a sob, blind rage barreling through her fists. Eugenio spit at her and she narrowly missed being hit with crimson saliva.

Sima reached for the sword she'd knocked from Eugenio earlier. His eyes widened as the tip of the blade slid across the surface of his skin, leaving a dribbling ribbon in its wake.

"Fight!" she yelled. "Fight for your fucking life, Eugenio. Isn't that what you told me? Before you walked out, leaving me there to die? I want to see you fucking fight."

"Queen Cosima," Eugenio panted, body tense with pain. "Hey, you knew the King wouldn't let you die. We were just having some fun."

Vincenzo's hand gripped Eugenio's windpipe, sealing off his air. "I can't kill you this way, but your body needs air for consciousness. Can't keep me from ripping your wings off with my bare fucking hands if you're sleeping, now can you?"

Eugenio's feet kicked weakly beneath him as Vincenzo hoisted him higher up the wall by his throat. Vincenzo's eyes blazed, wrath soaking the room as he watched the Guardian writhe beneath his hold.

"What do you want me to do with him?"

Sima's hands trembled, fighting the urge to drop the sword. She reached for Eugenio, forcing him to look her in the eyes. She wanted him to know she was unbreakable, that however he'd hurt her in the past, it would be she who won. Cosima had made it here without his help and she would send him into the void herself.

Eugenio's face purpled, and soon he would faint.

"Turn him around," she commanded.

Vincenzo nodded, dropping Eugenio to his feet, and releasing his hold on the man's neck. Eugenio panted, reaching for his vulnerable throat in the same manner Cosima had that time the Guardian choked her in the past. Sima averted her gaze.

"No, come on," Eugenio said between gasps, eyes wide. "You can't kill me."

"Cosima," Vincenzo said, "I can do it if you need me to."

"Turn him around," Sima repeated, staring at Eugenio. She raised the sword in the air above her head.

"I'm sorry, all right? I'm sorry."

Vincenzo's jaw clenched as he turned Eugenio around and forced him to his knees. "Whenever you're ready."

Sima looked up at him, seeing the future clearer than ever before in Vincenzo, and brought the sword down on Eugenio's wings, severing them from his body.

"Through here," Cosima said, pulling Vincenzo behind her. "The servant's tunnels. I recognize the entrance. We might have trouble finding our way through. I don't know how they're mapped underground."

He allowed her to lead the way, managing a pace just below a jog, his free hand clutching his side. The sword she had stolen from Eugenio bogged down the too-large belt around her waist. Sima swallowed hard, heart still pounding from the chaotic adrenaline that came from her first kill. The time would soon come to kill again.

Sima had taken Eugenio's life, the realization like a venom seeping deep inside her flesh. Her emotions pulsed as her heart shook inside her chest. They came to a stop. The servants' tunnels were full of gray stone, the only place on the islands that wasn't overtaken by crystals.

At the top of a small set of stairs lay a door leading somewhere within the Palace. Sima's brain was turbulent, and she braced a hand against the wall as she took a deep, shuddered breath.

"You did the right thing," Vincenzo said, placing a hand on her back. "He hurt you and who knows how many others he's done it to, or would do it to, if he continued."

Sima nodded. "Eugenio was one of the worst ones. He mocked me time and time again. The things he's done, the things he's talked about with the others in front of me…" She closed her eyes. "I'm happy he's dead."

"If you poke your head through that door, do you think you'll be able to figure out where we are?"

"Yes, I think so."

Footsteps sounded from further down the passageway. Vincenzo grabbed Cosima's wrist and pulled her down a hallway. The two flattened against the wall, ears scanning for threats. A slender, pale woman with dark hair clad in a brown servant's uniform ran past.

"Ivo?" Cosima's voice was hardly above a whisper, but her friend swirled in their direction immediately. "Ivo, by the Spirit."

"Cosima!" Ivo dove into Cosima's arms, wrapping tightly around her. "One girl who cleans the prisons claimed she saw you. You're here, you're really here."

"I am, friend. I am here. Yet so are you. Why have you not left the islands like your sisters?"

"I refuse to leave until every one of my sisters is free from the Archipelago. Not just that," Ivo eyed Vincenzo, lowering her voice a touch, "I found more of my people's history. Our records had been stolen by the King, all hidden across the three islands, most of it beneath the ground. It seems other Hexia were reclaiming the texts bit by bit and storing them out of sight like me."

"We will help you," Cosima said, resting her hand on Ivo's shoulder. "This is Vincenzo. He is a Guardian from the Ombra District."

"I will do whatever it takes to save those documents." Vincenzo offered a warm smile, which Ivo returned. "And your sisters."

"Where do we go from here, Ivo?"

Ivo bit her lip, contemplating. "The few remaining servants here are being observed. Aurelio cannot contain their power, but the Guardians are still forcing them to work."

"How many are left?" Cosima asked.

"Forty, maybe more."

"How did the others get off the islands?" Vincenzo rubbed a hand behind his head.

Ivo smiled. "Vipus. There aren't many left. We'll have to figure out another way to get all the girls out of here." Ivo looked at Sima. "Are you sure it's safe for you here? Maybe we can get you out of Aeria and back to the Ombra District."

"He found me last time," Sima said slowly. "I don't think I am free anywhere. The only way I will be free is if he is dead, or else Aurelio will always come for me." Her fists balled. "More than that, I refuse to run anymore. There are more than beasts from the veil in Ombra. The Shadow District is overrun with monsters made from the bodies of the dead."

Ivo gasped. "It's worse than I imagined. My sisters have fled to the Ombra District. What will become of them?"

"Rani Guardians on our side will help guide them to the main city if they come across them, even without direct orders to do so. Do you know where within Ombra they might have gone?" Vincenzo rubbed his chin with his hand.

"There is a small settlement on the north-eastern border where our coven once lived prior to our capture."

"That is incredibly far from the Portale del Regno Stellare. It is likely they will be safe, as long as they do not come across the infected," Vincenzo said.

"The girls who remain…" Sima said. "Where are they?"

"All are in the Palace above us. About ten are in the kitchens, twenty assigned to cleaning, and ten attending the King. Those will be the hardest to find. The girls in the kitchens are closest, and there are only two Guardians with them while they cook."

"Which way to the kitchen?" Vincenzo asked.

Ivo led them to the entrance to the Palace kitchen through the passageways. The halls were emptier than before, the silence eerie. At the top of the stairs, Sima peered through the door, spotting two Guardians walking toward them. The larger one spoke vividly of his desire to sleep with an Ambrosi woman, as the other nudged him with his elbow. The larger one went down first, thanks to Vincenzo grabbing him in a headlock and quickly knocking him out.

The smaller one was feisty. The Guardian reached for a second hidden blade that Sima had missed, two vipers striking at once. Sima used a morsel of her power to slow time, gaining an advantage over the Guardian. She wasn't sorry to see the Rani's hand roll down the steps with wet flops, and she wasn't sorry when the base of her blade skewered the Rani through the abdomen. Cosima removed her sword from the man's body and pushed her.

The Guardian followed his missing appendage back into the earth, as Sima pulled Vincenzo forward down the left side of the hallway. Ivo remained in the passageways, waiting for them to return with her sisters. Cosima and Vincenzo found the girls huddled in a corner, eyes shadowed with fright.

"Come," Cosima instructed. "We are here to save you. We will make sure you make it out of here."

Vincenzo and Cosima ushered the women back down the stairs and into the passageway. Vincenzo was gaining strength by the minute, wounds no longer seeping blood, and skin no longer torn to shreds. He led the group to Ivo, who embraced the girls with tears.

"Thank you," one said. "My name is Indigo, this is Vel."

Sima recognized them as the same two she had helped in the Nuvola Palace gallery. Indigo, with glowing brown skin, black-framed glasses, and inky purple-blue hair, held the hand of Vel. Vel's white hair was straight and ended at the base of her neck.

"It is my pleasure." Cosima bent in a small bow. "We wish to get you home."

"How will we retreat without Vipus?" Vel asked sheepishly.

Cosima's mind immediately flicked to the Emblems. "How far away is the Emblems Headquarters from here?"

Ivo shook her head. "It isn't too far, but we will have to be on the lookout for Guardians. They seldom come to these passageways unless they are searching for the girls. The entrance to the Headquarters is locked, however."

"What's the plan?" Vincenzo asked, hand cradling his side. "Because I know you have one."

Sima dangled the keys stolen from Eugenio's body. "Eugenio was the Emblems' kiss-ass, just like Caelian. I know for a fact that one Emblem has access to his own stable of Vipus. It's one I don't think anyone else knows about."

"How do you get the Emblems to give you the Vipus?" Ivo asked, arms wrapped around Indigo.

"When I touched a Guardian, it showed me a memory. I received a memory for Vincenzo, too. Once I found the thread, I started weaving things into his Fate. If I can replicate that ability, I can secure us a way out of here. There's one specific person I think really needs some screws loosened."

The Emblems maintained control over the day-to-day lives of the Guardians, instructed to manage what Aurelio could not be bothered to do. Aurelio's only interest in Guardians was in maintaining his threatening presence over them.

The Emblems were the exceptions. They were the personification of brain-washed, blind followers he so desperately needed to obey every beck and call. The Emblems were Rani, the few that could lead, a rare opportunity for their kind. Instead of being honorable, they were despicable, aiding and abetting all the insanity Aurelio had put in order. They stood to gain what all the Ambrosi did: a lush, luxurious life.

As they darted down the passageways, Cosima held the blade before her, prepared to defend the girls with her life. Her mind flickered with thoughts of Aurelio, and though she could not see him, she could sense him. He was here, in the same way he was everywhere, haunting her. Fighting the bile scolding the back of her throat, she flew down another path as Ivo gave directions.

Vincenzo kept pace beside her, large scabs forming around his wings, bruises beginning to fade more blue than purple. She couldn't help the creeping feeling wisping at the back of her neck, screaming at her that Aurelio was right behind them.

As they flew up the stairs Ivo selected, Sima allowed a temporary wave of familiar fear to wash over her, to let her body feel the anguish she was so used to carrying. She dipped herself deep into the unforgiving iciness of it, determined to remind herself why she was going to do this, and why she was going to fight her way out of here.

Fight for your fucking life.

She would.

Cosima inserted the keys. The girls huddled out of sight in the tunnels, waiting behind them. Vincenzo's hand was steady against her shoulder blade in a quiet reminder of his support. The door flew open, and four men stared at her like she was a wild animal on a rampage.

She was.

It took seconds to register who they were. The one closest to them was in the middle of smoking a cigar, playing cards held in his hands.

"So typical. Men with all the power usually sit around doing nothing," she said with a smile. Whoever she was before this, whoever she would be after, faded into nothing, until unforgiving hatred found her veins. A power and strength innate to her came out in ever bigger waves, washing her until she was dripping with it.

Until they could see it in her eyes.

She reveled in the smell of their fear. Only one of them looked prepared to put up a fight.

What happened to the men they used to be? What happened to the Rani capable of smiting an enemy on the spot at their full capacity, capable of leveling cities when working in tandem?

These were not fierce creatures, they were fattened pigs. The man in the middle still shed powdered sugar from his morning pastry, its evidence further plastered across his jacket. They dressed like the business managers of Aeria, playing dress up as Ambrosi, and did not wear armor.

Vincenzo loomed behind her, his wings surpassing both their bodies. It must have pained him, but he put effort into intimidating the others as best he could. She drew the sword from its stolen sheath around her waist, and met the eyes of each of them slowly, working her way to the right. The whites of their eyes glimmered beneath her heat. All except one. He was the biggest, the only one who seemed to be muscular, yet he hesitated.

"Don't do it, Remo," the sugary one said, eyes sliding to the trembling fingers on his only weapon. "You heard what Caelian said she can do. Aurelio wasn't lying when he told us he'd sic his dog on us."

"Aurelio will dangle us from the edges of the city if we don't stop her," he said, determination conjuring in his brow. He unsheathed his sword. "Caelian is a scared punk. See if your golden boy will save us now, Volfango."

"I love that you're brave," she said. "I think it's kind of cute."

She raised her sword, swiping to the left instead of toward Remo. Volfango's hands gripped his throat as a sea of blood flooded the table. He wouldn't die from bleeding out, but he would experience the sensation of it, and until he had enough energy heal the wound, would incapacitate him. As he slumped to the floor, his wings folded over him in a last-ditch attempt at self-preservation, unwilling to remain fully vulnerable.

Instead of severing his wings, Vincenzo took her sword, aiming it toward the shocked Rani. Remo was pale and firmly planted in his seat. She lowered herself to her knees and reached for his skin. Slitting his throat wasn't necessary for this part, not really, but it was undeniably an effective technique to subdue him.

Time slowed, the warping of sound and space around her secondary to the one slow, precise breath she inhaled. The memory she found herself in was more than enough to work with.

"Volfango," Remo said in the memory, gesturing to the woman beside him. "This is my wife, Casilda."

Sima arched a brow at the Ambrosi woman. Ambrosi kept far from the Guardians, always deeming them to be lesser beings. The only Guardians good enough, it seemed, were the Emblems. Remo was slimy, even if he wore fancy clothes and left his position. He could drink wine with the others, no longer cast to the side. Casilda wore a long burgundy dress, her blond hair swishing around her hips as she brought the glass to her mouth. She did not meet his eyes during the introduction.

Volfango smiled at Casilda, Sima seeing everything she needed in his eyes as he took her in. They knew each other better than they were letting on. A perfect opportunity for Sima to exploit threads already in existence. The line found her easier than it ever had before, the strings laying out the possibilities before her.

This wasn't something she knew would work, but it was her best shot. Cosima could not force Volfango and Casilda into an affair, but as Sima wove chance encounter after chance encounter, they would fall into it on their own. Small shimmers of her magic yearned to confirm it by glimpsing the future, but she wouldn't be able to know if it worked until she was out.

For good measure, there were a few other chance encounters Sima could make happen with what little information she gleaned about his life from the time she had known him. Volfango was rumored to be one of the first Rani to give support for Aurelio. A new line bubbled to the surface—a line that led straight for her husband.

Cosima could barely contain herself, and her laughter echoed in her ears as she wove. She planted dozens of minor changes. Cosima figured it was a better strategy to enact a dozen minor changes, than to lose her shot all at once if the alteration was too large and it snapped.

She let the threads fade away and transported herself back to the present.

Chapter 25

When she returned to the surface, tiny, insignificant shifts to her environment caught her attention. The wine before them smelled of fermented peaches. The color of the men's suits were different hues than before. Vincenzo pointed a sword at the whimpering group. Men who would've chewed him up and spit him out if Aurelio had assigned him to Aeria and not to Ombra, that is. Volfango, however, was not on the floor with a slit throat because of her. Instead, his mutilated corpse slept beside Remo, wings roasting in the fire pit as the Emblem Chief lit a cigar, hands trembling.

"You're a witch," Remo said, ashing his cigar atop Volfango's corpse. "You know that?"

"I'm aware," Sima said slyly, rocking back and forth on her heels. This was the beginning of the fun she would have. Pain and torture were one thing, but she could mess with their minds, their lives. "Though I can't make him do what he wouldn't have done already. I mostly just hastened the inevitable."

Remo took another long drag before letting the smoke billow out across the table.

"What do you want?"

"Happy to hear that you are willing to be reasonable," Vincenzo said, letting the tip of his sword press into the chest of the sugar-covered Rani Guardian, who was trying to reach across the table and take Volfango's glass of wine. The Rani stared up at him, a wipe to his mouth sending sweet sprinkles raining from his chin, before he relaxed back into the chair.

"I want out of here," Sima said. "I want to go and for Aurelio to not find me."

"You know we can't do that, even if we wanted to."

"Yes, you can. I know you can leave Aeria whenever you want. Just because you dirt-bags prefer to stay where it's safe, and gamble with the lives of others, does not mean I will allow the same behavior to continue any longer than it has to. You have ways out of here, and I want them. Where are the Vipus?"

Remo eyed Vincenzo carefully, taking in the sharp metal pointed at his friend's chest. His eyes flicked to his fallen brother beside him, the person whose life he had taken with his own hands for a betrayal that sent him to madness. That same madness still lingered there, not enough time having passed for it to hit him yet—what he had done to his friend.

Then he looked to Sima, giving her a crazed look—the look of a man truly dumbfounded and unsure of what to do next. Helping her would mean that Aurelio would have him killed, but not aiding her meant he was prey. She could wreak havoc on everything he loved.

Cosima's power reserve dwindled, but she would not let them know. Messing with Volfango had taken more out of her than she had planned, but she was already running low after helping Vincenzo only minutes ago. There was nothing more she could produce beyond hot steam, but putting on the show would be no problem. Especially with Vincenzo helping drive the threat home.

She allowed herself to take him in for a split moment, to assess his injuries, to scan him for pain. He could handle himself well, and the sight of him lit hope in her for better days. A day where they were far from the hell they were in. His hair was split down the middle, cleaving into two opposite colors. He was the embodiment of light and dark, night and day.

Cosima knew Remo would not agree to letting her leave. She itched to find out if her changes had gone according to plan. If so, the Emblem would be so paranoid about a particular key, he would bring it everywhere with him. He was so molded to the idea that someone would one day come for it—the gears turned and his facial expression soured as it clicked for him.

She was the one coming for it, and there would be no stopping her.

Vincenzo moved without a signal from Sima, as they operated on the same calm wavelength. She lunged, using the empty chair to gain leverage, before running atop the table and tackling Remo to the ground. Blood from Volfango's body splashed as they collided with it. Sima, not letting the moment go to waste, gripped his sword firmly. Vincenzo sliced directly through the chest of the Rani before him, cleaving his wings from him in one fell swoop.

The sound of the bone and tissue snapping sent the third trying to flee from the room, his plans in vain as Sima snatched his ankle, slamming him face-first into the corpse of his friend. Adrenaline coated her in a film of insatiability, a thirst for more blood than she'd be able to spill in one day.

How many had watched? How many had seen the bruises and said nothing? How many had decided it was not their business to say something about a man being a monster? The questions tumbled within her skull. It confused Sima, how injustice did not make them thirsty for vengeance as it did her.

Once their wings stacked four high in the furnace, Sima dangled the key she pulled from Remo before Vincenzo.

"Let's get them out of here."

Ivo had made use of the time Cosima and Vincenzo had spent fighting the Emblems and collected eight more girls on nearby cleaning jobs. Ivo jogged toward them just as Cosima and Vincenzo entered the servant's tunnels.

"There are twelve missing. Those we located are too near the

King to rescue. However," Ivo panted, "I say we get this group out first."

Vincenzo nodded. "Are there enough Vipus for those we have now?"

Sima shook her head. "I'm not sure. Ivo, you need to get us to the Southern wall, where I escaped the first time. The stable is near there. It's hidden beneath an enchantment that will only reveal for this key."

Sima held it up.

"Follow me," Ivo said. "Everyone hold on to one another. No one is getting lost."

"I'm going to stay a few steps behind in case anyone comes up while our backs are turned," Vincenzo said. "You are strong enough to protect from the front." He touched her arm lightly, sending a parade of sensation up her limbs. "Let's get these girls out of here once and for all."

Cosima nodded tightly. The group pushed forward, coming across only one additional Hexia as they made their way to the South. Once there, Cosima ventured out alone to the surface. Her legs peddled beneath her as she ran toward a small smoky quartz tower fashioned into a marble pedestal.

The contraption detected the key's presence. A panel of black marble reseeded to reveal a keyhole. Sima held her breath, trusting that her changes had come to fruition as she desired.

The key turned in the lock with a relieving amount of ease, and Sima threw open the door to reveal the interior of the stables. The winged beasts inside were Aeria's Vipus—Wyverns bred to be smaller and stealthier by mixing their genes with serpent creatures native to Haelos. Even so, they towered above Sima, eyes like the sun staring down at her.

Lengthy, razor-sharp fangs protruded from their scaled mouths. Their bodies were smaller, for precise maneuverability in the sky. The one in front of her was forest green, her scales shimmering as she stepped out of the stables and into the light. She stretched her fragile, thin wings out, fanning them in the sun while shaking her head.

Sima ducked her head back in, counting fourteen more. Each could hold two people. Cosima stepped outside, sending a quick whistle through the air. Within seconds, Vincenzo and the others were running toward her.

Sima held open the door as they tumbled into the stables. Working fiercely, the Hexia instinctively leaped into the saddles, and guided the Vipus into the fresh air.

For the first time, Cosima realized it was nearing dusk as nine Vipus launched one-by-one into the sky. Each held two women, leaving five more for any others they could help to escape.

Indigo and Vel waved goodbye, before gripping the reins and sending themselves plummeting toward the surface. Ivo kissed three of her fingers, then held them up in a silent salute.

"You can go with them," Cosima said.

"No." Ivo shook her head. "My job is not done."

Sima slipped her hand into Ivo's. "Neither is mine, then."

"Bad news," Vincenzo held a finger to his temple. "The connection between myself and the other Guardians is blaring with alerts. They realize we have escaped, and they are about to search the tunnels. All remaining Hexia are being rounded up. Looks like our rescue attempt has suddenly increased in difficulty."

"We're on the main island. Ivo, didn't you tell me there was a tunnel leading to the center of Innamorati?"

Ivo nodded. "I can get us anywhere in Aeria, as long as we remain hidden."

Sima glanced up at Vincenzo. "There must be a way to stop Aurelio."

"The Astral Atheneum," Ivo said. "We have to go now. If information is anywhere, it's there."

Cosima's heart belted songs of terror as they retreated underground again, cool stone replacing darkened clouds. With the aid of Vincenzo's tele-bond to the other Guardians, the three evaded others long enough to reach the threshold between the Palace and the main island, Innamorati.

As their feet crossed the boundary, Sima once again felt lighter, air filling her lungs in unrestricted breaths. She placed a hand on her chest, steadying herself as they continued. Though she had returned against her will, she moved now without Aurelio's approval. It was an achievement all in its own right, and Cosima's confidence rose slightly.

"The Atheneum is on Iridicenza. It has been under construction, but because you left, not much progress has been made. This means the wards that would normally keep us out are down."

"Right," Sima swallowed. "He hasn't granted me access in years. I'm slightly nervous about what we will find."

"We can cross that bridge when we come to it," Vincenzo grimaced, "because it seems our luck is running out."

"That it is." A Guardian strolled in front of them, emerging from the darkness. "I thought I might find you here."

"Caelian," Sima's voice cracked. "How did you find us?"

"Some Queen you are, to be so out of touch with the ins and outs of her own kingdom. Though I suppose you're really just a traitor now, aren't you?"

"Watch it," Vincenzo bit out. "Don't think you're coming any closer."

"So, the rumors are true," Caelian said, smoothing back his brunette hair. Burgundy feathers became visible as he stepped closer. "You are truly spitting in the King's face, cheating on him with this lowly grunt. Where did you even come from? I've never seen you before."

"Ombra," Vincenzo smiled, drawing his blade.

"Even worse than I thought," Caelian sneered, revealing his own sword. "I will relish in the way it tastes to return you to the King. I am the only one who has realized you slaughtered the Emblems. Truthfully, I should thank you, really, for the rare opportunity you've granted me. Once you're back in his hands, I will finally live the good life as an Emblem."

"All of this so you can drink wine and dance with Ambrosi women?" Sima's blade was firm beneath her grip. Her fingers flexed, tightening her hold.

"You misunderstand me," Caelian said, hand on his chest. "I

crave more than luxury. I crave an equal playing field. For once in my miserable life, they won't look down on me for the body I was born into. Guardians are second-class citizens, existing only to cater to Ambrosi."

"You have become jaded, brother. We do not exist to cater to Ambrosi. The people who need us are powerless—utterly defenseless. Without them, there is no us."

Caelian laughed. "You are asleep, *brother*. The King is right about all of them. They are parasites, not worthy of our defense."

"It is not up to you to decide," Cosima said.

"Says the one who abandoned her people."

"I did no such thing," Cosima's voice rose.

"Selfish br—"

Vincenzo cut him off with a swift swipe of his blade into the armor along Caelian's side. The impact knocked the air from his lungs, anger overtaking his features. Before he could launch an attack in return, Vincenzo dropped low, a spinning kick colliding with his knees, bringing Caelian to the ground.

Vincenzo pointed the tip of his sword against the soft flesh of the Guardian's neck. "You talk too much," he growled. "Give me one good reason I shouldn't kill you right now?"

"I have friends coming," Caelian's twisted smile beamed at Vincenzo.

"Let's go," Sima tugged on his arm. "We have Ivo with us."

Vincenzo forced his blade through Caelian's shoulder, the Guardian squirming and gasping beneath it. "I'll leave you to it, then." He tugged his sword free, leaving Caelian in a bloody pile on the floor.

Ivo trembled as she ran, clearly terrified about their narrow escape. Sima frowned, glancing behind them to see if any Guardians followed. Relief washed over her at the empty space that greeted her eyes.

"The bridge from Innamorati to Iridicenza has been closed since the day you left. There is a hole, making it unsafe to walk on. We are going to need you to fly us across, Vincenzo," Ivo said.

"One at a time," Sima added. "There's no use risking an injury this soon."

"I agree," he said, meeting her gaze. "Ivo first, then you."

"Yes," Sima replied.

At the end of the hallway, through an open archway, was a sturdy bridge. Crafted of obsidian compacted beneath sheets of peach aventurine tiles, the bridge offered a passageway between the two islands. A glass enclosure eclipsed the guardrails, sealing the bridge from the sky. Spanning the entire width of the bridge was a gaping circular hole, cracks shooting across the floor.

"May I?" Vincenzo gestured his intention to pick her up. Ivo agreed, and once in his arms, Vincenzo's wings lifted them a foot above the ground. He took her across, not glancing down as he passed the hole. He placed Ivo on the stone of the passageway.

Sima chewed on her thumbnail as she waited, glancing back every so often. Anxious thoughts peppered her mind, shouting at her that failure was imminent. Before she could break beneath the weight of it, Vincenzo returned.

"My Queen," Vincenzo said, holding his arms out to her. "Your chariot awaits."

His embrace was comforting around her body. She held onto him as he lifted them above the ground. As they neared the hole, Sima tensed, averting her eyes. His wings trembled, painful waves causing them to dip closer to the floor, unable to carry them. Blood dripped down his back as he tossed Sima from his arms.

Sima slid onto the stone ground beside Ivo. Vincenzo collided with the crystal tiles, wings twitching between his shoulders. Sima stepped, only to find herself stopped by Ivo. Loud cracks emanated from the failing bridge as it gave way beneath him.

A deafening scream exploded from Cosima as Vincenzo fell from the sky.

Chapter 26

His body froze—Vincenzo halfway through the hole—his weak, injured wings helpless. Sima cursed herself for not realizing carrying the two of them would be too much for his still recovering body. Sima's hands shook as she held them in front of her, pausing time with a tendril of magic.

"Breathe," she instructed herself. "Breathe."

Sima glanced at Ivo, who was also unmoving beside her. Her brain flew through remedies for the situation. A change in Fate would drain whatever was left of her power until her stores replenished, but doing nothing would have Vincenzo plummeting toward the surface with no way to keep himself from colliding with the ground.

Threads found their way into her hands, and in the same way Cosima had saved Vel and Indigo in the Palace, she stitched a resolution into the world around them. The repairing of objects was simpler. Often the universe around them demanded only a substitute in its place, not undoing the damage, but simply diverting it into a different host. The bridge leading from Innamorati to Iridicenza was one of two bridges, the other leading from Innamorati to Perpetuo, the third island.

Sima swallowed hard and made the change.

As her eyes fluttered open, Vincenzo lay bloodied on unmarred peach aventurine and obsidian, the damage redirected successfully.

She rushed to him, no longer fearful of the weight of her footsteps along the tiles on the bridge. She released her hold on time, her two companions in motion once again. Vincenzo groaned as he turned onto his side.

"What happened?"

Sima grabbed onto him, inspecting his wings. The skin along the outer corners pulled back, revealing muscle, blood, and tissue beneath. She winced, turning to face him.

"You are hurt. There was damage to the bridge, and I—well, I moved it. Vincenzo, I should have done it first. I should have known you couldn't carry the both of us. I don't know what I was thinking."

"Shh," Vincenzo said, "You can lament another time. For now, we need to make it to the Astral Atheneum."

"My stores are completely empty. If there is anything that requires my magic, I won't be able to help again."

"We won't need it," Ivo said behind her. "We will find our way out of this."

Vincenzo tipped his head in agreement.

Sima and Ivo offered the Guardian their support as he stood up, wings shivering in pain behind him.

"At least they're moving," Vincenzo said. "Sensation and movement mean they're still attached to me."

"We need to hurry." Ivo bit her lip. "What if the other Guardians catch up with us?"

"While I was going down, I heard the Guardian we left behind communicating the direction we fled. It is only a matter of time before they find us or figure out where we are going."

"The Atheneum is nearby, but if we take a different route, there is a lesser chance of us being caught." Ivo pulled Sima by her hand down a passageway to the left, gray stone blocking out the night sky from the bridge. Vincenzo followed loyally behind them, trusting Ivo to lead them to safety, all without complaint over the throbbing pain.

As they spiraled through endless hallways and turns, Sima's heart thumped loudly inside her chest.

I won't go back.

The words were incessant, an affirmation of the reality she was carving for herself. She was no longer a victim, she would sooner die than obey another command from the King. The ability to decide without coercion or threat was fresh, yet undeniably vital to the version of herself that emerged once the taste of freedom danced upon her tongue.

"Here," Ivo ducked down a hallway with two massive golden doors crafted of tourmalinated quartz. The ornate entrance towered feet above them, garnished with expertly crafted suns and stars among beds of delicate swirls and spirals of metal. The door handles were made of solid angelite crystal, capped on each end of the cylinders with shimmering moonstone.

"Even the gate inside the servants' tunnels looks like this?" Vincenzo touched the adorning metal, then knocked against the tourmalinated quartz. "This thing must be half a foot thick, at least."

"It's new. The construction on the Astral Atheneum was interrupted, so this is all the progress they've made, beyond minor demolition projects to clear the perimeter to make room for more statues of the King."

"Self-absorbed, pompous jerk." The words fell without Sima's intention, her fists curling. "How do we get inside?"

Ivo pointed to the top of the door, where a slender gap was barely visible above the door. "I will go inside, unlock it, and open the door for you both. Like I mentioned before, the warding is down for all but the top level. The King isn't concerned with keeping our planet's records secure, but that is to our advantage today."

"To think I was worried when you told me you've been sneaking around the Archipelago."

"The King underestimated my people when he imprisoned us. As if stopping our powers killed our spirits, too," Ivo said. Sima offered Ivo a steady hand as she placed her feet between gaps of golden metal and began climbing. "He'll pay for his insolence."

Sima let loose a small laugh. "My brave friend, you inspire me."

Ivo reached the top, hiking a leg over the thick crystal and through the gap. Her uniform scrunched along her back as she slid through. She offered Sima a small wave before disappearing. Sima tapped her foot and chewed her thumbnail, silently drowning beneath wishes for Ivo's wellbeing. Vincenzo stretched his back by twisting side-to-side, a small frown the only evidence of his discomfort.

"How are you?" she asked softly.

"I will be fine," he said, blowing a lock of hair from his face with a puff of air. "How are you?"

Sima wrapped her arms around herself. "What if there's no information on how to break the bond between me and him inside? He warded only the top level. Wouldn't he hide it away?"

"We won't know until we are inside. I know it's hard for you to be here, especially with the way you returned, but we will make it out of Aeria and back to Ombra. He found you once, but we'll take better precautions. We'll hide you better."

"My body screams at me to flee, but my heart refuses. I fled once and all it did was get Ivo and the others wrapped up in the violence. The next time I step foot in that Palace, I am going to kill him with my own two hands."

Vincenzo nodded. "I understand, and I will fight with my life to bring you the opportunity."

"What he did to *her*..." Sima's voice was hushed. "Ivo is here, saving others, refusing to run, even after what he did to her. You heard Yadira."

Vincenzo's eyes widened. "Yadira."

"What is it?"

Vincenzo shook his head. "It's probably nothing, but we saw her only moments before the King arrived. Perhaps he trailed her."

Sima buried her head in her hands. "When will the nightmare end?"

Clicks on the other side of the door caught their attention. A creak left the hinges on one side of the double doors as they opened. Ivo's cheeks were rosy as she pushed with all her might. Vincenzo took over, holding the door wide as Sima rushed through. He closed it quickly behind them. Ivo latched each of the nine locks along the back.

The hallway before them was lined to the ceiling with stacks of books and loose paper. It made the pathway narrower, and the three walked in a single file line.

"There is a staircase at the end," Ivo said, leading the way. "It will take us to the main level. From there, we will make our way to floor five. Floor six is off-limits. However, floor five may have what we are looking for."

"I'm not sure what exactly we are searching for. Will the answers lie in a book, a scroll, files?" Sima sighed as they began climbing the tourmalinated quartz steps, footsteps echoing through the empty stairwell. "My preparation to one day be queen never involved discussions on ending a royal marriage."

"Don't worry," Ivo said as they reached the top and ventured through the angelite archways. "We will be victorious. There are three of us, and if we work quickly, surely we will have our answers."

The library around them bore the same lavender-painted walls and extensive murals along the ceilings as it did the last time Sima was inside the Atheneum. Bookshelves lined the walls, endless rows of books arranged by color and topic. The floor beneath them, composed of checkerboard ash and walnut wood paneling, clicked softly. Greenery poured from decorative pots littered tastefully throughout.

Floor-to-ceiling windows along the back wall revealed the stars from the night sky. Magic from the Light Reserve lit orbs around the library. Without another word, the three climbed flights of stairs. An unending silence surrounded them. Sima would have once found comfort in it, but instead, the sensation of being watched overtook her. The weight of the risks piled high upon her shoulders as goosebumps lined her arms.

At the fifth level, the architecture changed from elaborate decorative displays to a quiet, subtle ensemble. Here, the shelves touched the ceiling, and no windows brought reminders of the outside. Books filled every inch of their eyesight, regardless of where they turned. Five black and gold marble tables with black wooden chairs sat in the center of the room, neatly covered in books two feet high.

"Where do we begin?" Vincenzo asked, walking up to a table, and flipping open a book. "There are so many."

"Have you heard anything from the other Guardians?" Cosima asked.

"No, they haven't arrived here yet. They are still in the tunnels. I think they thought the door was enough to keep us out."

"It looks like the books are organized by topic, though there is no indication of where they begin and end." Ivo stepped onto a ladder affixed to the edge of the bookshelf. "We will have to read the titles and discern for ourselves if the groupings of text will be meaningful. For example, these here deal with the maintenance of the Archipelago."

"That could be helpful," Cosima walked over to Ivo, scanning the titles. "The Light Reserve is vital to maintaining Aeria. Maybe there is a way to cut him off, even if we can't break the union."

"These along this wall are for the Ombra District, though a lot of them are missing," Vincenzo said.

"That was me," Ivo said sheepishly. "I have been saving what I can, mostly what pertains to my coven, the Hexia."

Sima's eyes stalled over an enormous book with no title along the spine. It was bound in animal leather, rare for books in Haelos. "How old do you think this one is?" She tugged it loose from the wall of texts, straining her arms beneath its weight. "By the Spirit, this is hefty."

She flipped it open, reading the title page within.

"*Tome of Eternity*," she read aloud, "*Section 1: Lessons of Damnation and Arrogance*. What kind of book is this?"

She turned to the first page, skimming the introductory section. It claimed to hold arcane knowledge, a collection of other books bound into one. That explained the uneven nature of the pages, though Sima was curious about the contents more than the book's appearance. A loud bang echoed through the library floor, causing Cosima to drop the book.

"Sorry," Vincenzo said beneath a pile of pages. "The shelves aren't as sturdy as they look."

Sima reached for the Tome, realizing it was open to another lesson, detailing ways to seal the planet from outsiders via the Portale del Regno Stellare. "Wait," she whispered, "could the answer be in here?" As she thumbed through the pages, illustrations of the veil and the archipelago flew by.

"These are instructions on how to rebuild the Archipelago to restore it to the Spirit Goddess's vision upon creation. It says here every planet has an Archipelago crafted by the Goddess."

"Anything on the Light Reserve?" Vincenzo asked, dusting himself off.

"There must be a way to disconnect the King's connection to the power of Aeria. Without tapping into Ambrosi magic, he won't be able to access a majority of locations in the Archipelago." Cosima chewed her lip.

"Huh," Vincenzo said. He bore a strange expression as he scanned the pages.

"What is it?" Cosima asked.

"There is a section about blood heirs. Apparently, by being chosen by the Goddess, you have abilities not granted to anyone, including Aurelio. It mentions something about you being able to pass through barriers, even when others cannot. You can also manipulate the Archipelago with rituals."

"I don't recall anyone telling me of these abilities."

"Is it enough to stop the King?" Ivo gasped.

"Maybe we could secure the library and lock him out." Vincenzo stared down at Sima. "You would be safe here until we come up with a permanent solution."

"We would have to get the King out of Aeria in order to do so," Ivo said, pointing to a section further down the page. "The only way to bar him from the Archipelago—he must leave first. Then a new barrier can be established."

"He left once to find me. Perhaps he would do it again." Sima turned to Ivo. "I can shut down the Light Reserve and draw Aurelio down to the surface of Haelos. Once we are gone, you reverse it, allowing the power from the Ambrosi to resume control. At that point, we will need to get me back to Aeria to finish it."

"Will this really work?" Ivo swallowed tightly. "What if something goes wrong and you can't make it back, either? What if he doesn't follow you?"

"He will," Vincenzo said. "The Guardians say he is on his way here now."

"I knew he would look for me. The Temple at the center of Innamorati is where we go next. If we make it in time, we can perform this ritual and disable it."

"Cosima, you must go *now*." Ivo hurried to a table, using a piece of paper and pen to draw them a map. "Use this. It will take you back to the main island. Take a Vipus and go to Eternita. With these spells, I can bring down the barrier, at minimum. Once you return, all you must do is put it back up and complete the ritual. I will leave the book in the Temple."

"Are you sure?" Cosima's brow furrowed.

"Eternita is safe. It is the one place the King has no access to." Ivo slipped the Tome from Cosima's hands. "I will take care of this. You can trust me."

"How will you make it to the Temple?"

"I am faster than both of you and I have been all over this island. They won't find me. Go, and return once it is safe to reclaim your throne."

Cosima's eyes welled with tears. "You have done enough."

"Repay me when you return, my Queen." Ivo bowed deeply, before running down the stairs with the Tome beneath her arm, leaving Vincenzo and Cosima alone.

Vincenzo and Cosima followed Ivo's instructions, weaving through the halls with speed. Their lungs desperately gasped for air as they ran, breath ragged. Vincenzo's connection to the Guardians indicated they were closing in on the Astral Atheneum from above, unaware of their departure.

"Any Guardians we come across, let me manage them. I am getting stronger, especially after that bit of downtime inside the library."

"Not a chance," Cosima replied, removing her sword from the sheath along her waist. "Not after you almost died on me a second time."

"You sure try hard to keep me alive. You're making me think you like having me around," Vincenzo flashed a bright smile.

Sima rolled her eyes, the corners of her mouth tugging upward. "Maybe." She wondered where Ivo was, if she was safe. Sima frowned.

"She will be all right," Vincenzo said, as their feet crossed from stone to peach aventurine, guiding them back to the main island. "We are drawing the King away, remember? He will follow as long as we show him you're leaving."

"Show him I'm leaving?"

Vincenzo's face went blank as he pressed a finger to his temple. "There are a couple up ahead. Get ready."

Blades met flesh as three Guardians whirled into their path, materializing from shadows. Cosima deflected the one who advanced toward her, returning with offensive swipes of her own. Vincenzo held off the other two, though evidence of his struggle marked his brow with sweat.

The Guardians were stronger, uninjured, and wildly more trained than Cosima. She slowed none, refusing to let doubt interrupt the flow she found. Her magic would not aid her this time, but Sima bet she could outsmart them. When the moment allowed for it, Cosima dove down a hall, becoming familiar with the endless twists and turns of the intricate tunnels.

The pursuing Guardian dragged several feet behind, becoming victim to the confusing layout. The Guardian sped up, running himself directly into Sima's waiting blade, perched at neck level. Gurgling tore from his throat as she wrenched her sword from his skin.

"Cosima," Vincenzo shouted. "Where are you?"

"Here, I'm over here."

"Kill him, or he'll alert the others, if they haven't already."

Sima nodded as Vincenzo flipped the man onto his stomach. The blade came down upon his feathers, leaving his wings in a pile beside the Guardian's corpse. Cosima and Vincenzo ran hand in hand toward the Vipus stables.

As the door flew open, Cosima was thankful to be above ground, drinking fresh air once again. Disbelief washed her extremities in a tingling wave. Without stopping, she inserted the key, revealing the five sleeping Vipus. Snorts and grunts left the creatures when they woke, but luckily, the two they selected easily slipped into saddles.

Sima tugged on the reins. It took three rounds of trial and error before she got the Vipus to respond properly. Vincenzo did the same and launched into the air above her. The one beneath Sima needed little guidance after that, leaping to the sky behind them. The two directed their new winged friends downward toward the Eternita District.

The commands became more intuitive with time, her Vipus more than content to be subjected to the commanding pulls and tugs. They only suddenly descended with terrifying jolts twice before Sima learned precisely what not to do. Vincenzo struggled as much as she did thankfully, the two of them erupting into hysterical laughter.

The cool air blew through her hair, her dark locks flying wildly behind her back, the sensation invigorating. For a second time, Sima had fought for her freedom, and for a second time, she had won. Vincenzo let out a wild whoop as he raised one arm above him, and the creature rolled its body and wings in a spinning dive. Sima let delight penetrate the residual anxiety and adrenaline, forging into it a crazed moment of happiness. She followed suit, laying her body tightly against the neck of her Vipus pulled the reins taut, and sent them barreling straight down toward the surface after Vincenzo. They moved so quickly, Sima almost didn't notice the shadow flicker above them.

Chapter 27

What confidence Sima had uncovered was shredded to pieces as arrows started whistling past them. Vincenzo hollered for Cosima to watch out, but the Vipus moved without command. Her ride instinctively began to serpentine through the air, avoiding metal intent on spearing her wings. Sima knew the arrows flying by them were laced with paralytic, a signature move of the Guardians from Aeria.

"No!" Sima yelled, hugging tighter to her Vipus.

"Don't look back!" Vincenzo's voice was bright with panic. "Keep going. Don't look back."

The two Vipus spiraled through the air as four Guardians strained to keep pace behind them. The Vipus were faster than the Guardians, the distance between them growing, but not quickly enough.

"They are calling for the others to tell the King, our plan is working!" he shouted.

Sima increased her grip on the reins. If the Guardians were alerting the King, there was a chance their plan would unfold successfully, and Aurelio would attempt to follow them.

The ground was fast approaching, the entrance to Eternita within reach. Sima yanked on the reigns and the Vipus craned its neck as it obeyed. The creature's powerful muscles strained, stopping their descent just meters above the tree line. Eternita was heavily forested, unlike the barren lands of Ombra.

Only a small strip of land was available for them to land on. The barrier sealed the rest, preventing outsiders, and the King, from entering. Sima gazed upward as she ran toward the shimmering dusty rose-colored bubble surrounding the District. The bubble in Aeria was only visible as it slammed shut and was invisible at all other times. She reached one hand outward, expecting to be denied entry. Instead, her palm passed right through.

The trees granted them cover, but it would only be a matter of minutes before they were found. "Go," Vincenzo said as he landed beside her. Sima stepped through and warm wind with floral scents accosted her face. Her hair hovered around her as the breeze brushed across her.

"What about you?" Sima said, eyes glued to the movement of brush and leaves in the distance. "He hasn't followed yet."

"It's a long shot, but I told you I maintain some very tense connections with this District…" he trailed off, approaching the bubble in the same manner Cosima had. A breath escaped her as he slid through, both hanging their heads in relief. "Thank the Spirit. Seems those connections are worth more than I thought."

"Are you all right?" she asked finally.

A small cough. "If I am being honest, I don't have much fight left in me. If this didn't work, I thought for sure you'd be dragging my corpse to Ombra later."

"Don't talk like that," she said. "I would have left your dead body behind, and you know it."

That earned her a smile from him. Sima pulled them further into the trees and closer toward the city, unable to relax until she knew they had lost the Guardians hunting them.

"The Guardians after us won't be able to follow us in here, but we might run into trouble." Vincenzo pointed. There were other Rani Guardian walking the streets, strangely wearing armor adorned with Eternita's Crest, and not Aeria's. They looked Vincenzo up and down, but none made any moves toward entering the alleyway.

"Why are they wearing that armor?"

"I wondered that myself," he said, rolling one shoulder in a stretch as he spoke. "Aeria forbids us to don anything other than Aeria regalia. I wonder how long it has been since Aurelio has been here, seeing as how every damn Rani Guardian I see is wearing it."

"Everyone except for you," she pointed out. That would be yet another problem to solve. *He may move around with less suspicion if he fit in.* "Did you notice anything else that's off about them?"

Just as she finished asking, three more walked in front of the entrance to the alley. They behaved similarly to the others, simply making eye contact, scanning them from head to toe, and continuing on their way. A shiver tingled down the middle of her back.

"Do you think they recognize me?"

He shook his head. "I doubt it. The people of Ombra only knew about you because the people of Ombra cared when they heard of the King's captured wife fighting back. The people of Eternita used the confusion and chaos to push their self-interests. Any citizens of the Ombra District devoted to the cause Aurelio considers the enemy, or at the very least, not of importance."

Sima ventured forward, peering around the corner to get a better glimpse of the new world around them. The sight of the city brought tears to her eyes. This city was small in comparison to the other larger ones they saw from the sky, but it was still buzzing with people, even in the middle of the night.

Thankfully, the citizens showed no interest in them, as Faeries of all kinds went about their business. The expertly-crafted city towered above, with fine detailing in every crevice. Trees tied intimately to the infrastructure, and branches snaked around buildings, growing alongside them. Vines sprawled up white columns and across the length of parapets fashioned to the edges of roofs. Sprites zipped past, faint trails of light and sparkle left in their wake. If she weren't so close to vomiting, she might have absorbed the atmosphere more.

Fae built each building with aesthetics in mind, and it was clear the architects of Eternita were not the kind to skimp on details.

They had considered the smaller Faeries, too, and intricately carved designs lined the bottom of the walls beside tiny doors. Those in this District lived in pure ecstasy, life bursting from all angles, alive as though nature itself had aided in the construction of this place.

Cosima spotted two Fae children with delicately pointed ears. The Fae sourced their magic from the world around them and considered themselves to be the protectors of nature. This vast, unfamiliar environment overwhelmed Sima's senses.

She pressed her back against the wall of the alleyway and sank to the ground. Cosima stared into the empty space before them, breath leaving her in small shakes. She angled her face toward the sky.

"How do you know me? When I touched your Fate in the prisons, I saw your past. You were looking at some kind of painted picture of me." Cosima planted her gaze firmly on her feet. She was tired.

He sighed, joining her against the wall. Sima's arms wrapped around her knees. She angled her face away from him, hoping to conceal her tears. The warmth of his hand on her shoulder was more comforting than she wanted it to be. Everything that had transpired between them felt like proof she would never be free of Aurelio.

"You are not from Haelos, not like the Ambrosi who are born here," he said, his deep voice ladened with caution. "You're here more like how Ostrum or Doc are here. *In* this world, but not *of* it."

She lifted her head, sniffling as she turned toward him.

"You come from the Eternal Kingdom, but you wouldn't tell me more than that. We met secretly, and I thought it was because you were ashamed of me."

He smiled, his eyes glossy from the tears that jumped free from his lashes. "You were so beautiful, just like you are now. I couldn't keep myself from talking to you. I knew my place. It's the same there as it is on Aeria. Rani are nothing, less than nothing. We are bred to die for you, not bred to love you. But I did, Sima. You loved me, too."

Sima joined him in shedding tears, the banging on the distant wall in her mind as loud as ever. Even if she couldn't remember, there was not a part of her that sensed he was lying. Since their first meeting, Vincenzo had drawn her in—in ways she could not deny.

"How did I get here?"

"You were taken, Sima," Vincenzo said, grief in every word. "Someone took you from me, two days before we planned to run away together." Another pained sob bit back by teeth. "After you went missing, I threw myself into training while the Eternal Kingdom sent Scouts to search for you. Even they wouldn't reveal your true identity to me."

"The day you were called to come to Haelos," Sima said softly.

"I felt unprepared when I got the blue slip. Then, I came here, not expecting to find you so quickly. I thought about marching right through the doors of his office and skinning him, but he is stronger than me, physically. So, I bid my time, focused on becoming stronger and keeping the Ombra District as safe as I could manage. I couldn't risk you getting in the crosshairs until I had an army behind me."

His hand on her shoulder pulled her closer to him as he rested his forehead against hers.

"The reason they sent me to Ombra, in my mind, is because he saw the way I looked at you. He saw the way I looked at *him* when I saw those bruises on you. I was still too weak to take him on with the way he's slain my kin. Being in Ombra—it benefited me. It gave me purpose, it gave me wisdom and techniques. Then I saw what they thought of you. I knew then I couldn't give up. These people mirrored what you meant to me, so I took care of them. I loved them because they were the type of people who loved *you*."

She swallowed hard, the lump in her throat not budging. Tears streamed from both of their eyes, but she couldn't stop herself. She had denied the million impulses to do it before. She wouldn't wait any longer. Her hands wrapped around his face, pulling him fiercely into a kiss. He kissed her back with a mirrored appetite, wrapping her in his arms and pinning her tightly to his chest. His body was rigid, tense from all that had occurred, but it softened ever so slightly against her touch.

It snuffed out the fire burning on pain, replacing it with a softer ember of hope. She had lost everything once before, and then again, when she had left Aurelio. He kissed gently along her neck, breathing in her scent before planting his lips flush against her warm skin.

If the moon hadn't lit the alleyway above them with her lunar rays, perhaps they would've stayed there longer, entwining themselves in safety for the first time. However, there was no safety, only illusions of such. They were in a foreign city. Ivo was to disable the Light Reserve, and they were to draw in the King.

She stole another small kiss before he pulled away, offering her hand up once he was standing.

"You always make the plans," Vincenzo said, brushing a lock of her hair away from her face. "Would you oppose me taking over for once?"

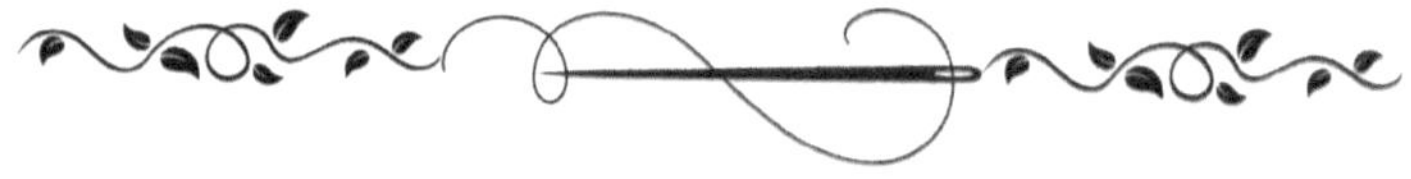

Sima's screams thundered through the city, tears streaming down her face as she beat her fists on his chest.

"Don't do it," she slurred between fits of screaming rage and outright sobbing. "I have nowhere to go! Oh, please," she said, going completely limp in his arms, resulting in him dragging her kicking body by her jacket collar down the street.

Curious eyes peeked behind curtains, but once they spotted Vincenzo—rather, once they spotted a *Rani*— they were content that the situation was being dealt with. Enough reactions like that, and Sima would start believing his plan was going to work.

She amped up the theatrics, calling Vincenzo all kinds of mean names and insinuating insults about his manhood, as a group of armed Rani sauntered past.

"You really got the short end of the stick on clean up," one jested, adding, "This is why we stopped granting access to the human District."

Vincenzo simply dropped his chin, embarrassed to be the one who had to deal with this mess. As long as she threw a fit this public, other Rani would be hard-pressed to get close enough to be associated with her. Besides, they thought she was human and weak.

"If he can get her that far before she snaps on him," another said, not even bothering to turn her head toward them as she walked arm-in-arm with another. "Ones who put up that big of a fight nowadays are always bat-shit. Don't they say coyotes chew their own legs off when trapped?"

The others laughed, their voices harder to hear over her own bawling as the distance between them increased. He bristled, just barely, enough to tell her they were in the clear. Sima raised her head, spotting the prison entrance.

It was indoors, at least.

Though Eternita's Guardians did not wear Aeria armor, their ranks were the same as in Aeria, which aided Vincenzo in knowing which type of guard was behind him. Insignias across their chests bore the telltale artwork of the Ambrosi. They approached the group just outside the prison and Sima continued the theatrics, dropping to her knees.

"Please. Don't send me back!" Cosima sobbed.

"Another jobless human, depending on Eternita for everything. Typical. You're lucky Eternita is a gracious land," he taunted, kicking his boot into her thigh. "Usually, they don't beg for the cells as nice as you." The few Fae around looked as if they couldn't be bothered to help, tilting their noses up and averting their gazes.

Vincenzo walked in front of her, leading her with chains, tugging hard enough to send her stumbling forward. All a part of the show. She didn't need him to reassure her of that. There were three guards with them, one in front of Vincenzo and two behind them.

The tantrums stopped. Only small sniffles escaped her now. One guard looked back at them, sneering at the sight of her. She gave back a toothy grin, one that made him swivel forward immediately. Vincenzo hid his smile, muscles flexing in his jaw.

As the cell door opened, it was time for her to truly let loose.

She bucked with might into the Rani, leading her inward, the crunch of the cartilage in his nose delicious in her ears. She bucked again, this time earning some teeth to the back of her head.

"That hurt," she laughed as he fell onto his back. She straddled him, still giggling as she wrapped the chain binding her wrists around his head. Seeing what was incoming, he tried to fight it. Sounds of the fight the two guards gave Vincenzo echoed through the small cell.

"You crazy bitch!" he yelled. "Get her off me, one of you, get her off me!"

Sima gazed up at Vincenzo from the purpling Rani Guardian beneath her. He was clumsy and uncoordinated as he tried to fight her off, fumbling and hesitating every chance he got to attack her back. Sima was not skilled. She had picked up some tricks in Ombra, but this guard was as lazy and out of shape as the Emblems.

"Glad everyone here has such a comfortable life," she murmured, flashing wild eyes at him, relishing the way she saw it frightened him. Then it happened, her magic suddenly flooding her mind with memory.

Sima saw a young Fae girl walking arms linked with another. Their blond hair swished behind them as they walked, their dresses catching the light with shimmers of gold and olive. What he did next had Sima scratching for the surface, blindly raging toward killing him with her bare hands for the blood he had shed.

He was a monster, not the man of honor he paraded as. The girls hadn't even settled into immortality. He took their lives, hurt them, and went to work every day like he wasn't a murderer. She hated men who took what they wanted no matter who got hurt in their pursuit of it.

Depraved creatures.

She did not have the time to sit and sort through his life. No immediate strings held an answer that was promising. Others seemed willing to allow his sinister actions to continue. Sima decided it would end in this moment, one way or another. She could not go back and take their pain away or reverse death, but she could put down a predator.

Maybe it was the white-hot anger coursing through the riverbeds of her veins, or maybe it was the banging against the wall in her mind again, but she wanted it to end, for him to die already.

Once her eyes rolled back into place and time resumed, Sima gave him a little taste of his own medicine. Opening her jaws as wide as she could, she clamped down around the soft flesh of his throat, tearing at it with her teeth. They sunk into his skin, yet still she clamped harder.

She would make sure she filled the last few moments of his life with agony.

Vincenzo's shadow appeared on the ground before them, Sima looking up like a predator snapping the neck of its prey. He wiped his bloodied sword against his pant leg before motioning towards her with it.

"Want me to get him?"

Reluctantly, she let go. Vincenzo killed him, and the two began stripping their corpses. Once inside the Guardian's clothing, Sima felt at ease. The armor was too large, but it was warm. Vincenzo slipped his wings through slits along the back, the fabric taut along the skin connecting them to his body. Monstrous scabs surrounded his injuries, a gruesome but welcome sign his body was actively attempting to heal.

"What's your plan now?" she asked.

"I say we make our way to the Executioner's Office. From there, we should be able to obtain enough information about this District to make our way to the Fae Palace up north. I want to get us close to the Queen. I've had my fill of running around in the dark. If you are going to be taking back Aeria, perhaps we can come to an agreement about how this place will run."

Sima nodded slowly. The Queen of Eternita was the same person Aurelio had sent Cosima after not long ago. He had accused Solara of allowing crystals imbued with magic to flood into the human world. "I think that is a wise decision."

They jogged up the steps, stopping at the command room they

spotted on the way in. It held four to five guards at a time, but only one chair sat at the desk. She snagged slips of paper tossed across the tabletop. It appeared to be the list of inmates, as well as a schedule for the Guardians on patrol.

Before they left, Vincenzo gave the room a once-over, double-checking for anything important they might have missed. Sima glanced around, her vision narrowing on a notebook with the words "Discipline Log" written across the top. Sima flipped it open and read the contents. The guards geared every punishment toward physical pain and psychological humiliation. Sima's stomach turned as she slammed it shut.

"Something strange is going on here. The Guardians wear the crest of Eternita. They treat any humans within their walls horribly, and now this." She gestured to the log. "It's disturbing what the men get away with inside these prisons."

"This place receives shipments of inmates from the bigger cities twice a week," Vincenzo said. "This cell block spans miles underground. It seems Ombra wasn't the only District that made use of hiding beneath the surface. This schedule marks a shift change. Some Guardians are due to rotate back to the main city. Their replacements will relieve them within twenty minutes."

Remaining out of sight was made easier by their possession of the schedule. The Guardians had handed them a silver platter by detailing their every scripted move at the top of a map of the grounds. She would make them pay for their callousness, their complacency. The entire first floor was made up of the temporary holding cells, the space and equipment needed for processing and documenting incoming prisoners, and the room where the Rani would leave their belongings at the start of their shifts.

Inside it, jovial voices told her they were unaware of what was happening in the prisons below—at least for now. A sword sat propped against the outside door, placed there haphazardly by whatever guard had sauntered in last. Their loss was her gain, her fingers wrapping around the hilt as her other hand guided it into the sheath on the dead Rani's belt.

Part of her wished that rising up against her husband did not come with the death of so many Rani, especially when Vincenzo was the entire reason she made it this far. Defending her, aiding her, fighting beside her, it all required slaughtering his comrades in the process. She wondered if it bothered him as she made a dash for the stairs leading upward to the top floor, wondered if whatever they had before was worth all the pain and turmoil he went through to get her back.

Vincenzo halted at the entrance to the Executioner's quarters. The flowery detailing carved into the wood contrasted with the dreadful acts carried out in the rooms, Sima arching a brow as she examined it. The work on the wood panels consisted of intricate hand-carvings, offset only by the silver door handles, which bore one large lock.

Something in her screamed with alarm as voices trailed from inside the room. She turned to Vincenzo, who stood with his fingers pressed to his head, face unreadable. "Stand back," he whispered.

The door opened, and before them stood a Rani Guardian. The Rani made no outward signs that she was making eye contact with Sima in a dead Guardian's uniform. Sima was sure her pulse was audible as her body froze. Behind the woman was a round table littered with empty bottles of wine and playing cards, and another Guardian who laughed as he stood up.

Vincenzo and the woman locked eyes in an intense stare.

"Time for shift change," she said, simply brushing shoulders with Sima as she walked to the main floor. The other Guardian emerged, peering behind her.

He, too, cemented his gaze on Vincenzo. After a moment, he turned to Sima. "What, did they run out of your size or something?"

"Something like that," Sima said plainly.

"Whatever," he said, waving a hand to the Executioner as he exited. "Same time tomorrow."

It wasn't until the door locked behind them that Sima realized why her gut was warning her this entire time that something was wrong.

Chapter 28

The Executioner was not sitting in his office, like Cosima was expecting. Instead, his head was sitting, still trickling blood, atop the desk. A monstrous portrait of him hung behind the desk, a mockery of the scene before her. Above the red ribbons lay pale gray skin, pointed ears, and wisps of black hair. His eyes were closed, the muscles in his face lax. It was a pristine office, beautifully decorated despite the nature of his occupation. Perhaps the meticulous design distracted him from the despicable acts he carried out every day—or, Cosima reasoned, better hid his true nature.

Sima reigned in her reaction to the sight, wondering how she hadn't spied any sign of this on the Guardians. She swallowed a scream, of frustration or horror, it didn't matter. Yadira sat twirling a knife, slivers of mahogany spiraling from the hole formed in the tabletop, her ankles resting upon a stack of papers.

"Cosima, my friend," Yadira smirked, wings fluttering behind her in wide, slow swings. "It seems we have finally caught up to one another. It wasn't very nice of you to flee like that, on the back of a Vipus, no less. Though, I wish you knew how it felt to truly fly, your soul intertwined with open air."

Yadira was in polished golden armor, one reserved for the King's most favored Guardians. Along her deep brown skin were shiny black cracks, sprawling beneath her eyes and trickling down her neck. Her eyes were bloodshot and empty in a way that unnerved Sima.

"It was *you?*" Vincenzo growled. "What happened to you?"

"What have you done?" Cosima took a shivering step forward, hands trembling wildly before her.

"I did what was necessary. The Eternita District has restricted access to the King, and more so, are harboring two traitors. Our devout leader has ascertained a way through these barriers, and I am proof of its success."

Cosima's breath stalled at the base of her throat. She swallowed stiffly. Hurt washed the tips of sore muscles, burning in Yadira's betrayal. Sima slid a lock of midnight behind her ear, drawing in a breath. "Why are you here, Yadira? I will not go back. You know this."

"Turns out," she said, sitting up, "you can be quite useful. Shame to waste all that potential by killing you. I will bring you back alive."

"You are the one who brought me to the surface of Haelos for the first time. Why would you change your mind now? I have this whole new life to live, and you're telling me I will have to do it without my friend by my side?"

"Friendships are nothing when it comes to the greater good of Haelos."

"What are you talking about? You didn't agree with Aurelio either. What has gotten into you? Is it something he did to you? We are on the verge of figuring this out, I can feel—"

"There is no keeping safe from him, you fool. I refused to acknowledge it, but that didn't keep it from being true. I was just a small little rat in Aeria, living a plush life. Unbeknown to me, my pathetic feet were traipsing atop devastating secrets. I believed my transfer to Ombra meant the chance for better days on the horizon. I was merely a pawn in a much bigger game. Tell me, how do you know which enemy is your greatest? Can light adjudicate the depraved desires of demons? Is it worth it to persevere? Should we cease our hold on existence?"

"Our hold on existence? Why are you talking like that? Yadira, whatever secrets you've uncovered, we can expose them together. Our enemy right now is Aurelio. He forced you to endure his acrimony the same as me. He does not care for the people of Haelos. Your mission is to protect the people of this world, the whims of the weak-willed, and their traditions be damned. Why give up when we are so close?"

Sima's knees buckled beneath her. A grueling desire to vent her frustrations overcame her, one she could not heed. Yadira was no longer a friend, no matter the reason she had drawn this line in the sand.

"Ombra is more than underground tunnels and festivities, Cosima. There are contraptions there that have no business being in the hands of Guardians and sorcerers. How did the mission convolute into allowing the weaker people of Haelos to run rampant with lethal magic?"

"Weaker people? You really believe yourself to be above them?"

"No, friend. I know myself to be above them, for I must be to guide them. How can I show them the path by which my own eyes are not privy? I am a shepherd, as all my kind before me. Believe me capable of divine will, and I shall show them inviolability."

"You don't sound like yourself, Yadira." Vincenzo slid his blade from its sheath.

"How can I be?" she spat. Brown curls pooled before her face as she slumped forward. "With everything I know now, how can I go back?" A breath calmed her, before she began again, "Vincenzo brainwashed you into thinking he persuaded those Guardians to keep his secret. He indoctrinated them! You know what they call him in training?"

"That is enough, Yadira. Stop talking," Vincenzo's command was rough across his tongue, intertwined with heavily leashed anger.

"They call him the Hive, because he can summon a thousand little worker bees, all thinking and feeling in one gigantic mass. They all have come to realize he left them with distorted recollections of what transpired in Ombra. They couldn't spill his secret if they wanted to. Why do you think someone like that would have worked so hard to make sure we became friends, hm?"

Cosima shook her head, staring in disbelief at Vincenzo.

"It's not what you think. I promise you I can explain all of this after we secure Aeria."

Yadira laughed. "Convenient, isn't it? He will divulge as soon as the Crown graces his skull."

"I am not interested in any throne. Do not speak about what you are too small to understand."

Sima blinked at his word choice. *Too small.* "What is that supposed to mean?"

Yadira used the tip of her bloody knife to clean beneath her fingernails. "No wonder Aurelio easily trapped you into performing his bidding. You follow so blindly! He is *very* interested in leading, just not the Archipelago or Below. He wishes to rule the Eternal Kingdom. That is his entire prophecy. Did you not see that?"

She left Sima lost for words. Her mind flicked back to the pieces of his fate that were unalterable, the very prophecy Yadira was referring to. She shook her head, the shock not dissipating.

"If you don't stop," Vincenzo said, pointing his sword at Yadira, "I will make you."

"Let me be the one to enlighten you, since we're such good pals. Aurelio is one of twelve brothers, all born with the same destiny, filled with powers we cannot even comprehend. Every conniving one of them is fixated on ruling the Eternal Kingdom. Only one can rule, the other eleven must be slain. Vincenzo plans to lead you into the same trap, though he will use you to kill Aurelio."

Comprehension escaped Cosima. "Use me to kill Aurelio?"

Vincenzo's lip curled in a snarl. "That's not true. I will kill him myself if I have to."

"How many brothers remain beside you and Aurelio?"

Cosima turned to Vincenzo, sweat slipping down the side of his face in broad streaks. "Brothers?" Cosima's voice was soft, barely above a whisper. "You're his…brother?"

"We were never going to be free. Vincenzo was using you all

the same as the King. Each with an agenda, a sickly ulterior motive."

"It's not what you think," Vincenzo said, refusing to meet her gaze. His eyes remained locked on Yadira. "I promise I have no malicious intentions toward you, Cosima."

"This whole time? Which brother are you?"

"The baby brother he would happen to be." Yadira's teeth flashed brilliantly beneath her full lips as she smiled, clearly enjoying the pain marking Sima's face.

Vincenzo's jaw tightened. "I'm his half-brother. We share a mother, but another man sired all eleven other brothers."

"Your wings, your memories of being a Guardian…"

"I'm sorry," his eyes flicked to her for a moment. They were taut with grief. "It wasn't supposed to come out like this. What did Aurelio tell you, Yadira?"

Yadira erupted into maniacal laughter. "We *all* thought you were a Guardian. He is tenacious and thoughtful. How many centuries do you think he has been planning this? He told me everything, your entire history."

"How could you hide this from me?" Cosima drew her own blade, poised in Vincenzo's direction. Emotions tangled into an indescribable mess within her, dampened further by overwhelming shock.

Yadira's face went completely blank as her eyes rolled back into her head. Vincenzo dropped his sword as his hands flew to his ears, covering them, as he fell to his knees. Gasps of pain left his mouth.

Cosima's heart rattled her rib cage, unsure if she should come to his aid. "Stop it, make it stop! Don't kill him!"

Yadira's eyes returned to normal. Vincenzo sucked in air as he struggled to get to his knees. "It requires energy of unparalleled magnitude to kill him or any of the Sacred Twelve. They are descended from the Goddess, born of the womb of Ehses. Aurelio laid it out for me in great detail." She swallowed hard. "That's when he started pulling back the skin on my hands." Reflexively, her fingers ran calming strokes across them, faint scars along her flesh.

"If he knew it was me, then why didn't he just kill me?"

"He wanted to leave you to die slowly," Cosima said, "To force me to bear witness."

Yadira sighed. "Yes, quite the man for dramatics. That being said, it is time for us to return, my friend."

The sound of Sima's blood pumping wildly through her veins echoed in her bones. "I refuse to go back. I have tasted freedom, and even the tallest prison walls couldn't keep me from finding it again."

Yadira wiped a rogue tear from her cheek, her other hand gripping the hilt of her dagger. "I loved you as a sister, Sima. Why did he have to take that from me? Will my wings smolder in a fireplace, too? How many will die for your selfishness?"

Cosima shook her head. "You endured days at Aurelio's hand while I suffered for *fifty years*. Did you know the Guardians I killed deserved it? Do you know what kind of depravity I witnessed?"

"Only more will follow. This world is not worth saving—or better, I should say it will not survive, whether we fight for it or let it perish. The King spends his time wisely, and while on Haelos, he has been preparing for pandemonium on an unbelievable scale."

"Don't listen to her. We will free ourselves from him." Vincenzo once again gripped his sword, though he seemed wary.

"So noble of you to care about those at the bottom of the food chain. I'm sure the politics never end for you, do they?" Yadira picked at her teeth with a nail. "You cannot comprehend what the King is doing beneath all of your noses. I found out the hard way."

Breath left Cosima's lungs as Yadira stood, unhooking her chest plate to reveal a blood-soaked white shirt beneath. When she lifted it, Sima gagged as Yadira revealed a large, stitched wound spanning the length of her entire abdomen.

"Gruesome, isn't it? This is how I slipped through." Yadira poked a finger through her own flesh between sutures, poking roughly at her insides. "Aurelio's newest experiment, and I was the first successful host."

"Host for what exactly?" Vincenzo furrowed his brow.

"Four lively crystals in a thick glass shell." Yadira tapped on her stomach. "All sewn nicely into place."

Confusion hit Cosima first, before it cracked into something with more of an edge. Sima was crumbling internally, as if every piece she had put carefully into place was falling into her core all at once. The ridges of safety she had grown accustomed to were slipping through her fingertips. Her hands balled into fists.

"How?" was the only thing Vincenzo asked in response, his eyes wide and frantic.

"I would rather die than go back," Cosima whispered. Alarm rang through Sima, and instead of waiting around for what Yadira, and Aurelio, had planned for her, Sima used a morsel of her power to slow time. She spirited through the door, before releasing her hold on the others as she ran.

"Where are you going?" Yadira growled behind her. A noisy squelch from the snap of bone into brain chased the sound of Yadira's blade slamming through the thick skull of the Executioner.

Sima fled, willing her feet to move faster as she scurried down the steps, intent on taking her chances back out in the city surrounding the prisons. Neither Vincenzo nor Yadira followed, though faint sounds of a scuffle trailed behind her until she reached the outside. She was unsure how to accept that Vincenzo was the brother of her mortal enemy. The memory of their kiss was now slimy, unrecognizable. Whatever bond they had was stitched of deceit.

Sima noticed the shadow in the sky above her, one set of wings trailing her. *Yadira or Vincenzo?*

It didn't matter. The blended crystals inside of Yadira left her victim to Aurelio's wishes, and Vincenzo shared his blood. Sima would gnaw the flesh off any piece of her body restrained beneath metal. She would not return to the King. She hoped for Ivo's safety back on the sky islands and continued toward the houses built on the ground directly above the cells.

Feet loyally followed the map they had seen prior to reaching the Executioner's office as she left the prisons behind her. Sima had taken excruciating mental note of everything around her on the way in and easily found the correct path. It was not a complex route, though her muscles begged for rest, not from fatigue, but from inner turmoil. She blinked away tears, staring hard at the wings above her through its shadow beside her.

Cosima had earned her freedom and rebuilt her life, facing uncertainty with courage. She had reformed broken walls within herself, treacherously, even when progress was slow. She had protected herself, even when held in Aurelio's grasp, even when reality was full of hallucinations and drug-fueled binges. The agony almost made her miss those times. They were horrendous, but they were certain. Sima played wife how she needed to, and coped how she could. The unknown at one time was enough to scare her into submission.

Was I just Vincenzo's cheap attempt at stealing the King's greatest weapon?

Her hands trembled into balled fists at her side, feet plundering forward, unwilling and unable to stop. It was so familiar to her, this moment in time. Fear gripped her, filling like viscous fluid in every bit of free space inside her body. Sima dropped to one knee, her head bowed. She allowed her dark hair to flush out the light of the day beginning to break across the mountains.

One breath. Two. Three.

The winged shadow came upon her again, and Sima's staggered inspirations came in heavy waves as she twisted skyward. Yadira floated there, her golden armor glinting like the sun at its highest peak. Images berated her mind as she rose, dirt covering the armor she bore.

One breath. Two. Three.

There was no request for her magic, yet still it came in unpredictable waves. The onslaught of images did nothing to slow Sima. Either Yadira would kill her, or she would get to where she needed to go. Strength met bone, energy met muscle. She powered onward, refusing to dwell on why it was Yadira above her, and not Vincenzo.

The subject of her search came into view. The records in the office of recently released inmates had listed her target's address as one only a few blocks from the prison. They reserved those homes for faeries attempting to reintegrate into Eternita after release, the threat of being submerged beneath the surface again, one they could not forget. Beneath every step, only vertical distance and soil kept the former prisoners from captivity.

The sheet detailing the prisoners and their crimes had initially given Cosima the idea, though she never imagined she would follow through on the plan alone, without Vincenzo's help. Again, tears fought against her eyelids, threatening to stop her in her tracks. She was only minutes from reaching it when another set of wings took to the sky. The shadows danced around each other, the battle continuing.

One breath. Two. Three.

Sima yearned to turn around, to remove the crystals controlling her friend at whatever the cost. Yadira's aid had led Cosima directly to her destiny, even if she, too, worked for the King now. The interior of the house, what Kismet held next for her, Cosima was unaware, but intuition guided her through the modest wooden gate at the front of the small property.

Yadira and Vincenzo drew nearer, Vincenzo shouting at Cosima to wait for him. Sima ignored his pleas as she bolted for the front door.

"Please, listen to me. I will explain the best I can, give me a chance!" Vincenzo hollered from feet above her. Metal collided with metal as the two launched at each other relentlessly.

"Come with me, Cosima," Yadira taunted, "Save your people from the King's wrath in the way only you can. Let's go home."

Home.

The word tugged at Cosima's might, a foreign, ill-fitting descriptor of the torment she endured for half of a century. "Leave me alone!" Cosima barked.

An arrow flew past her, lodging itself inches from her head into the side of the home. Wood splintered the air around Sima. She ducked, shielding her head with her arm as a hand wrapped around the brass doorknob. She threw open the door, her foot narrowly crossing the threshold as Vincenzo and Yadira landed.

Chapter 29

"Who the fuck are you?"

It was the appropriate way to treat someone barging into his home. In fact, she didn't blame him for being freaked out. He took one look at her face and nearly fainted. She rolled her eyes, slamming the door.

"Enchantments—you have enchantments, right? Seal the door. We have to seal the fucking door, the windows—just for like five minutes!" Sima started pushing furniture in front of the door, completely ignoring the fact that the paint covered man looked ready to pee his pants.

"I have—" He stumbled to his feet, still weak in the knees. "I have some, I have—why are you here? Who's out there?"

"Simon, you're Simon," she said, blowing a piece of hair out of her face. "Come here and help me with this, or get the damn enchantments, please."

His footsteps receded down the hall before he came back with a small vial.

"That's *it?*"

"It'll buy us maybe ten minutes. If we're lucky. I don't really need this sort of thing here." Simon paced back and forth, running trembling hands through his jet-black hair. Smooth brown eyes were visible beneath large-framed glasses, balancing on his small nose. He wore plain tan pants and a burgundy top with holes in it.

"Yes, you do," she said, frowning as her eyes settled on his latest works. One a half complete portrait of *her*, which explained why he nearly shit himself when he saw her. The other was another monster, similar to the ones she saw during the Day of Return. The creature was in the middle of eating what remained of a woman.

This is what he is seeing in his head?

He followed her gaze. "Is this why you're here? I'm sorry, I just paint what I see. I can't help it."

Sima poured the potion in front of the door, reading the instructed phrases listed on the side. It bubbled and smoked before it exploded in a flash of light. When Sima opened her eyes, the enchantment masked the windows and doors on the outside of the house in rosy pink panels of magic.

"This is exactly what got you arrested, isn't it? Anti-Aeria propaganda, they called it on your sheet."

He looked down. "Yeah, something like that. I can't help it. It just comes to me. It's impossible for me to resist the urge to paint it, sketch it, mold it, whatever it takes. I have to share them, to make them real."

"You're the prophet the Guardians on the Archipelago were talking about."

"Prophet is a heavy word. I'm not sure it's appropriate. I have visions, but sometimes I wonder if it's a torture method more than a blessing."

His explanation sparked something strange in her, but Cosima had minutes, not hours or days, to sit here and decipher his words. "You're human, right? How did you end up in Eternita?"

He chewed on his lip. "They stole me from the Prisma District. They told me it would save me from being found and destroyed by the King of Aeria—your husband, I guess—and instead, they threw me into the prison."

"Soon to be *ex*-husband," Sima murmured.

"The Eternal Kingdom put Ambrosi here to protect this land, to protect Haelos. What do they do instead? Drink wine, take days off, fuck each other stupid at parties? While people on the other side of that wall—" he jutted a finger toward Ombra, "are suffering and dying, being picked off one by one slowly, and no one is doing anything."

"I am trying to put an end to this, but I need your help. You must know something the others don't. Those running this District are watching you in whatever capacity they can manage. Your knowledge is priceless."

He softened a fraction, opening his mouth and then shutting it. He stared down at his painting of her. Although it was half-finished, she could see that it was yet another with the vacant look in her eye.

"Why do you paint me like that? Like I'm made of wax or something, not a real person."

"This is the only way I have ever seen you," he said quietly, averting his eyes. "The images of you have been coming to me since I was a child. I kept painting. I kept trying to show the world what was happening because of King Aphelion. Instead, I made myself a target."

"Have you seen anything about crystals?"

He nodded, rummaging through a pile of paintings as he spoke. "The human lands, the Prisma District, are mountainous. In order to move from settlement to settlement, one must brave the rocky terrain and scale the sides of gigantic cliffs. Before I was born, humans gave their weapons to the previous king, leaving us vulnerable."

Sima swallowed. "My father is the one who closed the human lands, though. I wonder if this decision only damned the lives of those within."

"We are quite tenacious people. Humans crafted more weapons and engineered siphons to use crystals found across the Prisma District. Though, without the ability to fly, it can take some time to spread new weaponry or knowledge."

Sima nodded. "That is why the King is so concerned with destroying all who employ the magic of the crystals. Your people have learned to wield them and he wants to stop it from spreading."

Simon pinpointed the artwork he was searching for and pulled it from the stack. He turned it to Sima, the brilliant colors popping from the canvas. It depicted three crystal butterflies, each crafted of a different stone. The top was ruby, the middle sapphire, the bottom emerald.

"I can't tell you how many times I have seen this in my dreams. At the time, I questioned people high and low, but no one has seen these before. I don't know what they are for. I have heard the same phrase when it appears, though."

"What do you hear?" Sima glanced at the doors, double checking the enchantment was holding. No sounds from outside permeated the barriers.

"*Pure blood will wash them clean, none left alive to deny its resonance.*"

Sima blinked a few times. "Do you know what it means?"

He shook his head. "I told you it is more of a curse than a blessing. The visions have only become more cryptic and terrifying with time. Others tell me that the Goddess preaches through me, and my comprehension is unnecessary for the spread of her word."

"Do you know where the crystals are stemming from—or of any way to stop the King of Aeria?"

Simon pondered her question, taking a seat before a sturdy easel with a sizable, unfinished portrait of Cosima taking shape.

"I can tell you the pieces that stick out to me, but I warn you, not all of it is decipherable, at least to me. When the Goddess speaks to me, she occasionally tells me stories alongside the visions. At nine, she told me the story of a great Celestial Empress with rivers of space for hair and the sparkle of suns brighter than ours in her eyes. This Empress commanded all until she grew tired of the responsibility."

As he spoke, he picked up a paintbrush and began repainting the eyes, glancing at Sima now for reference. It felt odd, being a model in this way when he had completed half her face before she arrived, but she allowed it since it calmed him enough to speak. Little dollops of paint from thin tubes were chosen, Simon mixing colors seemingly at random, until he concocted the perfect shade to match her eyelashes. Sima complimented the changes in her head.

"Then she created twelve women to help her rule. When these

daughters, too, grew weary with time, they would pass it down to their daughters, and so on." Simon tapped his foot as he worked. "At thirteen, the Goddess sang me a song about beautiful white feathered birds with broken necks falling through stormy clouds. The birds knew better than to fly in those conditions, yet hubris lifted their wings to the sky anyway."

Sima chewed her nails, nearly crawling out of her skin as the minutes passed. Simon hardly made progress, still delicately placing eyelashes with gentle sweeps of his brush.

"Another that seems worth mentioning involves what I believe to be the protective shielding around Eternita. The seal works for more than protecting Eternita from unwanted visitors. Along the borders, it blocks all light and sound. The people here notice none of what occurs in the Ombra District. When I was sixteen, on my birthday, the Goddess came to me, yet again, with a song."

The dead look was disappearing more and more as her eyes rested more naturally, and the Sima in the painting mirrored her flaming determination. She liked it, even if her gut was roiling with alarms bells. He turned to her, interrupting his painting for the first time.

"*Empty vessels, adorned with care, returned to the soil. Light and souls home-bound, ever loyal. With no call from Death, they will be turned away. Unable to return, they wander as their bodies decay*," Simon's voice followed the rhythm, though he spoke instead of sang.

"Perhaps it has something to do with these creatures." Cosima pointed to fungal beasts with multiple heads depicted in a painting nearby.

"Those beasts are coming from this land. I heard them at night while in the prison. There was non-stop shrieking echoing through those cells. It takes a firm grip to avoid descending into madness, especially when they're louder at night."

"The deformed monsters are coming from *Eternita*?"

Simon's head dipped. "I heard of the threat to my people. No creatures from the veil would have found their way to Prisma without demolishing this District first. I think they round them up here, and deposit them elsewhere, for other Districts to deal with."

Sima couldn't bear the energy building in her legs, soon to pace a hole right through the ground at this rate. The shock threatened to knock her off her feet. "Is there anything you have heard alongside visions of me?"

He chuckled. "I figured you'd heard it by now. It's always the same story. It is foretold you for you to save Haelos, and to slay a brother of the Sacred Twelve," he touched a hand to his chin. His eyes swayed back and forth as he resurfaced the memory. "From darkness came order first, not existence. A woman to touch threads and alter their weave in an instant. Her hands to test the tides of time, undoing power in its prime."

"I've heard others mention a prophecy, but..." Sima trailed off, realizing the barrier faltered. She cursed beneath her breath, racking her brain for an exit. Cosima searched around the small home for an alternate way to escape.

"There's only the front door," Simon said with a frown.

Sima withdrew the blade from her waist and planted her heels on the ground.

It was only then that she spotted it.

Ivo.

A small painting along the front wall, her friend's beautiful face recognizable. Sima ran over, tossing the other paintings out of the way, earning a grumble from the human artist until she had it. Then, she wished she had never seen it.

The image was of a very dead Ivo, her stomach gutted, organs covering the floor in wet, bloody heaps. Her fingernails were torn back and broken, the fingers bent in all the wrong angles. Her face was picturesque, reflecting none of the horror encompassing her body. Instead, she appeared peaceful, her expression soft. Her ocean eyes were open, revealing no fear. Somehow, it only disturbed her more.

Sima vomited.

Simon ran over, tossing a small metal bucket beneath her.

The magic around the doors and windows wavered, allowing in the commotion that was occurring outside. From the exterior, the sound of several voices escaped the barriers. All the worry Cosima held suddenly vanished, replaced by a furious wound. She couldn't wash herself of the dread. The image of her dead friend was plastered on the insides of her eyelids, haunting her.

"When did you paint this? Is this true?" she rasped, bile burning her throat, tears dripping into pools of her vomit as she lay across the small tin waste basket.

His mouth pressed into a firm line.

"I painted it only this morning. It is there to dry. Who was she?"

Was.

Ivo was dead. Sima shook her head, internally begging to wake up from the bad dream or horrible hallucination she was caught inside of. It hit her then, the shame and guilt. "Are your visions always true?"

"Yes," he responded, turning away from her.

"By the Spirit, Ivo." Her lips trembled as she spoke, her voice hushed. "I'm so sorry. I left you behind. Why would I leave you behind?"

Oblivious to her plight, Simon snatched a paintbrush from the table beside him. "If they want to kill me, or arrest me, they'll have to come drag me by my ankles like they did last time. I will use every second with the one thing that makes this wretched life worth living. My art is who I am—separate me by force." He plopped back into his seat, resuming the painting.

Sima whimpered, believing she deserved the cruel mockery Fate had aligned for her at this moment. Simon painted his model while ignoring its real-life counterpart.

Within just two hours, Cosima had lost the three people closest to her. One to crystals, one to inexcusable lies, and one at the hands of Aurelio. Her future would be spent constantly on the run until she or someone else could murder the King. Until then, every friend, every act of kindness, would accomplish nothing beyond earning death in return. She was cursed. She was contained. The pounding of her heart made her head pulse, pain scattering across her scalp in an intense headache. She gripped the trashcan, heaving again as she faintly picked up on the sound of the door slamming open.

The commotion grew only slightly louder. Sima could not focus on anything other than the agony seeping into her bones. *I betrayed Ivo; I left her for dead.* She had saved Sima's life just to give up her own in return.

Was it worth it?

Hands grabbed her, pulling her away from the portrait. Sima's hand grasped for Ivo, too weak to fight back. She allowed herself to go, sealing her eyes tight as she fought the urge to heave again. The headache did not relent, even as she covered her face with her arms. A guard she didn't know cradled her, her tears warm against the cool metal of his Eternita armor.

Chapter 30

Simon struggled for a long time, just as he said he would. To her horror, one Guardian used the wooden base of his blade to knock him unconscious. It took only four blows, Simon was human. He couldn't take a beating, not like the stronger beings in Haelos. His battered face swelled and swirled purple and blue around his temple. He had gone limp; she feared it was more likely he was dead, too.

It was the only time she opened her eyes, to witness another image she could never unsee. A different Guardian threw Simon over his shoulder as he took to the sky. The one carrying her followed, Sima shuddering from the icy wind. She curled in on herself, ashamed that they had caught her. Fear whispered in her ear—Aurelio would force her to go back to a place where the people branded her a traitor and deserter.

The Guardians restricted their ascension to a couple hundred feet above the ground. Their destination was not Aeria, and they were not turning her in to Aurelio, at the very least. Instead, they began the long flight toward the largest city in Eternita, and away from the one built directly above prison cells. Trees, homes, buildings all blew past them in a blur. He maneuvered out of the way of obstacles, but otherwise, set himself dead straight. She didn't know long she lay there, unmoving and defeated, but it was almost a slap in the face how little the Guardian had done to restrain her.

Sima held a similar sentiment about her power that Simon did about his. Cosïma did not consider it a blessing; it was a curse. The threads she wove snapped more often than they held. She could sew a hundred, and only one would come to fruition. Her control wavered, and she could not alter her own Fate without involving others.

She peeked an eye at the Guardian carrying her. His reddish black hair rustled in the wind. He set his square jaw tight, his wings making broad strokes to propel them forward faster. He was aware she was looking at him, but he did not look back. If she had any fight left in her, if she thought it would make any difference, she would try to glimpse him once they landed.

Her hand begged to use her power to fight for freedom once again. But all she could think about was Ivo. The first time she met Ivo was over twenty years ago. They had assigned her as a servant for the Palace for showing exemplary skill. It was only now that Sima understood they sent Ivo to the Palace for her will to be broken, for her to stop showing signs of any skill other than blind obedience. Occasionally, Ivo was quiet, or reserved, but more often than not, she was cracking jokes with Sima while brushing her hair or telling her stories of her life on Haelos.

Tears came again, her arms rising to hide her face.

The swish in her stomach told her they were descending. Magic shielded the Palace in mist and fog—the glamor allowing only shady glimpses of what laid beneath. They made their way towards a rose-colored portal. Tall marble statues of Fae standing thirty feet high marked the entrance to the Palace. Each statue bore the same armor as the Guardians, and elongated ears adorned with massive pieces of polished gold jewelry glimmered.

Sima was curious about the number of Guardians surrounding them. She wondered if Aurelio had noticed the considerable number of missing Guardians, and if he suspected they were all here, hiding, working. Sima took a steadying breath at what the packed entourage meant.

They existed to protect the Queen of Eternita from Aurelio.

A small huddle of Fae and other faeries living in Eternita gathered outside, awaiting to be granted access. The Guardian's feet barely touched the ground before he set her down. She straightened out her clothes where discomfort bit at her, internally devoid of emotion. The only thing her body did was hurt, until the pain became mute, too.

Two people not three feet high ambled by, their pointed ears peeking out behind delicate swoops of hair. They carried small baskets of divine-looking green and yellow fruits. Sima's stomach turned. Her empty stomach craved nutrients, and her tired body craved rest. With the sensation toppled in another wave of shame. She preferred the numbness.

Four small pixies flew past, zipping like dragonflies through the admittedly beautifully wooded area. They had built this city with such meaningful intention. The city absorbed nature, working with and around it. It was only when she was on the ground that she got a full view of the intricate miniature roadways through the leaves in the trees.

Her head whipped as she tried to follow them. The Guardian grunted, his lip curled in a sneer. He motioned with his sword toward the portal. Sima had half a mind to make a run for it, jumping into the riverbed with the water nymphs and merfolk to escape. Instead, their laughter set her spine stick-straight.

She was invisible, and the world was carrying on as if what was happening to her meant nothing. As if all the pain and suffering she went through, in the end, would mean nothing. A low rumble shook the ground beneath her feet as storm clouds began gathering in the sky. She didn't say another word as she stepped through..

Fresh herbal scents bombarded them as they emerged on the other side of the portal and enchantments. The smell overwhelmed her, adding to the churning in her stomach. Looking toward the sky made her feel dizzy. Sima wondered if they had transported her to another world. The misty storm now was nowhere in sight. Surrounding them were bright, endless skies, and fat, fluffy clouds trundling by.

The horizon in all directions proved to be the same. Vast

emptiness greeted her, nothing beyond the sprawling grassy fields and the Palace. It sat regally, the wild vegetation brushing against its walls from the warm spring breeze.

She turned back towards the Guardian who only stared at her with an incredulous look on his face. She realized it was an expression meant to motivate her to keep walking, so she did, heading up the ivory stone paved pathway to the main entrance. Her head hung low as she walked, unable to look at Simon, unconscious and bleeding in front of her. His blood began trailing into her line of vision, the pounding in her ears growing.

As they meandered through the hallways, Fae passed them, discussing upcoming holidays, gossiping about dating circles, and the latest enchantments available to the public. Their easy-going nature stung like salt rubbed into an open wound. They split off from Simon without so much as a nod between the Guardians. Simon disappeared down a dimly lit hallway.

Her Guardian overlapped her, leading the way to the third floor. Surrounding them were tall, pure white pillars with thick green leaves twirled around them. The ceiling in every room featured extravagant hand-painted murals of winged babies floating around clouds, some holding bows, others had tridents and scythes. The walls were dressed in powder blue paint, and golden statues throughout depicted various animals.

She considered running several times, but the over-pour of Guardians left no genuine opportunities. A dissatisfied sigh left her as she picked at her fingernails beneath her sleeve. Her Guardian slowed to a stop, a sneer blemishing his face as he looked back at her.

"We could do without the theatrics," he growled, turning forward again.

"Am I being held captive?" Cosima glanced down at the ornately designed carpeting beneath their feet.

His shoulders straightened as his body went rigid, but he did not slow again or answer her question.

The populace consisted primarily of Fae and an assortment of sprites. It wasn't hard to figure out why they used the sprites here for messaging and spying. They were impossibly quick, if they let you see them at all. Their wings were delicate and translucent, colors varying in all shades of the rainbow. Most appeared elemental, conjuring water, fire, or plant matter, but some manipulated lights, shadows.

The ability to manipulate lights and shadows granted a mischievous few the means to change how others saw them, giving them optical illusions on demand. The two running alongside her in the hall stuck their tongue out at her as their faces morphed into rectangular mask-like forms, echoing devilish expressions. She smirked, thankful for the bit of humorous distraction they brought.

They had intended to irritate her, but it was enough to clear her mind for a moment. Before Cosima witnessed the sprites torment others, her Guardian abruptly turned down a hallway. She followed, growing confused as he entered what appeared to be a bedroom.

The walls were the same powder blue, and a sizable pastel pink comforter was draped across the plush bed. From where they stood, Sima noticed there was a bathing chamber attached to the room. "What are we doing in here?"

"You are to bathe, sleep, and eat. When the queen has decided what she will do with you, I will return."

Cosima blinked at him. "Sleep? Here?"

"Unless you'd prefer to bake outside in the sun, yes."

He spun on his heel, closing the door behind him. Before Sima could make another move, an electrified yellow barrier of enchantment arose over her door.

The Fae, she thought bitterly. *To say they are skilled at enchantment is an understatement.*

Sima relished the opportunity to be alone, finding her way to the bathing chamber where a circular gray-stone tub sat along the wall beneath a hazy window. Sunlight illuminated the steaming water already filling the tub to the brim. Without thinking, she shed the stolen armor she'd been wearing and dipped herself up to her shoulders.

Tears burst from her eyes, rocking her chest in heavy waves. She sobbed, allowing the salt from her tears to cover her cheeks.

The relief the warm water brought her sore, tired body was overwhelming atop the mountain of emotion that now ran freely through her.

"Yadira, Vincenzo, Ivo," she whispered between whimpering cries. "I'm alone again."

Alone.

The word repeated without pause. Loneliness was something Cosima had learned to fear with time. When she had been locked in her rooms, isolated from the outside world, it was the company of others she craved the most. Being around people while in the Ombra District had brought her comfort, but now it resurfaced with pain.

"I can't let anyone near me ever again." She pressed her palms to her puffy eyelids. "But I don't want to be alone. Not anymore."

After what felt like hours, Cosima pulled herself from water that had long since grown cold. She stepped into a fresh pair of clothes, frowning at the ill-fitting ensemble. The purple skirt was too short, ending midway down her calves and exposed her hips at the top. The matching purple top pressed tightly to her skin, emphasizing her chest as it clung to her ribcage.

She pulled back the comforter and climbed into the bed. The void of sleep took her swiftly.

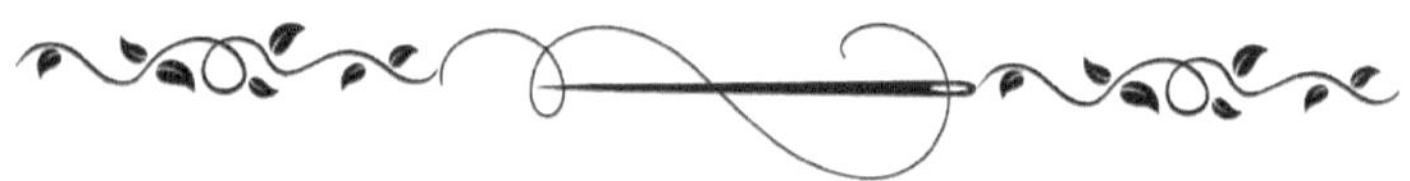

It took more than a day for a Guardian to fetch Cosima from the room. Sima would have been unaware of how much time had passed if he hadn't told her. She spent nearly all her time alone, unconscious, fearful of reality. He led her into a large meeting room, equipped with a wide oak table with a polished finish, and a dozen cushioned chairs.

Flanking the walls were three slender but muscular Fae. The two women bore similar chestnut streams of hair, one pulled up, one flowing freely down to her midsection. Curls in the man's hair shimmered like sunlight, blond spilling over his soft features. Fae were beautiful. Sima understood why they had been so strongly associated with Aeria in the past. Their alliance, it seems, did not withstand Aurelio's capture of Haelos.

The women inspected Cosima as the man instructed her to sit. Their faces revealed a steady lack of emotion. It wasn't as uncomfortable as Sima thought it would be, being left alone in a foreign Palace, unsure if she was a hostage, prisoner, or bargaining chip. The man seemed at ease. Nothing about his body language, or theirs, indicated much of a threat.

"Who are you?" one said, flipping her long hair to rest behind her as she got comfortable in the chair across from Sima. Her eyes were smooth like jade, which paired well with her other subtle features. Her face was relaxed, and Sima detected no anger or malice. Cosima figured it was a good start if they were attempting to calm her.

"Queen Cosima Aphelion of the Aeria Archipelago," she said, tilting her head, holding the woman's stare.

The Fae only blinked.

"Why are you here?" the same woman asked.

"I was hoping you'd tell me," Sima said tensely, growing irritated. "No one has told me why the Guardians brought me to this Palace."

That earned her a curious look from the ponytailed one. Her hair swished like potions swirled in bottles, magic wafting off her in powerful waves. Sima had been too busy drowning in her misery to notice it when she walked in. Sima's scowl faltered an inch as goosebumps fluttered up her arms.

An orange aura simmered an outline around the woman with the ponytail's tan skin. She warmed the room like summer, summoning the feel of the breeze and open sky. It was comforting, gentle. Against her better judgment, Sima closed her eyes and let it envelop her. Unseen wind caressed her, feeling strangely akin to the moon. Cold, vibrant, pure.

Unfamiliar emotions rose in her, tsunamis of grief and detriment accompanied by delight and anger in jarring waves. Yet

Cosima's face remained blank, no outward markers of her inner turmoil appearing. Only deep emptiness anchored the ravenous pit of conflicting feelings.

As quickly as it came, it was gone, leaving her feeling more alone than before. The Fae wore strange looks across their faces. A wall built somewhere within her mind toppled, and a flood of images battered her brain. A disturbing lack of context made the memories feel as if they were being forced to fit in her brain, whether they belonged or not. They came seemingly out of order, images of her as a child jumbled alongside images of her just a few days ago. They washed together, colors blurring and mixing like smeared paint behind her eyelids. She remained statuesque, not out of choice, but out of the sheer panic raging through her veins.

There was a reason brains refused to recall so much at one time, why memory worked the way it did. Her mind struggled to maintain composure. Aurelio popped up, repeatedly, his likeness burning holes into her visions, as adrenaline began coursing through her veins.

Still, she did not move. Still, she did not break.

The three Fae sat motionless, and the only movement was the magic rippling off of them. The man's ears twitched as they tuned to the sounds of her panicked heart.

Images of Ivo came next, causing her right eye to twitch, covered in a shiny sheen of water from the tear she held back desperately. Misery bled openly as the memory unfolded, her friend laughing about a girl she was seeing secretly. Ivo had hidden the relationship from everyone, except Sima. In the end, Aurelio had Ivo's girlfriend murdered. It was not a simple job to work the Palace and her partner could no longer tolerate it. She acted out to be reassigned. Instead, the kingdom punished her with death.

Sima bent over, preparing to vomit. Bile burned the back of her throat. Part of her savored the way it hurt, savored the way it seared her flesh to remember Ivo so vividly, intrusive images of her dead body painted on the canvas fighting its way in repeatedly.

"Enough," the male said, slapping his hand across the back of one woman's shoulder, brushing large locks of her hair over her face as she tipped forward. That ended the misery, bringing rise to more pleasant, amped energy. Without intending to, but not caring enough to stop, she felt herself lean into the warmth again. It was as though she were being embraced by someone familiar, someone safe. The thought of Ivo still made her chest ache, but it no longer weighed her down.

The trio continued to eyeball her. The awkward silence made her want to crawl out of her skin, but before she could lash out, the one with the ponytail broke it first.

"Why do you show no reaction? I can feel my magic crawling all over your mind, but you barely blink."

Sima pondered her question for a moment, slowly meeting her gaze.

"What is your name?" Sima asked the woman fidgeting with her ponytail.

She blinked before responding, "Tasia." A finger jutted toward the other Fae woman. "Aspasia."

The man cleared his throat. "Ioannis."

Without meaning to, Cosima snickered. In a freakish show of coordination, all three of them cocked their heads slightly to the left, eerily searching for the humor.

"Are you triplets or siblings or something? The names, the strange dead stare, and mirrored moves. Plus, you all have the same eyes." It was true. Each of them bore enormous blue boulders for eyes, the color pure enough to make Sima uncomfortable.

Tasia crinkled her nose.

"What do you mean? We don't even look alike," Aspasia said, swishing her hair as it fell back behind her shoulder. The look in her eye showed she had little faith in that statement. *Was she telling a joke?*

"They're twins," Ioannis said, reaching into his pocket and pulling out a piece of hard candy. He popped it into his mouth, tucking it into his cheek as he talked. "I am their half-brother."

"We share a mother," Tasia said. "Why do you not show a reaction?" She leaned forward against the table. "Please, the last time this happened, he died before I could ask him."

She arched a brow. "I have a shitty husband."

Tasia leaned back, contemplating the answer.

"You really don't know why the Guardian brought you to us?"

"No."

Aspasia laid a hand on Tasia's shoulder. The two of them shared a knowing look before Tasia said, "*He* sent you to kill our mother, we believe. We were unsure of your intentions, though we knew you to be a pawn of the King."

Sima's lip flickered with the heat that filled her at the word *pawn*.

"We laid waiting, terrified, feeling insane with not knowing whether you changed something in the past, and we would simply never know…"

"Or worse," Aspasia said, "You changed something in the future, and only time would reveal our Fate."

"You are not speaking of Solara, are you?" Sima said, stunned. If she was a future queen, she would be in a proper meeting chamber, not a side room. It was the Fae district, so the spaces were all of annoyingly exceptional quality, but the lack of purpose to this one was not something that could be painted over.

Ioannis's eyes flickered with suspicion.

"Solara was her first decoy name. Among Fae, there is a type of magic that preys on one's name. Your name is more than just what others call you, it is who you are. To take your name is to take everything. The sitting queen, our mother, was assigned her name, Solara, at birth. No one has referred to her as such since adolescence. I am surprised you have heard it."

"It is true then, that you had your hand in her Fate," Tasia said.

"I glimpsed," Sima said, deciding against mentioning the Drago, "but I changed nothing. I couldn't bring myself to do it. Am I at risk here, of falling victim to your name magic?"

Aspasia smiled. "It doesn't work on anyone born…*up there*. Wherever you all come from. We tried."

The corner of Ioannis's mouth tipped up. "We tried—hard."

Understanding settled into her.

"You are capable of the magic then?"

"All but Tasia; she has a couple more interesting tricks to make up for it. She is the future queen for a reason," Aspasia said.

"When do you take the throne?"

"We have until the Summer Solstice. My coronation will be then, to hold with tradition," Tasia said tightly.

"I have tried to urge her to move it closer, to assume her position, her power, now."

"And I have told you time and time again, no. We pass traditions by upholding them every chance we get. We are the example by which others will follow. Our people are not in a place to be unsure of their new queen making abrupt changes."

"She's right, Aspasia. This is not the time to shake the boat. We are going to stick to our roots, and they are unaware of the true extent of her magic ability. The throne is a highly public position, and she needs more time to practice without others watching her every move," Ioannis grumbled.

Sima admired their matching form-fitting tactile gear, equipped with blades as long as arms at their sides. There was one on each hip. Their power hummed, incapable of being concealed.

One of them noticed her attention, and whatever she saw in Sima's eyes made Aspasia grimace.

"Hey," Aspasia said, nudging Tasia with her elbow. "Enough. Stop spilling secrets to the enemy. Let's move onto the part where we kill her."

Chapter 31

"You brought me all this way, only to decide to kill me?" *What a waste of time*, Cosima grumbled internally.

She blinked, and time came to a screeching halt. It took Sima a moment to notice the change, because one of them kept moving, blinking, breathing, and watching her. Someone had frozen them solid.

Tasia was behind it.

"You're not the only one with magic to manipulate time. These powers I possess, they are strange, and they do not match my sister's. We may be twins, but she bears the mark of our parents. I do not."

"A mark?"

"The name Fae is just one name given to our kind, the one most prefer. In her creation of our universe, Ehses limited the number of souls for the Fae. When we die, our souls are recycled and returned to the planet. They do not leave, as the souls of others do. I hear this is unnatural for Goddesses to do when in charge of souls. As we age, we forget all memories of the past, and the only evidence becomes our mark"

Tasia twisted, lifting her ponytail, and revealed a red symbol on the back of her neck. It was a series of interlocking circles wrapped in thorn-covered vines. "Mine does not match my siblings or my parents'. Beyond this strange difference, for whatever reason, in this reincarnation, I am blessed with the ability to transmute time as I please."

"How do you do more than pause it?"

"I recently mastered the creation of what I call 'pockets'—longer moments within another. If you watch closely, those around us still move, but at a significantly slower pace. The family name magic, for example, I don't have it, and it doesn't work on me. Instead of being suspicious, they theorize I am a shield of sorts. I have deeply hidden my abilities from the public—however, I have been in contact with people in Ombra. Consider it an allegiance of sorts. They help me discover more of my power, and in exchange, I provide them priceless information about my kingdom."

"You're informing on your own kingdom?" Sima asked, averting her gaze toward Tasia's frozen companions.

"I don't plan to kill you."

"Oh, thanks," Sima said blandly. "The traitor said she won't betray me."

"You have zero reason to trust me, but I have a feeling you will."

"What makes you so sure?"

"I have been in contact with Vincenzo, a friend of yours, I am told. He believes helping me could one day help you. As you know, our kingdom sealed Eternita years ago. Has anyone told you why we sealed our District from the King? It did not happen when he took the Aeria Archipelago."

Sima perched a brow. Though grief weighed heavily on her shoulders, her curiosity swirled alongside the desire to detach the King from the throne. "No, I haven't heard the exact reason."

"The King received knowledge of a fiercely hidden ability within my family. I came to know why my mark differed from the others, why I gained powers others did not. I can transfer life-force at will. There is one caveat—this ability must be passed down. We are forced to find a successor."

Sima nodded. "When I saw your mother's Fate, your grandmother was transferring her life force. She did the same with you?"

"Yes, and the powers accumulate more with each generation."

Sima pondered it for a moment. "How long do we have in here, in your pocket?"

Tasia cocked her head to the side, expression blank.

"Ninety-seven minutes, if my math is right."

Sima blinked.

When Sima didn't respond, Tasia explained, "I have gotten excruciatingly good at this, and at wielding my other powers. We won't be down here that long, however. I promise."

"Do you trust them?" Sima jerked her chin toward the frozen siblings.

"With my life. But not with the lives of this District, or yours."

"How should we spend our time here, then?" Sima rolled her neck. A gentle popping ran along her spine, relieving tension. "Since you clearly have need for me."

"Yes, *that*," she said, her mouth pressing into a thin line. "Are the rumors from Vincenzo true? You can manipulate Fate, as well as time? Describe to me how it works. I am curious how it unfolds."

"Why would I do that? All I know about you is you sealed your entire District off, causing the other two Districts to suffer immensely, all to hide your power from the King."

Tasia's face turned a shade of gray and she frowned.

"I suppose I should explain my interest. It is believed that only Fae in the royal bloodline can perform the transfer of life force to others in the family. However, this is false—a*ny* Fae is capable of life force transfer if gifted the ability by the royalty. My family has tried to keep this secret. Despite sealing the District, King Aurelio imprisoned Fae from our bloodline to perform the transfers himself. For years, he has been abusing their powers as well."

Sima chewed her lip. "I don't understand. What do you need from me?"

Tasia turned to her siblings and sighed. "I need you to tell me how your power works."

Cosima crossed her arms in front of her chest. "I don't know how to describe it. Fate feels like a string, and I attune my mind to the feeling of it. I can almost feel it on my fingertips and then I tug."

"Can you manipulate the past or only the future?"

"I can alter both, though the past is more complex. I don't have to reform one outcome, I have to change potentially hundreds. The more mundane the moment, the easier it is to change. That being said, the future is more straightforward, but is less likely to actually occur when the time comes."

"How do you cope with manipulating people's future, changing whatever you deem to be mundane, forcing people into lives they would never live?"

"I cannot make anyone do what they wouldn't. It didn't take long to figure that out. The Fate changes that take the best are the ones with roots already, especially if the target was already indecisive. I push them the other way, and often they run toward it, happy to be given a direction. Where is Simon?"

Tasia rolled her eyes, toying with the hair in her ponytail.

"He is none of my business. He gave us much, but gave us many headaches, too."

Sima thought for a moment, eyes latched on observing how little the others had moved in all the time that passed.

"You will get no help from me if Simon dies. He's a prophet. He knows valuable information."

"As if you actually have a choice here."

"Or what? You'll give me up to Aurelio?"

A sneer flickered across Tasia's face, clenching her jaw.

"You think too lowly of me. You were a captive of his, yes? Then I have no interest in further traumatizing you. Vincenzo begged enough on your behalf for me to reconsider holding you captive here, as well. However, when I show you why all the Rani Guardians in Eternita have joined the rebellion, as well as why there was sparse communication between us and those of Ombra, you will understand. Maybe then you lend us a hand with your powers."

"I don't let anyone tell me how to use my abilities. I am tired of that role."

"It benefits all of Haelos for you, Cosima Aphelion, to grow your power."

She bristled. "Why does everyone think I am capable of so much? This is a horrible power, isn't it? A curse? Something others will always want to use me for? What kind of life is that, running from those who only wish to use me, only to end up in the arms of more users? I feel as though the end of the world will be my fault. Those threads, I can't see the outcome until after I resurface. The effects aren't predictable. Who is to say what is the right move and when?"

"You are," she said firmly. "*You* were given this power, not anyone else. There is a reason for it, there is a reason for it all. As much as King Aurelio believes himself to be all powerful, he is nothing without you. The Archipelago is crumbling with you there to undo his mistakes or thwart his attacks. If you cannot force anyone to do what they would not already, there is a specific family member of mine I believe would do well under these circumstances. We can begin there. I will alert Vincenzo."

"No," Cosima said softly. "I don't want to see him."

"Ah, so that is why he has not pushed to speak with you since you arrived. Perhaps there is another friend you wish to see. I believe her name is Yadira."

Sima stiffened. "What happened to her?"

"Well, the King is becoming more emboldened, and had infiltrated the barrier enchantments with his use of crystals. We removed them from her body, of course."

"You removed them? Is she all right?"

"She is under careful watch, to ensure the stones leave no lasting side-effects, but yes, she is all right."

"Can I see her?" Sima scooted to the edge of her chair.

"Soon, yes. In the meantime, may I question you further?"

Sima slumped back into her seat. "What about this time?"

"Why are you resistant to Vincenzo?" Tasia leaned forward, tapping her fingernails along the table. "I learned quickly how valuable of an asset he is. Each individual in the rebellion, spanning across every District, owes their life to him. If he had not rescued the Ombra District and secured the Star Realm Portal, who knows what kind of mayhem would have found us?"

"Yes," Sima said bitterly, "It is mighty convenient that Vincenzo took over and fixed a mistake your kingdom helped create."

"You misunderstand me. Vincenzo is more than someone who has altered the course of repercussions for my actions. The passing of information between the two Districts has given me hope that one day our world can recover from the hate and the murder the King has spread. Vincenzo is powerful, knowledgeable, and, more so, kind. I should think you would be quite interested in him."

Sima huffed. "You only know what Vincenzo has revealed to you. There are plenty of things he does not speak about."

"Why should he reveal everything? Perhaps it is because of my Fae heritage, but our people are quite keen to mask our true intentions, even if they are not ones filled with malice. His secretive nature allowed years of expansion and growth to occur right beneath King Aurelio's nose."

Sima pondered Tasia's statement for a moment. "What kind of queen do you want to be?"

Tasia rolled her eyes, releasing an exasperated sigh. "It's not something I like to think about when I don't have to. We are not talking about me, anyhow."

"How can you expect to rule if you don't have a solid idea of what kind of queen you will be? What do you stand on? What do you stand up for? Where do you draw the line between tradition and innovation? What will you do when *King Aurelio* discovers what you've done here, and he makes thousands upon thousands of people pay for it? When he makes *you* pay for it?"

"We have always been aware of the risk."

"And that makes it justifiable? To send all these people to their deaths—*painful ones?* Do you know how you can kill Rani? Only by cutting their wings off, and then sending the killing blow. It is a barbaric, painstaking process, and you are damning them all to it, without even having a good reason you do it!"

"Enough," Tasia hollered, "I have a multitude of reasons I do this. A good leader is someone who can handle bearing the weight of losing lives, don't you understand? There is a responsibility in knowing how many lives are worth risking for how many you can save. It will always be on my head, every death. I have to be strong enough to decide for myself, anyway. When you are fighting fire, you can't expect to not get burned. You just hope you can keep it from spreading."

And just like that, time resumed.

Sima nearly suffered whiplash from the flow of time resuming its usual pace, but she did her best to keep up with the suddenly flowing conversation. She had forgotten completely where they were.

"Fine," Ioannis said, "Just know that it's on you if she goes all crazy and gets her hands on your destiny or whatever."

"Deal," Tasia said, standing up and making her way toward the hall. "Cosima, I have something imperative to show you."

Sima followed her blindly, legs moving automatically. She couldn't tell if she was afraid of Tasia or not with the way she could so easily use her power. There also was the looming expectation from Tasia's trusted siblings that Sima was to be killed by them. She questioned it then, the conditions under which she might die. She was half-immortal Ambrosi, lending her healing powers and strength. Would there be a special trick to killing her completely? She grimaced at the idea that Aurelio could force her to endure a painful cycle of healing, nearly dying, and healing again. Until she grew too tired to keep the life-saving measures in motion. Sima swallowed harshly at whether death would be comforting darkness or filled with nightmares, like she feared.

Tasia led her into a wine cellar, impeccably organized and well stocked. She meandered around the many crates, storing wine until she stopped before a blank taupe colored wall.

"I hope I am not making the wrong decision by trusting you with this," she said, touching her hand to the wall. A ball of light accumulated over the top half of her body before it moved in one swift pulse toward the brick. A green sigil illuminated against the wall, composed of strange drawings. The brick shuddered and fell away, revealing a passageway.

Cosima grew impossibly overwhelmed by the sensation of magic and the numerous passageways, but nevertheless, she followed behind, the brick sewing itself back into position behind them in satisfying clinks. A ball of light illuminated the room in Tasia's hand. Sima arched a brow. The woman couldn't have *that* many more powers hidden inside her, could she?

Tasia's ponytail swished across Sima's face as she turned to look at her. "This is what I thought might get you on board with the rebellion."

Sima peered over Tasia's shoulder to reveal the room did not contain more wine. It held cages. Hundreds and hundreds of cages in every size imaginable. Iron bars marred with rust, miniature prisons stacked high to the ceiling. The sight chilled her to the bone. Sima attempted to pull in a breath, only to find it stuck.

"What the hell is this?"

"*This,*" Tasia hissed, "is the biggest shame of my people. They used them in farming those considered to be lesser faeries. They captured them years ago, but no one went looking for them. Turns out, they were in this Palace the entire time. They forced the faeries to breed, then they killed them and harnessed their life force. Vincenzo mentioned to me you met Santoro and asked him about the crystals."

"They're being farmed for their life forces?"

"They are being made into weapons, Cosima. Much stronger than those party trick crystals King Aurelio talked to you about. Do you know where those monsters are coming from?" She gestured to the empty cages. "They turn into wretched beasts when they are drained completely of their life force. It is not their time, so death cannot take them. I do not have it in my heart to tell Vincenzo I believe the fungus is growing to break down their bodies back into nutrients."

Sima immediately thought back to one of the songs Simon had uttered. *With no call from Death, they will be turned away. Unable to return, they wander as their bodies decay.*

"The fungi are not the cause. They are part of the natural order of the planet, still trying to be carried out," Cosima spoke softly.

"Only it can't. Death won't take them, so their bodies will continue to function until nothing is left of them. Then, I fear, I do not know what becomes of them. We do not know if their life force *is* them, but for their sake, I hope their souls find passage."

"What does this have to do with Aurelio?"

"Everything, Queen Cosima. Everything. He did not start it, but he has progressed it beyond my worst nightmares."

She pulled a small pin from her pocket. It was a viper wrapped around a blade. Sima could not hold back her gasp, recognizing it immediately as the same one Ivo wore.

"Where did you get this?"

"From the belongings that get discarded. Some keep alive purely for breeding. It allowed the operation to explode without us being any the wiser. They selected people they thought no one would care about. During the migration of people out of Eternita and back into Ombra, Fae killed any stragglers or imprisoned them. They were damned to a life of *this* or drained immediately of their life force. Aurelio chose our planet to capture. I suspect itt was always in his plans to harness as much of the life force crystals as possible."

"The Sacred Twelve," Sima gasped. "Aurelio told me himself the crystals can kill Ambrosi. Does that mean they could kill him or his brothers?"

Tasia nodded slowly.

"You were right. There is no way I can walk away from this."

"I would like to teach you all I have discovered about channeling my magic. Anything to help free us from the King."

Ivo's face flashed behind Sima's eyelids every time they closed. "I will make it happen, one way or another." The gears began turning in Cosima's head. "You will need to get me Simon and a Guardian."

A voice sounded from behind them. "I have one right here, begging to be at your service," said Vincenzo.

Chapter 32

"Get away from me!" Cosima said, pushing past Vincenzo. His feathers slid across her skin as she maneuvered around his wings. At one time, she would have delighted in the sensation. Instead, she shot him a deathly glare, causing him to step backward.

Vincenzo placed his hands up. "I won't force you to do anything you don't want to, but please allow me the chance to explain. You have every right to be angry with me, but at least hear me out, and then decide how you feel."

"I don't need time to decide how I feel," Cosima stood with her back to him, arms crossed in front of her. "You should have told me."

Tasia quickly grew uncomfortable and excused herself, leaving Vincenzo and Cosima standing in the hidden room filled to the brim with cages that had once held people. Cosima sighed. What little fight she had mustered now slipped like sand between her fingers. Her shoulders slumped.

"I heard about Ivo. I am so sorry. You should not blame yourself. He gave you no choice but to flee."

"Easy for you to say when she wasn't your friend. Ivo meant everything to me. When I had no one else, not even Yadira, I had her. She was the one to wash the blood from my hair and untangle it gently. When he banned me from the library, she risked her life to bring me books, all to make me smile." Tears fell down her cheek. "She didn't deserve this. It's not fair."

Vincenzo sighed. "We haven't confirmed it yet. Maybe there's still a chance—"

"Don't," Sima interrupted, waving his sentence away with her hand. "Do not give me false hope. I can't bear it. You don't know what it'll do to me."

"I understand. I won't speak on it again."

"Thank you," Sima muttered. "Please, return me to my room."

"We won't be staying inside the Fae Palace, I'm afraid. It is too risky, as the queen is still on the throne instead of Tasia. Yadira has already been relocated. Now it is your turn."

Sima turned around and inspected Vincenzo carefully. He wore moss green armor with golden detailing, the metal sprawling like sunlight on a warm spring afternoon. His dual-toned hair was messier than usual and dark bags hung beneath his eyes.

"No," she said simply.

Vincenzo smirked. "You can't stay here. You can continue to hate me once you're somewhere safer. There are cottages in the forest near where you entered. Our plan did not work. Aurelio sent Yadira after us and has not yet left Aeria. We can devise a new one."

"Fine."

Sima followed behind Vincenzo, staring daggers into the back of his head as they walked. Sima gasped as they reached the corridor. Everyone moved slowly, almost frozen, clearly under Tasia's control. Sima's head swiveled, and she realized how worthwhile it would be to learn more about her power from the future Queen of the Eternita District.

The lack of meaningful movement around them was impossible to ignore. Even as they stepped through the portal outside of the Palace, Sima expected it to end. She was secretly delighted to find that the people of the city mirrored the inside, helping them escape without alerting others of their journey.

It wasn't until they reached the edge of the forest that the sounds of the city came alive once more behind them. Cosima looked back only once before slipping between the trees after

Vincenzo. Deep, full breaths swam in and out of her lungs.

"I am going to talk to myself now." Vincenzo said, ducking beneath a tree branch.

"Oh, really?" Sima rolled her eyes before doing the same.

"It's something I like to do. It has nothing to do with you, so you can listen if you want, or block me out. I spend too much of my time traveling around, and if I don't use my voice, I may realize I no longer know how to speak."

"Do as you please. This won't make me talk to you."

A deer with sharp pronged antlers poked its head from behind a tree, and Sima got a strange inkling that it was watching them, monitoring their every move. Its empty black eyes surveyed them tightly. The forest was breathing around them, full of more life than it was willing to reveal.

His head dipped in a nod. "In a place very far from here, there was a prince and his eleven terrible brothers. They called them the Sacred Twelve, but there was nothing seraphic about them. See, their mother was a wicked woman, unperceivable gifts lurking beneath her surface. It was as if the universe itself had underestimated the power that flooded her veins, and now the bloodstreams of each of her sons."

Cosima watched the canopy of leaves above them cast magnificent shadows across his back, the metal reflecting light in golden rays. Petite wildflowers encompassed the forest floor in sweeping purple and blue patches. Her chest ached, images of Ivo visible with each blink. As much as she wished she could ignore him, she listened closely, if only to distract from the pain that threatened to wipe her off her feet.

"Their mother was a High Priestess, one of a dozen Goddesses blessed with the gift of creation. Those twelve Priestesses govern the whole of the Eternal Kingdom, deciding when to expand and create, and when to destroy. Only one deity superseded the chosen Goddesses. That was Kismet."

Cosima's eyebrows raised. *Kismet.*

"Kismet cursed their mother for the unbalance she brought the universe and removed her from her position as High Priestess.

That is when she created her sons, drooling over her chance for vengeance. She bore eleven sons with a God named Luciano. Luciano, the Light God, granted his eleven sons immeasurable strength. Unfortunately for the Sacred Twelve's mother, Luciano refused to give her the twelfth son when he uncovered her plans."

"What did she have planned?" Cosima slapped her hand across her mouth, remembering her vow of silence. She cursed internally at what she believed was Vincenzo concealing a small laugh.

"Luciano realized the former High Priestess was raising their sons to take over the Eternal Kingdom. Each son was to romance a Priestess and lure them into marriage. Once all twelve were in position, the brothers were to murder their wives and seize control."

Sima garnered the feeling they were being watched and scanned the tops of the trees. There she spotted several tiny sprites, all wearing flower petals as clothing. One dressed in orange peony petals waved gracefully before her paper-thin rainbow wings fluttered and she disappeared. Directly in front of them, a reddish-brown fox walked with its head hung low as it moved out of their way.

"Ignore them. Tasia keeps a watchful eye on Eternita, and they know not to inform the sitting queen." Vincenzo held a large branch out of the way and waved her through. "With only eleven sons, the plan would fail, and Luciano threatened to reveal her misdeeds to Kismet if she carried another son. Desperate, their mother manipulated another God, Domani, and hid their child away. Domani is the God of Tomorrow, and it is his magic that created the planets for the High Priestesses to fill with their creations."

"That is your father?" The curiosity oozed from her skin. Vincenzo and Cosima walked side-by-side, giving her a clear view of the sad expression on his face.

"My mother is the one who created the people here on planet Haelos. Ehses, the Spirit Goddess, attempted to fulfill her plan by keeping me, the twelfth child, a secret from Luciano. She stored me with the Rani Guardians because my wings allowed me to blend in.

Wings are rare in Ambrosi, making it too suspicious to conceal me as an immortal. So she could think of nowhere better to keep me. I was to remain in the training camp until she sent for me."

A wooden cottage with a slender porch and tall glass windows appeared between the trees. Thick moss coated the roof, and candlelight flickered from within. Massive chunks of river stone paved the pathway to the front door.

Before they could reach the door, Vincenzo turned to Cosima. "You and I fell in love, and my eagerness to escape my destiny and live out my days with you was all that motivated me. Each day I spent in that training camp, I thought of you and the light you brought me. No longer did it matter that I was born to start a war alongside my brothers. The only direction I would follow is yours."

"Why did you keep it from me?"

"I thought you would recognize me. As you opened up more about what you endured in the Archipelago, I thought my admission would be poorly timed. I knew you would be hesitant to trust me if you knew the truth." Vincenzo rubbed the back of his head with his hand. "I wanted to tell you, and yet I hid it from you out of fear. I feel constant guilt for not saving you, for not knowing how to. Compared to my brothers, I am weak, and as a stowaway, I trained to be a Guardian, not an all-powerful member of the Sacred Twelve. I worried if you knew the truth, you would blame me for being unable to protect you."

Vincenzo's head hung. His words were a hot knife through her anger, dividing it in two. On one side, her rage ingrained itself in her, as natural as skin and bone. Then, something unfamiliar and quiet lay on the opposite end—hope.

"You truly came for me?" Sima stood tall, but she could not handle looking at him. Instead, she made eye contact with more sprites who gathered nearby to scrutinize them.

"And abandoned the Fate leashed around me for centuries by my mother. It has been so long since I saw Aurelio, I think he failed to recognize me at first."

"What about what Yadira said? She called you the 'Hive'," Cosima turned her head toward the wooden door beside them, suddenly aware Yadira was mere steps away.

"It is true. I possess powers of mental manipulation."

Sima took a step back from him. "How do I know you haven't used them on me?"

"You're nearly immune. All of my brothers possess this power, to varying degrees, and others exist that are capable of the same shielding as you. Yours isn't a full shield, but it prevents most applications of our power. At most, I have used my power to calm you, or help you rest."

"What about Aurelio?" Sima's fists clenched.

"I am unsure how effective his abilities are on you, but I would suspect your shield limits him or he would've controlled you outright. Instead, that block forced him to subdue you in other ways." Rage struck like lightning within his viridian eyes. "When I confessed I would die to keep you safe, I meant it. There are no more secrets between us, and if you never forgive me, I will understand. But please, allow me to protect you in whatever way I can."

Sima walked to the door and opened it. "After what he did to Ivo, he needs to be more worried about protecting himself than you need to be about me. He will pay for his transgressions."

Inside the cottage, a modest living area greeted Cosima, complete with two fluffy blue sitting chairs, a wooden side table, and a sizable rug embroidered with a sunrise over mountains. "Yadira," Sima called out, "Where are you?"

"Cosima?" Yadira's strained voice came from inside a nearby room.

Without thinking, Cosima followed her voice and threw open the door. Yadira was tucked into the bed, covered with a soft blanket. Instead of armor, she wore a loose tan top, and she had tied her curls up and away from her face. The last time she had seen Yadira, crystals riddled her face with deep black cracks. In their place now sat fading gray lines.

"Oh, Spirit," Cosima gasped, throwing her arms around Yadira in an embrace. "You're alive! Oh, you're alive. You tried to kill me not long ago, do you remember? I am relieved we can move beyond that."

Yadira coughed, causing Cosima to pull back with caution. "I agree," she whispered. "I never meant to bring you any harm. Please forgive me."

Cosima smiled. "There's no need to forgive you. At least they removed the crystals and now you are back to your normal self."

Yadira flashed a sad half-smile. "You cannot know how good it feels to be free of them."

"Excuse me," a voice said.

Cosima jumped at the unrecognized voice. "Who's there?"

Yadira laid her hand softly on Cosima's forearm. "He is a friend. Come in, Adelmo."

Adelmo stepped into the room with a sheepish grin. Lavender hair sprouted from his head, toppling over his elongated ears, which were decorated heavily with gold jewelry. He was tall, Vincenzo's height, and wore a tawny brown vest with a pure white shirt beneath. A colorful tie with Clementine, mocha, and olive swirls emerged from his collar. A small yellow chain connected a piercing on his nostril to an earring on his left ear. He bowed deeply.

"Apologies for frightening you, Queen Cosima."

Cosima felt her cheeks warm. "It's all right."

"I am here to be your liaison to the Palace, and, more specifically, to Princess Tasia. The Princess has requested that you three remain hidden here while we form a plan. In the meantime, you and I are to practice your skills and prepare you for the first stage."

"You mean prepare me to change the Fate of the Fae captured by King Aurelio, right?" Cosima took a seat on a wooden chair with a round cushion beside Yadira's bed.

"Precisely," Adelmo said. "Is there information you require to perform the change?"

"The broader my knowledge, the easier it will be for me to locate them." Sima tapped a finger on her lip. "It would be helpful to know more about their daily lives and habits to help me get a feel for threads that will stick instead of fraying or snapping."

"I will source this to the best of my abilities. I stocked the cottage with food, and please refrain from hunting while in our District. Animals are friends, not meals, here." Adelmo looked at Yadira as he spoke. "I have heard you are skilled with a bow," he added with a wink.

Yadira smiled. "You don't have to worry about that for now. I'm not sure I want to hold another weapon for quite some time."

Once Adelmo was gone, Vincenzo strolled into the room carrying two steaming bowls. Cosima took a bowl from his hand and inspected the contents. "You truly enjoy cooking soup, don't you?"

"Lentils, spinach, tomato and herbs," Vincenzo said as he handed Yadira her portion. "Soup brings me comfort, and it will bring both of you some much needed nutrients. I see you met Adelmo."

"He was nice," Cosima said. She blew a gentle stream of air across her spoon and took a bite.

"He will be back shortly," Vincenzo said, taking a seat on the opposite side of Yadira's bed. "Apparently, all three of us stink and need to be bathed."

Cosima turned up her nose. "I do not stink. I bathed not long ago."

Vincenzo cracked a smile. "We stink to the Fae. Tasia used her power to slow time to guarantee our escape because the Fae possess a superior sense of smell."

Yadira took small, slow sips of the broth. "What did she tell the others about Cosima's sudden leave?"

Vincenzo shrugged. "That's her fire to put out. All we need to worry about is taking those scent-masking baths and planning our next moves. I want to get us back into the Archipelago and take back Aeria once and for all."

Sima's heart thumped beneath her shirt at the thought of returning. Though wrath tumbled alongside her blood, an automatic fear response initiated, quickening her pulse.

"Don't worry, Cosima." Yadira laid her hand on Sima delicately, her eyes sodden with compassion. "We will enact your justice, regardless of the stakes. With Ombra and now Eternita's help, we will devise a fool-proof plan before we ever set foot on the sky islands."

"She's right," Vincenzo sighed. "He took us against our will, and your power was enough to buy us our freedom. There will be no stopping us once we have a formidable strategy under our belts."

Sima's head dipped as she fiddled with the ends of her dark hair. "I want to find Ivo—or her body, I suppose."

Vincenzo nodded knowingly. "We will. I promise you, we will. Together, we will bring her home to Ombra and allow her kin to perform the proper ceremonies."

A single tear slipped down Cosima's face. She quickly wiped it away with the back of her hand before meeting Vincenzo's gaze. Wrought-iron determination stitched into his expression.

"Aurelio's time is ending," Cosima's voice trembled as she spoke, "I won't know peace until he takes his last breath, and no divine intervention can sway me. I will bring forth his demise, and I will do it all with a smile on my face. I shall see that he regrets every breath he's taken, all while rivers of iron coat the insides of his lungs. Then we will see who was the truly powerful one."

4

The Retribution

When tribulation brings sinners to holy ground, hands high in
benediction, can the divine offer them relief, or do they fear becoming
unclean?
When their creations beg for answers, are the Gods capable of reply?

The children unsettle me.
They ask where they come from, and how, the scared God whimpers.
Too, they ponder, where it is I gain my existence, but even I do not know.

Chapter 33

With a deep breath in, Cosima submerged herself in the vat of purple tonic. Tasia was a strange future queen—that, Sima was sure of. Having things like this obscenely large tub lying around, whether for 'ceremonious' occasions, or otherwise, ultimately, was very creepy. The vat was a solid bowl carved of Black Obsidian and the stone was not fond of water, so it had been sealed, giving it a lightly glossed appearance. The coating did nothing to keep the stone from emanating energy.

It was sizable enough that Sima engulfed herself fully by merely dropping to her knees. The first dip had gone straight up her sinuses, burning as if it were poison. The sensation forced her to blow her nose four times before the pain ceased enough for her to go under again. According to Tasia's instructions, Sima was to dunk herself at least twelve times to build enough potion on her skin to completely neutralize her scent. It would last a week, perhaps a day or two more.

Then, they would be free to train and practice outside the cottage without risk of exposure. As her hair floated above her, fingers pinching her nose shut, she wondered if they had built the cottage around the massive tub or if magic was to blame for its position.

Her lungs burned, begging for a breath of fresh air. Sima ignored the desperate sensation as she felt her body absorb the surrounding darkness. She sat at the very bottom of the tub, a foot of water above her head.

Ivo's last words rang with a lifelike tone through her mind.

Repay me when you return, my Queen.

Cosima forced herself to endure the overwhelming urge to surface for a breath. Aurelio had taken Ivo from her, and no amount of denial would let Cosima forget what Aurelio had done. This was the moment to decide whether she would be weak, whether she would allow this to become her legacy.

No.

A loud gasp echoed through the bathing chamber, tonic splashing onto the tile below, as Cosima surfaced. "I won't stop here," she whispered in small pants. "I won't forget why you gave your life for me. Your sacrifice will not go silenced with my end."

On a nearby wooden table lay the viper pin Tasia had given her in the Palace. Cosima refused to be away from it, and though it did not belong to Ivo directly, Sima felt it was the only thing she had left of her friend. With wet steps, she found her way to the table and wrapped her fingers around it.

Cool goosebumps tickled their way up her arms, up to her biceps. She climbed back into the tub, thankful for the heat it brought back to her bare body. Her hair swirled like vines in a riverbed around her, her pale skin hidden beneath purple tonic. She unfurled her fingers to reveal the pin, holding just below the surface of the water. The purple hue seemed to melt into the vivid green drop at the end of the dagger.

Her fingers traced the intricate carvings, and Cosima's heart sped until all sound drowned outside of it. Without intending, her power flitted through her fingertips, revealing a memory. Cosima gasped, paralyzed as the vision overtook her.

"Please," a small brown-haired girl whimpered. The girl tumbled to the floor, heels digging into the cool iron beneath her feet as she peddled backward. "Get back, get back!"

"I always get the lively ones," a man growled as he reached for her. "Give up already."

Cosima's head swiveled as she took in her surroundings. They appeared to be in an abandoned home with cobwebs flanking her in every direction. The well-furnished home now breathed dust and sat in disarray. The tapestry hanging above the dirty fireplace depicted two Fae women in a loving embrace, sprites shooting arrows with heart-shaped tips at them from the clouds.

The man, Sima realized, was Fae, and the girl was Hexia. The pin holding her hooded cloak shut was undeniable evidence. It was the one Cosima was holding in the tub.

"This is her memory," Sima mused quietly. "Who are you, dear? What have they done to you, poor thing?"

Objects with highly personal value could be imbued with intense emotional energy. Those items allowed her to recall the memory that caused the rise in emotion.

The Fae man dragged her with a firm grip on her shoulders as he ushered her away from the seven large iron cages at the center of the room. The others were empty. He led her up the stairs. The young witch was nearly sent tumbling when the wood gave out beneath her step. He hoisted her by her arm in front of him, snarling as he pushed his white hair back. He exposed deep tan skin as he pushed up the black sleeves up his arms and reached for a dagger along his belt.

"You know what's next. Get it over with." He pressed the tip of the blade into the small of her back.

Her top lip wobbled as she entered the room, where an iron table fashioned with ankle and wrist restraints lay. Cosima shook her head as realization dawned on her. They were planning to steal this woman's life force in order to create a weapon out of it. The man picked up the Hexia girl and set her down roughly on the tabletop. "Lay down," he grumbled.

Only then was Cosima aware of others. Three more Fae men entered the room and watched as the first strapped down the girl.

"Is it going to hurt?"

A man with sea-green hair laughed. "Thankfully for you, no. We're not total monsters." His shoes clicked against the aged wood floor as he strode to the head of the table and gazed down at her.

"Why are you doing this? Why do you need my magic?"

"Not just your magic, your entire life force." His eyes were dark and earthy like tree bark, high cheekbones carving his face into that of a miraculous specimen. The sea-green hair came to a stop just below his elongated ears. "We are going to kill the blasphemous King of the Above and bring Haelos into an era of fortune. Only good things can come from his demise."

A man with apple-red hair cocked his head to the side, his lime-green eyes narrowing. "You are the sacrificial lamb of the evening. You are quite brave. Allow your passing to ensure a better future."

Cosima understood—the creation of the life force filled crystals had snowballed as a resistance effort against her *husband,* Aurelio. The white-haired one who led the young witch into the room left briefly and returned holding a small, yellowed scroll.

In a language Cosima could not decipher, the white-haired Fae began reciting what sounded like a song. It was melodic and slow. The green-haired one above her head held his hand over her chest. The girl whimpered, attempting to free her limbs. He winked at her, and at the same moment the tune ended, a stream of bright light burst from her chest and into the man's palm.

A small smoky quartz sphere, slightly smaller than his hand, appeared from thin air, absorbing the magic flowing from the girl. Her eyes rolled closed, and within seconds, her cheeks were gray and lifeless. Satisfied, the man rubbed the sphere clean on his black jacket before he slipped it into his pocket.

"That was the last one," the red-haired one said. "Let's set this one on fire. No tracks, remember?"

A long smile broached the green-haired Fae's face. "My pleasure," he said with a fraction of a bow forward. As their footsteps reseeded, Cosima eye's remained locked on the girl. Laughter echoed down the hall before the crackling of burning wood eclipsed it. Before the memory ended, Sima swore the girl's finger twitched.

Once returned to the surface, Sima shuddered as the weight of the memory settled across her shoulders. She sighed deeply, shaking her head to clear away the foggy cloud over her brain. The scene bothered Cosima; the image of the woman's body engulfed in flames at the end of the memory kept replaying in her mind with pinpoint accuracy. Her fists clenched, but she repeated the ritual as anger rattled like a loose animal inside her skeleton.

The scent of clover overpowered the other strange liquids Tasia had added, and the tiny confetti of leaves swirled around Cosima as she went for her seventh dip, fingers firmly clamping her nostrils shut. Monsters reigning terror in Ombra had animated corpses of entire generations of faeries, Echos and witches—all drained of life force. The smallest cages, meant for the sprites, concerned her the most. The cages bore teeth and claw marks, making rivets in the iron bars. According to Tasia, the magic of the Fae dampened around iron, allowing them to be held captive. Yet the sprites fought against the pain, desperate for escape. Hadn't that been her once, too?

Aurelio's capture of Aeria and subsequent treatment of the Below had increased the demand for intensely powerful weapons.

She twisted her hair to drain it of the potion completely. Tasia told her it would help with her scent as well as offer her protection. She wasn't sure what kind of security it offered, but the cleanse really did make her feel lighter and cleaner.

She rose and quickly dried herself off. Once dressed, Sima fitted the two blades given to her by Tasia into the sheaths at her side. They bore black obsidian like the vat, ovals of inky black displaying proudly from both sides of the hilt. They were long enough that they extended nearly two feet behind her, angled to avoid dragging along the ground. She swirled in the mirror, attempting to get her mind acquainted with compensating for the extra weight.

They were light, but every bit of additional weight could throw her off balance if it came down to it. She was taking her kingdom back, finally. Learning about herself, figuring things out with Vincenzo—that could wait. Her kingdom needed her, and it needed her now.

Sima stormed from the bathing chamber and hunted for Vincenzo.

He sat on the couch beside Yadira, and Adelmo stood near the door.

"Enjoy your dip?" Adelmo asked.

Cosima ignored him and grabbed Vincenzo's hand. He trailed behind her until they reached a thick patch of trees a few yards from the cottage.

"What is it?"

"I wanted to talk to you alone. I feel like I am going to burn right through my skin."

"What happened?" he said, arching a brow.

Sima revealed the pin she clutched in her right hand. "I had a vision. I saw the girl this belonged to. Four Fae men stole her life force and then burned down the home."

"I'm sorry you had to witness that," he said with a gentle, reassuring nod.

"That's not the point. I am *angry*. And I am not sad she is dead. I want to make people *pay* because she is dead. Because Ivo is dead. Why is the evil so far-reaching? Why are there deep horrors unfolding both silently and publicly and no one…no one does anything? It makes me wonder if there is truly anything I can do to save planet Haelos, or if it will be a never-ending battle against monsters of all shapes and sizes."

"Why do you want this?" Vincenzo asked. His green eyes were aglow.

"What do you mean? I think it is very clear why this matters to me."

"Is it?" Vincenzo asked. "I can understand why you would benefit from his permanent absence, why others would, as well, but that is not the end goal. You wish to remove him from the problem, so you may do what? What do you wish to see change?"

Cosima stared at her hands. "I know what it is like to not just be scared, but to be so terrified, all normal brain functions cease until you do whatever it takes to survive. I have wished for death, I have tried to bring myself to its door, and yet there, too, was fear. Not because I am afraid of dying, but because of all the things that called out to me about living, about breathing. What if I never tasted fresh air again? What about all the people suffering in the world behind me? When I imagine what exists in a time without Aurelio, I think only of the state of my world."

His eyes scanned her face, riddled with concern. Vincenzo laid his hand on hers with a reassuring squeeze before nodding for her to continue.

Cosima let out a breath and brushed her hair out of her face. "I am angry, down to the very pit of my soul angry. I cannot wrap my brain around the things people allow to unfold right beneath their noses, never daring a look. And I am tired of all the excuses and turned faces and people pretending their lives have nothing to do with the suffering of others. I am tired of keeping the peace, of being nice and acceptable. Others shun or mock me, but people on the other side do not adhere to their own preached morals."

Vincenzo opened his mouth to speak, seemingly unfazed by her abrupt, cathartic meltdown, but Cosima carried on. "Why is it enough that they are not us? Why is it enough that so long as the water never touches their toes, they won't care the world is drowning? How much longer can the suffering continue before one of us does something about it? That is what I want to change. I want to become the type of person who speaks up over injustice, and I want people by my side who commit to the same."

"You are already that person, and you have people who will go to the gutters of the Underworld to free you. We can fight for this together. You are precisely the leader you wished this world had."

Cosima wrapped her arms around herself as she allowed his statement to settle. The pain in her chest refused to disperse. "Tasia said leading is about knowing what lives are worth taking. The people of Aeria—I want to protect them, and yet so many of them have allowed the problems to worsen. Am I truly of a high enough caliber to bring change to their hearts?"

Vincenzo kicked a tiny brown rock on the forest floor with his boot. "Ambrosi are deeply connected to their immortality, and though they can live for the foreseeable future, it does not mean tomorrow exists for them. Part of the reason they were complicit in Aurelio's crimes is they, too, fear death. Perhaps more than others with mortal lifespans. For the humans, the Fae, the witches, death is a guarantee, an unavoidable end. They spend each day with the knowledge they will one day become dust, yet Ambrosi carry the idea they will never reach the empty void. I am unsure if there is any bigger threat than to take away their forever."

"Do you believe they will side with us if they knew we could remove the King?"

Vincenzo sighed. "When I came to Ombra, I had to decide. Either I could sit and continue to watch the way others treated these people, or I could do something about it. Immersed inside of their world, I couldn't help but develop love for them and hatred for those who put them in this position. *We* are what makes the difference. Someone must bear witness, someone must experience their pain and their suffering, and pass it onward. If no one else knows, at least we do, and we won't forget. Maybe it is up to us to inform the Ambrosi of the world below them and remind them why they should assist them."

Sima locked eyes with Vincenzo, tears streaming down her face. Her voice wobbled as she spoke. "We won't forget her, right? We won't forget Ivo?"

Vincenzo pulled her into his arms, wrapping them snuggly around her. "We will never forget her, I promise. She's not gone if she's with us. Always."

Emotion overtook her, blocking out all sensations other than the heaviness in her chest. For the first time in her life, Cosima unleashed the grief building in her chest, no longer restraining it for the sake of others. For decades she had scolded herself for showing any signs of weakness, and that shame had been mitigated only in her time away from Aeria. The others supported her, allowed her to speak on her past as much as she was willing, and offered their kind ears and warm reassurance.

Vincenzo's actions, however, went beyond a comforting gesture. Though she was thankful for the friends she made, and the compassion they showed, none brought her peace as thoroughly as Vincenzo did. For days, her mind lingered on the betrayal, wondering how she did not know his real identity. Then, his story in the forest had shifted her perspective, forcing Cosima to reevaluate the way she felt.

"I thought I hated you," she whispered against his chest. "And I wanted to hate you."

"I understand," he said, brushing her hair from her face. "I wish I never kept it from you. Listen." His fingers trailed her chin lightly. "I can feel your pain and I want you to know I always in awe of you. I admire the way you keep going and never give up. No matter the direction we go, I look up to the way you transform every force against you, all to fight for what's right. Don't let anyone, not even me, stop you from getting what you want."

She stared down at her palms, scrutinizing them for some sign that she was built to handle her power, built to withstand the weight that came along with it. When they fell flat against her legs, it was not doubt that filled her, or even motivation. It was something calmer, more akin to acceptance. She would do what needed to be done. She would learn intuitively which lives to take and which to spare.

"I will be the type of queen that others will respect for millennium. There is a world where I no longer live to be submissive to others or am forced to perform to earn my right to live. No more acting like the perfect doll, never faltering, never having an outburst. I know what we need to do, and I know exactly how we will bring the King to his knees."

Chapter 34

The field was a short hike away from the cottage, the path there composed of small hills to meander over and a gentle riverbank to cross. From there, they would cross the open grass field until they were far enough from the tree line to practice.

In the mornings, Adelmo would run Cosima through drills, painstakingly teaching her how to mimic the pockets of time Tasia created. It brought forth many pounding headaches and burned through her magic completely. The constant drainage increased her reserve, but she was gaining a grip over her ability. Still, she wedged small changes into the Fate of the kidnapped member of Tasia's family, unaware if her changes were fully fruitful.

In the afternoons, Vincenzo ran her through physical exercises, meant to boost her overall strength. They focused on her abdominal muscles so she could better wield the long swords at her sides and improved the muscle tone in her arms for accuracy and speed. The training made her mind and body exhausted, for which she was thankful. It brought her relief from pain and worry.

For two grueling weeks, Cosima stifled every urge to point a knife to someone's throat and beg them to take her back to Aeria. There was no telling if Ivo's plan worked, but there was also no sign of Aurelio. Although the crystals allowed Yadira passage into the Fae District, Eternita was secluded beneath the enchantments, and he made no appearances.

"If she was successful with the Light Reserves, wouldn't we have seen some sign she locked him out?" Cosima's arms were heavy and tired as she practiced her punches with Adelmo as Vincenzo was running behind.

Adelmo expertly danced around her throws, smiling all the way. His jewelry gave off gentle clinks as he moved. "Perhaps he has yet to leave Aeria—therefore, it will not take place until he leaves, right?"

"We're honestly not entirely sure. We only read through the Tome one time before we had to flee. My friend took it with her." Sima swallowed hard.

"You must have faith your friend did her best to bring you the opportunity. Only time will tell the level of success. For now, we are working on improving your abilities. You shall be a sharpened weapon by the time we launch our attack on the Archipelago."

"About that," Cosima rubbed her wrist, kneading out the tight muscle, "I have been thinking of the best way to use my power in order to help those in rebellion be successful at reclaiming the sky islands."

Adelmo straightened. "What have you come up with?"

"My powers cannot make anyone do what they wouldn't already do, but Vincenzo mentioned the Ambrosi went along with him out of fear or complacency. What if I show them he is not infallible?"

"How do you plan to show them this?"

Sima scratched her chin. "Simon is a gifted painter, and right now, his canvases are the only depiction we have of the horrors occurring in the Districts. I say, we distribute these, and sow the seeds of doubt against him. Also, the King must have replaced the dead Emblems with new Guardians by now. I know one Guardian, named Caelian, who is especially ruthless. He will step on anyone to get to the top. I think there is way I can unfold some chaos through him."

"I like this idea," Adelmo said, rubbing his jaw.

The trees behind them rustled, leaves parting around Vincenzo's tall frame and the outer corners of his wings. In the sunlight, the bone white interior of them was especially bright. He smiled at her, and she returned it. Though she had allowed herself a moment of vulnerability with him about Ivo, he had spent the past two weeks with her, still keeping a careful distance.

"Ah, my replacement arrives." Adelmo clasped his hands together. "I shall begin tending to Yadira."

Sima frowned. Yadira was recovering much slower than a Guardian should. Vincenzo suspected the reason lay in the crystals the Fae found in her gut, but there was no telling how long it would take her to fully heal. In the meantime, Adelmo attended to her wounds, took her for slow walks around the interior of the cottage, and cooked her meals.

"You started without me, I see." Vincenzo unsheathed his sword with gusto. "And I shall meet your disrespect with proper scorn."

"Yes," Cosima said, crossing her arms and unveiling the slender blades at her hip with a slow pull, "but what of your tardiness?"

Vincenzo arched a brow. "What of it?"

Cosima loosed a small laugh as Vincenzo began darting around the space in front of her, using his wings. The wind from it blew back her hair as their blades collided over and over. "Where were you?"

He jumped into the air, and stared down at her, blade directed at her face. "I unearthed an avenue to communicate with Calix and the others back in the Ombra District. They are all right, though I know not if I can claim the same for you."

She thwarted his attack, narrowly missing the opportunity to spear him by a few inches. She rallied again, aiming for his legs as he floated. His wings lifted him higher as he scowled.

"What else did you speak about?" Cosima's pulse quickened at the thought of her friends.

"They wish to join us, of course. They have continued to work on the crystals, and we might have sourced enough of them to be capable of bringing down Aurelio."

"*What?*" Cosima breathed. "So, there really is a chance of killing him?"

Vincenzo landed in front of her, lowering his sword. "It appears so. Calix and Alma also wished for me to inform you they miss you and will help in any way they can."

"Perhaps there is something they can do. The Hexia are powerful enchantresses, and though the King kept them captive in Aeria without their powers for quite some time, a bit of practice may have them back to a suitable baseline."

"You wish to use their enchantments how?"

"What if they could shield us as we made our way to the Archipelago, so no Guardians can shoot us with arrows in the sky?"

Vincenzo tipped his head to the side. "That's an interesting idea."

"We could move in waves. The first people who arrive can initiate the plan. Arriving unseen means we can sneak in droves of paintings by Simon. If we clear out his home, we are bound to find enough to line the streets before the citizens wake." Cosima sheathed her blades. "The following waves will come and find positions to hide. When the time is right, all of those on our side will be ready to attack."

"You have been thinking a lot about this, haven't you?"

"Yes. While everyone is distracted, you and I can search for Ivo, though my plan only works if the bubble around Aeria is truly down. We must also locate the Tome. If we're lucky, it will be in the Temple."

Vincenzo sighed. "If that is the case, stealth is going to be our biggest concern."

Sima's face glittered with determination. "We can do this—especially together."

Vincenzo nodded. "You have been improving over these last few days. I know you will do it if you have to."

"I will be all right," Cosima said softly. "Have you or Tasia agreed upon a date for our movement?"

"There is a new moon coming."

"The cover of nightfall will aid my plans greatly."

"The new moon is it then." Vincenzo raised his blade again,

and the two of them sparred until it left them panting again. Cool sips of water brought to them by Adelmo brought their breathing back to a steady pace.

Once Adelmo disappeared back through the woods toward the cottage, Vincenzo sat beside Sima in the grass and pushed his hair from his face. "There is one more thing I was asked to bring to you. I promised not to keep secrets from you, but I have been trying to find the best way to phrase it."

"I can take it," Cosima said. Her lips pressed into a line.

"The Doc was studying the drugs Aurelio was giving you. After we left, Calix found them and brought them to him. Once he analyzed them, he discovered concerning findings."

"Oh no. What is in them?"

"The first identified ingredient was Death's Mirror—*Mortoid*, as expected. However, along with it, crushed crystal fragments ground into a fine powder. You were ingesting life force crystal in order to amplify your power. He was bypassing your consent by forcing your body to utilize your magic while the Death's Mirror caps incapacitated you."

Cosima blinked several times, wondering if she heard him wrong. "There's no way I was ingesting those crystals. This entire time, he has been increasing my power through them?"

"You told me the most he gave you at once was three, right? You must have an incredible tolerance to the crystals. It is likely these magnified your healing capabilities, as well."

"Explains why he was so willing to risk my life. He was equally sure the crystals would help my body heal," Cosima murmured, chewing her thumbnail.

"How do you feel about this?"

Cosima straightened her shoulders. She wasn't sure. "I feel violated, like I have done something horrible by ingesting life force stolen from people. Alternatively, my impulse is to take them and use the increase in my power to ensure I kill him when I see him again."

"I can understand that desire. We cannot return their life force after it enters the weapon, but we can do everything in our power to make sure they do not create more."

"Perhaps this is the only justice I can grant them, to use their power for good."

Vincenzo nodded solemnly. "Perhaps."

"What is it?"

"It worries me," he whispered. "I support whatever choice you make, and I will defend you until my dying breath. But how do we know how much your body can withstand?"

Sima glanced down at her feet, unsure why she averted her gaze. "I appreciate the concern for my wellbeing. I am viewed as a tool to be used by others, usually."

"You are free to make your own decisions with me. I would not force you into anything," Vincenzo said.

"If that's the case, then see if someone from Ombra can bring the remaining capsules."

"The Doc can take out the *Mortoid*, to avoid the hallucinations." Vincenzo turned away from her. Cosima glanced up in time to spot his wings flex and shudder.

"What was that?" Cosima stepped forward with her hand outstretched. Her fingers ran along the fine feathers. Vincenzo rolled his shoulders in response to her touch.

"The pain hasn't completely subsided yet. I'm not sure why. It comes and goes."

Sima's fingertips pressed lightly against the muscle where his once terrifying wound had been open. Now the skin was a deep purple, as if his body was sealed shut with hot metal. The muscles beneath were taut with tension. A flicker of guilt chimed at the realization he had been training with her all this time, hiding his pain and discomfort.

"I'm sorry. I didn't realize you were so uncomfortable. Why did you not mention it?"

He turned to her and grasped his hand around hers and held her to his chest. "This is not the time for things to be about me. It is about you and people who need our help. It's nothing I can't handle."

"We could ask Adelmo. There has to be something they can

do.”

Vincenzo frowned. “No, really. I am fine. No need for anyone to fuss. I will contact Calix, and she will bring the crystalline powder—free of mushrooms. In the meantime, how are things coming along with our new Fae friend?”

Birds sang from the air above their heads as they flew by, and Sima shuddered. Never before had Cosima seen such expressive wildlife. Only a few species of bird frequented the Archipelago, and the exotic animals of Ombra were Echos in their shifted forms. Here, the creatures lived alongside the Fae, and they were given free rein. The weeks she had spent in Eternita brought her no closer to apathy. Instead, her interest in the life here only grew. Sima inhaled the fresh scent of the trees.

“Every day I grow stronger. We began trials this morning to speed up recall of my power. He gives me a description, like Aurelio would, as well as some facts about them. From there, I find the threads, plotting possibilities without making significant changes.”

Vincenzo smiled.

“What is it?” Sima asked.

“I enjoy seeing you embrace your power. You have come a long way. In the beginning, you thought there was no way to access your power without the drugs, and now you’ve shown us all you can. Even Aurelio underestimated you, which is exactly why we stand here today.”

“I’ll be more willing to accept compliments when I really nail down my abilities.”

“Don’t be hard on yourself. Only a couple short months have passed since you left the Archipelago, and you have stepped into your role more now than ever. Moments ago, you were suggesting plans for bringing him down and taking back your throne.”

Sima chewed her lip. “There was a time in my life I thought I would never regain the confidence or strength to do something about him.”

“And now?”

Sima smiled. “And now, I spend every waking moment

scheming."

"It's a good look for you. Quite the mastermind, and all."

"Oh?" Sima bit back a grin. Before she could continue, the sounds of someone shouting their names interrupted them.

"Cosima! Vincenzo!"

Sima turned to find Adelmo racing toward them, covered in blood. Vincenzo grabbed Sima's wrist, pulling her to his chest. He held onto her as he flew them across the field to meet Adelmo.

"What happened?" Cosima was frantic, bolting from Vincenzo's arms to grasp onto Adelmo. They dashed toward the cottage as he spoke.

"Someone attacked us." Adelmo pointed toward the dwelling. "Yadira and I fought them off, but she is still weak. I can't get her out of there. More might be coming."

"Is she injured? Are you?" Vincenzo's brow knit together.

"Yadira's pain is off the scales. I am concerned she has torn something within."

"What do we do?" Cosima asked, running her hands through her hair, fingers cold across her scalp.

"We can't go back to the Palace. I'm afraid I don't know what to do until I can contact Tasia." The small cottage came into view through the trees, and Sima bolted toward the door.

"We will defend her until you can get word to Tasia and return," Vincenzo said from behind her.

Adelmo sprinted toward the Palace, moving majestically like a fleeing deer, and disappeared into the forest. Cosima bolted through the doorway and found Yadira clutching her gut with one hand, and a bloody weapon with the other as she sat on the plump sofa.

"Yadira," Cosima breathed, dropping to her knees beside her friend.

"Hey," she said weakly.

"It's all right, friend," Vincenzo said, slipping the blade from her hand. "We're here, it's all right."

Cosima gripped the Guardian's hand tightly in hers and brushed a small kiss across the back of it. Yadira smiled softly at her. "Do you remember all the times you told me you wished you could be more like me?"

Sima nodded. "Yes?"

"Lately, I want to be more like you. You are brave, you haven't given up. The day *he* found you again and took you back—it was my fault. The crystals were already in me at that point, and I led him directly to you. I am so sorry, to the both of you."

"That is not your fault. Please don't apologize for that," Sima said.

"We've got some visitors," Vincenzo growled from his position near the window.

Cosima stood up and found her way to his side. Outside the dwelling were four Fae men wearing clothing much too fine for them to be fighting in. The elaborate designs reminded Cosima of everything in this District: over-the-top and artful. Their hands gripped daggers, and the taut expressions on their faces revealed their intentions. The fight was not over.

Without thinking, Cosima pressed her hand to the window and halted time. Leaving Vincenzo and Yadira frozen behind her, she crept outside and stood beside the men. She ran her finger along the forehead of the one closest to her, and let the threads flutter forward.

Chapter 35

Sima worked quickly, no longer wasting time. Her time with Adelmo practicing this very skill had done her well, and with well-versed hands, she began threading. Even with limited information about the intruding man, Sima found his path simple to maneuver.

She gathered the man's name was Ewan, and he was originally a piece of the Royal Fae Guard—before the Rani Guardians swamped their position. His disdain for Aeria, and especially the Guardians, was palpable, and Sima followed the invisible scent her instincts noticed. She stitched together an obscene amount of scorn for Guardians, one that far tipped the scales to push him beyond the realm of rational thought. Blood-lust would consume him, and the fire would burn through him in seconds.

The others were of a similar sort, though two pushed further into panic and the depths of their fears instead. When time resumed, the sight of Vincenzo emerging from the home had a split effect. Two stuttered, hesitating behind a mentally self-imposed barrier as their companions pushed forward with blinded rage.

The attacks were sloppy and wrathful, each movement sending them toppling beneath the force of their own weapons. Vincenzo experienced little resistance from them, and though they were fairly well-trained, they were still no match for the Guardian. He sliced through each of them cleanly, as if their bodies were made not of flesh, but of silk.

Between flutters of her eyelashes, the sight before her became bloody and still. Vincenzo's chest heaved with weighted breaths as he locked eyes with her. "It's done," he whispered.

"For now," Cosima replied, just as quietly. She turned on her heel and headed back inside what Cosima now considered a sitting target. Without words, Vincenzo helped Yadira to a stand, and Cosima slid beneath her arm. The three slowly made their way outside, interrupted by Adelmo's return.

Two Guardians flanked him, both draped in Eternita armor. The common red-black hair of the Rani spilled from their scalps and hung on their shoulders. The taller one of the two bore a small gold hoop through her lip and was holding Adelmo as they flew through the trees. She met Sima's eyes with deadly precision.

"Where do we go?" Vincenzo asked the Fae man. Several deer with intimidating sets of antlers pressed closer, no longer lingering in the tree line, instead standing mere feet from the group.

"Princess Tasia requests your return to the Palace. These Guardians will carry Yadira."

"What about the queen? Aren't I considered her enemy?" Cosima asked.

Adelmo nodded tightly. "The queen is aware of your presence. However, fortune favors you. She will cease attacks in exchange for your services."

"My services?" Cosima took a step back as the largest deer broke formation and strode before her, stopping an inch from her face. She stared into the black pools of its eyes and dared not a blink.

Adelmo cleared his throat. "You may speak with her if you like. She can—she can hear you."

Cosima's line of sight bounced between the Fae man and the animal in front of her. "What do you want me to do?" Cosima shivered. She found herself unnerved by speaking to the Queen of the Eternita District in this way, but she pushed herself to explain. "I want you to know my hand on your Fate was not a malicious one. In fact, I made no changes to your Fate at all. King Aurelio Aphelion ordered me to, and though the option lay within my hands, I did not alter any piece of your life. The only thing I know of your life is your birth, and nothing further."

The deer cocked its head to the side at a near unnatural angle. It blinked before the entire herd bolted through the forest, leaving the group behind. Cosima looked to Adelmo and the other Guardians for an answer, but their faces offered no answers.

"Yadira," the taller Guardian said, reaching for Yadira's arm. "Come."

Yadira slipped easily into her arms, though she studied the woman's eyes intensely. "I thought you were dead," she mumbled. "So, this is where you've been hiding."

The woman looked away from Yadira and sighed. "Many of us sought refuge in this District after being discarded for dead in Ombra. Eternita was the only chance for me to continue to serve without the King knowing I was alive."

"It is enough for me you are alive," Yadira said, her face stoic.

Cosima's heart tugged at the realization the two were once friends. Vincenzo tapped on her shoulder and motioned with his hands that he intended to carry her and fly her to the Palace. Sima wrapped her arm around his shoulders as he hoisted her up.

The group silently made their way to the Palace, the whistling of the wind the only noise. Cosima's mind wandered repeatedly, questioning if she had conveyed her point to the queen effectively, or if she was now marching straight into a trap. Cosima had slowly trusted Adelmo, but panic surfaced at the thought of being betrayed. After all, Adelmo worked for the Palace. He was Fae. His loyalties were never with Cosima, no matter her mission.

The moment they reached the entrance of the Fae Palace, Cosima immediately noticed the frozen bodies of citizen and Guardians surrounding them. Tasia had used her powers to once again freeze those around them. Through the towering doors, Cosima spied Tasia twirling the end of her ponytail around her finger as she tapped her foot.

Tasia turned toward them and threw her hands up. "What is taking so long? You act as though I can do this all day." She spun and stomped away, leading the group up the stairs and into a plush seating area. The doors closed and left them alone. Cosima took a seat in one of many chestnut chairs surrounding a long oval table.

Vincenzo spun the chair beside her to make room for his wings and sat. Cosima searched for Yadira and nearly panicked when she realized they were alone with Tasia.

"She will come in a moment, do not fret." Tasia waved her hand. "My mother is coming to speak with you both. I thought I had a handle on the Faerie friends in the forest, but apparently my leash is waning. Nevertheless, after many tough conversations with her, my mother agreed to spare you under the condition you use your powers for her."

"What does she want?" Cosima wrapped her arms around herself.

Tasia shook her head. "I don't know."

"What happens if she doesn't agree?" Vincenzo's jaw tightened.

"I will protect you long enough to flee the Palace once more. From there, you would be on your own. Perhaps you would require a return to Ombra."

"It's not safe," Vincenzo growled. "I have been keeping in contact with my District, and Aurelio's worst is flooding it, searching for her. We can't go back, not yet."

"What?" Cosima breathed. "You didn't tell me that."

Vincenzo shook his head, but Tasia cut him off before he could speak. "Why else would you have remained in my District?"

Cosima balled her fists. "I thought we were working together to take back the Archipelago and defeat Aurelio. Am I mistaken?"

"If you can accomplish what my mother asks, you will gain the aid of every Guardian in this District. Otherwise, we are more limited in numbers, especially now that we must move in even tighter silence."

Cosima nodded. The door to the room opened as a Guardian stepped inside. He moved over and allowed the queen to enter. Cosima recognized her sunlight yellow hair and fragile white eyelashes, exactly as they had been when Cosima glimpsed her as a baby. The queen wore a slim but elegant amber colored dress. Gold earrings hung on her lobes, bearing giant jade gemstones, matching a carved butterfly pendant around her neck.

Though she was the queen, Cosima couldn't help but notice the distinct lack of power coming from her. Tasia and her siblings were unbearable with the weight of their magic, yet none wafted off her. Her elongated ears were delicate, as were her facial features. She appeared to be the same age as her children. Cosima blinked, wondering if it was an illusion.

"You are the Queen of the Aeria Archipelago." Her voice was crisp and sounded regal, reminding Cosima of how her own mother once sounded when she held the crown. Cosima swallowed.

"Yes." Cosima almost called her Solara, the name the family had given her at birth. "I'm afraid I don't know what to call you."

She smiled, before taking a seat in the chair her Guardian pulled out for her. "Queen Silana is fine."

"Noted," Cosima said. "What is it you want from me?"

"Direct," Silana responded. She held her hand out, and the Guardian placed a slender glass of ruby red wine into her grasp. She took a slow sip. "I heard what you told my companion in the forest. I have been considering whether I believe you. However, I can also recognize how incredibly useful a power such as yours can be."

"I don't allow others to use my powers," Cosima's gaze hardened. "It is ultimately up to me how I use them. I am uninterested in being useful to others."

Silana's expression soured, and Tasia's gaze bounced between them, the whites of her eyes showing more than usual.

"Is that so? Not even if I were to provide you a blade I can guarantee would slaughter King Aurelio upon your success?"

"We have plenty," Vincenzo bit out.

"Plenty," Silana laughed. "How can you be so sure?"

"How can you?" Cosima retorted. Her magic flared at her fingertips, begging her to use it, but Cosima shoved it away. The queen had led the creation of weapons made from lifeforce, and only fear lined Sima's gut as she thought of what it must have taken to craft a weapon she was so confident in.

"I know much more about Aeria than the King would like. I suspect this is the reason he came after me so viciously for all these years. My daughter tells me she showed you to the containment area. I am sure you think of me as a monster, sacrificing my people to craft a defense, and on some days, I likely would agree with you. However, I will sacrifice a few to save the many. I know this weapon will work because I have spent decades crafting it."

"The situation has gotten incredibly out of hand," Vincenzo said tightly. "Those crystals are causing problems across every District and have led to the death of humans. How can you be so irresponsible and ask us to trust you? Do you know how much has gone into trying to undo the horrors you have created?"

Silana narrowed her eyes at Vincenzo. "So, you would rather we do nothing?"

"Enough arguing," Cosima said, slamming her fist on the table. "Tell me what you want from me."

Silana glared at Vincenzo before turning back to Sima. "I want to come to some agreements between the two of us on how the world will run after his demise."

"Agreements?" The word made her uneasy.

"As you witnessed, protection of my people became vital due to the burning star that is the King. He scorched everything in sight, with no rhyme or reason. I simply want to ensure this does not need to happen again. To my dismay, you traversed through my boundaries."

"Get on with it," growled Vincenzo.

Silana huffed. "You are able to amend Fate, yes? We could explore the extent of your capabilities and give rise to a world where my people are stronger than ever. Your power could grant us that. You can change the tides of Fate, you can bring favor, fortune."

Cosima's mouth went dry. She had not considered using her abilities in such a way before. "How much meddling are you trying to do?" she asked.

"Who is to tell how Aeria is run after his demise?"

"I am." Cosima clenched her jaw.

"For now," Silana said, with an amiable smile. "Ambrosi of any kind are too cocky. One day, you might misstep, as well. I believe the people of this planet should decide how to run this planet instead of leaving it up to islands full of invasive, pitiful immortals."

"Is it wise to insult the woman who had her hands on your Fate before and could do it again?" Vincenzo said, his head leaning to one side as the two locked into a staring match.

"Tasia seems to think you're not the threat he preached you to be," Silana replied simply.

"I will deal with whatever fires you set later. I want the blade. We are moving under the next new moon."

"Is this the best decision?" Vincenzo whispered to Cosima.

Cosima ignored him. Silana eyed her carefully for a moment before she snapped her fingers. The Guardian placed a thin brown notebook in her hand. Silana slid it across the table to Cosima.

"If I do this for you, once Aurelio is dead, the walls here come down and your Guardians go back to defending the Star Realm Portal. Your District must locate all the reanimated bodies and eliminate them, as well as cease all production of those crystals."

Silana furrowed her brows. "You wish to eliminate a profitable avenue out of fear."

"You are killing people to make them!" Cosima stood up, causing the table to shake.

Silana met her eyes. "People will always have to die. There are worse things in our reality than your husband Aurelio. How will we handle them then? I am the only person concerned with actually protecting this planet. How did he find us in the first place?"

"Cosima is working hard on protecting this world, and it would do you well to stop considering her the enemy. She has this planet's best intentions in mind." Vincenzo said.

"Mother," Tasia said quietly. "Perhaps it is best we save this for another time."

Silana snapped her fingers, and this time, the Guardian pulled a dagger from its sheath along his waist and handed it to Cosima. Cosima wrapped her fingers around it. She gasped, feeling the energy pulse within the weapon. The jade embedded in the hilt mirrored the ones Silana wore, and its pull was magnetizing. Before she could change her mind, Sima grabbed the weapon and the book from the table and walked toward the door.

"You will lend me every Guardian in Eternita for the resistance movement under the new moon. Or I *will* come back and make you regret defying me."

Once they were in the hallway again, Cosima spotted Yadira sitting on a floral-patterned sofa nearby. Her skin was full of color once more, and no sweat marked her brow from pain. She immediately noticed Cosima and Vincenzo's hardened faces and stood up to walk beside them. Though not fully healed, the down time had given her enough strength to walk with only Vincenzo offering an arm to balance her. The others in the Palace remained frozen as they exited.

"Where are we going?" Yadira asked.

"Ombra," Cosima replied.

"Cosima," Vincenzo said. "Please, it's not safe there. They have invaded the underground, and very few spots remain untouched. Since we left, he has been bombarding it with Guardians to scout for you. We are making our move on Aeria in only four days. Our time is best spent here, preparing."

"And sit and wait in the cottage for Silana to decide she still considers me her enemy and kills us in our sleep? How can we trust we are going to be safe here until it is time?"

"That won't happen," Tasia said from behind them.

Cosima turned to her. "You never told me your mother hates all of Aeria and wishes to lead it herself."

"It is not herself she wishes to lead. It is me."

"You want to rule the Archipelago? There is no way for the Fae to do that, no matter what you desire."

"That may be true," Tasia replied, "But there is no need for Aeria at all. Perhaps this world is better governed by the people who inhabit it."

"I've heard enough," Cosima growled.

"She is misguided, but she loves our people. She won't hurt you in your sleep. I promise you will be safe for the next few days, and she is going to dispatch the Guardians here to aid your movement. I will go with you to the cottage and when the time is right, we will all make our move."

"We are going with my plans then," Cosima said, turning her back to Tasia and continuing to walk. "I know precisely how we will make a move against Aeria."

Once they were back at the cottage, Vincenzo got to work cleaning up the blood with a cloth and bucket. The bodies of the Fae slaughtered in the field out front were gone by the time they returned. If crimson did not fill the dirt, Cosima would have thought she imagined their existence all together.

The air between them was thick, and Cosima excused herself to take a bath. The large obsidian tub still sat in the center of the bathing chamber. She filled the vat with steaming hot water and tossed in various herbs for her scent as usual.

Her skin marbled with pink from the heat of the water as she washed her hair. Her mind firmly fixated on plans to overwhelm Aeria and take back her kingdom. Each time Tasia or Silana's words wiggled their way inside her thoughts, she pinched her nose shut and held herself below the water until the desperation for air cleared her head again.

Where is my little dove?

Aurelio's voice haunted her brain, the stress seeming to make it more lifelike than it had been in a long time. She shook her head, as if it would make the sound of it cease, but it only grew louder.

You think you can kill me? It's a shame you haven't learned your lesson.

"I can do this," Sima whispered to herself. "I am strong enough for this."

You've never been strong enough to lead. Aurelio's voice echoed in her head. *You were happy to meet me, happy to let me take over so your weakness wouldn't infect our kingdom.*

"If only you could convince me again I am weak, then maybe you'd still have a chance," she said harshly, voice still hushed. "I know who I am, and who I do this for. I know why I fight and why I wake up. I know none of those reasons have anything to do with you."

They'll never obey you as their queen, not after how miserably selfish you have been.

"Seeking peace is not selfish." She submerged herself and though his voice rambled on, Cosima found he, too, grew quiet during her body's quest for air.

It was then that the idea hit her, a plan for how to wipe out not just Aurelio, but all who eagerly lapped at his ankles and encouraged his tactics. Rani and Ambrosi alike were at fault, pushing beyond submission and into conspiring alongside him.

It finally made sense to Cosima why a man capable of slaughtering them all even took the time to make himself look good in front of others, why he would not force the Ambrosi to run the planet under duress but won them over with riches and leisure instead.

"You," she said to his voice inside her head, "You are truly terribly afraid of being alone. You could have come to this planet and spent your time killing us all. Instead, you made yourself the King, you cared what others thought of you."

A small laugh broke from her lips as she realized she would take everything from him, and more.

Chapter 36

"You really think it will work?" Vincenzo said, rubbing his chin.

"Yes," Cosima said, crossing one leg over the other as she sat at the table. Before them was a large breakfast with a slew of vegetable dishes she had never tried before. "I say we go to Aeria and use me as bait. We make sure this time that Aurelio makes it off the islands. Then we get to the Temple and turn it all back on, with him outside of it."

"How will you know how to lock him out if you cannot locate the Tome she used?" Tasia tossed her chestnut hair over her shoulder and picked at her nails.

"I think Vincenzo and I should return to Aeria as soon as possible and search the Temple and through all the servants' tunnels. It is important we use as little of my power as we can. This will cut down on unexpected fallout from changes that I cannot predict."

Tasia nodded. "Fair enough."

"The Guardians are all on board with collecting Simon's paintings, correct?" Vincenzo asked Tasia.

"Yes, they are aware of the plan."

"About that," Cosima said, stretching her hands in front of her, "I want to bring a few of the fungus covered beasts to Aeria."

"What?" Yadira said, choking on her sweet potato noodles. "No way, Cosima. You can't put everyone in Aeria at risk. What if that thing gets loose and starts killing Ambrosi children? Immortal children are the most vulnerable."

"I'm aware," Cosima said, "On the new moon, I don't want the citizens to remain in the housing areas. I want them all corralled into the center of each island. From there, you will shield them, and they can watch what unfolds."

"Is there no chance of the other Guardians agreeing to be on your side?" Tasia asked.

Yadira shook her head. "No chance. The majority of them are fiercely protective of him. Our brothers and sisters are lost to the maniac that calls himself the King."

"We shall do it your way, then," Tasia said, clapping her hands together. "I had a lovely breakfast with you all, but I am going to rest more to prepare to shield the both of you tonight."

Cosima dipped her head in acknowledgment. Yadira excused herself as well, and Cosima and Vincenzo found themselves alone together.

"I have plans for you, too," Cosima said once she was sure the others were out of earshot. "Your powers, the mind manipulation. Explain more of it to me."

"The further I extend it, the less impactful it is. The strongest reaction comes within a few feet, the weakest being a few hundred feet, and no further than that. I am also equally limited by how many I am trying to sway. Two hundred is harder than ten, ten harder than one. The power also fades if I am not actively concentrating on it."

"How long can you uphold it over a group of twenty?"

"An hour, maybe two, depending on how pliable they are. I have to be sure to not get injured, or I won't be able to use it all. When we were escaping Aeria, I couldn't focus well enough. To be honest, I refrain from using my power as much as I can."

"Why is that? You maintained control over the Guardians in Ombra."

"No, I didn't, Cosima," Vincenzo's hair fell in front of his face. "Not in the way you think. I used it on them until I could see their reaction to Ombra. All of them upheld the secrecy voluntarily when they saw what I helped build. It feels…wrong."

Cosima chuckled lightly. "I know that feeling well. Putting my hand into the Fate of others has an immeasurable weight to it. I never feel qualified enough to make decisions as grand as I do. Something so small can end up being disastrous. I feel as though I am molding with fire, terrified of it melting my flesh."

Vincenzo stood up at the same time as Cosima. She picked up her bowl, but before she could take it to be washed, he was standing in front of her. He lowered the dish to the table before wrapping her hand in his. "Whatever it is you want me to do, I will do my best to achieve it."

"I want you to use your abilities to keep others out of our way, however you find yourself able. The fewer people getting in our way, the better. We need to be direct. Once we have locked the King out, it will be up to us to find him and then," Cosima slipped out the dagger from Silana, "we kill him."

She stared up at him, searching his emerald eyes for any hints of doubt or fear. She found none. He was ready for this, as was she.

"Are you nervous?" he said, brushing a lock of hair from her face, his thumb gently trailing the tip of her chin. He now took his turn searching her for hidden emotions. He would not find many. There was a storm raging wickedly inside of her right now, the tantrum of a soul begging for a chance to hit back. She would not deny it.

"No," she said, swallowing. "There are injustices I have been trying to heal from for fifty years. There is a pain inside me, so ancient and integrated with who I am. I do not know where I end, and the rage begins. He broke my heart thousands of times; my spirit, a thousand more. And yet, I stand, and I fight. I think of the girl I was, I think of the girl I became. Those past versions of me deserve to be laid to rest, and there is only one thing I think will bring me comfort at a time like this."

"What's that?"

"Aurelio's blood on my hands. Tasia told me a good leader can think through which deaths are necessary in order to rule. I believe his is essential if we ever want Haelos to heal from the wretched things he put us through."

Vincenzo rubbed a hand behind his head, jostling his two-toned hair. "I told you he was in over his head once you realized how much power you hold. Being near you hasn't been easy. A selfish piece of me hoped you would recognize me the first time you saw me, and when you didn't, I was so close to breaking. I held in, and I am glad I have. You are worth fighting for. As we go back to Aeria and put our lives on the line, I want you to know that I do this for you, because I believe in you."

"Do you think my memories will ever return? What if I can never remember how I got here, or who we used to be together?" Her heart sped involuntarily as she pondered her feelings for him. Could she act on them? Was he truly safe to lean into?

"I will wait," he said, "as long as it takes for you to be ready. We can figure out what we are, if you want to be anything with me. If they never return, we will create a new future together."

Sima glanced down at her hand against his chest where it still lay. The beat of his heart was palpable through his shirt, and she could not ignore the heat building in her from his touch. She had spent many nights falling asleep at the thought of lying in his arms, yet part of her desired to flee from every situation that brought them close. She removed her hand, suddenly more hollow inside at the absence of his warmth.

"I wish I remembered you," she said, "but I have felt a pull to you from the moment I laid eyes on you. Maybe even longer, as my heart always yearned to venture Below the Archipelago. When we met, I was inspired by the way you cared for others. I think in some ways, I have learned what kind of leader I want to be because of you."

He laughed, and it was warm, like sweet herbal tea. Sima caught herself smiling at the tune of it. "If only you knew how I saw you, and if only you knew you never needed me to teach you strength. Somehow, even in this life, you are as much yourself as you were back in the Eternal Kingdom."

"How so?" Her heart fluttered beneath her ribs.

He leaned closer, the palm of his hand planted on her back, and pulled her forward. "Powerful." His voice sent goosebumps along her skin. "Magnificent, no matter the occasion. The way the world stops where you step, the way your essence commands attention. You are intoxicating, in every sense of the word, and my soul aches beneath the pain of missing you."

Sima's knees were weak beneath her. She was unsure how, but she missed Vincenzo, too. Her soul was plagued with the same pain, the same desire. She allowed her head to tilt forward until she could feel his breath on her skin. His viridian eyes were soft, devotion dripping from his gaze.

Their lips met in a quiet indulgence.

His arms locked her into a tight embrace, and Sima's skin tingled at the sensation of his body against hers. Their kiss was slow, with undeniably careful intention laced into each meeting of their lips. He held her, not as if he was afraid—instead, as if he was never more sure.

"I want you to know that I love you, and will follow you wherever you go, so long as you permit me."

His words cascaded over her with electricity, awakening something inside her. He loved her, and deep within her, somehow she knew it to be true. Cosima let her hand trail his muscular arm in gentle strokes. He smelled of sage and rosemary, and his lips were soft. She wrapped her arms around the back of his neck and let her hands weave through his hair. Vincenzo's hands slid across her upper back and shoulders as he pulled her nearer. His touch was home in a way she had never experienced.

She broke their kiss, cheeks flushed. Suddenly aware of their surroundings, Cosima pulled Vincenzo toward the room she had been occupying. He followed, and the moment the door closed behind them, time faded. To Cosima, nothing existed in the world but him.

Cosima fell backwards onto the bed, Vincenzo's body on top of hers. He held himself up with his arms, his knee in-between her legs. "I missed you," he breathed across her neck. Light kisses peppered her skin as he made his way down to her collarbone.

For the first time, her mind was truly quiet as she focused on the present. The way every kiss made her crave more of him, the way it felt so *right* to be with him. As if her body had never known pain, her body sang with pleasure as his hands made their way to her waist. She held his face as she pulled him in, dying to taste him again, to feel him.

"We will only do what you want to do, nothing more," he whispered lightly against her mouth. "We can stop whenever you want to."

She smiled as she kissed him. "I know."

"You're safe with me," he replied.

Her hand slipped down the front of him from his abdomen to the hard length of him. She grinned at the small groan that escaped him. He pulsed in her hand at her touch. His kisses increased in ferocity, and the heat between Cosima's thighs only increased.

As she removed her top, Cosima shuddered with her skin exposed. Vincenzo pulled his shirt off, revealing his muscular form, complimented by his white and black wings behind him. He lowered himself, trailing his lips down her stomach and stopping at her hip bones. His hands explored her body, making Sima moan as he pulled off the rest of her clothes.

Vincenzo's touch was inviting, warm in a way that mirrored only the brightest of days. His tongue against her skin was like touching the sky, and she bit her lip to keep from begging him to venture lower, faster. Her legs parted as she lifted herself closer to Vincenzo's face.

He happily obliged, smiling as he held Cosima's gaze and allowed his tongue to slip over her. Pleasure exploded through her body, and her hands immediately found their way through his hair. Her thighs squeezed together as he brought her closer and closer to finishing. Sima clamped her mouth shut with her palm over her lips to keep her sounds contained.

"You taste heavenly, as good as you look," he said as his finger slid against her with a teasing amount of pressure. He grinned, enjoying how wet he found her before his mouth was on her again, once again bringing her ecstasy. His finger twisted in and out of her as she felt her walls close around him, desperate for him to continue.

"Enzo," was all she found herself able to say. "Enzo."

She found herself enveloped in waves of building energy, the pleasure only intensifying as he continued. When she finished at last, she pulled a pillow over her face to muffle the sounds of it. Vincenzo left gentle kisses along the insides of her thighs. He moved at an easy pace, in no rush to end their time together.

Vincenzo moved his way back up the length of her body, fingertips running circles along her sides. Cosima could taste herself on him as he pressed his lips to hers. He laid himself in between her legs, his pants the barrier between her bare skin and his.

Cosima planted kisses along his jaw and down his neck as she eagerly tugged his pants below his waist. He laughed softly as he pulled them off and lowered himself on top of her once again. The warmth of him was enough to make her dizzy with desire. His hard length rested against her, sliding up and down with teasing motions.

"Please," she whispered as she wrapped her arms around him. "I want you. Please."

"Anything you want," he whispered back.

Gasps of pleasure escaped Cosima as the head of him parted her and he slipped himself only partially inside. He worked his way in and out, plunging slightly deeper each time. Her hands gripped his shoulders as she bit softly into his shoulder to keep from crying out. He was unlike anything she had felt before and it took everything to remain composed enough to stay quiet.

Before she could stop them, the words tumbled from her mouth. "I love you, Enzo." Her cheeks flushed. From pleasure or embarrassment, she didn't know. She didn't regret the words, yet Cosima had only known to associate love with humiliation. Now, it took on an entirely new association—one of safety and trusted intimacy.

"I love you," he said, lifting himself to better look into her eyes. His gaze locked onto her and as he continued to work himself in and out of her, she fought to keep her eyes open. She clamped down on her bottom lip with her teeth as her eyes rolled back. "I love you," he repeated.

The pressure between her thighs only seemed to build, until her mind lost the ability to form coherent thoughts, blinded by pure enjoyment. Her walls were tight around him, as if she could hold him inside of her forever. Cosima felt the muscles in his back tense, and his eyes fluttered shut.

Realizing he was close, Cosima wrapped her legs around him, pulling him deeper. She could feel him spill inside of her, the warmth within enough to bring a smile to her face. The high from their joining caused small laughs to escape her, purely in denial of an experience capable of leaving her so breathless.

Vincenzo panted as he lifted himself off of her, only to find her legs had not released him. "Not yet," she whispered. He grinned, swaying his hips to move in and out of her at a slow, steady pace. He nibbled along her neck, hushed confessions of love escaping his lips. His pace increased, and soon she was again panting his name.

Pure bliss was the only way Cosima could think to explain it. As he withdrew, he looked her in the eyes with a delicious grin of satisfaction. She curled into Vincenzo's arms, his chin resting on the top of her head. A sigh of exhaustion and delight was the only sound between them before she drifted off to sleep. There was never a place more comforting to Cosima than within his embrace.

Chapter 37

"This must stay on your person the entire flight there," Tasia said, slipping a gold necklace with a ruby pendant in the shape of a teardrop over Cosima's head. "As well as the blade. Your enchantment concealing your person will last only long enough to get you to the third island, Perpetuo. From there, it will need time to replenish before you can use it again."

The sun had nearly set, the sky a brilliant display of cosmic purples and pinks. Stars twinkled dimly as night approached. The wind blew Cosima's hair chaotically. She reached back and tied it into place. Tasia was wearing a full black ensemble, outfitted with the same two blades as Cosima and Vincenzo. They bore black obsidian like the vat, ovals of inky black displaying proudly from both sides of the hilt.

"That's when I'll begin luring the King." Cosima patted the sheath containing the crystal blade given by Silana. "Vincenzo and I know exactly how we're going to do this."

Vincenzo gave a curt nod. He wore forest green and gold armor across his chest and along his arms. His eyes were brighter than usual. "We've agreed upon a plan."

"All right. Cosima, I wish you luck. Remember, after you successfully draw away the King, you must hide until the new moon. On that night, reinforcements will come precisely as you have detailed, including all my mother's Guardians. Vincenzo, I will make sure your points of contact receive these instructions."

Clutched within Tasia's hands were instructions meant for several people. Calix, Alma, and Monte were as vital to the operation as Cosima herself. Vincenzo slipped his hand into hers. She turned to find him smiling softly at her, his eyes warm. "It is time for justice to lay her steady hand on our lives. It's time to take it all back."

"I'm ready," Cosima said, marveling at the sensation of his hand in hers.

Without another word, she climbed into his arms. Tasia cast her enchantment across the ruby pendant, and a dusty shadow fell over the two of them. They glanced into each other's eyes, before Vincenzo launched them into the sky, the bubble shielding them from the view of others.

Barrier slightly muffled the sound of wind, and all that came to her ears was their breathing and the pulse of his wings. Perpetuo in the sky above them was the smallest of the three sky islands of the Aeria Archipelago.

Stress and nervousness left a dampened effect on her body. Though she could acknowledge their presence, the emotions did little to dissuade her.

Cosima had chosen Perpetuo rather than the main island, Innamorati where the Nuvola Palace and Temple were located. Instead, she would use the same tunnels Ivo did to slip unseen into the Temple.

"The tunnels will allow us to make our way to where Ivo attempted to use the Tome of Eternity. With any luck, we might find it. I know Ivo, and I think she would have stashed it prior to her capture, no matter what it took to keep others from getting it."

"I trust you," he said. "We are approaching. Are you ready?"

"Yes, completely."

She half-expected their plan to sour immediately, yet their feet connected to the dirt of the place she called home. The Guardians patrolling nearby were none the wiser and continued their rounds without taking notice of the two of them. As long as Vincenzo stuck close to her, he would remain shielded.

Vincenzo tapped twice on her shoulder, indicating he was using his power. He cast a wide but gentle stream of calm to all nearby. Placating the Guardians was easier than killing them.

Staggering slabs of quartz seemed to spurt from all directions, the island nothing as she remembered. Her path stuck closely to the crystalline walls of buildings and alleyways, slithering her way to the entrance she was seeking with Vincenzo only steps behind.

The metal door stuck out immediately amongst the cold quartz, and Cosima scanned around them. When she knew it was clear, she opened the door and she and Vincenzo slipped easily inside. Down a spiral staircase, they came upon tunnels with gray stone not yet replaced with more valuable crystals.

Vincenzo used his star-fire to conjure a small light within his palm. Cosima marveled at the miniature galaxies illuminating his hand. He ventured in front of her and continued down the narrow shaft filled with pipes, sensors, and valves. This area maintained the water supply for Aeria. Part of the magic harnessed from the Giving kept Aeria floating, and the rest went into the conjuring public necessities such as access to water, or heating and cooling. She could feel the power source calling to her.

Dust and sediment covered everything in thick layers. It left Sima feeling unsure if anyone ever properly maintained it. Steam blew randomly from small gaps in piping, and water dribbled from a generous, unknown source. Rust formed on the metal that had long since eroded, sediment creating hazy clouded spots on every surface. They followed the line straight down, avoiding any of the turns.

"I don't think anyone has come down here in quite some time," Cosima said.

"You're right. Do you know what we're looking for?"

"Not entirely. I remember how to get to the Temple. It was the last time we saw her…"

In some places, roots broke through the ceiling of the passageway, leaving piles of dirt and dust several inches thick along the floor. Whether it was the nerves or something else entirely, Cosima couldn't stand the silence between the two of them.

"Tell me more about your upbringing. Have you always known you were the son of the Spirit Goddess?"

Vincenzo paused in front of her and spun to face her. "It wasn't revealed to me until I was nearing the end of my adolescence. I thought I was an orphan, and probably why I became so close to the Rani Guardians I was raised alongside."

He faced forward and continued on. His wings were compact against his back in the slender hallway. "The scar on my face came the day one of my brothers attempted to kill me. His name is Amadeo. I was unaware of my mother's plans until the day he came for me."

"Why did he try to kill you? I thought she wanted you all to rule the Eternal Kingdom."

"Kismet."

Cosima shivered. The more she learned of Kismet, the more she feared her retribution if Cosima ever stepped too far out of line.

"Kismet eventually learned Ehses's plans for the twelve High Priestesses. To make her pay for the unbalance she created with the creation of her sons, she damned us all. Kismet stole our Fates, setting into motion with her powers a prophecy. Eleven brothers would die in the search for the strongest and most capable of leading. Kismet is to grant the winner rights to marry her daughter, and therefore lead alongside her in the Eternal Kingdom when Kismet steps down."

A twinge of pain and jealousy grappled within her stomach. Part of her was confident Vincenzo would be the surviving brother, which meant he would be married off to someone else. "What of Amadeo then?"

"He attacked me and used his power to manipulate regeneration to prevent me from healing. It wasn't until he held me down and cut into my face that he explained who he was...who *I* was."

It all made sense to Cosima. "Aurelio was planning to attack one of your brothers, Carmine, by luring him here and killing him. The crystals were to help him kill Carmine. All of this is because

Aurelio wants to rule the Eternal Kingdom?"

"You don't know quite how much power that is, truly. He would not be in command of one world, but *every* world, in every universe that exists out there."

"That means, if you survive, *you* would be in command of all of that."

Vincenzo rubbed a hand behind his head. "I suppose it does. I haven't given it much thought. Until I met you, I was merely waiting for the day one of my stronger brothers would come to find me. I wouldn't go down easily, but I never expected to survive. I killed Amadeo and went about my usual life. Then you changed my entire trajectory."

"When did you realize Aurelio was your brother?"

Vincenzo sighed. "When I arrived and learned you were up there, in the sky, and I was in Ombra. The Guardians discouraged me from attacking by speaking to me about my prophecy, unaware of who I really was. They spoke of him being a brother of the Sacred Twelve, destined to rule."

"I think the reason my father was so willing to allow Aurelio to marry me and steal the throne was because of that threat. The longer we spend away from him, the more surreal it feels. I went from spending every waking moment afraid of him to having small glimpses of peace." Her cheeks reddened. "Especially since being with you. I think I refrain from dwelling on the idea of returning to him in favor of my dreams that one day he will simply be a horrid parasite from my past."

"He will fade from memory. We are going to end this together. If ever you decide you do not wish to face him, know I have prepared many years for this, and I can take over. I also know if there is anyone who deserves the justice of spilling his blood, it is you." He flexed his fingers at his sides as he walked.

Cosima studied him from behind. The duality of his nature. A fierce protector, a powerful warrior—and yet, equally compassionate, romantic. Vincenzo mirrored the mastery of light and dark. His aura was a magnetic field, drawing her in relentlessly. The longer they spent near each other, the stronger her attraction to him became.

"I want to do it. If ruling means learning when to take a life, I hope only good can come from his demise. It is a proper lesson in defending my home from invaders."

Vincenzo let out a harsh breath and his star-fire flickered, momentarily casting them in spurts of darkness.

"What is it?" she asked.

"I will always respect your wishes, but this is not your home. You were born in the Eternal Kingdom. Maybe the Priestesses can undo my mother's shackles on your memories. We will return there soon, and sort this all out."

Cosima felt her gut swirl. "You expect me to one day abandon these people? Who is to rule? Where will I go?" She could not fathom leaving behind the world she thought was her home. If it was true and she was merely held captive here, she paled at what would become of her after he was gone.

"You come home with me. We beg Kismet for forgiveness. I swear to peace, promise to them I am no threat, and hope they let us live out our lives together. If not, we will find somewhere to hide together." He reached back and held her hand. The two of them wandered forward at an angle, allowing their hands to dangle clasped together between them.

"You sound insane. However, I also cannot deny a piece of me relishes in the idea of spending an eternity by your side, no matter the view." Spending time in bed with Vincenzo had severed whatever imaginary ties remained between Cosima and Aurelio, and now she craved freedom even more. She could only envision a life where she could choose for herself, never to be directed by others again.

"Precisely my feelings, as well. I can picture it now, the two of us finding a new planet to live on, enjoying the open world around us." Vincenzo slowed. "Look there, the sign says this is the way to Innamorati, to the Temple."

Sima stepped forward and examined the small map painted on a sheet of metal. They would come across a split path and needed to divert to the left to reach storage. The other direction led to a dead-end area meant for maintenance Ambrosi to perform tests. Considering the state of their surroundings, it had been out of use for quite some time.

The endless walls of the tunnels made her head dizzy. She was relieved when finally, they came upon a black iron door affixed to the wall. Sima tried the handle and realized it was locked. Vincenzo used his arm to guide her out of the way before he sent a burst of his star-fire at the lock. The lock melted away, and with a croak, the door opened. It revealed a room beneath the Temple where others left offerings to the Spirit Goddess.

Inside lay four massive crystals, one to mark each of the elements. There was Iolite for water, Angelite for air, Peridot for the planet, and Hessonite for fire. All wore these gemstones on Haelos, though Sima would have never thought grandiose deposits existed. Each polished and carved obelisk stood three meters high.

"Which one is the right one?" Vincenzo asked.

Cosima shook her head, her heart pounding in her chest. Before she could panic, her first private conversation with Tasia surfaced in her mind. Tasia had advised her to let it come to her without force. She took three steady breaths in through her nose and out through her mouth.

Her hands grazed each of the four stones, hoping she would remember the spell. Pieces floated in, enough for her to gather the first stone to use, the Peridot, but not enough to know how. Her magic flared and though she knew not what her intuition was picking up on, Sima turned around and made her way through the passageway. The only thing behind her eyelids was the painted map they saw on the way in. Vincenzo lit the way from behind her, their shadows reminding Sima of hallucinations she had once endured.

Inside the maintenance room, Sima's gut swirled with unease. Something was off about this room. Surrounding them were stacks of papers, books, and discarded items. "Do you think Ivo came in here?" Cosima said, her voice shaking.

"It's possible," Vincenzo said. He held his palm up to examine a mountain of papers. "I think these belong to the Hexia girls."

Cosima's eyes widened as she began flipping through them

alongside him. It was true. Ivo had told Cosima the reason she was going through the tunnels was to recover their history and important literary works from the Astral Atheneum on the last island, Iridicenza. Sima's vision blurred from tears as she realized this was the place her friend was storing what remained of her people's culture and past.

"The Tome is here somewhere, I know it," Cosima said, balling her fists to keep from shaking. "If we find it, we know she made it this far, and all we need to do is lure Aurelio off the islands. Then he will lose all control over the islands."

It only took minutes for Cosima to be violently close to ripping her own hair out. Frustration was not enough to describe the feeling that hung in her chest. "I'm here with you. We will find it. They haven't spotted us yet. We can do this."

Sima nodded, before taking a huge breath in through her nose, and holding it for a moment. As she let the air out, her mind erupted with images. Cosima could never see the memories of those who had already passed on, yet it was as if she were seeing Ivo with her own eyes, right before her.

"Memories from items, but never those who have died," Cosima whispered.

"What?" Vincenzo's voice was deep and distant.

All she could do was sit frozen as images of Ivo layered one on top of the other, her friend scurrying in and out with assorted items in tow. Each time she was alone, each time her face conveyed how unafraid she was. Sima was proud of Ivo for her commitment, for her bravery. Then it came into view, the Tome. The night Ivo died.

Ivo came running in, her forehead slick with blood. She stuffed the Tome of Eternity beneath her arm and her eyes were wide and rabid with fear. Ivo stuffed the Tome behind a pile of other works before she darted from the room again and disappeared.

Cosima blinked, and the vision was gone.

"What happened?" Vincenzo said, holding her steady by her elbow.

"I saw Ivo. I think she might be alive."

Chapter 38

Cosima's hands trembled as she plucked the Tome of Eternity from its hiding place. Papers fell at her feet, yet she ignored them and brought the book to her chest. It pulsed with energy as it had the first time she encountered it. Inside, there was a tiny, hand-written note from Ivo on the vital page they required.

"I did it. If you're reading this, I was successful. I am going to hide. I love you. Ivo." Cosima read aloud.

"It's time then, for us to lure him out," Vincenzo said. "We bring the Tome with us, and we get him off this island no matter the cost."

"This will be the fun part," Cosima said, storming out of the room.

Following the tunnels to the Palace was easier for Sima now that she believed Ivo was still alive. The hope was a small ember, but enough to keep her motivation piping hot. The dead of night was the perfect time for this, no loud rampant attacks like the day she first left. This time, everyone would sleep in their beds, blissfully unaware of Sima stalking around. She glanced down each corridor she passed, counting the doors as she made her way to the food stores. The kitchen kept excess stock in one room in the servants' tunnels—flour, sugar, and more.

The sound of a voice had them ducking down a corridor, bodies pressed flush against the wall, careful to avoid the door to someone's personal chambers. Whoever spoke didn't come closer, but another voice joined it soon after. They poorly attempted to keep their voices hushed, but it was clear they were unaware she was here.

Petty chatter, nothing more.

She grit her teeth and pushed off the wall, steps cautious at first. It didn't take long for the voices to fade. The food stores were directly beneath the kitchen, for easy access for the staff. Vincenzo lifted a large tin of oil onto an empty cloth sack, then tied a piece of thin rope to the bag and pulled.

The tin slid easily across the floor, and Sima trailed behind Vincenzo. They once again made their way to the Emblem Headquarters, where they had recently slaughtered the four leaders.

The pang in her gut didn't slow her. If anything, it made her pull harder. As she suspected, the singular hallway that led toward the Emblem Chambers was now blocked off with iron gates. The change came in response to their last fight here. Without pause, Vincenzo opened the gate with a blast of star-fire, as he had done earlier.

It was eerie how quiet the tunnel was. She stared back at the gate, wondering how she had been lucky enough that there weren't barriers like this everywhere when she was escaping. She thought of how different everything would be if she and Ivo had gotten stopped by a heavy iron gate, and she never made it off the islands—never made it to Vincenzo.

They came upon the stairs that would lead from the servants' tunnels, up to the bedrooms of the newly assigned Emblems. Vincenzo withdrew his weapon as he walked in front of her. Cosima tipped the oil over, unscrewing the cap enough to leave a small river behind her. She wanted to make every bit count. Cosima was thorough, coating the entire floor with a thin layer of the slippery substance. Her muscles ached as she hoisted the tin up along the steps to the Emblem Chambers, knowing Remo's predecessor would be inside, sleeping. Exactly as she had planned.

A shiver ran down her spine as Vincenzo opened the door, delighted to find herself inside an occupied suite. A small kitchen area to the side, two separate bedroom chambers with private bathing rooms, and a discarded coat and boots by the other entrance. The new Emblem Chief was snoring peacefully from within one room, his door ajar.

So comfortable for someone who hasn't earned it.

The Chief was a Rani Guardian, which meant what she was about to do next wouldn't kill him—but that wasn't the point, not yet. She just wanted to hurt him and hurt him badly. She grinned ear to ear as she marveled at her work. The entire suite, including Caelian and his precious feathers, Sima coated them all in oil. She used a modest stream of her magic to pause time, careful not to be wasteful. She walked backward towards the door that would lead to the main corridor.

Caelian was one Guardian who had taken pleasure in her capture and had not hesitated when offered a chance to join in her torment by Aurelio. Not everyone knew what she endured, but he did, and he did nothing to stop it.

Once they were clear, Vincenzo turned and lit the flames with star-fire, and the two ran hand-in-hand as Caelian's screams echoed behind them.

The heat tickled her skin as waves of fire enveloped the passageway and all of Caelian's suite. He had gotten what he wanted. It was Sima who had motivated Remo to take an interest in gaining a predecessor. Caelian was the easiest option. Aurelio already had a sort of friendship with the Guardian. She let her laugh reverberate in the tunnel as the panicked sounds he howled came from behind her. Perhaps his saviors could get in once they had put the fire out enough to rescue him.

Plus, the Emblem Headquarters were closed off enough from the rest of the Nuvola Palace that she could almost guarantee he would crawl out of the fire a melted mess before someone could get to him. Her thighs burned as she rounded the hall leading back toward Aurelio's chambers. The commotion in the Headquarters was sure to draw as many Guardians as possible away from him. Oh, how she delighted in it.

Cosima was on the main floor, and her knowledge of the Palace kicked in automatically. She knew where to duck and where to hide when voices sounded. She knew which storage closets were unlocked, which meeting rooms were vacant. The list was endless, yet she chose the path of least resistance, directly through the main corridor, up the stairs, until she reached his bedroom chambers on the fourth floor.

The primary staircase would be empty this time of night, and any traffic would head anywhere but for Aurelio. Unless they were Guardians and were on their way to him right now. The voices grew louder. She hissed, crouching behind a large art display of a fish dangling the sun like a charm from his tail. His merry expression completely opposed hers. Its glazed surface left a ghostly mirror of her reflection as she hid.

Vincenzo ducked behind her and whispered in her ear. "Lucrezia, Ulrico, Ermete. They're arguing about whether alerting the King to the fire is the right decision. They're scared to piss him off."

Sima peered around the corner. The same Guardians who had been in charge of the Archipelago before the attack bickered amongst themselves.

"For all we know," Ermete said, scratching his skin incessantly, "this is a small fire. Has anyone actually checked it out?"

"Oh, please," Lucrezia said, her voice beginning to fade as they continued up the stairwell, "as if the King cares about anything repairable. He is going to be furious if we come to him before we figure it out. You would know that if either of you were worth your salt enough to be in Innamorati."

Sima crept slowly behind them, fingers dragging lightly against the railing as she ascended.

"Big words from the girl who missed all the signs from the last attack. Plus, the actual Queen escaped on your watch."

"Watch it, Ulrico," Lucrezia snapped back.

"Maybe this is another attack. They can bring the rebellion here. I'll finally do what I should have done and end each of them," Ulrico growled.

"Maybe the Queen is back," Lucrezia said.

"I doubt it. You know what happened the last time Aurelio brought her back? I think she's gone for good," Ermete said. "Come on, please let us go look at it before we wake him up."

"We lost a couple of guys that night. Such a stupid risk, all for the Queen who does nothing but sit around like she's molded of clay. She could at least be pleasant," Ulrico said.

"Stop it," Lucrezia said. "It can't be easy."

"What precisely do you mean by that? You know any talk against the King is forbidden. What comes next for you, Lucrezia?"

"Shut up," she shot back as their footsteps faded down the hallway towards the King's rooms. They stopped, Sima halting her own steps as the trio went quiet.

"What does that mean?" Ermete asked after their pause. They must have been communicating with other Guardians.

"Shit, the fire is reaching the ball rooms, meaning it's gotten pretty far." Ulrico cursed. "Let's go, I am waking the King."

"Wait," Lucrezia called, "Someone really should be there to put it out. I'm turning around."

"I can go by myself," Ermete said, his footsteps descending toward Cosima.

"Please," Sima said, her swords drawn, one pointed directly at Ermete's chest, the sharp blade drawing a small dribble of blood. "I think we should stick together, friends."

"What the hell?" Ulrico raged. "Drop it, bitch."

Vincenzo unleashed both swords from his hip. Ermete froze with his hands up. He wasn't wearing the chest plate to his armor; he had likely been sleeping when the alert about the fire came in. Ermete appeared more afraid of Cosima than he did of Vincenzo. Ulrico growled and swiped at her with his blade, only to be stopped when it clashed against Vincenzo's.

"I just want to talk," Sima said, cocking her head to the side.

Before they could react, her blade was through Ermete's chest, spearing him like a hunk of meat over a fire. She withdrew it, nearly losing her footing with the effort it took to be free of him. It was far from fatal for a Guardian, but it would hurt enough to keep him down while she went for Ulrico.

He was ready, fending off her advances with his blade. Blood coursed through her veins, frenzied pulses from a heart too far from giving up. It was loud in her ears, deafening the sounds around her. She couldn't hear the sound Lucrezia choked out when Sima suddenly changed targets, spinning her blade through a thin, weakened area of armor between the shoulder and arm plates. Lucrezia's arm dangled wildly, and surprisingly, despite all the spurting blood, she merely clutched her severed arm and fell to her knees.

Ulrico's blade slid across her cheek and across the bridge of her nose. She winced, her dodge not quite fast enough. Cosima's grip tightened as she lunged for him at a maddening pace. The tiger in her had finally broken free of its cage and there was no putting it back. She was bloodthirsty.

Ulrico's feet backed over the stairs, and Sima did not give him a moment's rest, lunging again and again. They were on the third floor, one floor beneath Aurelio's chambers. She pressed him deeper into the sitting area on the landing beside the steps. He hardly seemed aware that he was feet from the railing, too overwhelmed by her attack. It wasn't because she was stronger, or that she was more skillful. The subtle hesitation was coming from somewhere else.

Before she could back him over the railing, she yelled, "enough!"

They panted, Ulrico wiping the sweat off his angular brow. It was then that they both clocked it, a minor cut above his brow. Barely visible, no more than an inch across, iron crimson flowed. Satisfaction bit into her, curling around her feet like a devoted presence.

"You're scared, too, of what I can do," she said, reining in the urge to laugh at him. "Even if you won't admit it."

"I was doing my rotation in the prisons, and that asshole wouldn't shut up down there about you. King Aurelio said we're all going to get it one day, because you can change Fate. He said you can do it without even being near the person," Ulrico stammered, lip trembling. He pressed his mouth into a line, swallowing tightly.

Sima tossed her head back and stared up at the sky. She imagined the stars in the ribbons of night outside and sighed.

"Thank you for telling me that," she said, snapping her head back to look at him. "I don't know if you're a piece of shit like the rest of them, and I do not have the time to find out. However, I am conflicted about whether you should die for that reason alone. You're scared. It means you might be trainable later. Or," she tucked her blade beneath his chin, scraping along the skin, "you have reason to fear someone who can see into your life."

He shook his head vehemently.

"No time to find out, though." She clicked her tongue, pursing her lips in contemplation. "Oh, well!"

He cried as she sliced into him, hinging straight for the flesh in the crook of his neck. He fell to his knees, tumbling forward as she cleaved her blade free. His wings lay exposed, but she resisted. A plan of this magnitude, crafted with delicate threads, would require patience. These three Guardians, the three Captains, were all at her mercy. Her luck was a sign the universe breathed her blessings in the wind.

Sima didn't know if they all deserved to die, simply for being Captains. These Guardians actually performed their duties, unlike the Emblems, whose mere existence was ultimately political. It helped show the influential Ambrosi that Aurelio had tamed the Rani Guardians deeper into submission. At one point these three had given every order, no one moving without their say. Now, all three of them lay injured enough she could deal the killing blows with a much lower risk to her own safety. Yet again, she resisted.

Lucrezia swept like a ghost into the room, her severed arm no longer dangling; instead, she clenched it in her remaining fist. "I wasn't supposed to hear. Honestly, I wasn't supposed to know. I was doing my rounds, and the door was open. It's just like me to be worried something was amiss. Those doors should never be open."

Sima was confused and lowered her blades as she met her agitated stare. A beast, persisting at all costs. She could respect that. "What did you see?"

"You need to find your mother, Queen Aphelion."

That was new. Better than being called a traitorous bitch, she supposed. "My mother?"

"Costanza. She is Hexia. You knew this, yes?"

Cosima couldn't tear her eyes off the blood dripping rhythmically from the Guardian's wound. Vincenzo swayed back and forth on his feet as if he was struggling to decide whether to kill her. "Yes."

"She is the one who put the enchantments in your brain. She is gifted. The High Mother of the Coven."

"Why are you helping me?"

"How do we know we can trust you?" Vincenzo asked roughly.

"I can't explain it, the way it feels to disobey a command from the King. It's torture, indescribable pain. I eventually stopped resisting and convinced myself I was doing the right thing for Aeria. The Ambrosi here, they don't care for any of us. I don't know how they convinced us they did. I have heard what they say about the Guardians, what they say about Haelos. What they plot. Why was Costanza meeting with the King at all hours of the night, and why do they only ever speak of you?"

Lucrezia looked at her then, angling her face until her bloodshot eyes met Sima's. She was trembling, though her wound no longer wept. Sima was face-to-face with the outcomes of her own decisions, and yet Lucrezia showed no hostility in her expression. Only defeated apathy. "I don't care what they do to me now. I have had enough of this life, this stage of it, or the whole thing, I haven't decided. My time as a puppet will cease now."

"You can join my side. Help us take back Aeria."

She chuckled, a hollow laugh. "He locked the portal. No one can come from the Eternal Kingdom. We would fight a losing battle."

"How is that possible?" Vincenzo asked.

"That's just my guess," Lucrezia said as she dropped her arm to the ground, Sima wincing at the sound of the thud. "It will regenerate. I do not need it," she added, dully watching Cosima's expression. "How can he get things from other realms? That is a question perhaps you can answer."

"Me?" Her mind flashed to the Drago's nickname for her. *Realm-walker.*

Lucrezia nodded. "You are opening the door, Cosima. You are the key." Lucrezia fell forward, a flash of shadow flaying her wings from her body. Sima wouldn't have known what happened if her severed wings didn't sit at the feet of a Shadowborn. Half-Rani Guardian, Half-Viipir. A deadly combination that lacked the Guardian lifespan but made up for it with increased strength and the ability to move within the shadows.

She blinked.

"It is imperative," the Shadowborn said, "that you enact whatever plan you envisioned, because the King is on his way down."

"Did you kill the other Captains?" Vincenzo asked, running his hand through his hair.

"If you knew how those Guardians felt about the world, you would recognize that I am on your side," the Shadowborn grumbled. She took him in—inky hair like hers, but blood-red eyes, a trait only known to the Viipir. His wings were extremely similar to Rani, if not smaller. He did not wear Aeria armor. He wore what appeared to be plain black tactical gear, similar to what they wore in Ombra.

"Are you going to help me, or stop me?" Cosima asked.

"Just because some things happen in the dark," he said, disappearing behind a cloud of thick smoke, voice echoing from where he once stood, "doesn't mean they are not seen."

"Let's go," Vincenzo said, wiping the blood from his blade onto his pants. "He said Aurelio was on his way down."

As if speaking his name caused him to manifest, Sima felt the terror coating her skin as he came into view at the height of the stairs.

"What a pleasant surprise, dove," Aurelio said. He wore satin navy blue sleeping clothes embroidered with waves like the sea. His blond hair was in perfect alignment, and his golden eyes simmered as they met hers.

Her heart jumped within her chest, but she refused to succumb to fear so easily. She pointed her sword at him, mentally reminding herself of the more powerful dagger in her belt. Although Cosima did not intend to meet him on the staircase, his attention was precisely what she was asking for.

Cosima stopped time, turned, and fled. Once a far enough distance away, she allowed time to resume enough for him to witness her leaving. Aurelio was remarkably fast, but he could not entirely overcome her pauses, especially with how skilled she had become at wielding her time magic.

Vincenzo positioned himself behind her, but Aurelio ignored him. His eyes locked onto Cosima, and anger rippled off of him. Cosima kept her pace, repeatedly jumping time to ensure the gap never closed between her and her miserable *ex*-husband. Each time she turned to find him still hot on her trail, a piece of her begged to quit, begged to curl into a ball and retreat.

However, a louder part of her egged her on, pushed her legs harder and further than ever. Cosima sent a silent, desperate plea to Vincenzo to be exactly where he needed to be by the time she got there. Aurelio's wings lifted him to the sky, the gray feathers invisible in the dark sky above her.

Cosima's power left in floods from her fingertips, placing Aurelio in a smaller pocket of time, even slower than the ones before. She could not let him fall too far behind. The plan depended on him leaving the bubble surrounding the Archipelago once again.

She spied the barrier marking the edge of the island. A plunge to the world below greeted her as her foot pushed off the fence and sent her tumbling downward. Cosima turned to find Aurelio already above her, making an equally fast descent toward her. The wind howled in her ears, pausing as she landed in Vincenzo's arms.

"Got you," he said, before using his wings to propel them out of Aurelio's reach. "How are your reserves?"

"I'm going good," Sima replied, feeling the electric energy in her extremities. She was fatigued, but she maintained more than enough of a supply of her power to keep the pursuit going. If all else failed, she would hold him in a pocket long enough for them to flee to safety. Sima's mood soured at the thought of giving up.

"I am tired of chasing you!" Aurelio hollered from behind them. "You will regret this. Your new tricks will do nothing in the end!" Blinded by rage, Aurelio's eyes flickered with the heat of his hatred for her. It seemed almost foreign now, like he was a part of a nightmare and not her waking reality.

"Almost," she whispered against Vincenzo's shoulder as she peeked back at the King. "Almost there."

Vincenzo's muscles worked overtime to push them further ahead, baiting Aurelio to fly outside the boundary. Relief washed her the moment she knew they were in the clear. It lasted only a moment as Aurelio sent blasts of his star-fire in their direction. Vincenzo dropped them lower in the sky, narrowly evading the attack. Cosima used a larger pulse of her magic to halt time and buy them the opportunity to lose him.

"*Now*," Cosima said, tightening her grip around Vincenzo.

He rounded back toward the Palace, leaving Aurelio behind them. If all went according to plan, the seal would lock Aurelio out of the Aeria Archipelago, allowing Cosima to locate the procedure to sever their marriage bond. The Tome sat in a sack tied around her, the weight of it unregistered in her brain as panic cleared her thoughts.

The farther they got from Aurelio, the more Cosima knew she should release her hold over him, but she couldn't make herself do it. She wanted to buy them time.

"Let it go," Vincenzo reassured. "We are close. Let him go, save your power. Think this through."

Cosima nodded, and as her breath exited her body, Aurelio reanimated, realizing they had evaded him. Sima waited for Aurelio to bounce off the invisible barrier, only he didn't. Instead, he began gaining on them, and Cosima burst into tears, realizing their plan was not accurately unfolding.

She loosed one last hold on time and scrambled to pull the Tome of Eternity free. Innamorati came into view and before Sima knew it, their feet planted on the ground. Her reserves were becoming lower than she was comfortable with, but she narrowed her focus. Cosima's hands tore open the book to the page marked by Ivo's note.

"Shit," Cosima cursed.

"What is it?"

"I know what happened. We have to return to the Temple and place a new protective shielding around the island before he gets here, because it is now too late for the primary one. The lockout requires one last spell." Cosima trembled. "I hope my powers can hold him off long enough."

"Time to find out," Vincenzo said, before launching them through the air toward the Light Reserve once again.

Chapter 39

Once they reached the Temple, Cosima ran out of steam, and let loose her grip on time. Face to face with the four large gemstones for the second time, she flipped through the Tome of Eternity and found the page. It walked through the steps, including the order by which she was to remove them.

"It says there is a talisman representing Aeria," Cosima said mostly to herself. A circular piece of gold the size of a dinner plate sat in between two of the elements on the wall. The Tome offered no translation for the symbols, but it resembled the face of a tiger, Cosima thought. Where she imagined eyes lay two sparkling diamonds, the only adornment added to the talisman.

First, she removed the Peridot. It detached smoothly, and when the Archipelago did not snap in half as she feared it might, she continued onto the Angelite. Vincenzo gently took each piece of stone from her hands and positioned them against the wall. She moved onto Iolite for water and finally, the burning orange of Hessonite. As the crystal marked for fire left the reservoir in which it sat, a loud buzz collided with their ears.

Their hands clamped tightly over their ears as Vincenzo shouted: "What do we do now?"

Cosima bit into her lip to keep from crying out over the pain from the deafening buzz and continued reading. As the Tome commanded, Cosima cried out the name of the island they stood on—Innamorati—three times. She lifted the Peridot and replaced it. The ground beneath their feet trembled as she fit the Angelite back into the proper place.

"Hurry!" she called.

Vincenzo quickly placed in the final two gemstones. The instructions called for a blood offering to create the new seal. Cosima pulled one of her blades free and her eyebrow flickered as she sliced into her palm. With her hand overflowing with crimson rivers, she slammed it down onto the talisman.

The buzzing finally halted, and Sima found a pounding headache in its place. The ground continued to wobble and sway, reigniting fears it would crack and send her hurtling toward the surface of Haelos. Vincenzo ripped off a section of his shirt, grimacing as he wrapped it around her bleeding palm.

"With luck, I have sealed him for now, unless he knows of a way to bypass the bubble," Cosima said, examining Vincenzo's job at bandaging her wound. "Now we find Ivo."

"Where do you think she is? You never told me what led you to believe she is still alive."

"I could never witness the memories of those who pass on, but I could see her hiding the Tome. She must still be alive if I can see those moments. If I could choose what I saw, I'd try to find her that way, but I can't." Sima sighed and chewed her lip.

Vincenzo pressed a finger to his temple. "They're panicking up above." His face slacked with relief. "He's out, Cosima, he can't land on Innamorati. He's diverting toward the other islands. They are about to head our way. We need to leave *now.*"

Cosima's chest ached, and she stumbled. It was working. She brightened. The idea of surviving, after all, seemed more realistic. She allowed Vincenzo to lead the way. Her head still pounded, and Cosima was dizzy. She struggled to keep her feet moving beneath her.

"What's happening?" she whispered before she toppled to the floor. Black encroached on her vision, blocking out the sight of Vincenzo leaning over her. A song played in her mind at such volume she couldn't understand a word coming from his mouth.

It was the same song that had played in Ombra by the water fountain. She blinked, vision fading as the music swelled in dramatic symphony. She could make out the moonlight shining through the stain glass ceiling. The sensation of being in his arms enveloped her.

The next time she opened her eyes, she was on the cold floor and shadows violently swayed in a haze before her. She tried to think, to speak, but sleep came in lamentable waves. When consciousness surrounded her once more, she was in a storage room for cleaning supplies previously used by the Hexia girls. Her head rested on Vincenzo's shirt, and his scent was a positive sign she stood a chance at remaining awake.

"Hey," Vincenzo said softly.

Cosima blinked several times, but he was no clearer in her vision. *What is happening?*

"I think the seal took power from you. You were already running low from feigning off Aurelio, weren't you?"

Cosima gave one slow blink. His hand rested lightly on her shoulder, and her eyes shut as she breathed in his scent once more.

"We are almost inside the Palace. You take all the time you need. Maybe laying low will help the search for us to die down. Besides, now that you've locked Aurelio out of the main island and Palace, all that's left is to wait for the new moon, and help will arrive." He stroked her hair gently, and Cosima found the sensation soothed her. "I've gotten us as far as I can for now."

Her head swam, jumbling up any words she intended to speak. She allowed herself to enjoy his touch before drifting off to sleep again. When she opened her eyes, no longer was she in a small closet full of brooms and buckets. Instead, she was wading through a pond filled with murky black water.

The trees in every direction were dead and bare. The water seemed to stick to her skin in a way that sent horrified gasps from her mouth. Her mind filled with thoughts of unseen creatures grabbing her legs from beneath her as she ran from the pond. Hands grabbed at her feet and ankles as she reached the edge, and she fell to the dirt.

Cosima hissed, realizing her arms were scuffed and bloody, but the hands grasping at her were gone. *Or did they not exist? Had I tripped?* She scurried to a stand before taking off into the dead forest she found herself in. Aurelio's laughter pierced her mind. Sima pounded the bony edge of her palms into her forehead as she ran, hoping to drown him out.

"Stop it!" Cosima cried. "Enough!"

The sound of dirt beneath her feet became muffled and unrecognizable. She opened her eyes and slowed to a stop. She was in a hallway in the Palace, only it looked the way it had before Aurelio's arrival. Questions tormented her brain, and she wondered if she'd gone mad.

Why do you remember being a child? Who is your actual family? Where do you belong?

The string repeated like an incantation, casting her failure into reality, but she pushed it aside and began walking down the hallway. A small orb of light attached to the wall illuminated it, and murals decorated the walls with images of baby Rani Guardians floating in the clouds, alongside stoic looking Ambrosi children waving hands to the sky.

She recognized the hallway as the one leading to her mother's primary bedroom. Even as the Queen, Costanza never shared a bedroom with her husband. Cosima tiptoed along quietly and rested her ear on the door and listened for any signs of her mother inside.

"Come, my daughter," Costanza called from within.

Cosima startled and stumbled backward into the wall. *How did she know it was me?*

The door unlocked, and her mother peered around the door. Her beautiful high cheekbones were flushed red, and her onyx hair was matted to her forehead. Costanza's eyes were puffy and swollen as she gazed at Cosima with anger.

"Mother," Cosima whispered. "This isn't real. The Palace doesn't look like this anymore, and you wouldn't be able to see me if I were in a memory."

"We have only a bit of time, and this was the only way I could think to reach you." She stepped aside and motioned for Cosima to enter. "I am not the High Mother of my Coven for no reason."

Cosima stepped in and marveled at the way the baby blue and satin white bedroom existed exactly as she remembered it. Costanza closed the door behind her and turned to Sima. She crossed her arms across her chest. A lengthy cerulean nightgown hung over the tops of her feet.

"Dark magic is at force here, Cosima. There is only so much I can tell you because there is only so much I understand. I would normally never risk this sort of summoning spell, but we are running out of time. Your father and I wished for a child. We were faithful and kept our promises to the Goddess in hopes she would bless us with a baby. Ehses brought you. At first, you appeared to be but a child, only a few years old. On her command, we were to step down and hand you the crown when you came of age after your arrival. It was not until she disappeared that her illusion dissipated for no one but me. I, alone, realized you were young, yes—but not a child. Her twisted magic could change your brain, the body you inhabited, but it could not conceal your soul."

Cosima placed a hand over her chest, her pounding heart palpable. "My soul? It was the Spirit Goddess who kidnapped me and brought me here?"

"I tried to figure out how to break the curse upon you, but I have never been successful. You honestly believed you were our child, and I could not turn my back on you, even if I struggled to accept your place in our lives. I cared for you as you appeared outwardly, and not as the restrained woman you were inside. Before you were able to take the crown, you met Aurelio."

Cosima's cheeks flushed. "He is her son." She shook her head, wondering how she had failed to make the connection before. "Was this a trap? Ehses planted me here, knowing her son would one day come for me?"

"I cannot give you those answers. But I can give you something else. The reason no one rescued you." Costanza's face stitched with a lingering sadness.

"What is it?" Cosima hand's shook. She crossed her arms and

squished her hands into her sides.

"You are the key to the Star Realm Portal. Without you, there is no opening or closing. The waves of beasts through the veil coincided with Aurelio's requirement of you to use your power. While he sent you off on tasks, you would open the gate, allowing him to leave Haelos with thousands of the crystals."

"How did I become the key?" Sima's mind jumped to her short, strange conversation with Lucrezia.

"When you inherited the Crown, it granted you the ability. I only became aware it was a possibility once Aurelio manipulated your power at the start of his reign."

"A Guardian told me she saw you meeting with Aurelio all hours of the night."

"Are you aware how powerful the Sacred Twelve are? Rumor is that all of them possess some level of mind control. You are their biggest nightmare. You can shield them. Aurelio has had to resort to using drugs and fear to control you because he cannot order you around as easily as he would like. The reason he came to me was to make sure I kept your memories sealed away. He was always terrified you would remember your old life and where you came from."

"Is there any way to undo it?"

"I can only remove what I created. The ones by the Spirit Goddess, if they remain, will have to be taken down by her. I have never uncovered the key to undoing your bindings. There is something you must know." Costanza seized Cosima's arm in a tight hold. "Listen to me! Because you are the key, each time you use your power, you risk opening the portal for very brief periods of time."

"Does this mean I could open them on purpose, too?"

Costanza shook her head and released her grip. "I advise against that. There are ways to create a selective filter on what goes in or out, but one wrong call and you might let in even worse demons than Haelos has seen to date. I am not an immortal like you, but I know very well to resist creating pure chaos. Using your Fate altering abilities is already dangerous."

"I know this," Cosima bit her lip. She had long feared the consequences that would come along with her alterations. "If I am the key, then there is hope for me returning home—to my real home—isn't there?"

Cosima glanced down at Costanza's feet and realized a pool of blood was growing larger and approaching where they stood. She jumped backward. "What is that?"

Costanza glanced at the wardrobe where the cause of the mess originated. "About that..." Costanza said slowly. "Those crystals can truly kill Ambrosi."

"Is this in reality, or your memory?" Cosima gasped.

"A mixture of the two," Costanza hummed. "I told you the situation was a tad dire, didn't I?"

"Who did you kill?"

Costanza walked over to the wardrobe, Cosima's heart pounding in time with her footsteps as she followed. Her mother grimaced, her brows knit together. "Step back," was all she said before she threw open the door and the body of Cosima's father fell out.

Sima jumped back and clamped her hand over her mouth. Her father was the very man who had conspired with Aurelio prior to their wedding. There had never been a need for the death that fell upon Aeria at Aurelio's hands, and now, Cosima would never know why her father had allowed him to take those lives to convey a message of power and control. "Why?"

"He deserved to die. He was evil long before Aurelio came, only more secretive. I have done you a favor. He handed the keys to Aurelio with his tail between his legs."

"I saw him—I saw him talking to Aurelio the night before the coup," Cosima stammered.

"Your father knew precisely what Aurelio planned to do. The only reason I have complied is to protect you and your sister. He *let* them die, Cosima. He let Aurelio round up my entire Coven before my eyes and enslaved them. I have been chained as much as you have."

"Ivo..." Cosima whispered. Costanza's eyes flickered, and a

lump formed in Cosima's throat. "What is it?"

"She's alive," Costanza said, staring down at her feet. "They captured her, and Aurelio tortured her, but I healed her. She discovered Aurelio is the son of Ehses when she broke into the Astral Atheneum. She was threatening to expose more of his truths."

Cosima's knees threatened to buckle. "Where is she?"

"On Iridicenza." Costanza frowned. "Hopefully, alive."

"No," Cosima shut her eyes to stall the tears. She had only been successful in sealing the main island, Innamorati, but now it was obvious. Of course, Ivo would hide on Iridicenza, near the Astral Atheneum. It had once been the second-safest place in all of Haelos beyond the Nuvola Palace, because of its intensive warding. Warding Aurelio had destroyed right before Cosima fled. She swallowed tightly.

Voices sounded in the hallway. Costanza's head snapped toward the door. "Go," she said, placing her hand in the air, aimed at Cosima. A puff of blue energy pulsed toward her, and Cosima was once again flying through the darkness. The void held her as she plotted her next moves. How would she get to Ivo if leaving the Palace meant Aurelio could attack her again? At least he could not access the Light Reserve, which kept him from shutting down Aeria and sending it toppling from the sky.

Cosima could not alter her own Fate, or she would have gone back and sent her and Vincenzo toward the Astral Atheneum immediately after sealing off the Light Reserve and the Palace. Instead, she sank back into her body. Her limbs were as heavy as sandbags and her eyes refused to open. Her mind swirled, making her feel as though she were on a sinking ship and not as though she were funneling back into her body.

She was relieved when her nose picked up on scents of vinegar and lemon. Cosima was still in the closet with Vincenzo. Her entire body lit with tingles as sensation returned. Something shifted around her before she felt his hands on her shoulders.

"—back?"

"Huh?" Cosima muttered. She could not seem to understand

him.

"Are you sure you're back?" Vincenzo said the words slowly, worry heavy in his green eyes.

"At least I can see," Cosima said. She could move her body, though it felt exceedingly heavy, and she attempted to push herself off the floor.

"Here." Vincenzo reached for her and helped pull her upright. He wrapped his arm around her and held her against his side. The slow speed at which her head moved to face him was excruciating. Vincenzo laughed softly. "You're all right. You were out for an hour or so. Take more time if you need."

Cosima nuzzled against his bare skin, realizing his shirt had been acting as her pillow while she was speaking with Costanza. She could not decide yet if it was the truth or a monstrous nightmare, all made up inside her mind.

"Why would your mother have kidnapped me and brought me here?" Cosima said against his skin. Vincenzo recoiled. "What?" she asked, as he frowned.

"I suspected, but I uncovered no proof. The only explanation I have come up with is perhaps she found out about us, our love. We planned to run away together. Perhaps she wanted to stop me and force me to follow her plan."

"I need to see the Tome. My mother has reason to believe I am the key to the Star Realm Portal, and that is because of my power. No one came to Haelos. Perhaps there is something inside about how we can get in contact with someone from the Eternal Kingdom. Could there be a way to speak with a Goddess?"

Vincenzo shook his head. "I'm not sure. I only know of traveling through the portal, but one must be a certain strength to survive, if not moved with the help of a Goddess."

"Ivo is on Iridicenza, in the Astral Atheneum. How do we go there?"

"Are you sure that is the wisest decision? Leaving could draw him there if he has not ventured there already. We should wait until we have people to back us up."

"I can't wait any longer, Enzo." Cosima resented the blush that rose to her cheeks in using a nickname for him. She cleared her throat, ignoring the perplexed look on his face. "We left her before, and I am not leaving her again."

"If you wait until the others show up with reinforcements, we wouldn't need to flee through the tunnels and risk our lives." His hands touched the gold and ruby pendant around her neck, given by Tasia. "Soon, this will regenerate and allow us to move safely toward the library, without exposing ourselves to the mercy of whatever unexpected outcome lay ahead of us. Think about the resistance movement. It is safer if as many of us target Aurelio as possible."

Cosima let it simmer. "How can I wait, all without knowing if she is all right?"

"You have my word. We will go for her at nightfall. Until then, you can get your strength up. There's no way you have a full reserve already."

Cosima grimaced. It was true. Her reserves were a measly quarter of the way full, not nearly enough to go after Aurelio and hope to win. Enzo laid his head against hers, and Sima sank into him. Sleep begged to have her, and as exhaustion tickled at her senses, she obliged.

Chapter 40

Cosima woke to find herself tucked beneath Vincenzo's arm, curled into his side. He moved as she did, allowing her to sit up straight. Her eyes settled on the brooms leaning against the back wall to the storage closet. The shelves were full of clean towels, fresh linen sheets, and various natural remedies for keeping the Palace tidy. With the escape of the Hexia girls, it was no wonder the closet had been undisturbed during her rest.

"Is it time?" She rubbed her eyes with her hands. "I want to find Ivo." Even in her short slumber, Cosima had dreamed of her.

"Almost." Vincenzo stood and meandered over to the door. He pressed his ear against it and reached for the knob. Cosima froze as he opened it and inspected the hallway, before gently shutting it again. "Don't worry, the only people who would think to check this room are Rani Guardians, and I will hear them coming. I didn't realize the Guardians on Aeria used the ability to speak into each other's minds so frequently. It was a pleasant break of quiet while you slept. No close calls."

Cosima nodded, thankful for the reassurance that her slumber had not put them at risk. She truly needed the rest, and her body no longer ached with fatigue.

"How are you?" Vincenzo's eyebrows knit together in concern.

"Better," she said sheepishly. "I have never hit the bottom of my reserve that quickly or intensely before. It was like nothing I have experienced before."

Vincenzo frowned. "We should keep this in mind, Cosima. If we plan to use any more rituals from the Tome, you must take into consideration what it does to deplete you. You may have to choose between hunting down Aurelio and securing Aeria with the guidance left to us inside this." He reached for the Tome of Eternity from where he had stashed it after they hid inside the closet. A stack of white towels flopped onto the floor. He nudged it out of the way with his foot.

"If I kill him, I will have all the time in the world to fix up the Archipelago."

"That's true," Vincenzo said, sucking on his teeth. "However, going after him is risky. I say we comb this text for anything useful and produce a better plan."

"The trio," Cosima said, resting her head against her fingers. "Calix and the others will be rounding up Ambrosi to help expose them to the truth. I refuse to let Calix close to Aurelio like last time. After how he hurt her." Cosima's free hand curled into a fist. "However, I have use for Ostrum. Yadira was telling me previously Ostrum has been successful at making it within the Astral Atheneum, even through its strongest wardings. Perhaps, if we are otherwise locked out, he could find his way inside and create an opening."

"Interesting plan," Vincenzo said, rubbing his jaw. "Though, good luck talking Calix out of getting another shot at the King after he knocked her unconscious."

Cosima dug into the Tome and skimmed the heading of each new section to see if any of it was of interest. For the sake of time, she could not read through each individual ritual. "Two Ambrosi found the Archipelago, sent directly from the Eternal Kingdom to oversee the islands. Although the Founders are not royalty, they maintain balance amongst the power the crown holds." Cosima glanced up from the book. "Tomasso and Ginevra have been incredibly complicit in Aurelio's crimes. They are the founding Ambrosi, and still found themselves wrapped up with him."

"Do they know what he has done to you?" Vincenzo's jaw

clenched.

"Perhaps not the entire series of events, but I am sure they witnessed at least a portion of the abuse." Cosima chewed her lip.

"Is everyone in Aeria aware? All the Ambrosi?"

"No," she replied. "I don't think so. I am sure many are aware he is not pleasant, but over the years, he has truly blinded the immortals into believing he is their true king. Decades have passed, and they were all willing to believe Haelos was truly being care for, even without them lifting a finger to provide for them."

"Does it mention anything about what to do if the Founders are not upholding their responsibilities?"

"No, but it mentions that they can connect our portal directly to the Eternal Kingdom easily and quickly. After we finish with Aurelio, we are finding them."

"What's this?" He pointed to the new page she flipped to. "Replicating reality for viewing?"

Cosima's eyes quickly skimmed the text. "This sounds similar to what Ostrum has put into place, but there are instructions on how to connect this to the Eternal Kingdom." She swallowed hard. "We could show them what happens here tonight."

Vincenzo nodded tightly. "We should do it."

"We won't know how they will react. Your mother…"

"I don't care," he said, waving a hand. "She has dug her own grave. In my head, I was born to be of use to her. I can think of no better resolution than her receiving the punishment she deserves in part by my hand. I am unequivocally devoted to you, Cosima."

Cosima felt heat rise to her cheeks. "You make me believe there's more out there for me than the pain I have endured. Being with you is safe, and in that space I have only grown stronger."

"Don't attribute too much to me," he laughed. "You only needed shade from constant rain. You are more than capable of bringing down Aurelio, and I have known this from the start. Remember how hard you have fought to get here and let it fuel you. Your story doesn't end here."

Tears streamed down Cosima's cheeks as the words crashed against her. "My story doesn't end here," she repeated.

Before Cosima knew it, it was time. The Guardians from both the Ombra and Eternita Districts transported those entwined with the rebellion to the Archipelago. It would be mere minutes before the Devout Rising flock would land, concealed with small, veiled enchantments to shield them from sight. They would come in silent waves, the rebellion Guardians using their connection to the others to help others stay hidden out of sight. Cosima suspected the Aeria Guardians would be on higher alert than usual because of Aurelio's exclusion, but no word on Aurelio's response came to them.

Her mind begged for resolution, for an answer. "I feel he is hiding on one of the other islands. There is no way he would subject himself to the surface of Haelos, especially when he despises it so. If he is on Iridicenza, that puts Ivo at risk. If he is on Perpetuo, there is a greater chance he will sense something amiss as the rebellion is landing there."

"The closer we are to Iridicenza, the more I will be able to discern from the communications of the Guardians in the area. It is time to move." He brushed a quick kiss against her forehead.

Once they exited the hallway, Vincenzo moved like an animal stalking a scent trail with silent efficiency. A Guardian's wings came into view as Cosima trailed a few feet behind Vincenzo. In seconds, Vincenzo had subdued him and held him against the wall with his arm against the other Guardian's throat. Vincenzo pressed his palm against the man's head and shut his eyes.

The Guardian with olive skin and hazelnut hair was fraught with apprehension. He struggled against Vincenzo's grip, but no sooner freed himself. Instead, when Vincenzo opened his eyes, the Guardian's eyes shot wide open as well, now glowing a deep emerald green. Cosima gasped and when Vincenzo looked at her, so did the other Guardian.

"He goes first," Vincenzo said, releasing his grip. The Guardian merely turned on his heel and headed up a flight of stairs.

"What happened to him?"

"I can concentrate my power and move into someone else," he said, eyes blank. "The weaker willed, the better. Come, we must follow him. If there's too much distance, the connection will diminish. I can only do this once, but this is precisely the moment I was waiting for. Let's find the others and get to Ivo."

Cosima stuck closely to Vincenzo, ducking when he did and creeping along the shadows until they reached the surface. They were just outside the Palace, in the main city. The brainwashed Guardian sauntered down the street, his eyes still aglow but dimmer now. Cosima flattened herself against the walls of nearby buildings, ensuring she stayed away from any outdoor lighting. The sky was a deep black, the moon missing among the stars.

Her breath was heavy and conveyed her worry, but Vincenzo acted as though he did not notice. His attention was spent puppeteering the Guardian. When necessary, they dove out of sight or made a slight detour to avoid being discovered, but Vincenzo quickly closed the gap each time. He impressed Cosima with his ability to keep them cleverly hidden. He was remarkably vigilant and thought quickly on his feet.

"Wait here," he whispered into her ear. "I am going to make sure the path is clear and move this huddle of Guardians out of the way. We can save Tasia's enchanted necklace for crossing into Iridicenza."

Cosima wanted to follow, but she agreed. If he was making her stay behind, there was a reason for it.. She reached for the pendant around her neck, reassuring herself it would soon be time for it to shield them once again. The shadows in the corner of her eye moved and Cosima flinched. She turned slowly, but in the darkness, there was not much she could make out. Vincenzo had asked her to remain behind in an area with no outdoor lighting for cover, and she was nearly blind in the darkness.

Cosima gingerly withdrew her blade and stilled her breaths to better hear. Her time with Aurelio had taught her this skill with incredible precision, always seeing with her ears to sense if he was nearby. Her senses returned no indication of her *husband*'s presence, but of someone else entirely.

Star-fire erupted from the palm of a Rani Guardian. He was tall, with short red-black hair and slender wings the color of fresh blood. He stalked toward her, his barely-visible face stitched with a ghastly grin. Cosima realized he was not alone. Beside him were the last two people Cosima expected to encounter.

The Founders, Tomasso and Ginevra.

The Rani Guardian reached for her at the same moment she swung her blade. Though she had intended to save all of her magic for Aurelio, Vincenzo's absence meant she would be the only one able to ensure her safety. She would not go with them. She slowed down time, placing him within a pocket before releasing it just as her blade collided with him.

Cosima didn't hesitate, not when her thighs pushed themselves to the maximum driving her and the blade towards him, and not when he crumpled around it. Her magic spilled onto her weapon. It was singing to her, telling her exactly where to strike, when to move. She didn't need to glimpse him. Her blade knew him intimately, and it was hot for revenge.

Tomasso and Ginevra looked mildly intrigued by the situation, watching as Sima sliced at their Guardian with relentless fervor. She let her body twirl to its invisible tune, her power flowing freely into the blade. Her attacks became more brutal, snowballing until she speared him straight through to the ground, pinning him just above the crest of his wings. A threatening position for someone whose mortality resided beneath those feathers. They both panted, his blood smearing them.

"I don't understand," the Guardian choked, his feet aimlessly kicking. "I can't get a hit on you."

Tomasso laughed.

"Time away has done you well," Tomasso said, adjusting the hem of his coat. "Perhaps we were right. She would have benefited from training."

"She intimidated the King too much for that," Ginevra chuckled.

Sima clenched her teeth, looking up from where she stood over the Guardian.

"I have a theory I've been working on," Sima said, "If you're up for hearing it."

Ginevra smiled, as beautiful and as awe-inspiring as always. Her smile sent off alarm bells in Sima's head, Ginevra hemorrhaging waves of a twisted magic.

"Tell us, Cosima Aphelion."

"I think," she said, standing and resting a lazy arm atop the blade, the guardian squirming beneath it, "you know exactly how poorly Aurelio has been running Haelos, and you never once tried to stop him."

Something like contempt flashed across her sculpted features.

"I also think," Sima continued, "that you know how to track the King's exact location. It's that ring of yours. Aurelio has a similar one. You will tell me exactly where he is, and then maybe I will let you live."

It didn't take more than ten seconds for Ginevra's mask to deteriorate. She picked at her ring, attempting to hide it when she felt Sima's eyes on her. But it was enough. The ring indeed communicated the location of someone else, just like the ring Vincenzo had given her.

"You dare threaten me? You think because you ran off with some Guardian that now you are better than us all? Naive girl, you will wish Aurelio killed you properly instead of letting this charade go on, all for minimal benefit. You weren't even a useful captive. Your magic failed half the time."

The insult didn't land. Far from it. Instead, Sima felt her power continuing to seep through the blade, invisible arcs of energy vibrating the surrounding air. She could sense it, all the magic she had been coveting, saving for the perfect moment.

"Funny how you all will take the inventions of the people Below, but face away from their demise."

"Enough," Tomasso said. "I do not have time for your games, child. What is it you think you will accomplish? I give you his location and you walk to your death, or worse, you live, and it all begins again. You kill us and you disrupt everything those of Aeria know and trust. How will you mediate the chaos? You think having a good heart is enough? We *all* had a good heart, one time or another. It favors you none, especially in a place like Haelos."

"Is that it? You submit to him because you fear there is no

chance at his defeat?"

"Have you not been paying attention?" Ginevra snapped. "He's been shipping them off to other realms, depleting Haelos's stores. We were overzealous in our creation of Aeria. We used the crystals to run the Archipelago and left the rest to the planet. It was only a matter of time before Aurelio realized they were incredible reservoirs for power. Your world is emptying, and you know of nothing of it."

"How is it possible? What about the other continents?"

Ginevra paled. "They are all dead."

She flinched at the wave of confusion. "All of them?"

Ginevra nodded.

Tomasso cleared his throat, his jaw clenched. "Some of us made the same mistake as you, girl," he said, "trusting someone so fully while being lied to so completely. What do we have to show for our shame? A bigger mockery than before, if you can believe it. Other magic types once existed, hundreds of them. Haelos was special because the magic on this planet is older than most of the Goddesses." He shook his head, grinding his heel into the dirt. "This is all we have left. When it no longer suits Aurelio, we shall go, too. So, no girl, I will not tell you where he is. I have had enough of seeing good people march to slaughter."

"That's why he never speaks of them," she said, horrified enough that she retracted the blade from the apex of the Guardian's wings. He twitched but remained on the floor. It wasn't about Haelos, it was about bleeding them dry and destroying the planet. "If you're not planning to bring him to me, why are you here? What do you want?"

"Our silence keeps this world still functioning. The moment the Eternal Kingdom catches on to what is happening here, the High Priestesses will destroy Haelos without a second thought. We want to stop you from making that happen."

"Cosima," Vincenzo said from the sky, descending quickly and withdrawing his weapon.

"Vincenzo. What a pleasure." Ginevra shifted on her feet but made no sudden movements.

"We are clear to go," Vincenzo said in a hushed voice. "I sent the Guardian to Perpetuo with a message for Tasia, and they know about our plan. What's happening here?"

Cosima levied her gaze at Ginevra. "She says the High Priestesses will destroy Haelos."

"Why would they destroy this planet?" Vincenzo asked.

"Because," Ginevra said through her teeth, "we are nothing to them. They care not for what happens to the people of this planet. Those in the Eternal Kingdom claim to want to protect the products of creation, yet when a mistake occurs, they merely wipe the slate clean again. The only one she might care about is you, isn't that right, Vincenzo?"

Vincenzo took a step closer, baring his teeth, a low growl shaking his chest.

Ginevra smiled, brushing a curly lock of her hair out of the way. "Aurelio told us long ago of his brothers, the reason the Sacred Twelve were so powerful. Half-Ambrosi, half-God, supposedly. Yet you are supposed to be the weakest one. Another brother gave you that scar, isn't that right?"

Tomasso stood like he was carved of marble, the only movement slow blinking from his unfocused eyes. It set off an unease in Cosima she could not shake.

"Enough," Vincenzo said, running a hand through his wild hair, a blur of white, black, and gray. His blade now veered closer to Tomasso, though the Ambrosi hardly showed that he noticed. "We have places to be, Sima. We can't spend all day with these two."

With a swift swoop of his blade, he severed the wings from the injured guardian. His corpse was limp, and it appeared to cause the two Ambrosi nothing more than irritation.

"Give me your ring," Sima said, moving to Vincenzo's side, positioning her sword for attack.

"You don't understand what you are doing," Ginevra snarled.

Cosima had listened to enough of their rambling. "You are complicit in all the death Aurelio has left in his wake." She lifted her blade and swung at Ginevra at the same moment Vincenzo locked onto Tomasso. Sima and Enzo bore blades with power heightened by crystals strong enough to kill Ambrosi.

Anguish and confusion flooded Ginevra's eyes as the pain registered. The Founder, like all immortals, never truly expected her end to arise. Without intervention, the Founders would live on forever, but now, it was Cosima and Vincenzo who cut them down.

Cosima grimaced as she slipped Ginevra's ring off her corpse. She slipped it over her shivering fingers as Vincenzo used the pendant to activate the barrier shield to hide them away. The two pulled the bodies from where they lay and tucked them deep into alleyways.

Vincenzo lifted them into the air, no longer at risk of being seen, and flew toward Iridicenza. Cosima couldn't help the increased thudding of her heart within her chest as the ring illuminated brighter and brighter the closer they got.

Aurelio was on the same island as Ivo, confirming Cosima's worst fears. Her chest felt too heavy to lift for breaths, but she kept her chin up, unwilling to stop now. She would not give in, not when they were so close to victory.

"I'm coming, Ivo," Cosima whispered. "I'm coming."

Chapter 41

"Cosima, stop," Vincenzo said, reaching for her arm to pull her back.

She shoved his hands off her. "She's in there with him! Ivo is in the Atheneum with him. Let go of me!" The ring from Ginevra had led them directly to the Astral Atheneum. Horror slicked her hands with sweat as yet another memory of Ivo's flooded her brain: one of Ivo sneaking into the library, just as they had witnessed her doing before, but this time alone. "This is the only place she would go to hide. She is in there."

Vincenzo wrapped his arms around her and held her tightly, despite her attempts to fight him off. "Take a second to breathe and think this through. The faster you storm in, the more likely he is to harm her. We take this slow. We do it the right way."

Cosima slumped as he released her and hung her head in her hands. The ring on her finger was glowing with a blinding light, indicating Aurelio was incredibly close. The Astral Atheneum construction had not ceased, as Sima had hoped. Instead, it had been finished quickly. Towering walls of labradorite had created an entirely new shape out of Haelos's most important library.

At one time, the Atheneum had been crafted of white pillars and intricate crown molding, hand-carved by Ambrosi artists. The windows had been inviting and allowed in floods of natural sunlight. The labradorite now blocked out the windows, and bloodstone sealed the pillars. There was no telling what remained of their vital historical catalogues.

"Wait a minute," Cosima said, reaching for the pillar near her. "Aurelio showed me a piece of bloodstone. It was the first time I learned of the crystal's ability to wield power. This labradorite is the same material Aurelio used to harness Hexia power."

The stone hummed beneath her touch. It was made of brilliant shades of dark green, trails of what looked like drops of blood ran across the pillars in mesmerizing patterns.

"He's built a fortress," Vincenzo said quietly. His head snapped to the noise coming from behind them. "They're here."

From the shadows emerged Calix's fiery red hair. Beside her, Alma and Monte, both armed heavily, and though their faces were stoic, Cosima could feel a nervous energy emanating from the group. Though Sima desperately wanted to throw her arms around her friends, her desire to rescue Ivo overwhelmed her senses. She offered a tight nod to the trio instead.

"Where do you want us?" Calix asked.

"I need you to get a message to Ostrum." Cosima turned toward the heavy crystal doors that reached feet above their heads. Warding encompassed the whole of the entrance, visible only with the light of Vincenzo's star-fire. "He'll know how to get inside. Tell him to meet me there."

"Meet you there? How are you getting inside?" Alma arched a brow. "Look at those wards."

Beneath Vincenzo's light, the wards shimmered with a faint green and yellow sprinkle of color, carved directly into the labradorite. Sima touched the door. Within seconds, the warding began pulsing with an indigo light. The trio stumbled backward as one of the double doors creaked open several inches.

"Aurelio has grossly underestimated me. He overlooked a key fact—the wards he places on the Archipelago come to fruition only because of his relationship to *me*, the chosen heir. These will never work to keep me out just as Eternita could not keep me out."

"You were planning to do this the entire time," Vincenzo said, surprised. "If I didn't stop you, you were going to march in there alone."

"We can't come with you, can we?" Monte asked.

"Draw him out," Calix growled. "Don't you dare go in there alone."

Cosima slipped her body through the opening in the door before the others could object. Their panicked cries from behind her slowed Cosima none. Only when Vincenzo's voice rang above the others did she stall.

"*Please*," he cried, "you come back to me. Whatever you do, come back to me in the end."

Sima returned and held his hand through the door. Vincenzo brushed a quick kiss across the back of her hand before pulling it to his face. Their eyes locked through the gap and Cosima read the fear in his gaze. She expected him to beg her not to go, but he whispered, "I knew it had to be you. You can do this. Just come back to me."

Cosima nodded. "I love you," she whispered.

"I love you."

Vincenzo's hand hung in the air after she released him, as if in denial of her departure.

Cosima dialed her attention back to the task before her. The trio had brought along Ostrum von Toadsage to Aeria, not because he was particularly inclined to help, but out of his own morbid curiosity. After the conversation with the woman she had grown up believing was her mother, Sima knew precisely how to motivate the wizard to come to her aid.

She drew her blade, walking further into the library. Yadira's tale of a robed man breaking into the Astral Atheneum despite the strict warding aligned perfectly with the wizard. Ostrum could simply appear where he wanted.

So, he did.

"Cosima," he said, quietly, looking around sheepishly, "tell me it's true right now, or so help me, by the Cosmos, I'll curse your children's children."

"Hi, Ostrum," she said at a normal volume. "Yes, it's true. I know why you and Doc are stuck here. I will help you in exchange for the terms Calix has given you."

"Yes," he said, squinting at her. Sima would never get over the sensation of meeting a wizard, and by the Spirit, he really fit the description. He pulled off his miniature spectacles, huffing a hot breath before rubbing them clean on his cloak. "I can arrange that. More importantly, you're sure you harness the remedy?"

"Positive," Sima said, extending her hand. "You know how this works. Were you able to source the documents from Doc Santoro?"

He reached into his cloak, pulling a scroll tied neatly with a ribbon. He slid it into her hands as his head swiveled around the room. Obsessed with research, with finding his way around the other realms, Doc Santoro had precisely collected the information Cosima needed to open the Portale del Regno Stellare—the Star Realm Portal. In exchange for their services, Cosima would open the seal and allow them to escape Haelos.

Sima stashed the scroll away and handed him the Tome. She held her hand out for a handshake.

Ostrum was wary as they shook on their agreement, scrutinizing her face as he did so. The slightest glimmer of magic breached her eyes. It was the same energy Vincenzo had witnessed in her on the Day of Return. He smirked, eyes flashing with surprise as she clasped her free hand around his and the Tome.

She blinked, releasing him.

"This is much to my delight, Queen Aphelion. So, it is. Continue as you may. The magic will follow, and so will the eyes. The Tome is now in good hands. Oh, before I forget."

Two capsules fell into her palm. The thin clear shells revealed a fine black powder inside.

"Obsidian," Ostrum said. He disappeared with not so much as a puff of smoke. Sima blinked, eyes wide as he reappeared to add, "Good luck, I suppose. Goodbye."

Cosima shuddered, allowing time to resume. Sima tossed the capsules into her mouth, and even as a part of her cringed, she swallowed them dry. She swirled on her heel, following the ring, and her gut, to her husband's final day.

Ostrum's ability to broadcast to other realms paired with the rituals from the Tome would allow them to connect directly to the Eternal Kingdom to reveal Aurelio's injustices. Cosima figured the Goddesses would be less likely to wipe the planet completely if others witnessed their peril, how innocent the people of Haelos had been in Aurelio's schemes.

The library had six levels, all devoted to the various strands of knowledge needed to run the city in the sky, as well as manage the upkeep of Haelos. Several stacks also held important historical information about the people who lived there. Ambrosi were to maintain extensive records as they cared for those on the surface. However, this practice had collapsed during the last fifty years, evidenced further by the general disarray on the main floor.

Entire continents had been wiped out, for a reason she couldn't discern. This world was practically empty, bled dry by a parasite who planned to bail once he finished his plots. There was a reason he had chosen Haelos to impress his mother.

Though her thighs burned, Cosima reached the sixth-floor landing with scorching wrath, goosebumps encompassing her skin at the feeling of it. She hesitated only long enough to scan the document Ostrum had given her. The enchantment was long, but she let the final words simmer in her mind.

The ring reached its highest alarm. He was not only here—he was feet away. She glanced around the landing. It was a comfortably sized sitting area, and the exquisite detail was impressive, but hollow. She scanned for signs of Aurelio or Ivo, coming up short.

"Not used to the tables being turned, are we?" she called down an empty hallway, its expressionless design a dull collage of cream-colored furniture atop red jasper floors. "The fortress you built is hiding behind wards linked to my birthright, the Archipelago."

Cosima turned into the large room at the end of the hallway. She stopped in her tracks as she spotted someone. With a deathly shadow looming around him, Aurelio appeared relaxed, puffing on the Void Vine. He hummed a soft tune, one that her had grip tightening on the blade. Their wedding song floated through his disgraced vocal cords, the very sound of it becoming her guide, begging her to move her blade to his throat.

That would come soon. Cosima stepped into the room, the door auspiciously closing firmly behind her. It latched, and her husband bestowed upon her one fragment of attention, a bored glance.

"Tell me," she said, striding for the open chair beside his, "why did you never mention Vincenzo?"

"Is that what he's calling himself these days?" Aurelio asked, the sneer on his face a clear communication her hit had landed. He had showed his hand before, having used Vincenzo's pain to hurt her. "I knew him only as the worthless runt he is. My mother was desperate when she conceived him."

The room was a sanctum, sacred knowledge teeming from where the books sat along the shelves. Crystals of all kinds lined the walls, illuminated by invisible sources of light. She could describe the sight as nothing short of holy. She allowed herself to take it in, to breathe in the shift of air inside. This room wasn't hollow like the exterior suggested it might be.

Above them, a light fixture hung with a thousand tear drop gemstones. As though angels wept from the ceiling, the rainbow of light peppered every inch of the room. The radiance wavered as she stepped forward.

"I never knew you cared so much for your mother," Sima taunted.

His face was full of subtle disapproval, her former lover unable to contain his scorn fully. He had played the role a thousand times to the Ambrosi.

"Why do all this performing?" she continued. "Do you truly crave the attention more than outright control?"

He blew a puff of air out his nose, rolling his eyes. A cloud of smoke built a hazy cloud before them. Though the wave of dread building in her veins threatened to submerge her, she forced down her contempt and waited for his reply. He showed no sign he had noticed the pocket she created, though it was clear he continued to underestimate her.

"I can't control how the feeble view the strong," he said simply, ashing his cigar directly on the cold stone. "If the people adore me, who I am to turn them away? It is no matter to me how meaningless their lives are to me. I would slay millions more if it meant securing my position, the position ascribed to me by the powers higher than any creation. Once I am in control of the Eternal Kingdom, I will crush every useless planet however I desire. Together, my mother and I will unleash a new era of creation. One not bound by morality, but as I see fit." He held her gaze, testing the waters. Aurelio wore an intricate black suit with stormy clouds stitched in black thread across the jacket, paired with a velvet green tie. Tourmaline adorned his cufflinks, replacing the solar ones he wore habitually. The stone protected the wearer.

"You're scared," she said, not daring to break eye contact first. He feigned bravery, scoffing, but Cosima could sense his apprehension. "You're using all these crystals to craft yourself a hiding spot. You feel you need these weapons to survive."

"What did my poor brother get wrapped up in your mind? I suppose it is true. You really are fond of him, aren't you? I thought it was merely a passing fancy. Oh, I never told you that story, did I?"

Cosima's jaw tightened. "What story?"

"Where you come from, truly."

Cosima swallowed hard, but she kept her breathing level. "Tell me."

Aurelio laughed deeply, his perfectly molded hair unmoving as he tossed his head back. "My mother has always adored me more than my brothers, even if they deny it. Since the beginning, it was I with the strongest attacks, with the ambition needed to complete the task set before us. Even as the plans changed, and only one brother would be left alive to rule, immediately I knew it would be me, for there is no one of finer caliber for the job."

"When she uncovered the relationship between the two of you in the Eternal Kingdom, she knew precisely how to make you pay. See, the truth is, *dove*, you are incredibly gifted. It is a shame you do not have the grit to use your power properly, but it was enough to reward you with capture instead of death. Trust me, I have learned from this foolish decision. You should have been killed, instead of becoming a pawn for my mother."

"The Spirit Goddess captured me, all for loving Vincenzo? Our union must be quite influential, especially if, according to you, he was doomed to die, anyway."

Aurelio ground his jaw. "Make no mistake, I left him alive simply because I believe him to be that little of a threat to me. My brother…he is identical to me. All of us are wicked. How are you sure I am the worst? He perhaps is a better liar, but don't forget how enamored you were with me when we met."

"Before you showed me the true side of you?"

"Precisely," he spat. "I can go back to playing those little mind games if it makes you happy. You're quite a costly woman to maintain, primarily in spirit. You've had your fun rolling in the mud with the pigs, playing pretend. It's time to remember exactly why you were put here—to be mine. You know what your worth amounts to." Another long drag of his cigar. "Submit, or don't, I don't care. You know as much. I'll always take what's mine."

"How do I remember being a child here?"

Another of Aurelio's hearty laughs shook from his chest. "Your body is merely a vessel. She is the Spirit Goddess, capable of bending space and time for creation. She can craft memories, a body, manipulating your soul in whatever manner suits her, so long as she is on a planet, and not in the Eternal Kingdom."

Cosima snapped to her feet, the blade pointed firmly against Aurelio's chest. The dagger in her belt was the one to deal the killing blow, but Cosima felt she wasn't ready for it to end yet.

A contemptuous smile coasted his angular features.

"You can't kill me, Cosima."

She bristled at the mention of her name. Sima shook it off. "Want to bet?"

"What's the point? Seriously, *Yin*, I've had enough of the act. You don't know the first thing about what I've been doing behind the scenes. Maybe you never will. I'll find a way to break you again, to make you forget it all, over and over. I'll do it until you're sick.

I'll do it until you beg me for death. You can try to kill me, Cosima, but my soul, too, shall be reborn."

Sima blinked. Time slowed further. The sound of what she thought might be footsteps in the hallway distorted as Cosima stared down at the man who had tormented her for fifty years. A piece of her remained terrified and begged for respite, but a louder command came from within to end it finally.

"You may never understand the depths to which you altered my life. You may never comprehend the utter desolation you forced me to endure. I realize now, there is no thread of Fate one could pull that would erase the harm you have done, no world in which your recognition of it would smooth it over. Thankfully, I have realized there is no need for you to understand. I am more than what you preached to me I was. I realize now you attacked me relentlessly, not because I was weak, but because I was strong. You kept me in the dark out of intimidation."

His brow twitched. She forced her eyes open wide to watch his body flinch as Sima released the hold on time and her blade exploded through his flesh.

Release.

It was pure ecstasy, his blood on her tongue, in her hair, dripping down her arms. She took her time, unfolding pocket after pocket. Still, he moved with refined force, making measured leaps away to avoid her attacks. Her magic poured into the blade, lighting it brightly with an opalescent shine. Cosima swung, aiming for the crook of his neck.

Aurelio produced his own blade within seconds, the crackles of his malignant power weeping a dark maroon from the weapon. A hand slicked back his hair, mixed with his own blood. Cosima's slice was not enough to slow him. He launched himself at her, knocking her to the ground. She slipped from his grasp with a neatly timed pause, careful to monitor her reserves. She could not be foolish enough to run herself dry.

"You will never amount to anything without me. No one is interested in a defiled, broken woman. What use are you to the world without me to give you purpose?"

Cosima let loose a scream as her blade pierced him along his left side. Before she could slow him, he sped backward, preventing her from pinning him. This time, he prepared his own attack, slicing into her upper arm. She cried out, peddling away as she regained composure.

Aurelio chuckled, bringing the blade to his tongue, and tasting her blood. "Careful, dove."

"Never again," she whispered.

Wind rustled her hair as Aurelio flew at her. She shrieked as they fell backward. His hands wrapped around her wrists and pinned her to the floor. Her feet peddled kicks in his direction, but Cosima was no match for his physical strength.

Panic flushed defensive action clean from her veins and left paralytic in its wake. He leered closer, his breath hot on her face. "Look at me."

She refused and scrunched her eyes shut.

"Look at me," he screamed.

Cosima flinched, and reluctantly, she met his gaze. The wrath that swelled along his facial features frightened her.

"What will become of you when you fail the others? What happens when you are a leader no one will follow?" Spit flew as he spoke, his eyes dizzy with rage.

She surveyed him, and her blood threw a tantrum in her body as it pulsed heavily beneath the surface of her skin. Her eyes dragged up his sculpted chin, the fierce lines of his cheekbones and sharp brows. Hardened honey marbles glared at her, his eyes narrowing with scrutiny. His piercing gaze portrayed every nightmare, conveyed every threat, but Cosima was not the same woman she had been when she was with him.

No, Cosima was *much* different now.

"I'm not afraid of you anymore," she breathed.

He cocked his head to the side and scoffed. His grip tightened around her wrists until she yelped in pain.

"I am the only one who knows the truth about you, *Yin*. You are worthless down to the middle of your core. You mean nothing to no one and if given a chance, you will fail everyone every time.

You are not the person you've deluded yourself into thinking you are. Sure, others may come to you now. They may stand by your side. That is because of your proximity to me. When their pity runs out, you will have nothing to show for it. You will never rise above me, and I will break you again and again until you understand."

It was Cosima's turn to laugh.

She reached for her magic, relieved to feel it come easily. Instead of pausing time, Cosima channeled her affinity for inciting natural consequences. Above them, the crystalline light fixture hung on loops of metal. The sound of the metal splitting beneath the weight of hubris caught their ears. The colossal display rained from the ceiling and shattered around them.

Aurelio tucked away beneath his wings, and Cosima rolled onto her stomach and covered her face. The sharp points of the carved stones pelted them like daggers, slicing feathers and flesh. Aurelio no longer wished to play games and lifted a hand directly at her.

Time slowed the galaxies of his starlight blasting toward her. Cosima scrambled out of the way, hardly feeling the hundreds of small cuts across the back of her body. The starlight blew a giant hole straight through the side of the Atheneum.

He flew to the damage, and for the first time, they both once again witnessed the Archipelago at war. Outside, thousands of Guardians fought to the death mid-air. Wings and limbs tumbled downward, and blood coated her home.

"The end of your reign is here, and you can deny it no longer." Cosima stepped forward, aiming her weapon at him. Magic skidded across the blade in iridescent ripples.

"I hope they all die," Aurelio snarled. "I hope every last one of them pays with their life for your idiocy."

"You are a sad man, *Yang*. How empty you must feel being so hollow within. Is that what keeps you up at night? The knowledge you have *nothing* inside of you, not one salvageable piece?" Cosima levied her blade.

His eyebrows flickered with surprise at her retort.

"You have no idea what I have been planning. You think so small. You are incapable of comprehending the true intentions I hide. I told you I *chose* Haelos for a reason. Planets like this are rare. Among the trillions of universes, crystals as powerful as this are unheard of."

"Then how did you find it?"

"My mother favors me for a reason. I have my father's strength, but it is her wit that I have taken to like flesh to bone. She created the *Alfrii* and recycled their souls within as an experiment of sorts. She could do as she pleased to these souls, and she toyed with them. One day, her playthings came to her with pretty little rocks on altars. Within them lay infinite potential. That's when *she* began enlisting the pointy-eared fools into doing her dirty work. Mother has much to attend to, and thus, Haelos became my responsibility."

"You said I was a pawn for your mother. How?"

Aurelio tipped his head back and laughed. His feathers ruffled as he turned and stared out of the gaping hole. Chaos still consumed the outside world, and he relished in it.

"You won't get that information from me. Perhaps Fate will favor you enough to tell you herself, or I'll kill you before she gets the chance. Who knows what is next for you?"

I do, thought Sima.

Time slowed, sweeping symphonies of ever-growing silence further into the distance. She slid the weapon from its sheath and marveled at the weight of it in her hand. Energy from within flooded into the dagger and light burst from the jade affixed to the hilt.

"Enough."

Before his face could convey his understanding, Sima pressed a kiss to the side of it, and launched it into the air. It whistled, the sound of it divine in her ears, and as it spun, she allowed time to resume fully. The dagger barreled into the flesh of his eye; the hilt halted by the bone of his eye socket.

He crumpled, landing with a heavy thump to his knees. Cosima approached slowly, remaining weapon aimed tightly.

"Want to know the best part—" she said, pulling his face up from the ground, staring deep into his remaining golden eye, "about these disgusting crystals you and Mommy made? They are going to end you, because I can think of no better justice for whatever soul lost their life for this to happen."

Cosima wrapped her hand around the dagger, pressing it farther into his skull. She removed him with a heavy push backward, a hollow thunk resonating through his skull as he hit the ground. He groaned and spat a mouthful of blood over her. It was rain in a drought; it was touching heaven for the first time. A swing of her leg had her boot lodge into his side.

"Get up," she said, "I said *get up*. I need you to know that I am doing this to you because of the fucked-up way you are." She sliced her blade into him again, using the hold on his flesh to turn him over.

"Do you get it yet?" She slid her blade along his abdomen, admiring the way the stone glistened, covered with his blood. "You slaughter innocents, you believe yourself godly enough to take their lives, when you are at heart a pathetic man. You fear me deep down because you know you are nothing like me, nowhere near as powerful. I was only fragile because I fell victim to your lies and manipulations. The one thing you never expected was that I saw a life for myself on the other side of you. This is not where my story ends."

Iron crimson poured heavenly rivers across his body. "You are nothing," he grumbled.

"Why could I never change your Fate, Aurelio?"

His remaining eye rolled to her. A heavy cough interrupted his laugh. Aurelio's finger tapped his forehead. Cosima cocked her head to the side, not comprehending.

A hollow, gasping laughter escaped him again.

A sound echoed from the hallway outside. Cosima remained still, resisting the urge to follow the noise.

Ivo.

Somehow, Cosima knew. She could sense her friend.

Don't do anything stupid, Ivo. Hide.

"Ah, the lamb returns," Aurelio growled. Scarlet flecked saliva slid down the side of his face. "I assumed she finally gave up."

The door flung open with a hefty blast of wind. Ivo stood there, surrounded by swirling papers.

"Queen Aphelion!" Ivo shouted. "Are you all right?"

"Get out of here!" Cosima cried. Aurelio shifted beneath her, and before she knew it, he was across the room with his hand reaching for Ivo's neck. When she halted time, he was only inches from her friend. Cosima gasped for air. "Ivo. What were you thinking?"

"I won't let you fight him alone, Cosima. I told you I would always be here for you." Ivo slipped away from Aurelio's frozen form and ran to her. Cosima threw her arms around Ivo, and though she knew her power was dwindling, she couldn't resist embracing her friend.

"I thought you were dead," Cosima said. "Stand back."

Aurelio's sudden absence interrupted them. Cosima was on the ground, dizzy with pain, before she could understand what happened. Ivo screamed. She shook off the haze and scrambled to pause time.

He would have to die *now*.

Before he could break her hold over him, Cosima stabbed the dagger into the back of his neck, a primal yell of anguish and fury hot on her breath as she pulled it down into his spine. The sensation of her rage blinded her, and the last of her power flooded into the weapon as she dealt her largest blow.

With no fuel, her hold on time ceased. Aurelio's knees hit the floor stiffly. Blood trickled from him, his gray wings painted with evidence of her unrelenting dedication to her freedom. The Atheneum trembled beneath their feet, but he did not move.

Cosima crept forward. Her hand weaved into his hair and pulled his head back. His eyes were a dull yellow, lifeless.

Ivo, brandishing Cosima's discarded blade, ran full force toward the once-powerful King. Her body twisted as she came to a stop beside his battered body. A razor thin crimson slice encircled Aurelio's neck. Cosima could only stare as his body abandoned his head, and the two pieces of him fell in separate wet thumps across the floor.

The only sound was of their ragged breaths. Exhaustion and adrenaline vied for space in her body. Cosima shared a look of timid disbelief with Ivo.

"He's dead," Ivo breathed. "Now we know for sure."

"He's dead," Cosima repeated. She stumbled over to his head and pulled it further from his body by his ivory hair. Horror swelled in her gut, and she let his head tumble to the floor for good measure.

The world around them erupted into tumultuous rumbling. The crystals surrounding them began toppling to the floor, shattering into pieces. Cosima wrapped her hand around Ivo's and pulled her toward the exit. The ground was unstable beneath their feet as they ran down the stairs. Ivo slipped, Sima narrowly grabbing her elbow in time to keep her from falling down.

The walls of the newly renovated Astral Atheneum crumpled, dropping in chaotic crashes. Cosima felt her skin being peppered with broken shards and she wept blood where he had cut her open. She and Ivo used their hands to shield their eyes.

Cosima prayed the stairs would not give out beneath them as they neared the second floor. "What's happening?" Cosima cried.

Ivo offered no answer, intently focused on remaining upright. The walls beside them lost all sense of stability, as Cosima realized the building was collapsing in on itself. Just as her mouth opened to scream, a flash of black and white wings came into view.

Chapter 42

The Astral Atheneum erupted into dust and a cacophony of crystal shattering. Vincenzo hurtled them all to safety, the three of them covered head to toe in abrasions and cuts. As Vincenzo released her, Cosima collapsed to the ground.

A thick sob fought its way out, causing her to fold in on herself. Vincenzo kneeled beside her, rubbing a reassuring hand across her back.

"He's dead," she whispered. "He's dead."

"I know," Vincenzo said just as softly. "You did it. He can hurt the people of this world no more."

Relief only brought powerful waves of tears. As she lay on the ground and cried, all the friends she had made along the way now stood around them. Through hazy eyes, she could see they, too, had gone through quite a fight.

"More Guardians than expected put up a fight," Vincenzo said, stroking her hair gently. "We have slain all who opposed Aurelio's death, and we spared those who relinquished their positions. The island is ours once again. You did it, Cosima."

At that, she sat up and scanned the small crowd around them. The trio stood wiping their swords clean with cloths produced from their belts. Tasia, Aspasia, and Ioannis—the Fae siblings—engaged the Ombra trio in light conversation. Cosima realized that even though some were injured, the crowd sang with victory.

Daylight erupted along the horizon, promising to bring renewal with it. "How did you convince them?"

Vincenzo tilted his head toward the growing number of people surrounding them. "We distributed Simon's paintings across the islands. The Ambrosi woke to the chaos to find the truth from Below right before their faces. Some were doubtful, but others were curious. Not every immortal was aware of the suffering taking place Below. It will be interesting to see how this resolves in the coming future."

The crowd murmured quietly around them as Cosima gathered her breath. These were her people, those of whom she believed she must protect as the proper Queen. It was always supposed to be Cosima who led them, who renewed their devotion to the people Below. Yet, as she took in Vincenzo's emerald gaze, she knew, ultimately, it was not supposed to be her.

Cosima could not deny that Ehses had placed her in this position all in an attempt to punish her for loving Vincenzo. When the Spirit Goddess discovered her youngest son's relationship with Sima, she had stolen her away. *Who, then, is fit to lead them?*

Suddenly, her body signaled something was incredibly out of place as the mirage faded around her home. Cosima glanced at Vincenzo, but bright flashes of memories crowded her vision. The images were indiscernible, fluttering at a speed she could not interpret. Vincenzo wrapped his arms around her to steady her, but it only worsened the flood.

"Are you all right? What's happening?" Ivo whispered, dropping down beside Cosima.

"I-I don't know," Cosima said. "I can't see. It's too much."

A wave of calm embraced her skin. Tasia's voice whispered something too soft for Cosima to hear to someone nearby. Tasia's magic slowly suppressed the panic building in her chest. "Can you hear me?"

"Yes," Cosima said, tears streaming down her cheeks. Her eyes blinked furiously, but nothing made it end. "Something is happening. There are so many images."

"Some of the restraints on your mind are coming down," Tasia said, "releasing a flurry of memories. It will take time before you can understand them. The images may be out of order and without context, it is impossible to discern what they mean. Give it time. Let the floodgates open. We will get you somewhere with more privacy."

With that, the sensation of being picked up by Vincenzo encompassed her body. Sima leaned into his comforting scent as the images surged behind her closed eyelids. The noise of nearby Ambrosi and citizens from the Districts on the surface faded and the sound of running water overtook it.

Vincenzo placed her down on a plush chair and asked for her permission to undress her and place her in the tub. She nodded her consent, her head dizzy. Once inside the tub, he washed her hair diligently. His muscular hands took their time removing all knots and matted blood. He removed the shards of glass from her skin with precision, minimizing tearing.

The memories finally came to a stop and left her with a pounding headache. Instead of opening her eyes, she lingered in the maze of her mind. Nothing made sense, and she feared the onslaught would begin again with one wrong move. The memories piled atop one another, bringing her no closer to understanding. A stream of water crested her scalp as Vincenzo rinsed the soap from her onyx hair.

"Vincenzo," she said.

"Yes?" he replied, wrapping her hair in a towel.

"Where do we go from here? What do we do next?"

"I think the next step is for you to open the Portale del Regno Stellare again and allow those from the Eternal Kingdom to arrive. The Rani Guardians are protectors of those on other planets, but those who care for the Ethereal Realm are called the Trine Scouts. I believe they would come to us and take us back home."

"What happens to you? Aren't you at risk of being killed by one of your brothers? Who else is still out there?"

Vincenzo's brows flickered. "Don't worry about that right now. You focus on replenishing your reserves, so you have enough to open the gate and demolish the seal."

Cosima allowed one eye to open and peek at Vincenzo. His skin was bloody still, but he had changed into a fresh shirt and washed his hands before he touched her. He offered a smile.

"Is this real? He is gone and now I am free?"

"You're free."

"What becomes of the people of Haelos? Who shall lead them?"

"That is for the High Priestesses to decide. Ehses is not the only Goddess capable of choosing royalty for the Archipelagos. Any one of them can decide."

A knock sounded from the door. Ivo's face was visible through the crack in the door. "Something is happening. A strange, giant beam of light is coming from the Ombra District. You must see for yourself."

Vincenzo nodded. Once Ivo closed the door, Vincenzo lifted Sima from the tub. She got dressed quickly while Vincenzo went to investigate. As Cosima walked down the hall, she realized they had gone back to the Palace. This was the first time in decades she could leave her room freely, and Cosima couldn't shake how that fact lingered over her head.

At one time, she had thought herself a lost cause. Cosima had doubted herself and questioned every move, consistently shadowed by his oppressive desire for control. The more he had distanced her from the authentic version of herself, the easier it was to restrain her, to manipulate her. He had believed he'd subdued her enough that she would never fight back, and now it was her who continued to live, to grow.

The girl who once believed death would be sweeter than life now only saw a world of possibilities, a future untapped. Her justice would not lie in Aurelio's departure from her life alone. It would sprout from who she was after him. For every time she cried and thought her misery would go unheard, for every night full of fighting and cruelty, and for every hole that felt too deep to crawl out of, Sima embraced her freedom.

As she walked the halls where he had confined her for the last fifty years and made her way down to the main floor, Cosima could recall only sparing pleasant moments, those precious times because of the love from Ivo or Yadira. The two women had stayed by her side, even if it risked their lives to do so, and Cosima was grateful. Sadness held on inside her as well at the idea that her future could mean leaving them behind.

Cosima gasped, covering her mouth with her hand when she spotted it. It was true. The beam of light was overpoweringly bright. Cosima shielded her eyes and stood beside Vincenzo. He wrapped her hand in his and stood with the other, blocking the Portal from view.

"I believe this means you won't need to unseal the Portal after all," he murmured.

"What?"

"The Trine Scouts have come through the Portal. They're on Haelos."

"I'm ready," Cosima said. And she was. "I want to know what is next for me, for us." She spotted a mess of black hair and bright blue eyes running toward them. "Ivo," Cosima chirped as she embraced her.

"They're taking you away, aren't they?" She studied Sima's eyes nervously.

"Yes, I'm afraid so."

"When are you coming back?"

"I'm not sure."

Ivo paled but nodded slowly. "You did it, you freed us from him. Now, this is your chance to live a life without him. Don't waste this opportunity."

"It's them," Vincenzo whispered.

Two men walked closer to them, wearing mocha-colored suits, trailed by pastel green capes. The men watched Cosima and Vincenzo tightly enough to convey they considered them potential enemies. She took a small step back.

"I'm right here," Vincenzo assured her. He squeezed her hand.

The closer the Trine Scouts came, the higher her panic climbed. The men halted a few feet in front of them and crossed their arms across their chests. Both were tall, Vincenzo's height, with long blond hair. Angular, strong features composed their faces.

"Cosima Aphelion?" one man said clearly.

"Yes," she said, mustering an evenness to her tone that concealed her fear.

"You are to come with us and return to the Eternal Kingdom. You must come before the High Priestesses and plead your case."

"My case?"

"Demolition of any planet in violation of the standards set forth for each Archipelago is a standard outcome. However, because one of the High Priestesses were privy to the Aurelio's true intentions laid forth in his last moments, you are being granted the opportunity to plead your case."

The other one spoke this time. "If there stands to be a convincing enough negotiation on your part, the planet will remain, and they will construct a new Archipelago, and choose a new leader. If you cannot convince them, all here shall die, including the two of you."

"No!" Ivo cried.

Cosima's jaw fell open.

It was Vincenzo who spoke next. "There has to be some sort of misunderstanding. Why would we have to die? We have done nothing wrong."

"I beg to differ," the first Trine Scout said, placing a hand on the strange sword at his side. The metal was nothing like the weapons Cosima had seen on Haelos. "She has committed many egregious changes to Fate. This cannot go unregulated."

Cosima wrapped her arms around herself, and Vincenzo laid a protective hand across her back. "You're right," she said. "We will go with you, and I will plead my case. I will tell them the truth about what transpired here, and they will have no choice but to believe me."

The Scouts appeared uneasy with her statement but said nothing further. Instead, the two approached them and latched invisible restraints across their wrists. Though Cosima could not see the bindings, she could not free herself from them. Her heart thundered in her chest, but she persisted and followed their commands.

As they walked with the Scouts, she glanced back at Ivo. Sima waved them goodbye with tears streaming down her face. She wished they had more time. There was no guarantee she would ever see Haelos again with her own eyes, no guarantee she would see Yadira or Ivo again, either. In fact, she was not granted the chance to say her farewells to anyone, and with that realization came rampant worries. She pushed the twinges of guilt and resistance away, instead focusing on what lay ahead of her.

For the first time, Cosima saw the Portale del Regno Stellare with her own eyes. An imposing red rock mountain lay before them, the enormous center swirling with a burning orange glow. Sima was but an insect compared to the Portal. There was a low hum vibrating through the air from it. From the top, it sprouted the vicious beam of light they had witnessed from Above.

"Do you know if anyone has been looking for me?" Cosima asked the Trine Scouts. She wondered about her family, if they still wished to see her, if they existed at all.

The two shook their heads in tandem. "Until we verify your identity upon returning to the Eternal Kingdom, we can give no information. Either your memories will settle into place, and you will remember, or you will await information from the High Priestesses."

From where they stood, the light was less bothersome, drowned out by the warm-toned portal. The Trine Scouts ushered them forward. Cosima turned her head to Vincenzo and sighed. "We will have our time together. I know it to be true. I do not know why things feel as cumbersome as they do, but we will be victorious on the other side."

Vincenzo nodded, his green eyes smoldering with love for her. "I can't pretend to know why this strange existence works the way it does. I have searched the galaxies and found myself no closer to an answer until I met you. My soul has been waiting, biding my time, even before I knew you existed. Then they took you from me, and by the tides of Fate, I found you again. My stories may not make sense, but they will, and I will show you the same heart I gave you the first time."

Cosima was unsure what the future would hold, if they would truly be granted the time to explore the love they had for each other, or if their lives would be cut short. It brought her no peace to think of the horrid situation Aurelio had forced upon them all. His egotistical, insecure nature had left a path of pure destruction in his wake, and there was not a straightforward answer even when the dust settled.

"Whatever awaits us on the other side," Cosima said, "it was all worth it. I will never regret freeing us from him, and the strength I have found within is irreplaceable."

His bound wrists moved in her direction and floated in the air between them. A silent request. Cosima moved the same and their fingertips grazed one another. The Scouts grumbled but did nothing to stop them as they marched right to the threshold of the Portal.

"When they let us go at the end of all of this, will you promise me one thing?" Vincenzo said with an easy laugh.

"What's that?" Cosima said. She met his gaze once again and Cosima wrapped herself in the warm sensation brought over her by the love in his eyes.

"Promise me you will never stop fighting for yourself. You are powerful beyond measure, and the universe stands to change if for no reason other than you willed it so."

"I promise," she said, nodding her head once.

"And promise one more thing. Promise you will let me gloat once your memories come back and you realize we truly were in love the entire time."

Cosima laughed. "What if I change my mind and decide I want to go separate ways?"

He shrugged and the Trine Scouts tapped their feet impatiently. "I am pretty confident you won't. I was *really* good to you."

"Oh?" Cosima said, tilting her head to the side. "We will have to see if that's true, then."

With fingers interlaced, the two of them stepped through the Portal, led by the Trine Scouts. The fabric of space and time melted around them, contorting into magnificent displays of light as other worlds flashed by them. Cosima couldn't breathe and couldn't feel her body. Instead, she did the only thing that made sense to her at the moment, and she surrendered.

As the Portal transported them to the Eternal Kingdom, Cosima felt the Cosmos flow through her hair and across her skin. She felt the tapestry of life as she knew it fade away from being. All the curses placed on her by the Spirit Goddess fell away and though she did not expect it, events played out behind her eyelids.

Cosima was unsure of what she was witnessing at first until she realized it was a celebration of some sort. People clothed in extravagant gowns and suits swirled around with glasses full of glimmering ruby red wine. Music from violins and pianos hummed in the background, filling the space with tranquil noise. At the center of the elaborate dance hall was a girl with midnight black hair down to her waist.

A woman with matching black hair emerged, splitting the crowd in two as she made her way in. Her eyes were a richer brown, her skin a shade deeper, but the resemblance was undeniable. She looked related to Cosima. She stood wearing a long, flowing gown. Lavender silk fabric wrapped around her neck and sagged her shoulders and arms, concealing them. The woman was intimidating, and her beauty was striking. Cosima felt both the desire to run toward her, and to run away from her.

The girl in the center spotted the woman and darted toward her. Her dress was the same pastel purple, with silver stars hanging from the hem of her skirts. The two twirled around and around to the music, oblivious to the crowd of eyes on them.

"Cosima," the woman laughed, "slow down."

The image faded. Once again, flashes of colorful light crowded her vision. Cosima bucked against the invisible restraints in the celestial waves, desperate to see more.

Cosima had witnessed a younger version of herself, had glimpsed her mother's true face, and she would give anything to see it again.

Her feet now landed on solid ground, and Cosima blinked away the remnants of the beams from the Portal. Surrounding them was an empire in the clouds, remarkably more beautiful than anything Cosima knew from Haelos. The air was fresh and smelled strongly of a recent rainstorm.

Beside her stood Vincenzo and the two Trine Scouts.

"Welcome home," Vincenzo said and took a deep breath.

Shock stole every word from her tongue, so instead of replying, Cosima drank in the new world around her. The buildings were entirely gold or white, with craftsmanship she never thought possible. At the center of the city, a tower stood higher than all other buildings. The tower itself was sculpted into the shape of a blossoming lotus with delicate white and pink petals.

Cosima allowed her breath to bring her courage. Her family was out there, waiting for her. There was a whole life left for her to live, and she would not see that chance squandered by others. Her legs moved her body forward, rigid from the travel—but that discomfort meant she was still alive. Her mind rumbled with the workings of a plan to prepare for what lay ahead.

From now, until the end, Cosima Aphelion's destiny was hers alone to command.

Glossary

Above- the name given to the Aeria Archipelago, referencing their position 'above' the surface of the planet in the sky.

Aeria Archipelago- a collection of three sky islands, home to the immortals and winged Guardians.

Alfrii- the name given by the Ambrosi for the Fae. It means 'elf'. These are creatures with powerful abilities to manipulate nature, among other things, and have pointed ears.

Ambrosi- Immortal beings with internal power capable of powering the Archipelago and allows them to care for the people of the world they are set to care for. The founders come from the Eternal Kingdom, then all Ambrosi are then born on the planet they serve. They are capable of dying, but it is a difficult process.

Astral Atheneum- the largest library in all of the Aeria Archipelago. This library is home to all recorded history and artifacts since the creation of the Archipelago. This stores not only vital information for the operation of the Archipelago, but also keeps detailed information on the inhabitants of the world below.

Below- the name given to the surface of the planet, referencing their position 'below' the Archipelago.

Day of Return- a holiday celebrated by the inhabitants of the planet, more specifically, the Shadow-types from the Ombra District. During this holiday, all souls from those who have passed return to the Eternal Kingdom via the thinning of the veil.

The Depths- the name given to the vast, underground city below the city Speranza in the Ombra District. Thousands live below the surface, hiding from beasts, as well as the Archipelago.

Drago- a large dragon creature residing in the In-Between. These creatures are tasked with defending the slumbering souls of those who have passed on, until it is time for them to be born again.

Echo- a shadow-type capable of shifting their bodies to match naturally occurring animals or plants. They are capable of making themselves smaller or larger. Every Echo is capable of forming into a Hawk.

Eternal Kingdom- a kingdom that resides in the Ethereal Realm. Here, there are twelve High Priestesses who rule the Kingdom and are responsible for creation of life in other realms. This is where Ambrosi come from, as well as where Rani Guardians are born and trained.

Ethereal Realm- realm where Goddesses, Ambrosi, Rani and more are born.

Eternita- Eternita is a District on the surface of planet Haelos. This District is home to the Faeries, including the Alfrii (Fae), sprites, dwarves and more. The name means 'Eternity', in reference to the Fae's long life-spans. This District is full of lush, green forests and houses a plethora of animals.

Ehses (Spirit Goddess)- the creator of all the life on planet Haelos. She created the Faeries, Shadow-types, and humans. She did not, however, craft the physical planet. She was a High Priestess in the Ethereal Realm.

The Giving- a holiday in which all Ambrosi on the Archipelago forfeit a small amount of their power in order to run the Archipelago. This power is funneled into the Light Reserve.

Haelos- the planet where the Aeria Archipelago and Districts are contained. This planet contains many natural resources, including towering slabs of crystals.

High Priestess- a set of twelve Goddesses who rule over the greater Eternal Kingdom, beneath Kismet only. This is a highly coveted position, allowing the ability to partake in the creation of new worlds and people.

Hexia- a coven of witches enslaved to King Aurelio on the Archipelago. They are originally from the Ombra District. They are skilled at creating spells or enchantments.

In-Between- also known as tra paradiso e inferno (between heaven and hell). This is where slumbering souls rest until it is time for them to be reborn.

Innamorati- the largest island in the Archipelago and is home to the Palace where Cosima and Aurelio live. The name means 'The Lovers'.

Iridicenza- an island in the Archipelago, home to the Astral Atheneum. The name means 'Iridescent'.

Kismet- the Goddess gifted with the power to apportion Fate to the creations of the High Priestesses. Even those in the Eternal Realm are endowed with predetermined lives. Kismet seeks balance above all else. She is more powerful than the High Priestesses.

Light Reserve- this is where all the power from the Ambrosi is stored and distributed across the three islands in the Archipelago.

Mortoid- also known as Death's Mirror, Mortoid is a mushroom with powerful powers, highly enjoyed by the immortals. It is a hallucinogenic, capable of showing the user what death feels like.

Nuvola Palace- the Palace belonging to the Aeria Archipelago on the island Innamorati. The name means 'cloud' palace. This is where Cosima was held for fifty years with Aurelio.

Ombra- the Shadow District. The name translates to Shadow in reference of the large shadow cast across the District during the height of the day from the Archipelago blocking the sun. This District is primarily a barren desert, worsened by the shun from the Eternita District.

Perpetuo- the smallest island in the Archipelago, home to the Complaint's Block, where prayers and messages from the world Below are interpreted and responded to. The name means 'Perpetual'.

Portale del Regno Stellare (Star Realm Portal)- the gate that connects Haelos to the inter-dimensional roadway. This connects the planet to the Ethereal Realm, as well as many others. This gate can only be operated by the ruling family from the Archipelago.

Prisma- The human District on Haelos. The name translates to Prism. This region is mountainous and difficult to traverse from one city to another.

Rani Guardian- the winged Guardians from the Eternal Kingdom tasked with protecting the Ambrosi and life-forms created by the High Priestesses on their assigned planet. They are raised together to form strong bonds, and the only way to kill one is by slicing off their wings.

Sacred Twelve- the name for Aurelio and his eleven brothers. They are some of the only Ambrosi in history born with wings, marking them especially powerful.

Sotto il Cielo- 'Beneath the Sky' is the name given to the surface of planet Haelos. Similar to 'Below', but is primarily used by the Ambrosi.

Speranza- the largest city in the Ombra District, hiding the Depths underground. The name means 'hope'.

Trine Scouts- protectors from the Eternal Kingdom, occasionally tasked with "cleaning-up" the chaos on other planets.

Via del Profeta- the largest city on Innamorati, in the Archipelago. This is the city just outside of the main Palace.

Viipir- these are the blood-drinking, bat-shifters from the Ombra District. With advancements in medicine, they are capable of being in the sun with regular doses.

Vipus- these are large serpent-like flying creatures. They are thought to be the cross between gigantic vipers and wyrvens. They fly incredibly fast and were first tamed by the Hexia coven.

Void Vine- a smokable drug capable of causing euphoria, as well as anxiety.

Whisper Leaf- a smokable drug with a gentle earthy aroma and soothing effects.

-End-

Acknowledgments

Thank you to the amazing people who stood by my side through all it took to get this novel published. The only reason people have my book in their hands is because of the wonderful people who took a chance on my debut. Thank you to everyone who pledged through my Kickstarter campaign to get this novel funded and thank you to everyone from Booktok and Bookstagram who put effort into reposting my videos, showing up for me, and expressed your excitement for my book. You were my first ever supporters.

Those who love my novel, please know, all the amazing people below also contributed highly to getting this published:

Thank you to my sweet boys, **J. and A.** You two are the lights of my life, and the joy you bring me is otherworldly. The person I am today is hugely because of you two. Being your mom has taught me more than any other experience in my life, and I am thankful to call you my sons. To J., you are smart, so kind-hearted, and always ready to stand up for what is right. To A., you are silly, sweet, and attached to mommy's hip. I am so proud of you both, and I am so lucky I get to be your mom. Mommy loves you, from now until forever.

Thank you to my incredible **husband, Rafael**. Your love inspired me to keep going, even on the hardest, darkest days. You gave me a safe, welcoming space full of endless love, and my creativity flourished because of it. You have stood by me, never faltering, since the moment we met and without your encouragement, I don't know if I would have ever started writing. This book came not just from my sacrifices and dedication, but yours as well. I love you to the tips of my soul, and I would look for you in every lifetime.

Thank you to my **mom and dad**. Surprise! I wrote a book! Thank you for all the love you have given me. Thank you for never giving up on me, even when others told you to. Thank you for all the love you have shown my boys, and I know they love Oma and Opa very much. Thank you for seeing me through every obstacle, for letting me move back home so many times, and for supporting me however you could.

Thank you to my **psychiatrist**. You are the example by which I wish all in the behavioral health field followed after. You have gone above and beyond for me, and believed in me even when I didn't see it in myself. Every appointment you uplifted me and supported me. Your genuine excitement for my novel motivated me in ways I can't describe. Your passion and dedication to your patients is something I hope you are very proud of. Thank you for helping me get here, even if I know already you will tell me, "it was all you!"

Thank you to **Alexandra W.** for everything. For being by my side, even if there were thousands of miles between us or 10 minutes. For talking me through becoming a mom for the first time. When I think back on our memories, I think of how, when it came down to it, I always knew you'd be there if I called. I am so proud of the woman you are, and I am proud to be your friend. To the two girls who sat next to each other in English class who had no idea the journey life would take them on. Love you girl.

Thank you to **Jinapher Hoffman** for the incredible work you did on the front cover image. You are an amazing friend and fellow author, and your work will always mean something wonderful to me. You have such a compassionate heart, and I look forward to seeing how far you go with your books. Your success encourages other indie authors to keep going, and I hope you are proud that your wins are for more than just you.

Thank you to **RSK of Hyper Nostalgia Editing** for your priceless feedback and developmental editing. Your developmental edit helped transform this novel into the product I imagined in my head. You were fantastic to work with and I could not have gotten this far without your help and guidance. You are a truly talented editor and kind friend.

Thank you to **Makenzie Marshall** for your wonderful editing services. I could not have done this without you. You took my book baby into your loving hands and brought it back to me even stronger than before. Thank you for being here since the beginning and showing me so much kindness and support. You are such a gem, a wonderful friend, and a talented author.

Thank you to **Haven/Vydia_Moth** for the adorable, sparkly, beautiful work you created of my characters helping with my Kickstarter campaign. The friendship you and I have formed is one I value highly. You have been so supportive and I am consistently blown away by your talent.

Thank you to **Hope Garrity** for the jaw-dropping artwork of my characters for my commission. You were an overwhelming joy to work with and your professionalism went such a long way with me being totally new to the art commission space. Your work will always stay with me. I am grateful to have been in touch with such a talented artist.

Thank you to **The Voice of Hel, KJ and Zack R.** for the amazing narration snippets you have done for me. Hel, you went out of your way to do multiple narrations for me because you liked my writing. To a brand new baby author, you have no clue how much that meant to me. All three of you are talented and capable of evoking incredible emotion through your work. Please, never give up. I know you will go far.

Thank you to **Bri Hires, Lina Cichy, Raven K. Storm, Makenzie Marshall, Katia Black, Megan Turner, Jordan Hancock, and Erica Nichole Huerta** for being beta readers for me. You were all so vital to the process and thank you for taking a chance on me and my book and being willing to read through the roughness to offer me feedback. I truly am so lucky to have found every one of you. Your hard-work was not lost on me, and I will always feel so grateful for your help. I found the most incredible group of people and I love you guys.

Thank you to **Andrew Valenza from Valenza Publishing** for your support of my novel, but also for being a friend. You showed your belief in my book, even when things looked tough and impossible for me. Your belief in me pushed me to keep going. You are precisely the kind of person the writing world needs more of—a talented author, a dedicated partner to your wife (as evidenced through your books), and a supportive friend. I know one day we will make it big, and will be cheering each other on even then.

Thank you to **Zaylan Flynn** for the amazing contribution to my pen-name and for being so incredibly supportive throughout my entire journey. Your friendship has meant so much to me and I am happy we met through the writing community. You helped me keep going, even on the days I wanted to give up and throw in the towel. You're an amazing storyteller and I adore your creativity.

Thank you to **Bri Hires and S.J. Taylor.** You two are my "powerpuff" girls and I couldn't have done this without all your love and support. Thanks for keeping a smile on my face. The times when things felt overwhelming and confusing, I knew I could turn to you two. You are both incredibly talented authors, and I will be first in line to purchase every book you write.

Thank you to **Morgan Christensen.** Your friendship sincerely means so much to me and being able to travel on this journey side-by-side has been invaluable. You lift me up, you motivate me, and you listen when I'm going through it. I am proud to call you my friend, and I know you will go so far with your books. Here's to many more books by each others side.

Thank you to **Bex Gil** for offering me a lovely stand-in book cover to use during my Kickstarter campaign. You rock, and I hope you never give up. The world needs you, your books, and your heart.

Thank you to **Kelly J**. Kelly, you came right when the universe intended on you finding me, and I can't express how much your kindness meant to me. I was in such a low moment, wondering if I should continue, and you encouraged me.

Thank you to **A. Sayuri Miyaski, AJ Casey, C.K. Anderson, M.J. Lindsey, Anastasia Arellano, Stevi Lynn, Akita Sregor, Emma Mortimer, the Assist LLC, Soren Frosteson**, for all your support and friendship. At times when I thought I couldn't possibly do it any longer, you all gave me the push I needed.

Thank you to **you** for reading this book, for supporting me, and for making the world better, just because you exist.

About the Author

Jade Nioma is a Korean American debut-author from Arizona, where she lives with her husband and two boys. Jade has experience in the past working in rehab facilities, lock-down psychiatric wards, and on a specialized crisis team for those experiencing psychosis. She has a bachelor's degree in psychology and prior to attending her first master's level courses, Jade pivoted toward her life-long dream of writing.

When Jade isn't writing, you'll likely find her curled up with a book, journaling, or playing video games with her family. Close to Jade's heart is domestic violence awareness and mental health representation, especially after her own struggles with both. Jade hopes her writing will inspire others and show those who are struggling that their story is not over.